LAST SONG
BEFORE NIGHT

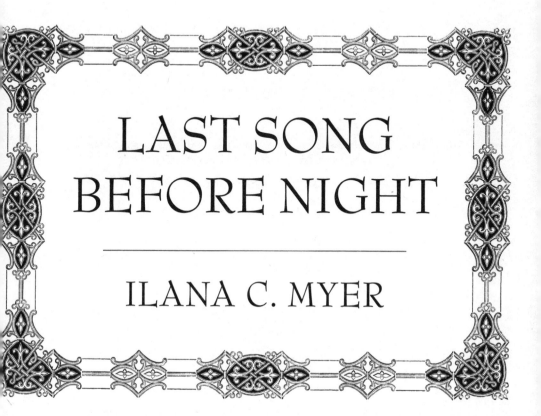

LAST SONG
BEFORE NIGHT

ILANA C. MYER

A Tom Doherty Associates Book

New York

LAST SONG BEFORE NIGHT

Map by Jennifer Hanover

A Tor Book
Published by Tom Doherty Associates, LLC
175 Fifth Avenue
New York, NY 10010

www.tor-forge.com

Tor® is a registered trademark of Tom Doherty Associates, LLC.

The Library of Congress Cataloging-in-Publication Data is available upon request.

ISBN 978-0-7653-7830-9 (hardcover)
ISBN 978-1-4668-6103-9 (e-book)

Our books may be purchased in bulk for promotional, educational, or business use. Please contact your local bookseller or the Macmillan Corporate and Premium Sales Department at (800) 221-7945, extension 5442, or by e-mail at MacmillanSpecialMarkets@macmillan.com.

First Edition: September 2015

Printed in the United States of America

0 9 8 7 6 5 4 3 2 1

For Yaakov

NORTHERN OCEAN

Bitter Falls

VASSILIAN

ACADEMY
ISLE

DYNMAR

STYRIAN HILLS

EIRNE

TAMRYLLIN

EIVAR

BLOOD SEA

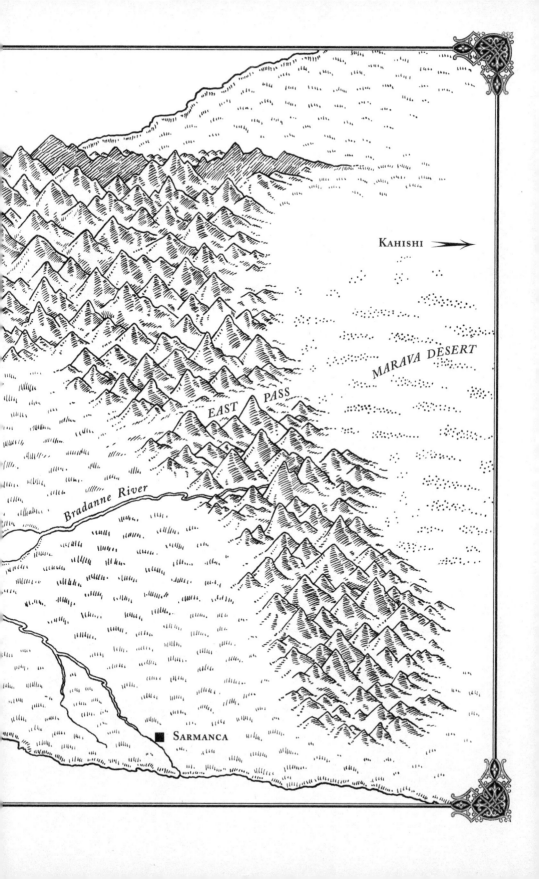

KAHISHI →

MARAVA DESERT

EAST PASS

Bradanne River

■ SARMANCA

Now that my ladder's gone,
I must lie down where all the ladders start,
In the foul rag-and-bone shop of the heart.

—W. B. YEATS

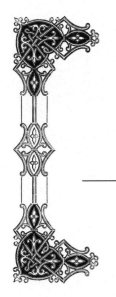

PART I

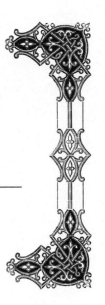

CHAPTER
1

MUSIC drifted up to the window with the scent of jasmine; a harp playing a very old song of summer nights, one Dane knew from childhood. The merchant smiled to himself as he scratched out the last figures in a column, the result of a long evening's work. This was why he liked to work in a room that overlooked the street. Especially now in summer, when the Midsummer Fair brought singers and all manner of entertainers to Tamryllin. But especially singers—Academy-trained poets whose art was the pride of Eivar even now, centuries after their enchantments had been lost. Dane's wife complained of the noise, but that was women for you.

She complained about a lot of things lately, despite the considerable wealth Dane Beylint had hauled to her door in all the years since they were wed. It was tiresome. It was worse than that—it exacerbated Dane's anxiety in what she should have realized was already a tense way of life.

Ships came in, ships went out—you never knew if your fortunes might sink with one of them. Certainly he had insurance, but those agents invariably tried to cheat you in the end. Just a month earlier, Dane had lost a ship on the seas in the far east, an entire cargo of jacquard and spices gone forever to Maia. He was one of the few merchants of Tamryllin bold enough—and with the resources—to send ships to those distant waters, which were said to run red with blood.

Dane didn't believe any such nonsense. He suspected the ships' captains liked to spin tales as a ploy to raise their rates. To say nothing of the insurance agents. But there was no question that it was risky, no question that he—Dane Beylint—was renowned for where he dared send his ships, how much he risked. Between his boldness and his informers at court, Dane kept his wife in silks and pearls, his sons standing to inherit an empire. And his daughter—she would marry well; there was no question of that.

His work for the day done, Dane saw there was an hour's worth of oil left in the study lamps. Rather than call the servant to light his way to bed, Dane paused to consider the black satin cloak, lined with gold brocade, draped across a chair. It had just arrived that day, to his delight. Inwardly he calculated its assembled cost: two sumptuous imported fabrics sewn together, the impeccable tailoring. The gold clasp he'd ordered on impulse, that would glitter at his throat under lamps. Yes, it was costly, but he was to attend the Midsummer Masque at the residence of the Court Poet himself; for that you spared no expense.

More valuable was the mask that Dane now lifted from the desk and set over his face, gazing at himself in the silver-backed mirror that was itself worth a fortune. His eyes looked back at him from within a frame of black, patterned with gold leaf. Even the evening lamplight danced on that gold. An ornamental sword, the hilt and scabbard perfectly matched, would complete the ensemble. He had commissioned the mask and sword from a master craftsman in Majdara; they were just different enough from the traditional Eivarian style that he was certain to stand out. And Dane liked the idea of standing out. He had deliberately not asked his wife to attend the masque with him.

That line of contemplation was a bit too stimulating at this time of night, when he needed to sleep. He had an eye on more than one alluring prospect at court; ladies weary of their arranged marriages and intrigued by a man who was experienced, by all accounts, in the dangers of seas that ran red with blood.

As if divining Dane's thoughts, the singer outside had ended his song of the summertime and now struck up a ribald ballad, its brisk rhythm drastically at odds with the hush of night. Dane couldn't make out the words—it was something about seduction. But then, most of them were.

His informers at court were helpful in these matters—keeping Dane abreast of a prospect's level of interest, of opportunity. Frequently absent husbands, for example, could be a convenience. But that was a frivolous use of his contacts' services; more often, Dane benefited from them in other, more substantial ways. When the king was on the verge of betrothal to his southland queen, years ago, it was Dane who had caught wind of it weeks in advance; who had procured an emerald so fine, so prodigious in size, it was still discussed at court to this day. A gift from the king to his intended bride, set in gold as a pendant for her to wear. Such acts tallied over years could consolidate a man's power, extend his sphere of influence even in a court as harshly glittering as that of the capital.

Dane lowered his mask, felt the warm summer air on his face. An owl called at the window, softly. The song was moving into its last phase, and Dane hoped for his wife's sake that the poet was nearly done. Well, and for his own sake, too. He would be heading to bed and hopefully sleep in just a moment. But first, as he stood at the window and observed the startling edge of the scythe moon, there were things to consider. Or savor.

Days ago, one of his informers had told him of something that was interesting . . . singularly interesting. An opportunity, in fact, not likely to arise again. Dane had sent a note to the palace, pressing his advantage. It was precisely through such shrewd stratagems, such creative mechanisms, that he kept his wife in exquisite fashions—not that she would ever appreciate it. His children were ungrateful as well, but then that was all but a given. Luckily, Dane found solace in his work and its rewards. Particularly the rewards.

Silence, now, at the window. It occurred to Dane that the song had cut off abruptly, mid-verse. He wondered if some enraged, sleepless citizen had knocked the poet flat. Dane had a liking for music, and even for poets—brash and arrogant as they were—and so hoped not.

Once again taking note of the moon, the scent of summer jasmine, Dane thought—not for the first time—that if he had not had a family to support, perhaps he too could have been a poet. Wandering from hearth to hearth, composing songs that would make even the most diamond-glimmering of the aristocracy tremble with admiration or lust. His singing voice, he was told, could be impressive when he put effort into it. But poets didn't have families. Even the greatest poet of the age, Valanir Ocune, was said to wander without a home. And such was Dane's nature—forever putting the needs of others before his own.

It was while occupied with this particular thought, this melancholy satisfaction, that Dane heard a new strain of music break the silence. But this was not music such as he had ever heard before. Dissonant, it ripped across the night. Across his soul. And then blackness before his eyes, and then nothing at all.

When Dane awoke, he was bent painfully backward over a hard surface. The room was bright with the glow of candles, the brightness nearly blinding. Dane began to scream.

The man in his line of sight held a knife outstretched. His face a mask of red. Another moment, and Dane realized both who the man was, and that the mask was blood.

"*Dane Beylint,*" the man said and swiped the knife at Dane's throat. Mercifully, it was quick, the main artery of the neck severed at once. Around Dane's now-slackening face, a pool of blood collected into a trough in the table. It was neatly done.

LIN woke with a gasp. She'd tugged the blanket from Leander and clung to it, though the room was hot. She was shivering.

"For gods' sake, Lin," Leander muttered blearily and made a grab for the blanket. "Give it back."

Her fingers went limp; she let him pull the rough fabric to himself. From the bed she could see the moon, a white grin against the night. Lin shook her head; that was not a helpful metaphor. But the terror that had pierced her lingered.

"What is it?" Leander said now. He must have felt her shivering.

Lin swung her legs out of bed and approached the window. Outside, she could see a back alley, and not much of that. The smell that wafted up from it had induced them to close the window even against the summer breeze. "I heard a scream."

"You were dreaming," said Leander. "Or . . . you know what goes on in places like this. Nothing terrible, though."

She was glad he couldn't see her, that his face was still buried in the flat mound that passed for his pillow. Nightmares were certainly not new territory for Lin. She didn't know why this particular one had bitten so deep. Already, the images were fading—the flash of a long knife, candles. But the tortured shriek—that was new. Worse than any nightmare she'd ever had.

"Leander, can I play us a song? Just one?" Lin tried to sound more casual than she felt. The harp was his, and he disliked for her to even touch it. And he had been sleeping.

But perhaps she underestimated his kindness. At times he could be generous. She had cause to know. "You're crazy," he said. In the dimness she saw him stretch his arms wearily. "I could swear you invented a nightmare to get your hands on my harp. One song."

She nodded, stroked the metal strings of the instrument with reverence. In that moment she was so grateful to be in this room and with this harp in her hands that tears pricked her eyes. "That's right," she said. "I'll sing you to sleep again."

THE eyes were watching her. But no—they were hollows, not eyes, cut into the mask that sat on her bedside table in a spill of moonlight. Yet Rianna felt watched as she pressed her ear to the bedroom door. Silence in the hallway.

A stab of guilt in her, briefly, at the sight of the magnificent mask, a gift from the man she was to marry. But then she was on the move again. She cracked the door ajar, smoothly quiet on hinges she had oiled earlier that day with this moment in mind. All that day her thoughts had been arrowing to now, past the toll of midnight when at last she could count on her father's being asleep. Even if he had stayed up very late writing figures in his account books or pacing the carpeted floor of his study, interminably, fueled by wine. A merchant such as Master Gelvan had many cares.

Rianna's father was not one of those men—most often wealthy—who locked their daughters up at night. And for years, she would have laughed at the thought. They would both have laughed. He joked that the seventeen-year-old Rianna was already as sober as the most venerable spinster, obedient almost to a fault.

She slid around the door, stepping carefully in satin slippers. These allowed her to glide on the tiled floor and then on the stairs that led to the rooms below. By night, the interior of the Gelvan house had an eerie way of reflecting moonlight from the white marble of the floors and pillars, of which Master Gelvan was so fond. He'd had the stone shipped from the quarries of the south at considerable expense. Rianna thought her own shadow on the gleaming floor was like a pursuing spirit, felt a shudder.

How Darien would tease her, if he knew.

A thought that was mortifying and alluring at the same time. Her ears drummed to the rhythm of her heart.

It was when she reached the door of Master Gelvan's study that Rianna heard voices. Her father, and one other. Her heart thundered now, but she kept her composure; she still had time to tiptoe past the study door—open only a crack—and escape to the main room and, from there, out to the garden.

". . . An itemized note on the body had his name," said the voice that was not her father's. Rianna thought he sounded familiar, and then realized—it was one of their kitchen servants, Cal. "It seems to confirm your suspicion—that there is a connection to the other killings."

"His blood was drained like the others, Callum? You are sure of this?" Master Gelvan's voice, low and urgent.

"I spoke with Master Beylint's servants. It was the same wound. But instead of the streets, Master Beylint was found in his own garden. The night guard is being questioned."

Rianna stood frozen. She clasped her hands over her mouth to stifle the sound of her breath. *The murders.* An ugliness that had begun in the past year, but always at a distance: bodies found sprawled in the more ramshackle streets, the poorer districts of Tamryllin. Master Gelvan would have concealed the knowledge from her if he could, but the servants talked. The killings were all done the same way: a knife wound to the throat, the blood drained and nowhere to be found. Six there had been so far.

Dane Beylint, the seventh, was a man like her father—a merchant, with close ties to king and court. And not found in the streets. His garden.

"I will go myself, tomorrow, to convey my condolences to the family," said Master Gelvan. "Thank you, Callum, for doing such good work. For the rest—the invitations go out tomorrow. And now I think there are some names we must add to the list."

Rianna crept swiftly past the study and toward the main room. *The invitations.* Her father was of course referring to the Midsummer Ball that he was to host this year, as he did every year. Everyone in Tamryllin who was of any importance would attend, including the king himself—and his Court Poet, Nickon Gerrard, said to be the most powerful man in Eivar. The entertainment would comprise some of the most skilled performers who had journeyed to Tamryllin for the festival. So it had been every summer for as long as Rianna could remember.

This year was different. Darien would be there, performing, along with his friend Marlen. This year she had her secret to conceal from the world . . . at least until the contest was over.

As she turned the handle of the second door she had oiled that day—which led out to the garden—Rianna thought of her father's voice calmly invoking blood and wounds. It was too strange. And Cal . . . ? With his heavyset frame and mournful eyes, Rianna had often thought he resembled a hound. That was, if hounds spoke of animal innards and turnips and the turnings of the harvest seasons.

What had Master Gelvan's kitchen servant to do with murders? Why was either of them awake so late?

Then the scent of roses enfolded her with the warm summer air, and Rianna almost forgot her disquiet when she caught sight of them waiting at the base of the cherry tree.

IT was a long time since Darien Aldemoor had last broken the law. The last time had been for the same reason, a girl. Marlen had been with him then, too—his friend's much taller frame lending itself, on that occasion, to reaching an inconveniently located gate bolt.

Darien grinned at the memory. His and Marlen's success that night had made them even more a legend among the Academy students, the lady in question a stunning creature who had inspired one of his most admired songs. She had soon afterward married a wealthy lord, as stunning creatures did tend to do. But not before Darien had made her famous, in image if not in name, from the Blood Sea south of Eivar to the bare mountains of the north.

"What are you smiling about, lunatic?" Marlen growled. His dark hair veiled his eyes in the moonlight.

"You," said Darien. "Now hush. We could get stopped here by guards." The street was quiet and steeped in scents of midsummer. Jasmine and honeysuckle twined in starry abundance on walls that sealed the mansions of Tamryllin from the streets. Darien thought sadness was distilled in those scents despite their sweetness, from the knowledge of how short a time they would last.

An odd thought to have while breaking into a rich man's home. Yet such thoughts tended to go to a reservoir in Darien's mind, to the place where songs were born. And then women wondered how he knew about sadness—and loss, and ravaging love—when otherwise a more cheerful person would have been hard to imagine.

A person who was now about to cheerfully commit a crime.

Darien muttered a prayer of thanks to Kiara for the slenderness of the moon. Then: "Follow me," he said, and moved to another tree. A rustling sound told him that Marlen followed, grumbling under his breath.

"Stop complaining," murmured Darien. "We will sing of this later."

"That we will," said Marlen. "If in prison, a tragic ballad. Otherwise, a farce."

"You're too cynical," Darien admonished him. *Down the alley,* he remembered. *A fault in the garden wall.*

They crept down the alleyway beside the mansion, where they reached the square into which the gardens faced. Each with its own high wall, affording the treasure of privacy to wealthy inhabitants.

Except the merchant's wall had a loose stone at its base. When Darien prised the stone aside—with both hands and a grunt, for it was heavy—there was an opening wide enough for each of them to fit through.

As Marlen brushed himself off with distaste, Darien surveyed their surroundings. Roses greeted them in a profusion that appeared white by moonlight, islands in a dark sea of thorns and leaves. A stone fountain plashed at the center, flanked by curving ornamental trees that were also in bloom. Stone benches were scattered under the trees with deliberate artlessness.

A rose caught Darien's eye that was unlike the rest: in the night, it looked almost black. As blood would look by moonlight, Darien thought, and unsheathed his knife to cut it from the thorns.

"Let's hope the merchant doesn't notice the theft of his precious red rose," said Marlen. "His only one."

Darien smiled. Only an Academy graduate would be so metaphoric in his choice of words—alluding not just to the flower, but to its intended recipient. "Follow me," he said. He wondered why he had felt compelled to share this experience with Marlen, who, though his closest friend, was unlikely to understand. But it was too late to reconsider. They approached the cherry tree where he and Rianna had assigned to meet.

"How long are we to wait?" Marlen asked. He spoke in undertone, though it was unlikely that his words would reach the house from this distance. That and the music of the fountain colluded to mask their voices.

Darien shook his head. "Why, did you have other plans tonight?"

"I might have."

"It *would* do you good to practice 'The Gentleman and His Love.' I noticed you kept slipping up on one of the chords."

Marlen flung back his hair. "I play it exactly as it ought to be played, Aldemoor," he said. "You'd do well to practice not smirking when we sing it. The audience is not to know it is satire until well into the third verse."

"I can't help it that your bad playing amuses me," said Darien. He grinned as he said it.

They passed the time amiably trading insults for what seemed quite a while before the door to the house opened, and a slim white figure appeared on the steps. The moon was silver on her long hair. And then she was running, dress and hair flowing behind her as she tripped into his waiting arms. She wore a nightdress, Darien saw, and was momentarily scandalized. But she couldn't know, he reminded himself; there had been no mother to teach her.

"There you are," he breathed into her hair. It was whisper-soft and smelled of jasmine, a summer scent. After a moment, he released her and presented the rose. She smiled, and even in moonlight he could see her flush. He knew Marlen would note this, and the chaste brevity of their embrace, and want an explanation. That part of it Darien didn't want to tarnish with too much exposure to his friend's mockery.

"Where can we go to talk?" he asked.

She looked down, her lower lip curling almost in a pout. "My father's plans changed at the last moment. He's home. Last I saw, he was even awake in his study."

"Awake? Now?"

"There was—there was a murder tonight," she said. "An associate of my father's, in his own garden."

"His garden?" Marlen said sharply. "That is strange."

"You two have not been introduced—apologies," said Darien.

"Rianna Gelvan, meet Marlen Humbreleigh . . . thorn in my side since our Academy days."

"Pleasure," Marlen said lazily, and kissed her hand. Rianna looked startled, but nodded and drew back her hand, her composure a testament to her impeccable upbringing. Well, almost impeccable, thought Darien. With a high neck and long sleeves, she had no doubt thought her nightdress proper enough. The less proper implications were a nuance that had not penetrated the high walls of this garden.

Though it seemed a killer had managed to penetrate a different garden that same night.

Darien shook his head. Strange things happened in the capital. He had lived isolated on the Academy Isle too long, his only occasional respite the nearby village—and even that was against the rules. He and Marlen had since traveled to many towns and cities in the past year, but none compared in complexity or size to Tamryllin, the queen of them all.

"Do you think it will interfere with the Fair?" asked Rianna. Her eyes were round.

"The death of a merchant? Surely not," said Darien. "Sounds to me like someone had a grievance against him." He clasped her hand. "Don't fret, love. The contest *will* happen. And Marlen and I are the best, and are sure to win."

"Humility is not a trait in which we excel at the Academy," drawled Marlen.

"Oh shut up," said Darien and laughed. "No use denying the truth, is there?"

"All the same, there's some stiff competition," Marlen pointed out. "The contest brings the best people from all over the country. We know most of the people from the Academy, but there could still be surprises."

"Like if Valanir Ocune were to participate," Rianna said with sudden sparkle, and it was all Darien could do not to beam proudly. He flung his arm about her shoulders as if claiming a prize; when she leaned into him, he thought she felt fragile, like a bird.

"That would be unfair," Marlen conceded. "Luckily, he is said to be wandering in Kahishi somewhere. Being the world's greatest Seer must be a demanding job."

"Didn't he ever win the Silver Branch?" asked Rianna, her head on Darien's shoulder.

"No . . . Valanir never entered the contest," said Marlen. "Tales have it that he didn't want the Branch, didn't even want to become Court Poet. Of course, that may have been just sour grapes, since he and Court Poet Gerrard were rivals."

Rianna shook her head. "I doubt the Seer Valanir Ocune has time for sour grapes," she said reprovingly, as if he had uttered heresy.

Darien smiled. "You'd be surprised what even the greatest men have time for."

"As our presence here at this hour would indicate," Marlen said with a bow. "Listen, I want to get into the house and see the space where we'll be performing at the ball."

"But you've seen it," said Darien. "We already performed there."

"Yes, but I need to see it again," said Marlen. "Any chance your father is asleep yet?"

"I don't know," said Rianna, confused. She leaned on Darien's arm as if for support. "It seems . . . a risk."

"So much the better," said Marlen.

At last they agreed that Rianna would return to the house to see if her father and the servants were sleeping. And indeed, the silence within was absolute. To make certain she checked the study, and even ascended the stairs to confirm that her father's bedroom door was closed.

"Thanks," Marlen said when she returned. "I'll be just a moment."

Darien shook his head. "I don't know when you became one of *those* poets," he said. "The space, is it."

"It matters," said Marlen, and vanished into the house.

"Well that gives us a chance to be alone for a moment," said Darien, and kissed Rianna's cheek. "I only wish we were really alone—I would sing for you."

"Soon?" she said, and rested her head on his chest. He was the first man she had loved, Darien realized, not for the first time. He was sometimes awed when he considered this. "You will at the ball, won't you?" she said. "Even if no one knows it's for me."

"I will," he said. "All my songs now are for you."

DARIEN felt a silence come over him when Marlen returned, after he had clasped Rianna's hand for the last time and watched her disappear into the house. In silence they crawled through the opening and into the alleyway.

It was only when they reached the streets near their inn that Marlen asked, a note of rare uncertainty in his voice, "So what's different this time?"

Darien knew what he meant. So often had they helped each other in the game of seduction, seldom competing since their tastes were different. Marlen's women tended to be unhappily in gilded marriages, dissatisfied as caged snakes. Darien gravitated to smiles, to laughter. But Rianna took him to a different place. Her eyes were still as the pools in the woodland of Academy Isle, and stirred within him a similar quietness.

"I think I love her," he said, shaking his head. "A Galician girl."

"Other than that," said Marlen, dryly, "what's the problem?"

"She's promised to another," said Darien. "One of much more impressive lineage than a youngest son of Aldemoor. And her father made mention of a winter wedding."

"Sounds like you'll need to move fast," said Marlen. He looked unusually contemplative, gazing straight ahead, his long fingernail tracing the smooth carnelian stone set into his Academy ring. Perhaps that was why he did not ask Darien the obvious question: How could he be considering marriage? Darien, of all people? Only Marlen himself was worse suited for it. They had never made a formal pact, but both had assumed that the next ten years of their lives would be spent much as the previous one had been: traveling, singing, adventuring. Marriage meant one woman, one bed, one home.

But Darien thought he'd never wanted anything more in his life than he wanted Rianna Gelvan now. Even if it meant one home. Life with her could be an adventure, lit by the gold of her hair.

"If only we had those lost enchantments the Academy masters liked to go on about," said Darien. "I could magic Rianna away from this place."

Marlen laughed. "If we had powers, Darien, you could likely conjure up an ideal woman of your own."

"A terrifying thought," said Darien. "That could be a song—of a poet who uses enchantments to create his ideal woman, the havoc that ensues. There is always havoc—at least in songs—when you get your heart's desire."

"Is there?" said Marlen. "I'd risk it. Though it wouldn't be some girl."

Darien was only half-listening. "I'll tell you what I need to do," he said. "That Silver Branch is worth as much as a kingdom."

"You think the merchant will approve your suit if we win?"

Darien wagged his finger at Marlen in mock reproof. "No, my Lord Humbreleigh," he said with exaggerated courtesy. "*When* we win."

CHAPTER
2

ALL her life, music was a secret. It was what you stole to the cellar at midnight or the deep pine woods to play, or sing. Verse was composed in greater secrecy still, by light of a single candle after dark. Even then, Lin had to hide the burned-out candle the next day, smuggle it out to the midden heap under cover of night.

But now music was a drinking song in a tavern performed to crowds of rough men, or more recently, a stately ballad sung to lords at their firesides. And tomorrow . . . tomorrow would be more than either of those things, much more.

In the humidity of the night, the streets were choked with the scents of summer flowers. Here in the capital of Tamryllin, music was like a dancer in the fullness of her youth wearing little to conceal her beauty, flaunting everything. To Lin, it seemed profligate to make something lush and voluptuous that was meant to be a mystery.

It was her northern upbringing, she knew; a chill she carried within her into this decadent and too-beautiful southern city. She had never expected to see it for herself. The imperial buildings by the water, glistening white as if polished a thousand times. The parade of art, from the gilded splendor of the king's palace to the sculptures and frescoes that adorned even the humblest temples.

The white city by the sea, it was once named, in a song made long ago by Edrien Letrell himself. The great Seer had loved the capital. Now poets named Tamryllin "the White City" for Edrien, because of words spun one night by light of a single candle. Such was the capacity of one man to influence others, centuries after he himself had died.

"Tonight is important," Leander was saying. He had dragged her into the tiny room they shared. "You can't wear—that. We will need to buy you a dress. Perhaps on credit? I don't know."

Lin was grateful that he did not comment on the sorry state of her clothes. For the better part of a year she had been wearing the same shirts and trousers that she had stolen from her brother's wardrobe.

"Leander," she said in a calming tone, "I have a dress. Look." She untied the bundle that lay on the bed they shared, shook free billowing folds of corn-colored silk. She stroked them with the back of her hand, and a rush of memory welled from the feel of the fabric, the bergamot scent that wisped in the air like smoke.

Leander looked awestruck. "I always said you were highly born."

"You have," she said. "An oversight on my part."

"In your disguise?"

She ignored the question. "Did the approvals come in yet?"

Leander nodded. "I stopped by the office just now. The songs are approved—we can sing them tonight."

"Good," said Lin. "I wasn't interested in recycling our old material. So we'll meet back here in an hour to rehearse?"

"Why? Where are you going?"

"To get some air," said Lin, and then almost laughed despite herself. Their inn was situated in the tanning district—the reason they could get a room to themselves—and the air was thick with the stench of the trade.

But her business took her away from the tanners, down an alleyway shortcut she had discovered weeks earlier. Only a month they had been living in Tamryllin, absorbing the atmosphere and excitement of the Midsummer Fair . . . and the contest. The last time it was held, Lin had been eleven years old and unaware of its existence. Nickon

Gerrard, long established now as Court Poet to the king, had been green in power. It was difficult to imagine such a time.

Now she was at the heart of it all. This was the worst time of the year, the locals grumbled, but Lin could tell they were proud. At midsummer, thousands of merchants, traders, performers and artists from around the world converged upon the capital city. Spices and silks from Kahishi, wool from the northern hills, damask and jacquard from the southwest, jade and alabaster from the farthest east, where it was perilous to go . . . and through it all the wine would flow, or so Lin had been told.

The alleyway was a narrow passage that snaked between walls of stone. The windows in the walls began very high, and were dark holes. Down some narrow, winding stairs, she found herself at a square, where an ornate fountain graced the joining of three avenues. It was sculpted with the arcane symbols of the tanning guild. Here was where the district began, and by taking the street to her left, she was leaving it behind.

During one of her night walks around the city she had discovered a temple, but had never entered. But tonight she was to sing in the presence of the king and—even more unsettlingly—the Court Poet.

Lin entered through bronze doors and was met with a curtain of incense and candle fumes. She had expected the place to remind her of home, had in fact been steeling herself. But it was simpler than the chapel to which she was accustomed, and brighter, as if the southland sun could pass through stone. The marble sculptures of the Three were lit with a soft gold-toned light, not the bloodless white that she recalled.

An old woman wrapped in a shawl knelt before the statues, bent in prayer. She made no sound, and the room was still.

The Three gods: Estarre, Kiara, and Thalion; brother and sisters. Estarre terrifyingly beautiful, sword upraised in a gesture of salute or challenge. Thalion like a male version of her, a sword in one hand, but a huge book in the other, and an emblem of balance scales carved into his helmet. These things—the book, the scales—were what linked him with his other sister, Kiara. Chill-eyed, shrouded in robes.

Her distaff held close, along with the secrets of the earthly world. She stood to the left of Thalion, Estarre to his right. There was significance in this, also.

Nearby, one of the candles had blown out in its sconce. A wisp of smoke danced a lazy spiral upward, vanishing before it could reach the mosaics that adorned vaulted ceilings far above.

Lin's mother had worshipped Estarre to the exclusion of the other two, which—if anyone outside the family had known—could have meant a charge of heresy. But of course, no one would ever have told.

It was Kiara to whom Lin turned, as all poets did in Eivar. She lit a candle and set it down at the altar amid a sea of tiny flames. Each of them the same, as if all the dreams and desires of people were indistinguishable from one another. The prayer of a female poet, perhaps the only one in Eivar, no different from a mother's prayer for her sickening infant or a farmer's prayer for a good harvest.

Or in this particular part of the city, the prayer of a tanner. Lin smiled.

A brisk sound in the silence: footsteps behind her. Lin swung around. She recognized the poet who stood there—tall and dark-haired, an ironic smile perpetually tugging at the corner of his mouth as if he enjoyed a private joke. Or perhaps that was just when he saw her.

"Good day, Marlen Humbreleigh," she said, softly so as not to disturb the woman who prayed.

"It's you," he said without lowering his voice. "Here to pay tribute to Kiara, I suppose."

"It must be your perceptiveness that makes you such a successful poet."

"Oh, I like that!" Marlen said, and laughed. "Like ice. Very good. Well if you must know, I'm here for the same purpose. We have a performance tonight."

"As do we," Lin said. "If you don't mind, Marlen, I'd like to pray in silence."

"We're at the Gelvan ball," said Marlen. "How about you?"

She sighed. "We are, as well."

Marlen narrowed his eyes, his mask of indifference slipping for a moment. "How did a ragamuffin girl get that, I wonder."

"The same way an arrogant, spoiled lord's son does, I'll wager," said Lin, and heard, as if from far away, the cold anger of her mother in her own voice. It was always with her, a flame that she tried to hold in check under ice.

And what would Lin's mother have made of this man? Lin thought she might know, but was not comfortable with the thought.

Meantime, Marlen had recovered his good humor, or at least the appearance of it. "I'll be seeing you tonight then," he said with a grin. "I can't wait to see how you look in your *best* shirt and trousers, my dear."

Lin knew Leander would be furious that she had "antagonized" this paragon of success in the poets' world—for that was how he would see it. Turning away, she knelt before the statue, bent her head, and shut her eyes as if she were alone. It was easy to forget about Marlen once she had closed her eyes. The silence returned, marred only by the guttering of candles.

I want only to help you, the man had said. The lively flicker in his green eyes belying the silver in his hair, the creases in his face. On the third finger of his right hand a moon opal, one of the rarest of Academy rings. It was he who had somehow heard of Lin and Leander, an unlikely team considering that there were officially no female poets.

"Why would you help us?" Lin had asked. They were sitting in the common room of their inn, and she knew Leander was deathly embarrassed that Therron saw they were staying in such a place. But the Seer didn't seem to notice the grime and noise. On his lips was a faint smile, as if he contemplated a memory that both amused and saddened him.

"There are flaws in the way things are done," said Therron. His voice was deep. "One is that only a man may become a poet, and certainly only a man may become a Seer. You are brave to go against the tide. I would like to see that bravery rewarded."

Now it was Lin's turn to smile faintly. "Thank you," she said, "but I am not brave. What I come from is far worse than anything I could choose. So in a way, I risk nothing now."

"Even if you fail?" There was a dead weight to the question, contrasting with the din of the laborers who crowded at the other tables.

She met his eyes, strove to hold his gaze. "I will most likely fail."

"You will if you allow no one to help you," said Therron, taking her hand. "Take this invitation to the Gelvan ball. Make it the finest performance of your lives. The king will be there . . . and more important, so will the Court Poet. It may be the start of something for you."

Lin looked down at their joined hands on the tabletop, and it occurred to her that he was not so old, and was fine-featured. And a Seer. "You have our thanks," she said, and withdrew her hand—now holding a small parchment that she knew might be the key to their fortunes.

"Yes," Leander echoed, starstruck. "*Thank* you."

"It is with your best music that you will thank me," said the Seer.

Now Lin turned her mind from these thoughts, attempted to focus on prayer.

Kiara, she thought. *Keeper of secrets. Help us make it our best.*

She opened her eyes. The old woman had gone; so had Marlen. The polished floor beneath her knees had grown warm. Lin heaved to her feet, felt an ache in her shins and knees from being pressed so long against stone.

MARLEN Humbreleigh considered returning to the shrine of Kiara to submit a prayer, but in the end decided that he did not care to after all. Let the dark goddess do her work as she saw fit. On the streets, he attracted no notice, just another poet among the hundreds who had thronged to Tamryllin for the Midsummer Fair. Once every twelve years they gathered here for the most prestigious of the contests, where the Silver Branch was won.

He passed a stand selling masks, with their hollow-eyed half faces.

There were many such stands around the city these days, for the fair opened with a masque. Marlen thought it an amusing custom considering that in truth, everyone's face was a mask.

Marlen had always been good at learning secrets. From the time he was tumbling his brothers out of apple trees in the family orchard—before they were allowed to be picking the fruit—bringing the ugliness of people's deepest thoughts to light was . . . an amusement for him.

It came out in his work: critics praised Marlen and Darien for their masterful plumbing of the depths of human nature. At least half that contribution was made by Marlen, who felt the forces of his own need stir by candlelight, transform into the shadows of other, imaginary figures. He and Darien had risen to fame by subverting the heroes of bygone days. Making them human, and sometimes worse.

Some critics of their songs took a different tack, despairing that the popularity of these young poets and the men who imitated them bespoke a cynical age. Occasionally they even proposed that such songs be banned, but the humor of the poets' satires was entertaining at court. At least, so Marlen had been told. As long as you did not mock the court itself, it was acceptable to satirize the heroes of old.

So much of the humor, he knew, came from Darien. Marlen was the shadow that danced in the periphery, sensed by critics who could not quite articulate the source of their dismay. That could be called a secret, too, he considered. The dark heart of their music.

But there was a difference between discovering a secret that could be turned into a song and one that mattered. One, for example, that could get someone killed.

Marlen had never discovered such a secret before the preceding night and now was not sure what to do.

It was Darien's fault, of course, for sticking his nose—and rather more—where he had no business. A Galician girl, and on top of that, the daughter of one of the most prominent men in Tamryllin. Marlen knew there was no use pointing out his friend's folly to him: Darien would do as he pleased. The world had long ago taught him that he could.

The lesson Marlen had learned was rather different.

And he really didn't have time to be thinking of such things, not with the Gelvan ball coming up. To play before the king and even the Court Poet himself . . . He ought to have been with Darien right now, rehearsing. But spontaneity was one of the main characteristics of their partnership, and it was too late to change old habits. Even now, at this most critical junction of their lives.

The Gelvan ball. Back to the house where Marlen had gone to investigate the space where he and Darien would be performing. Where he could not resist doing a bit of exploring while he was at it—and thereby discovered the merchant's secret, one that could cost the man his life.

That the Gelvan family was of Galician descent, at least on Master Gelvan's side, was well-known. That Galicians loved money was also common knowledge, and undoubtedly how Rianna's father had famously risen from street sweeper to become one of the most powerful men in Tamryllin.

But Marlen could now prove that Master Gelvan, trusted associate of the king, still worshipped the Unnamed God of the Galicians, an offense punishable by death. His careless exploration of the man's study had uncovered a bronze shrine behind a concealing tapestry, along with a stack of books in the Galician tongue that had been banned in Eivar for centuries. The Galician religion accepted the existence of no other god—there was only One, they said. Which of course meant that they did not accept the existence of the Three, bless their names.

In the past thousand years, most Galicians had been converted by the sword, which meant that most were dead. Master Gelvan stood as an example of how a man might shuck off an inconvenient heritage and become great in the eyes of the king and court.

And now, it turned out, he was a heretic. And tonight Marlen would drink his wine, and smile, and sing for the man's company.

It occurred to Marlen that he could not cease to think about this, to turn it over in his mind, because he was his father's son.

Will you always *be the shadow?* Marlen could almost hear him ask.

And opened the door to the inn where he and Darien were staying, into the spill of light and warmth where there was no sign, none at all, that his life was about to change.

LIGHT assaulted her in the vast room; from overhanging lamps with their multiple slender branches, from torches in wall sconces of decorative brass, from wineglasses reflecting light like a thousand flashes of bared teeth. Master Gelvan's house could rightly be called a palace, its parquet floors spread with intricate Kahishian carpets, wall hangings and paintings on the walls that Lin knew were each in their way special. Musicians played a teasingly frivolous, fashionable tune to which some were already dancing.

As Leander straightened his coat and glanced worriedly about them, Lin made her own calculations. The people who crowded the rooms were among the finest in the city. Added to that were contingents of foreign lords and merchants, here in Tamryllin for the week of the Midsummer Fair. Lin would have to be on her guard even more than usual. She didn't think Rayen would accept the invitation of a Galician, even one so highly placed as Master Gelvan, but she couldn't be sure. One advantage she had: with her hair hacked off and her body whittled to nothing, he was unlikely to recognize her right away. Nonetheless, tonight was a risk.

A flash in her mind's eye and she was in a different room: a cavernous hall hung with draperies of finest velvet and brocade, with tapestries centuries old. Faces staring from them that possessed her forehead, her eyes. And Lin herself in the midst of a whirlpool of guests who stared and whispered and no doubt speculated on her still-unmarried state. Swirling in the shadows with hissing whispers, the guests reminded her of spirits. Her goblet of wine raised to her eye as if to consider its clarity and bouquet, when in fact it was so she would have something to look at . . . something that was not any of those measuring eyes.

See anything you like? Rayen, a warm feather of breath in her ear. *Not that it matters, love.*

And then she was back beside Leander in the home of a Tamryllin merchant, on the verge of performing before the Court Poet and king.

"Lin, what are you thinking?" Leander said out the side of his mouth. He kept tugging at the cuffs of his blue coat, which she knew was a nervous gesture.

"That I've already begun to itch." It was true: so long had it been since she had worn a dress that her body now rebelled.

They had made the proper greeting to Master Gelvan where he stood by the entrance to greet guests, framed beneath an arch of fluted marble. He was a slender, tired-looking man with pale hair verging toward grey. His attire was scarlet, slashed with gold-threaded brocade. She could imagine the cost of obtaining that color. A ruby pendant on a chain rested on the merchant's chest, a plain gold ring on his left hand—though she knew his wife had been gone many years. He had acknowledged Lin and Leander with a nod, without indicating surprise at a female poet. She was grateful for that.

Now surveying the crowds, Lin said, "Oh, dear."

Leander jumped. Everything before a performance made him anxious. *"What?"*

She had caught sight of two black-clad men, impeccably groomed and indisputably handsome. Each wore an ornate harp strapped at his waist on a tooled leather baldric. "Them."

Following her gaze, Leander swore under his breath. Lin sighed.

"I'm sorry," she said. "I knew they would be here. I met Marlen today in the temple, and he told me. Quite pleased with himself, of course, though that is probably his permanent state of mind."

They made a striking pair: Marlen tall and brooding, Darien slender and blond, with those mischievous blue eyes. Both were the most celebrated poets of their year at the Academy, and possibly of the decade. In just a year out of the Academy, they had made a name even some Seers might have envied.

And who might compete with them? Lin thought. A female poet of little training? An Academy graduate who had, thus far, failed to make a mark?

She knew what her partner was thinking. "Leander, listen to me," she said. "Therron sent us here because he believed we have talent. A *Seer* sent us. We don't have to be intimidated by these men."

"They're better than we are," he said. "And they have two harps, which means they can do the more complicated duets. Where's the wine?"

She caught his arm in a way that she hoped was inconspicuous. They could not be seen to quarrel, not here. "You know what happens to your concentration when you drink," she said. "We can't afford any wrong notes tonight."

"You'll deny me wine from Master Gelvan's cellar after months of cheap ale?" said Leander. "Lin, where is your heart?"

She smiled, relieved that his good humor was returning. "Afterward," she said. "To celebrate a song well played."

And when that time came, she thought, she could do with a glass of wine herself. Pale gold from the mountain vineyards and poured to the brim, in the style of a northern man (or woman). The heat of summer hung upon them here, but she still was who she was.

Strains of a new piece of music were beginning, this one even more tinkling and lighthearted than the last. The musicians played on fiddles, tabors, and lutes, instruments of the moment. The merchant was nothing if not fashionable.

Avoiding eye contact with any of the guests, Lin saw that someone else had joined Master Gelvan under the arch: a stunning girl, gowned in emerald green. Her golden hair had been curled elaborately and then allowed to cascade from a hairpin crusted with diamonds.

That would be Master Gelvan's daughter, without any doubt.

The merchant had many treasures, but Lin thought, seeing Rianna Gelvan, it was apparent which was most dear.

Leander had left her side, off to seek wine against her wishes, or perhaps only women. He labored under the misapprehension that a poet's ring was all that was needed to make him an attractive prospect—that and his family's estate in a green valley to the southwest. Like many southern men, she thought, he had an exaggeratedly optimistic view of the world. A name for Tamryllin in more sentimental songs was "City of Dreams," but it seemed to Lin that dreams were just as likely to be killed here as they were to come alive.

Still, it was to this city that she had come, from dark forests and cold. Nothing else could frighten her now. And then Lin felt a shiver, smiled a little, at the bravado she knew was false.

In that moment she spotted the Seer Therron in an alcove to the side, out of sight of most of the guests. Their eyes met and he smiled, and it occurred to Lin that he might have been watching her.

No fear, Lin told herself, and moved to join him.

SHE watched him. As those around her sipped wine or chatted in sedate groups, Rianna kept her eye on Callum. Clad in his best jacket, he was pacing the room with a decanter of red wine, filling glasses for the guests. But at the very start, she noticed that after filling the glass of a particular guest—a middle-aged woman Rianna did not recognize—Callum had pocketed a note.

An itemized note on the body had his name, he had told Master Gelvan.

Her eyes narrowed, Rianna almost didn't notice Ned until he was nearly knocking into her. "What?" she snapped. "Oh, sorry. Really, Ned, I'm sorry." It had been his clumsiness, but she knew that was something he was just about helpless to control, long limbs getting away from him.

"What is it that has you so occupied?" he asked with a strained smile. Rianna sensed the hurt behind that smile, regretted that she had lost patience even for a moment. He deserved better from her. If she was going to elope with a poet instead of marrying Ned Alterra, she could at least be kind.

"What do you know of Master Beylint's murder?" she said, leaning forward so only he would hear.

His brow furrowed. "That's not something I'd expect you to be curious about."

"Why not?" she said. "He's a friend of my father's, or rather he *was*."

"It's a terrible thing," said Ned. "The Beylint family was supposed to attend tonight, but now of course they are not. My father donated for an elegy at the Eldest Sanctuary . . . I'm sure yours did as well."

"But Ned, what do you think is going on?" said Rianna. "Don't you think it's strange that he was killed exactly like those poor people in the streets?"

Ned shrugged. "Could be some sort of imitation. I don't know, Rianna. I hadn't thought about it, I admit." He ran a hand through his hair, a nervous habit that never failed to make it stand on end. "I didn't exactly come here to talk about a murder. I thought . . . I was wondering . . . would you like to dance?"

Then she saw it happen: Callum approached Master Gelvan, refilled his glass. And in a movement so quick it was almost sleight of hand, the note found its way to her father's pocket. Rianna drew a sharp breath.

"What is it?" said Ned.

"Nothing," said Rianna. She forced a smile. "Of course we must dance."

DARIEN noticed that Marlen was already working his way through a second cup of wine. It was unusual for him to do that before a performance. Though Marlen *did* pride himself on his ability to do anything while inebriated . . . and if women were to be believed, he did mean anything.

"I suppose you miss Marilla," Darien said acidly. "Why didn't you bring her?"

Marlen barked a laugh. "I'm not yet important enough to bring my *whore* to events like this. Besides, she'd probably try to seduce whomever she believed the most powerful man in the room. It would be embarrassing." He drained the rest of his glass. "This wine's foul."

Darien watched him narrowly. He'd begun to wonder if Marlen's taste of life in the capital had somehow . . . *changed* him. Talk of Marilla brought out a savagery in him that Darien had seen rarely in the years they'd been friends.

And women must come second, always, to the music. In more ways than one, one of Darien's lovers had once wryly observed.

He could not imagine Rianna saying such things, ever. It was at once wrenching and gratifying to be able to watch her from across the room, without—of course—ever daring to approach. But from a distance he was free to observe her gleaming like a jewel by light of the overhanging lamps. And then at her side—a lank interloper—there was the suitor. Rianna had told Darien his name, but he had stubbornly forgotten it, willed it into nonexistence. And in truth, the man *looked* almost nonexistent anyway.

"Before you get to thinking that I'm too wrapped up in my wench, you ought to see how you're ogling that child," said Marlen, startling him. "And not that it's your business, but I haven't seen Marilla in nearly a month."

"It's not my business," Darien said curtly. "And Rianna's no child. For the love of Thalion, she's about to marry that stick over there."

"Him?" Marlen raised an eyebrow, amused. "My. He must have money, or title. *Something* . . . not apparent to the eye."

Darien was about to reply when he noticed that a hush was overtaking the room: the music had stopped, the chatter all but ceased. Twelve men in the red and black livery of the palace had entered, each bearing a horn.

The Ladybirds, as Darien and his friends referred to the king's guards derisively. There to enforce laws like the approval of songs for their content and form, and the proper mode of bowing when addressing his majesty. Such men may as well split open and fly away, for all the respect they deserved. But as Marlen once pointed out, they did know how to use weapons. And poets who failed to get their songs approved ended up imprisoned, or worse.

Darien had seen King Harald only once, and Court Poet Gerrard only twice. It was an unspeakable honor that they had arrived here tonight, at the Midsummer Ball of a merchant. But Darien knew Master Gelvan was not merely a merchant: he had cultivated the king's favor, using his extensive resources for the greater glory of the monarchy. Of course, Galicians were skilled at that sort of thing.

Six men stood at attention on each side of an unrolled carpet, and in unison their long brass horns were uplifted and sang. Across the carpet, the king and queen progressed arm in arm at a majestic pace, allowing the surrounding crowds to pay homage with downcast glances and bended knee.

Clad in a ceremonial mantle of porphyry, the king was round and soft, as was the queen at his side. Harald and Kora had produced an heir as round and soft as themselves, a boy who was now twelve and rumored to be afraid of the dark and dogs. When Darien was a child, he had heard talk among the adults of the dwindling of the Tamryllin monarchy; Harald's father, a great ruler, had been felled by a sudden illness. Leaving only one, unimpressive son.

At the Academy, the students had often traded banter back and forth about the ineffectual monarch, though the more clever ones realized that that same monarch might be their avenue to success.

It was the figure coming up behind the king and his entourage that drew the eye much more: Nickon Gerrard, Court Poet and the king's favorite. Drifting from his shoulders the six-colored cloak that only he was permitted to wear. A handsome man who had aged gracefully, with a distinguished profile and only a touch of silver at the temples. His eyes sharp and clever, as if there was nothing that could evade his gaze.

Harald depended upon him for everything, it was said.

The music was starting up again. Master Gelvan lifted his arms as if to encompass the entire room and all the glittering people there and called for a dance.

Normally, Darien would have used this as an opportunity for flirtation. Now, knowing that Rianna was here and not with him, he hung back. It was then that he caught sight of a slight woman in corn-colored silk, her head covered with a silk cap set with a single pearl. Her face was all eyes, large and deep-set in a sharp, pale face. She looked oddly familiar. He recognized the man who accompanied her easily enough, for he was just a year ahead of them at the Academy.

"Marlen," he said, "who is that waif with Leander?"

His friend smiled. There was wine in his glass again, as if by magic. His eyes were glazed and a bit pink. "Picture her in a man's trousers and shirt, and you'll remember," said Marlen. "She's our competition tonight. It's a bit offensive, don't you think?"

"I wasn't aware it was a competition," said Darien. He was growing weary of his friend's mood and wished to be elsewhere. Such as, across the room offering a cup of scarlet wine to a girl in a green dress. And if he could not help but see the symbolism in that, then so be it.

The music must come first, he reminded himself. Rianna Gelvan was here, but so were the king and his retinue . . . and Nickon Gerrard.

Remembering that moment later, Darien would think, somewhat ruefully, that if he had known then who else was in the room that night, it would have eclipsed those names altogether. And likewise if he had known what was to come in the next hour, not long after the moon had crested the nearby sea.

THE green he wore matched his eyes, Lin noticed as she approached Therron. Nearby, a group of what appeared to be Kahishian nobility, dark-skinned and clad in shades of red and violet and yellow, were conferring in their own tongue. She had never seen any of the desert people until now. They were of course here for the Fair and the world-famous contest.

"*Erisen*," she said with a small bow. "I didn't expect the honor of seeing you again." And then she caught sight of the harp at his hip, saw it was of gold and that the strings were gold. A wave of longing swept through Lin, the like of which she had not thought to feel again.

She met Therron's eyes and wondered if he had seen that look of longing, for surely she could not have concealed it in time. "*The light of lamps and the songs of the hearth still call to me*," he quoted. "How could I have stayed away?"

She saw that he had no wine. "Will you be singing for us?"

"I believe so. Right now, though, I am admiring this painting."

Lin moved to stand beside him. Master Gelvan had a number of paintings and tapestries hanging in this room. This painting depicted a grey-haired man with a harp, surrounded by mountains, under a black sky where hung a full moon. Brightness emanated from the poet as if from his skin. In contrast, the mountains were nearly as black as the sky. The stone of the poet's ring gleamed like a second moon.

"Edrien Letrell," said Lin. "Of course. Sometimes I think everyone has a painting of him."

Therron smiled. "True, though this is finer than most. Edrien Letrell's search for the Path is a popular story, not just among poets."

"Perhaps because he returned triumphant," said Lin. "People like stories with an uplifting ending, or at least they did."

"We do seem to live in a time when nobility is often questioned— even mocked," said Therron. "Yet somehow the tale of Edrien endures."

Edrien Letrell, greatest Seer of his age. In the distant past, he had sought the Path to the Otherworld that for so long had been relegated to myth, was thought lost along with the enchantments. And he had returned refusing to tell of what he had seen—bringing only the enchanted Silver Branch from that realm as proof. Poets told of its ethereal shining, how each spring the branch blossomed with flowers and leaves that were lost again in winter. The branch awarded at the contest every twelve years was only a replica of the enchanted Silver Branch now housed within the Academy's Hall of Harps.

In Academy culture, Edrien Letrell was revered. He had occupied a similar space in his age as Valanir Ocune did in her own—was even more highly regarded, since he had found the Path. The poet who had told her of these things had done so with a mix of wistfulness and resentment. There seemed no end in the Academy to the measuring, the competition. Or so it seemed to her, observing from outside.

"We need such stories," said Therron. "I believe in the coming days, we will need them more and more."

Lin shifted her gaze to the Seer. He was still eyeing the figure of Edrien, and appeared lost in thought. The sounds of the ball washed over them: the tinkle of a woman's laugh, the measured patter of talk.

Suddenly, the call of trumpets: it had to be the king and his retinue arriving. Lin was momentarily grateful for the concealment of the alcove.

In that time the Seer hadn't moved.

"The king and Court Poet are here," Lin said to his profile. His nose was the slightest bit beaky, his eyes deep-set in shadow. "I suppose you have met them."

"Oh yes," said Therron, absently. "Many times."

She waited, but still he contemplated the art before him as if nothing else existed. At last Lin said, "I don't understand. What do you mean, we will need these stories?" Behind them the music started up again, this time a slower dance.

Now Therron did look at her, his expression seeming to shift in the lamplight from stern to tolerant and back again. She couldn't tell if he truly wanted to be speaking with her or wished for her to be off. She was about to do the latter when he said, "I'm going to the garden to tune my harp. Would you care to join me there?"

He offered her his arm, as a gentleman might a lady. She nearly laughed, though could not have said why. Instead, she wordlessly took his arm, allowed him to guide her to the tall doors that led to the garden and then out, into the midsummer night.

CHAPTER

4

DECEPTION could so quickly become a part of one's life, Rianna thought as she allowed Ned to lead her in a dance. In truth, Rianna was the one who was leading—another deception, long-practiced, and for his sake. The charade had never seemed irksome until tonight. She had begun to wonder what it would be like if just once, she could allow someone else to take the lead.

He was looking into her face very earnestly, as if searching it for clues. He had a habit of doing that—had been doing it for all the years she had known him, which was most of her life. But now that her father was beginning to talk of a winter wedding, of making their troth official, Ned had begun to do it rather more.

Rianna forced herself to meet his eyes. So often they had confided in each other, growing up. Ned the man was not much different from Ned the boy—serious, overly lank, clumsy. He had proved strangely resistant to the lessons ingrained in most of the nobility—in physical grace, in arrogance.

Rianna forced a smile. "Why so quiet?" she said. She dipped in his arms and allowed him to twirl her around, seemingly without effort. Her hand clasped his shoulder, lightly. His hand at her waist was a familiar presence; they had danced together thus since she had come of age.

Ned shook his head. "I think you know why, Rianna."

The blood rose to her temples, pulsing in her ears. If even one of the maids had spoken with another servant, with anyone . . . "I don't," she said, with what she hoped was a puzzled expression. And hated the necessity of wearing an expression with him as if it were a mask.

Ned sighed. She could not help but notice that he always looked awkward in his elegant clothes, as if they had somehow been fitted wrong. "I know you don't love me, Rianna," he said. "I know this marriage was not your choice . . . any more than it was mine."

"Well . . ." Her heart had slowed somewhat, but she still wasn't sure how to deal with this. The light melody the musicians played grated in her ears, a dissonant mockery of what she was feeling.

"I only hope that . . ." Ned bit his lip. "I hope in time you may come to love me. Even if it is not as I love you. I know I don't deserve you, Rianna."

It was too much, Rianna thought, and the dance was not sufficiently distracting. They turned together, facing the crowd of onlookers who were probably speculating about them right now. She had heard the whispers. That her Galician father had made use of her beauty to ensnare a lord's son.

How could these people ever grasp the truth: that she and Ned had known each other since they were children and that their friendship had led both their parents to speculate about it becoming something more? Her father did not need more gold—she was certain of that. What he wanted, she thought, was the stature that would come with Ned's family name. And she could hardly blame him—once a street sweeper—for wanting that.

"Ned, I love you as a friend—even as family," she said truthfully, in as low a voice as the music would allow. "I always have. You are right, though, that a marriage between us feels—strange to me. That it might not have been my choice."

He may have flinched a little. "I am sorry," he said. "Do you think, though, that I could still make you happy?"

Rianna thought her heart might burst. "It's very possible."

She had no choice, she reminded herself. Darien had assured her that he would devise a plan—but there was no plan that could spare Ned the betrayal that was to come.

Rianna had heard there were kingdoms, oceans distant, where men and women could marry of their own free will. Such a place *would* be far away, Rianna thought. Beyond the green hills and lakes of Eivar, over the expanse of desert and mountains of Kahishi, across the Blood Sea and the lands of the farthest east. Places she would never see.

Over Ned's shoulder she caught sight of Darien across the room with Marlen at his side and an ironic smile on his face. He was so much the opposite of anyone she had known in her life. Tonight, she would hear him sing.

It was quiet in the garden. Though a few couples had escaped into the evening and now whispered among the roses, most of the merchant's guests preferred to be where the music and wine were flowing.

Twilight was descending as Lin and Therron seated themselves on a bench in silence. Without a word, the Seer fell to tuning the gold strings of his harp. Lin felt a pang of something less pleasant now than longing. She thought it was unlikely, unless she killed someone, that such a harp could ever be hers.

There was another thought nagging behind that one, but she could not quite catch it. At the sound of his voice, melodious like no other voice she had heard.

"It was brave of you to come here tonight," he said, his eyes still on the strings, sharp nails plucking. The sounds like fading bells in the dusk. "To be introduced as a poet, with the king and the Court Poet present."

A gentle wind rustled the trees, stirring the scent of roses in the air. Lin shrugged. "We obtained approvals for the song. There are no laws about the sex of the person who sings them."

"True." Now he did look at her, and smile. "You could have been a lawyer, spared yourself such a flimsy profession as this."

"So instead of a female poet, a female lawyer?" She raised an eyebrow. "An oddity, either way."

He laughed. "Lin," he said, "who are you, really?"

And it was then that moonlight broke through the clouds, touched Therron's face. And like an enchantment—for so it surely was—the light picked out iridescent symbols in Therron's skin, radiating from his right eye. Lin recognized them as ancient runes—intricate lines that shimmered in the night, reflecting the light of the moon.

It was the last of the enchantments still in use at the Academy: the marking of a Seer. None but Seers knew how the mark was made. The rite was secret. Certainly the young poet who had taught Lin all she knew had been as much in the dark as anyone.

The moon illuminated something else, too: the moon opal on Therron's right hand, which shone with a pale flame. The thought that had been drifting at the back of Lin's mind returned, and this time she recognized it. She felt the blood drain from her face.

"I could ask you the same thing," she said, keeping her tone even.

He inclined his head to acknowledge her thrust, as if in a duel. "What gave it away?" he asked. "The ring?"

"That," she said, "and that I have never heard of any Seer by the name of Therron. Yet clearly you are a master whose name would be known."

Now he smiled, glittering cold. He seemed to be distant now, withdrawing. "I thank you."

Though it was dark, the mark surrounding his eye shone like a star fallen to earth. No, Lin thought, that was too hackneyed a phrase. Yet there it was. Light and laughter from the party drifted toward them through the wrought-iron doors, reminding Lin that she was to sing tonight. As was he.

Into the silence he said, in a different tone, "As I recall, you had a question for me. About our need for the tale of Edrien, in the days to come."

Lin shook her head helplessly. "Well," she said, still overcome.

His eyes looked very green. "Word has reached me," he said, "that the Red Death is in Sarmanca."

She inhaled sharply. The plague that had supposedly been key to the undoing of the great Davyd Dreamweaver, the last Seer to possess enchantments. Hundreds of years ago. But these were legends. Lin shook her head. "It's practically a child's tale."

"Tell that to the people of Sarmanca," said the Seer, but gently. Before she could speak again, he took her hand in his. "Reports have reached me—so far over a hundred dead."

"Why is no one else speaking of this?" Lin demanded. "All those people inside—do they know?" Sarmanca was far southeast, near the mountains that bordered Kahishi. Rayen had told of trees bearing red perfumed flowers the size of his head, their velvet petals carpeting the ground come summer.

"The truth about Sarmanca—and many other things—has been hidden from all of us," said the Seer. "Listen: the plague will not remain in the south. It will spread, reach Tamryllin, and at last the north until all of Eivar is stricken."

"So you're saying we are lost?"

His tone was stern now. "I am asking that you recall what it seems all poets have let themselves forget—that the true purpose of our art is not to perform at parties, nor to win contests."

"Our true purpose?" Lin met his gaze. The familiar anger sparked in her. "Look at me. If my purpose was to earn gold, or praise, *Erisen,* I would not be here."

For a moment the Seer looked surprised. Then he laughed. "Of course," he said. "You are right, Lin. I'm sorry—you are right. And that reminds me." He twisted off his Academy ring and, before she could react, was pressing it into her hand. "For safekeeping," he said. "Will you do that for me?"

"Why . . ."

"You might say it's a—precaution," he said. "Now come. We'd best go inside."

Lin stared at him, at the shadow his face had become in the dark, at the light over his right eye. "One question, then," she said. "Why did you deceive us?"

"I've enjoyed our meetings," he said. "Did you?"

Caught off guard, Lin nodded.

"Then take that with you," he said, "and try to think well of me." And then he was standing, brushing himself off, and standing taller than she had noticed before, the harp again strapped to his side. The glow of the mark seemed to spread to the rest of him, as if he were in his entirety illuminated, but she knew that was a trick of her imagination.

Lin felt a sense of loss without knowing why as she watched the Seer bow and then turn to rejoin the crowds. As he entered the sharp line of light from the garden doors, she saw a slight stoop in his walk but knew it did not matter—would not matter to anyone in that room, who would surely tell of this night for the rest of their lives.

DARIEN had told Rianna that there were no female poets, but that didn't explain the woman who stood at the center of the room and sang as her companion strummed a harp. Her sharp face was upturned to the lamplight, her eyes focused somewhere past them, past all the people there. The voice that rose from her frail frame was surprisingly powerful. It was a song of lost love.

Darien had sung a love song, too, a masculine rendition that Rianna was certain he had written for her. Marlen had stood at a respectful distance behind him, contributing only melodies with the harp and his voice. The words still echoed in her head:

> *Snow Queen of my heart*
> *a dark night slowly falls*
> *and if I lose you in shadow*
> *I will ever sing alone.*

His eyes had never met hers, but the music strummed her bones as if she were a harp, or her nerves were the strings. She was by now expert at keeping her face impassive.

Now this poet, Lin—she gave no other name—was singing, with her strong voice and the dress that was too big for her. The song was wistful, as if it were sung by an older woman looking back from the end of life. It brought tears to Rianna's eyes, though those had probably not been far off.

At the conclusion of her song, Lin was met with silence—and then, slowly, a flurry of gracious applause that almost immediately petered out, like a brief drizzle of rain. It occurred to Rianna that while she was fascinated by the idea of a female poet, others in that room might feel differently.

Lin and her partner took a graceful bow. Rianna's father came forward to shake their hands, then announced, "Thanks to all our esteemed performers—and good luck in the contest!"

More clapping, just as controlled as before. Rianna felt proud of her father, for he cut a fine figure tonight, and she knew many women were watching. She had decided that her best course was simply to ask him about his and Callum's strange behavior. No doubt there was a reasonable explanation.

Likely she had occupied herself with the business of Master Beylint so she would be distracted from her own deception, and Ned.

"Now for a surprise," Master Gelvan was saying. "We have here a guest of honor, returned from long travels abroad, who has agreed to sing for us tonight. Words cannot express how deeply honored we are to have him with us in our home. I present to you Eivar's greatest Seer—the one and only Valanir Ocune."

A greying man in green came forward with a bow to Master Gelvan. Rianna barely had time to register her shock—both that the great man was *here,* after so many years abroad, and that her father had concealed the fact from her. More secrets, she thought. She looked at Ned and saw that he was grinning. When their eyes met, they both nearly laughed aloud. How often had they talked of their longing to see Valanir Ocune perform, just once? And now, without any warning, he was here.

Yet as Valanir Ocune unslung his harp and adjusted the instrument in his arms, the applause that greeted him was just as measured and careful as before. Rianna wondered why.

"THE old bastard," Marlen muttered. "So he's back."

"That old bastard is only one of the most famous men in the world," Darien said dryly. He was feeling pleasantly warmed by the success of their performance, however weak the applause had been. A strange aura hung about the room tonight.

And now Valanir Ocune was here. It wasn't fair—it was just the sort of thing that could eclipse their hard work altogether—but Darien was pleased that he would get to hear the master perform. During Darien's years at the Academy, Valanir had been little more than a legend to the students. For more than a decade he wandered in foreign lands . . . performing for the sultan of Kahishi, it was said; vanishing for months at a time into the desert.

"Yes, but . . ." Marlen's color was high, and he spoke with a rare excitement. "Valanir Ocune and Court Poet Gerrard are rivals. Sworn enemies. And both *here.*"

Darien thought that was a little dramatic, but didn't have a chance to say so: a hush was flooding the room. Valanir, eyes alight, had begun to speak.

"It is good to be home." Each word, shaped with the precision of a rock carving, falling into a breathless silence. "This will be my first performance on this side of the mountain pass. The first, and perhaps my last. Who can say?"

Darien raised an eyebrow. He and Marlen exchanged glances. *His last?*

"I give thanks to Master Gelvan for hosting me here tonight," Valanir went on. "Here in this graceful home, which has so much of Tamryllin in it. The art, the music . . . and tonight, royalty and the Court Poet himself."

Inevitably, many guests' eyes shifted to observe the king and queen, the Court Poet beside them. Nickon Gerrard's face carefully expressionless.

"I wrote this song imagining the roses and the sea winds of Tamryllin, as I took shelter in a tent in the eastern mountains during the journey from Kahishi," said Valanir Ocune. He had begun to strum his harp, lightly, softly. "This song," he said, "is dedicated to my home."

"Did you know?" Leander hissed in her ear.

"No," said Lin. It would do no good to explain, and the music was beginning. She wanted to hear every note, every word. Despite the thing he had said which had made songs seem irrelevant. *The Red Death is in Sarmanca.*

And the ring that she had hastily slid into her pouch, hardly believing it was real. The ring of Valanir Ocune.

Try to think well of me, he'd said, as if her opinion of Eivar's greatest Seer, the man who had played for kings and sultans on countless occasions, was worth even a drop in the ocean.

The music had begun. Tears welled in Lin's eyes, and she could not even bring herself to move a hand to wipe them away.

Though the melody had already cut into her, Lin made herself pay attention to the words. It was a love poem written to a city, dazzling white by the sea. *Dedicated to my home.* She felt a tug of disappointment. The music was all she had imagined, but this banal sentiment was not what she expected of Valanir Ocune.

That, at least, was her thought during the first moments of the song. And then it changed.

Marlen may have understood before anyone else in that room what Valanir Ocune was about to do. With the exception of Nickon Gerrard, whom Marlen suspected had known from the start.

It was coded in symbols for anyone versed in such things: white roses, meaning death. *Towers stabbing the sky,* an echo of a lament for a city destroyed.

But Marlen did not think it was because of his education that he detected the early signs of what would come to be called "Valanir's crime" in the streets of Tamryllin. It was simply his nature to know the darkness in others. Sometimes, that was all he did know.

So while it might have been shocking when the idyllic summer in a white city darkened, Marlen was ready. He had already stopped watching Valanir Ocune as he sang, focusing his gaze on Nickon Gerrard instead. The Court Poet barely moved a muscle—it was impressive.

Who will sing for my city? sang Valanir. A minor key had crept into the music, almost without warning. A seamless transition.

> *Where the great ones are gone*
> *and the music a shadow*
> *of what was once our pride.*
> *No matter the color*
> *of the branch—silver, copper or gold,*
> *there is one surety:*
> *It is false. It is false.*

It was as far as he got. Marlen would later wonder if there had been more to the song, or if this was meant to be the conclusion, the place where the threads of music and words intersected and knotted together.

It was hard to tell, because the next moment saw Valanir pinioned fast between guards who had advanced through the crowd as onlookers gasped. But it was only when one of the guards punched the Seer's face with an audible crack that the silence of the room was shattered and people began to flee, crashing into one another in their haste, like horses urged on by a whip.

CHAPTER
5

The room had changed. Quiet reigned where once there had been the harsh ringing of the guards' swords. Where above the commotion, there had been the exquisite voice of Nickon Gerrard, coiling and rising.

How strange, Rianna thought, that the orders for the capture of Valanir Ocune should come not from the king but from the Court Poet.

But just as abruptly, the chaotic boil died to a simmer. The guards were gone, and so—noticeably—was the Court Poet, the king and queen, and Valanir Ocune. Guests were filing out the door with impressive efficiency and speed. Rianna wondered what it was they feared—they had done nothing wrong. While Valanir . . . he had gone beyond the already-serious crime of performing a song that had not been approved.

How far beyond, Rianna was not sure.

Ned had at first put an arm around her, as if to shield her from the unpleasantness going on; Rianna had shrugged him off, annoyed. But her father apparently had the same idea, for he emerged then from the crowds of departing guests, ignoring those who tried to bid him a quick, panicked farewell. It was as if all the rules of etiquette had been abandoned.

"Are you all right?" he asked Rianna.

"Of course," she said. "But Valanir—what will happen to him?"

Master Gelvan's mouth tightened. "I don't know, Rianna. Maybe nothing."

"Impossible," said Ned, who looked pale. "For a crime like this . . ."

"There is no way we can know what will happen, Ned," said Master Gelvan, cutting him off.

Rianna understood then that he was protecting her. *How much does he hide from me?* And now she remembered the note Callum had slipped to him earlier.

"I need some air," she said, and disengaged herself from Ned, from her father. They watched her worriedly but did not follow. She meant to go to the garden, to lose herself there among the roses until the last of the guests had gone. To think about all that had happened—with Valanir but also with her father.

That was when she saw Lin, the woman who had performed earlier. She had dropped to her knees, her skirts crumpled around her on the floor, her face caught in her hands. As if she had been knocked there, like a doll.

Timidly, Rianna approached her. Other guests were flowing busily around Lin as if she were a stone in a stream as they headed toward the door. Lin showed no signs of moving.

When she thought herself within earshot, Rianna called her name. Nothing. Rianna tried again, and again met with no response. Finally, she touched the other woman's shoulder and said her name again.

Lin jumped to her feet like a spring, startling Rianna and nearly throwing her backward. Her face was a mask of anger. Then it cleared abruptly, and she said, "It's you. Mistress Gelvan. I . . . I am sorry."

Rianna could see now that Lin's face was ashen. She thought of how Valanir had complied so calmly with his arrest, how he had departed the Gelvan home surrounded by guards with his head high—almost as if he were their commander. But for the fact that two of them held his arms roughly back from his body, while others shoved him from behind.

No need to be gentle, Nickon Gerrard had said.

"We lost a good man tonight," said Lin.

"Why?" said Rianna. "What will happen to him?"

It was beginning to frustrate her, this question. And the female poet, who had already intrigued her, struck her as someone who might answer her questions. Who might understand, as the men did not, that she did not need protection.

Lin stared into the distance. "He broke two laws," she said. "Both serious. But one—one could be considered treason."

The room around them was growing quiet.

"Treason—how?"

She could sense, more than see, that the other woman was drawing from reserves of patience to supply an answer. "The contest, the Silver Branch, all these were created by the monarchy in centuries past," Lin said. The rhythm of her words called up a memory of her recitation, earlier that same evening. "Any power a poet has in this land must ultimately have been bestowed by the Court Poet, who is himself an agent of the king."

"And Valanir Ocune was saying that poets must find the real Branch—instead of settling for the contest prize," Rianna said, trying to understand. This world, which had so abruptly entered her home, was Darien's world.

"The Branch of Edrien, borne from the Path of the Otherworld," Lin said solemnly. "Yet surely . . . surely that was a metaphor. He can't mean . . ." she stopped.

"The *metaphor* will destroy him," said a new voice. Marlen had come swaggering up to them, a glass of wine in his hand. He was smiling crookedly, as if this were all a joke.

Rianna fell back a little, not liking this new incarnation of the man she had thought of as Darien's polite, retiring friend. *Why is he smiling?*

As if he sensed her revulsion, Marlen suddenly became serious. "This will be seen as rebellion," he said. "An attack on the way things are done. Lin, you know what that means."

The look that passed between them was unreadable to Rianna.

A long pause, and then Lin said, "For me, it was always about the music. Not winning."

"How like a woman to say something of that sort," said Marlen, the unpleasant smile returning. "Everything we do is about winning. How would Valanir have become who he is, without that?"

Something cold overtook Lin's eyes. She straightened. "Is that so, great lord?" Her voice musical with contempt. "Tell us, then: what will *you* become?"

His smile too fixed, Marlen responded with a violent flick of his wrist, upturning his glass of wine on the floor. A sunburst of red splashed the pale floor tiles. Without even glancing down at his handiwork, he loped off and away from them.

Now Ned spoke. Rianna had not even sensed him coming up beside her. "What was that?"

The rage seemed to have drained from Lin; she now looked weary. Once again, she was small, her figure lost in a dress that did not quite fit. "I'm not even sure."

Master Gelvan had reached them, too. Rianna wondered what he thought of the crimson puddle that was spreading on the floor. How carelessly it had been flung—a mark of disrespect to this house.

Yet her father seemed unconcerned, did not even glance down, though she knew it was in his fastidious nature to care very much about the state of the tiles. Instead his attention was focused on the poet who remained. "My lady," he said, addressing Lin. "I am not well versed in Academy matters, but if I understand correctly, your career might have been unfairly cut short tonight. The shock must be great. You are welcome to stay the night here, in our home, if that would please you."

Rianna glanced at her father in surprise. *Cut short?*

Lin looked grave. "You are kind," she said. "So kind, and have already done so much for me by allowing me to perform in your home." She straightened again. "I will not impose upon you any longer, and in any case, I must find my partner."

"Very well," said the merchant gravely. "Please consider this, however: my daughter Rianna is now at the age where some tutoring in poetry and music would be of great benefit. And I noticed her interest in it tonight. Would you be so kind as to return in the morning, and we will discuss your availability, and your fee?"

So he had noticed her interest in the performances, Rianna thought. Often it was easy to think her father was too involved in his business affairs to observe details like that.

Lin bowed low, and her eyes looked now as they had when she sung earlier that night. Warm, wistful. "It would be an honor."

"Thank you," Rianna cut in, and herself bowed, though she was unaccustomed to the gesture.

Lin nodded, looking preoccupied. Letting the hem of her skirts drag in the wine that Marlen had spilled, she drifted away toward the door. "Now where is that drunkard," Rianna thought she heard the other woman mutter, before she was out of earshot. Leaving the three of them. *The family.*

She had a sudden conviction that she was not meant to be here.

"*Avan,* thank you for thinking of me," she said, and hugged her father. "Tonight has been . . . upsetting. May I have a few moments in the garden alone? Please?"

Though she had not addressed him directly, Ned bowed his head. "Whatever you need, always."

He looked so solemn and unhappy. Impulsively, she hugged him, too. The pain she felt on his behalf transmuted, for now, into a kind of excitement. It was the events of the night, she decided. And seeing Darien sing a love song that he had written specially for her, and watch her in her green dress from across the room.

MARLEN felt a pang of regret that he had spilled out his wine: the merchant's servants had cleared away the decanters from all the tables, and he was left with an empty glass. When really—despite his dedicated efforts in the course of the evening—he was simply not drunk enough. His gait was positively steady as he made his way to the front door.

Most of the guests had departed, but not quite all; and there were enough alcoves and shadowed corners in this room in which people might take shelter, hold conference with one another. Events of such magnitude must be mulled, made sense of, even on a sweetly scented midsummer night. Particularly because for some, they might present an opportunity.

Marlen's first thought was to find Darien, but it had since occurred to him that his friend, in his accustomed fashion, had probably chosen to take advantage of the chaos. Seeing his own opportunity there.

With one song, Valanir Ocune had upset the balance of everything for the poets of Tamryllin in this year of the contest. Marlen knew it, even without his father there to point it out, as he would undoubtedly have done.

Wine was not enough, in truth.

"Ah, my lord Marlen. The one. The only." It was a voice that had been trained, though was unmistakably dulled with drink. Marlen turned and saw that Leander was slumping, his harp banging ungracefully against his thighs. Posture was important for a poet: in bearing a harp, and in song.

"I can't argue with that, I suppose," said Marlen, though the "lord" reference was uncomfortably near to Lin's ringing contempt. Enviously, he noted that the other man still had some wine, a white-gold vintage of the north. Leander was familiar to him, and Marlen had sensed in him a weakness even as a student. He was someone who could easily be manipulated, thought Marlen, because he was never sure who he was.

"What happens now?" Leander said. "I worked with Lin because she has talent. How could I know . . ."

"You couldn't," Marlen said smoothly. "But now Nickon Gerrard will enforce the status quo with an iron fist, to ensure that poets know their place. And there are no female poets."

"She will understand, won't she?"

"She's a clever girl," Marlen said with a purposeful patience. As a boy, he'd liked to observe the wolves of the forest in their careful stalking of hares and deer. "Plain as the Three made her, but nonetheless a talent. What is her real name, Leander?"

Even as he asked, he was unsure of the reason for his interest. Perhaps because he had sensed something hidden there, and it was in Marlen's nature to take an interest in anything hidden, or forbidden.

Leander was staring at the floor now. "I don't know."

"I enjoyed your performance tonight," said Marlen. "Even without a partner, you can still win." And then wondered what impulse had made him say that. He didn't believe it for a moment.

Leander laughed, but it came out like a sob. "You don't mean that," he said, proving to be more perceptive than he appeared. "You and Darien are a pair of gods . . . sun and moon. No one has a chance against you."

A bit too roughly, Marlen caught the other man's arm. "Let's find you a carriage," he said. "You've got money? Good." He guided the man toward the door. Somehow, Marlen knew that he would not sleep tonight, and he couldn't stay another moment in the Galician's house. It was ironic, he thought, that the greatest poet of the age had been arrested in the home of a heretic.

An irony at present known only to himself.

Wine is not enough, he thought almost sadly. In the midst of these events, his own weakness bit near to the bone. *Sun and moon*, Marlen thought, finding himself pulled toward that darkness within—source of much of his talent, but not only that. *Sun and moon. Of course. Of course.*

DAYLIGHT from a begrimed window was just beginning to fall across the bed. It was really more a pallet, thin and stuffed with straw. Lin and Leander Keyen had shared it by keeping their distance. They had shared a bed this way in inns across Eivar, north to south. Months of travel, writing, composing, and singing together.

That was over now.

She had returned in the small hours of morning, exhausted, to find Leander packing his belongings. The way he saw it, he was doing her a favor, leaving her the room, which was paid for the next week. Finding one for himself would be nearly impossible just days before the Midsummer Fair and contest. He would probably have to share a bed with not just one, but perhaps three others.

She made a sarcastic comment about his sexual preferences. A reflex to mask her shock. Predictably, he was angry. Until he recalled the enormity of what he was telling her, after nine months on the road.

"You must understand," said Leander. He was pale and sunken-eyed. "This is my only chance. What you've done for me—your songs have made a name for us. But Valanir Ocune changed everything tonight."

"I know," Lin said, "but that is only the contest. I know I am certain to be disqualified. But after . . . ?"

"After, I can't risk it. I want to go on as before, really I do . . . but women can't be poets. Neither the Academy nor the court will recognize my work, as long as I am with you."

"So you assume," Lin said. Then she shook her head, more to herself than at him. She sank onto the bed, closed her eyes. "I must admit . . . you have surprised me." And then almost smiled, thinking that when it most mattered, her skill with words deserted her. Not for the first time.

She heard the floorboards creak. Felt his hand on her shoulder. A furious part of her wanted to shake it off, even strike at it with all the force she could deliver. But the rest of her was just stunned, even—and she hated herself for this—understanding. Well she knew the insecurities Leander Keyen carried within him . . . and, similarly, how unaware he was of them. He thought he could discard his burdens by discarding her. She could almost pity him for that.

"My songs," she said at last.

"Our songs," he corrected. "And I will always credit you, when I can."

At the door, she heard his steps halt a moment. She didn't look up.

"I'll miss you," Leander said. "I never found out who you are."

He closed the door with barely a sound. She heard his footfalls descend the stairs. And then silence, for it was nearly dawn, just before tumult in the streets would herald a new day.

Lin rested her cheek against the wall, which was pitted and stained. It was rough against her skin.

She had no right to be angry with Leander. Her position had been tenuous even before Valanir Ocune had done what he'd done.

But the real reason she couldn't be angry with Leander was that last winter he had saved her life.

They had met as they would someday be parted, in an inn. At the time she had been a specter, wasted and pale from a lingering illness she had managed to conceal by constantly pinching her cheeks, for the innkeeper would have expelled her into the cold if he suspected she was ill. She had no money for lodgings, only her voice and a song she had composed in her head. For the price of a song, she would be allowed some bread and soup, and a corner of the stables for the night.

People thought she was a boy, of course. She didn't know what would have happened if anyone had guessed otherwise. It was a backwater town, hard-bitten by winter, and its men were hungry not only for food but for comfort against the cold and dark.

On this night, from a boy, a song would suffice.

She remembered the way she had bruised her cheeks with pinching, begged some bread from the kitchens before getting up on a bench and beginning to sing. Her audience a group of men who were taking turns dandling the only other source of entertainment, one of the serving girls, on brawny knees. Her voice weak as she began, so that snickers and grumbling had rippled the air and turned her legs to water.

Except that she had spotted one man in the crowd who was not like the others. Leander had been thinner then, too, and swathed in a good fur cloak. But what caught her attention was his harp, a triangle of willow wood and brass strings reclining against his belted tunic. *Beautiful,* she had thought, drinking in the sight. It had been so long since she'd seen one.

Her eyes had traveled to his right hand, where sure enough a ring with a round stone gleamed in the light of the common room lamps. His was an aquamarine. She remembered the lore of the Academy stones. The aquamarine stood for *Clarity of heart, a soul of the green meadows.* Academy graduates did not choose their gemstones—the Masters chose, based on signs known only to them. Another remnant of enchantments that were otherwise long gone.

Seeing that made her sure that this was someone she could trust. Her voice strengthened and she trained her eyes on his face, singing only to him. She sang of winter roads and the hope of discovering light, refuge from the cold. His eyes flickered perceptibly, and she knew he had recognized both her talent and that she was not a boy, after all.

The other men in the room recognized neither, but they enjoyed her song, and before the night was out they had urged her to sing two more, popular ballads of the day. Several pennies were tossed in her direction, which she collected carefully into her cap. When she was done, Leander Keyen was waiting to talk to her.

It was simple, really: Leander was gifted by Kiara with an adeptness for composing melodies, but he was less skilled in the art of words. It was common for poets to work in pairs, as partners. Leander was a recent graduate who would need years of training and study before he could achieve the mark of a Seer. But to win the prize at the Midsummer Fair, or even come in second or third place—that could open up doors. The nobility paid the winners a high price to perform in their homes, and those who won the Branch itself could expect much more.

Lin had known all of this but had never thought it could be relevant to her, a woman with no training. Women were forbidden from even setting foot on the island where the Academy was situated, in a bay in the northwest.

Lin had had no plans for her life at that time; had been plunging headlong through the winter like a hunted deer, with no idea where she was going and with no thought to the drops ahead. In fact, a fall from the precipice had at that time seemed assured.

As they had headed to his room for further talks, Leander noticed that she was shivering, draped his fur cloak around her shoulders. When they finished their talk and made plans to meet in the morning, she took it off to return to him. "That's all right," he said, with a pitying glance at her thin shirt. "You can have it." He closed the door to his room before she could protest.

She had nearly cried then for the first time in a long while. In the course of the past months she had grown numb, had come to imagine herself a statue with bruised cheeks, impervious. Leander's unexpected kindness was like a sword wound. She would do everything she could, she had sworn to herself in that instant. She would help him win.

Lin never told him about her decision that night. Nor did she tell him that until that night, she had relinquished any sense of purpose. As time went on, he guessed that she was highborn, because of her education, and knew she was of the north, because of her accent. She showed him how to hunt in the deep woods and some tricks with the knife. But more than that she would not say, and he, with uncharacteristic wisdom, did not ask. Instead, Leander confided in her about his parents, his overbearing pack of sisters, and she had listened eagerly and with something akin to wonder. Her own experience of family was so different.

She grew to depend on him, and she never told him that, either.

That was certainly just as well, Lin thought now, rising to her feet at last. Mechanically, she began to throw her belongings into her pack. Then she remembered she was still wearing the dress. Gritting her teeth, she strained her arms behind her back to unlace the bodice.

This business of getting undressed and dressed again, of packing— it gave her a purpose. In just a few moments, she would have to decide what to do next.

Just last night she had met—even sat and talked with—Valanir Ocune, greatest Seer since Edrien Letrell himself. Hours later, in a malodorous inn, she was wondering if she could summon the strength to do more than cast herself, finally, to the cold embrace of the Three, as she'd once had a mind to do.

A singular contrast. Was there a song in this somewhere?

The Red Death is in Sarmanca. Valanir's dubious gift to her—a dreadful knowledge, along with his moon opal ring.

She would not think of what could be happening to him now. He had knowingly gotten himself captured; she was sure of that. But it was not comforting. Court Poet Gerrard hated him, it was said, for personal reasons. That would make matters worse, much worse.

Lin reached into her pouch, ran her fingertips over the ring nestled there. She now knew something—a potential future—and that made her responsible. Perhaps Leander letting her go was a gift in its own way.

Since childhood Lin had been haunted by a recurring dream, in which she stood at the summit of a tall, sheer cliff wrapped in ocean waves. No sign of life amid the bareness surrounding. A silence almost oppressive despite the murmuring sea. And just a short distance away, a marvel: a tree that from root to leaf was entirely silver, resplendent in the sun.

All the years, Lin had thought it no more than a dream. At most, a sign of the yearning in her that had begun long before she could even give a name to it.

Now she was not so sure.

Valanir had hinted that the Path to the Otherworld somehow was key. Lin recalled the painting of Edrien Letrell, a figure of light against black mountains. His face a dissonant mixture of wonder and resignation.

It was a dangerous road, and she was not Edrien Letrell—was not even a poet by the reckoning of most.

Danger did not matter to Lin; it hadn't mattered for quite some time.

CHAPTER
6

THE common room of the *Ring and Flagon* was packed that day. As the tavern most frequented by poets for centuries, it was the natural gathering place for Darien Aldemoor and Marlen Humbreleigh to tell of the previous night's events to the Academy graduates who surrounded them, gape-mouthed and seething with jealousy.

It was bad enough that the two of them were so talented, so good-looking, so painfully likely to win the Silver Branch. Even worse that all their success seemed to come with no effort whatever. While other poets practiced feverishly—especially so near to the contest—Darien and Marlen could most often be seen imbibing at their leisure, feet up on tables as they debated the merits of the region's wines. And, of course, they had their pick of Tamryllin women—that didn't even need to be said.

But to cap it off—as if to sprinkle great crystals of salt in the gaping wounds of other poets—it was Darien and Marlen, the oh-so-privileged, who had seen the first known performance of Valanir Ocune in Eivar since most of them had been children. That was, in fact, the turn of phrase that one particularly young, embittered Academy graduate had used in a poem satirizing their collective predicament: great crystals of salt, a gaping wound. He'd gained much laughter and applause.

And even more salt, heaped up: the two witnessed Valanir Ocune's crime and arrest. The arrogant pair had seen it all—were already working on a song about it.

Of course they were.

"Go on," said Hassen Styr, a strikingly tall, burly man and one of the more talented of the graduates. He was sprawled in a chair, head tipped back. "Tell us more about how special you two are." He yawned. Other graduates looked on with awe, especially the younger ones; only Hassen could say those things without sounding bitter or weak. It was his intimidating frame, no doubt, which was in itself unfair.

Darien laughed. His feet were propped on the table in front of him. He reclined luxuriously, as if holding court. At his side, Marlen was standing, a drink in his hand, the other hand tapping arrhythmically on the table. He had the air of a restless cat.

"You know," Hassen continued, "if you need any help with that song, I have some ideas. How about, *And then Valanir came home / got himself arrested / and made life miserable / for the rest of us*?"

"Ingenious," Marlen drawled, and downed the rest of his drink. "My money's on you, lawyer boy."

Everyone knew Hassen's father was a lawyer—he came of common roots, an unusual characteristic in a man who could afford to prepare for the Academy entrance exams and then spend seven years studying there.

"Clever," said Hassen. "I've begun to suspect that there is an unfortunate pollutant in the water at the Humbreleigh estates. Why else would the heir to all and everything be so often ill-disposed?"

Darien interjected, palm upraised. "Enough, both of you. Hassen, if you don't want to hear our story, that's your choice. We know it wasn't because we were special that we saw all this. Just luck." Before anyone could speak, he went on. "And it's true we can't foresee what will come of this. Valanir's crime reflects on all of us, as far as the court is concerned."

"That had occurred to most of us already." This from Piet, a thin, compact graduate whose face seemed contorted in a perpetually angry expression. His tone dripped acid. "Those of us not invited to royal balls are all too aware of our vulnerability with regard to the court."

"It wasn't a royal ball," Darien said mildly.

"Piss off, Piet," said Hassen. "What do you hope to accomplish with your sour grapes?"

Piet directed a venomous glance at him and spun on his heel, departing the room. He had done that several times a day throughout their years together at the Academy.

"I wonder about the times we live in," said Hassen now, in a different tone, almost to himself. The focus of the room had turned from Darien Aldemoor and Marlen Humbreleigh to the lawyer's son. He could do that sometimes, the baritone of his voice filling a room, even pitched low. "I know Valanir Ocune's crime may have consequences for us. Poets in a world where the Academy is not what it was, where we can be executed for any perceived infraction against the Crown. Who can believe Seers once were warriors who helped temper and balance the rule of the king? But right now, all I can really think is that the greatest poet of our age is imprisoned . . . or worse."

The room fell silent. Some men bowed their heads.

Hassen Styr said, "It *is* about us. In doing this, Valanir was sending a message to us. About the contest, about our desire for fame. I'm not sure it's a message we want to hear." Somewhere outside in the streets, harp music was playing, soaring even above the noise of Tamryllin on a warm afternoon.

A young poet, one of the new crop of graduates, said timidly, "You're saying . . . Valanir Ocune committed this crime for *us*?"

Hassen shook his head as if in wonder. "I suppose I am saying that."

A new voice, now. As deep as that of Hassen, but smooth as honey. Marlen Humbreleigh said, "And yet while Valanir Ocune undergoes torture in whatever way they enjoy at the palace—and I believe the Court Poet enjoys it—is there anyone here who would not switch places with him? Anyone?" No one answered. Darien did raise an eyebrow and shake his head. Undeterred, Marlen said, "I'll bet that whatever they are doing to him, Valanir knows his power . . . and laughs."

LIN felt like an interloper as she took a seat in Master Gelvan's solar. The graceful lines of the room, the serenity evoked by afternoon sunlight streaming in the windows, pink roses cut adrift in a blue ceramic bowl on the table, all served to remind her that she was unwashed, half-starved—a weed.

And the contrast: Rianna Gelvan herself, golden hair to her waist, framing her belted dress. She really was the most beautiful woman Lin had seen. The girl was now holding out a cup to her and smiling. She was most likely unaware of how she looked, hands outstretched to give, gold trailing around and about her.

Like one of the aspects of Estarre, Lin thought. The goddess was a fierce warrior, but in another incarnation blessed the land with abundant harvest.

She was tired, Lin realized, to be thinking this way. For her mind to drift to Estarre of all the gods. She accepted the cup and drank. It was sweeter water than from the pump in the tanning district.

"My father isn't here," Rianna said, and took a seat across from Lin at the table. "But won't you stay a bit? I . . . I loved your song last night."

Lin was puzzled. This girl seemed excited to meet her, or nervous. "I'm honored, lady," she said. "I wouldn't have expected my work to be memorable, after everything else that happened."

Rianna nodded, as if she had expected that response. In the distance, Lin heard the faraway and oddly plaintive music of wind chimes.

"I came to apologize to you and your father," Lin said. "I expected to be in the city for some weeks, but . . . my plans have changed. I will be leaving after the contest."

Rianna nodded again. "I understand. It is a pity but—I was surprised when you agreed. Of course there are things you must do. Someone like you."

"Someone like me?"

The girl's eyes were intent. "Tell me . . . *how* did you learn? I've been told—I've heard women can't be poets, or study at the Academy."

So this, then, was the root of the girl's apparent fascination. The freakish idea of a female poet. Lin smiled a little. "What you've heard is true. A woman would never be permitted to study at the Academy. Women are not even allowed to set foot on the isle, by law."

Rianna raised an eyebrow. "But how—"

Again, Lin felt her lips curl in a thin, closed smile. "A man I knew," she said carefully, "taught me some of the elements of poets' lore. But I know very little. All the more reason that I'm flattered your father saw fit for me to teach you."

Rianna shrugged. "I'm sure you can guess why he'd prefer a woman to teach me."

"Because you might get to like one of the men a bit too much," said Lin, and was surprised when Rianna bit her lip and lowered her eyes to the tabletop.

A memory: Darien singing a song to his lady, an unknown love. And across the room, Rianna standing as if heart-struck, the hand of her fiancé grasping at hers as if the man knew—consciously or not—that she was already far away.

"Darien," Lin said, with a rueful grin. At least after all that had happened, she could still find some source of amusement.

Rianna's eyes widened. "Did he—"

"Of course not," said Lin with a wave of her hand. "We don't speak. I'm far beneath him, you know. Valanir Ocune's bringing me into the party was a great honor. No—only that you showed something in your face when he sang last night. And besides, it couldn't be Marlen. Or, rather," she amended, thoughtfully, "I'd *hope* it wasn't Marlen."

"Because you don't like him?"

"Because he would hurt you," said Lin. "And I hope Darien doesn't do that. I think he wouldn't on purpose, but . . . what are you going to do? You have a fiancé."

Rianna fidgeted and studied her nails, looking very young. "When

Darien wins the Silver Branch, my father . . . he will allow it then. For us to marry."

Lin sat back in her chair. "Oh," she said. Marry? It seemed . . . almost quaint. She realized, then, how even imitating the life of itinerant poets had changed her in the past year, with their ideas about transient love.

"The poet who taught you what you know," Rianna said. "Where is he now?"

"Gone," said Lin. "As you can see, we did not marry. But I'm not beautiful like you."

"I've seen a lovely likeness of you," said Rianna. She drew a breath, let it out slowly. "The way you are now—that is a choice. I've seen how you can appear—Kimbralin Amaristoth."

It was a good thing, Lin thought, that she was sitting. Somehow she kept her voice casual. "It's true that wealth can buy a woman some beauty. And a well-paid painter is liable to be kind with the brush. Choice? There I disagree, lady—I do not have a choice in the way that you mean."

And now Lin saw that Rianna had been holding the tiny canvas all along, but reversed so that Lin couldn't see it. She turned it over. "This came with a note, asking that we report to Vassilian immediately if we see you."

It had been painted three years before, when Lin turned nineteen. To send to potential suitors. In the picture she was clad in a violet so dark it was almost black, setting off the elegant pallor of her skin, her kohl-rimmed eyes. A corset cinched in her waist, a contrast to the billowing swirls of skirt that seemed to devour the rest of the canvas. A window sent in shafts of sunlight to touch one cheek. She recalled her brother's instructions to the painter: *Make her fit to be fucked, by all the gods, and you'll be paid handsomely for it.*

For three days she had stood for hours in that dress, before the open casement, with instructions to be still. The artist sometimes swore under his breath as he worked, especially if she dared scratch an itch.

Looking at it now, Lin felt worlds away from that time, from that room, from the shadows that closed in on the girl in the picture like a lingering caress.

"I haven't seen this in some time," she said at last.

"Last night I guessed," said Rianna. "I don't think anyone else has."

"I very much hope not," said Lin, wondering at the calm in her own voice. "My brother is looking for me."

"You know a secret of mine now," said Rianna. "I will trust you, and you can trust me. Only—why would you do this?"

She didn't specify what she was asking about, but Lin knew. Why a life sleeping on straw, with no home and barely even a set of clothes? Why appear at a merchant's party and pretend to be no more than the dirt beneath his shoe?

"Please keep this between us," said Lin, letting the *why* hang between them. "Not even my partner knew my identity. If you want me to teach you in the time we have . . . if you want me to live . . . say nothing of this." Her stomach was churning. No one had said that name to her, *Kimbralin,* in nearly a year.

Rianna was looking up at her. Lin had risen to her feet. In the younger woman's eyes she read a kind of anxiety and excitement that struck at a buried chord in her. It was suddenly so familiar. And Lin knew Master Gelvan was not like her brother, and yet she was still afraid.

"In exchange for your secrecy, I will teach you more than poetry," Lin heard herself say. She drew the knife from her sleeve and let it fly. Spinning, the blade thunked into the wood paneling of the wall.

Rianna let out a gasp.

"Don't worry—it's a thin blade, I doubt your father will notice the mark," said Lin. Crossing the room, she drew the knife from the wall, held it up for inspection. Of her few possessions, her knife was the only thing she truly cared for. It could be deadly to do otherwise. Lowering it now, she looked at Rianna, saw shock and possibly fear in the girl's face. She said, "Even a lady of Amaristoth learns the art of blades. You should know these skills, as well."

CHAPTER
7

EARLY morning mist was stealing across the slate rooftops of Tamryllin, gently flooding the groves of pine, oak, and cypress trees beyond the city walls. Rianna's father jokingly referred to her bedchamber as her "tower," for the windows commanded the best view in the house. As a child, she had spent hours at a time gazing from the window, watching wind ripple the trees and birds cascade overhead.

Below, she could hear the song of wind chimes from the garden. It was the sound of home. The breeze, the chimes, the carpet under her feet—all of these were home. It was only now, at the thought of leaving these things, that she even noticed them.

But even without Darien, she had little choice about leaving. The box on her bedside table was a reminder of that.

Her father had never allowed her to go to the Midsummer Masque. It was a night of debauchery, and sometimes outbursts of violence. This year, Rianna would be going for the first time. But not alone. Nestled in the box beside her bed was a mask of exquisitely wrought gold, encrusted with sapphires and rimmed with blue velvet. Peacock feathers were caught at the top, to stream up and away from the wearer's face.

It was breathtakingly extravagant, and the message could not be more clear. Yet Ned had not left her interpretation to chance, instead enclosing a note. *In this color, I picture you Irine of the Lakes,* he had written. *You know the one.*

She did. It was one of the most famous of the old ballads. In saving a prince from drowning, Irine of the Lakes, queen of the water nymphs, had joined the world of men.

And more practically, the color matched her eyes.

When she thought of Ned, she wondered why, for her, love had to be such a painful thing. But she was also a little angry with him. He had left her no choice. She knew it was not in the way of things for her to have a choice, and still, sometimes, she was angry.

She thought of Lin fleeing a home that was one of the finest in Eivar. The Amaristoth family in their northern castle were known for the vast extent of their wealth and their impeccable lineage.

Rianna had heard tell of other things too: that they lived in the far north, despite deriving their income from estates in the southwest, because icewater flowed in their veins instead of blood.

Lin did not seem like ice. She seemed wounded, even in the way she walked, as if she navigated carefully to avoid a pain. But her voice recalled the song of a caged bird. Rianna wanted to ask her so many questions—about her brother, about the poet who had taught her what she knew. She knew it would be rude to ask any more.

She thought of the knife that had thudded into the wall of her father's solar, of the sudden flash in Lin's eyes, the instinctive baring of teeth. Perhaps women did have choices sometimes. Rianna didn't know techniques of the knife, but she would soon be hurting Ned just the same.

IN daylight, Master Gelvan's study was revealed as surprisingly simple. The only evidence of wealth was in the rows of bookshelves that lined the walls, for which Marlen imagined he must have paid several fortunes. Otherwise, a serviceable desk and chair and some tapestries were the only adornments in the room. Master Gelvan had to call in a woman to bring a second chair for Marlen.

Marlen was careful not to look at the tapestry shielding the back wall, where he had discovered the shrine . . . and just as damning, the books written in a language that was not only extinguished in Eivar but forbidden.

Today Master Gelvan was attired without finery. Marlen would have expected a Galician to dangle jewels from every available limb, but realized that he had never actually met one before this. And perhaps their love of money was revealed in more subtle ways.

Marlen's own father would have undoubtedly remarked that this lack of ornamentation could be attributed to the perversity of the Galician mind. Thwarting people's expectations for hidden purposes.

"May I offer you wine, my lord Humbreleigh?" said the merchant.

"I will gladly accept," said Marlen.

Again the woman was sent for, and returned with two glasses of wine on a pewter tray. It was a dark red verging on purple, Marlen saw; a taste confirmed it as an especially fine vintage of the south.

This gave him satisfaction. It meant the old man had taken note of Marlen's lineage and was groveling in a predictably Galician manner.

"I know your father," Master Gelvan said as he sat at the chair behind his desk and motioned to Marlen to take the second chair—which, unlike the merchant's, was padded with an embroidered cushion. Running a hand through his greying blond hair, the merchant—who seemed perpetually weary—studied the garnet facets of the wine against the summer sunlight that streamed from the window. "And knowing him," he continued, in an even tone, "I must say I'm surprised that you are here. To cross my threshold is to enter the lair of the Dark One himself, is it not? That enemy which, to my limited understanding, the Three are always battling?"

Marlen blinked. "I am . . . not my father," he managed, and set down his wine. And then was immediately angry to be so abused by this—when all was said and done—exceedingly common merchant.

"Most of my family fell by the sword, in an attack led by the company of Lord Percy of Humbreleigh," said Master Gelvan, in a calm, even monotone. "It was one of the last of the massacres, just as what was left of my people were crossing the border into Kahishi, attempting to escape. My mother did escape, after being raped. Thus do I have a dark-haired sister, the sight of whom reminded my mother every day of what she had lost. And yet I still found myself interested in what you might have to say to me, lord. Particularly since you included in your note that it is a matter of urgency."

"I can't help it if you're bitter about the past," said Marlen. This was just the sort of complaining—the endless whinging—for which Galicians had come to be hated in the first place.

A half-smile tugged at the corner of the merchant's mouth. "Yes," he said. "I suppose I am bitter about the murder of my father and the rest of my family. And all their friends. We Galicians are so odd in that way." He took another, contemplative sip of his wine. His pale eyes fixed on Marlen. "So, before I decide that I've wearied of this encounter—to what do I owe the pleasure?"

Focus, Marlen urged himself. It would not do to allow this man to provoke him. He was no more than a pawn in a larger game. And if Marlen chose, he could see the merchant drawn and quartered in the streets of Tamryllin.

Out in the garden, a bird was singing.

"I know your secret," said Marlen, without the preamble he had been planning.

The merchant didn't react. He simply waited.

"If you do as I ask—a small request—I will hold my silence," said Marlen. "If not, I will reveal to the authorities that you continue to worship your false Galician god."

Master Gelvan leaned back in his chair. "And how would you prove such a charge?"

"I have proof," said Marlen. "You would find out what it is in due course, should you force me to exercise that option."

"And what do you desire in return for this—secrecy, Lord Humbreleigh?" said Master Gelvan. In only one way did he seem changed, in that he appeared more tired than ever.

Now it came. Marlen had pictured this moment many times in his mind, but now . . . He clutched his wineglass in an unsteady hand, without the graceful precision in which he took pride, and drank deep until it was done. Feeling greater resolve as he set the glass down again, he said, "You are one of the judges of the contest, are you not?"

"Yes," said Master Gelvan. "Let me guess: you want to win."

"Indeed," said Marlen. "But for that, I need nothing from you nor from anyone—except, of course, the grace of our goddess Kiara. If I may invoke her name in this house."

"Your sarcasm is tiresome," said Master Gelvan. "Please proceed."

Once more, Marlen hesitated. Later, he would remember that he had done so, cling to it as if it were proof of something that mattered. But it was only a hesitation before he told the merchant, clearly and with his accustomed precision restored, what he would have to do to avoid being torn apart by galloping horses outside the high court of Tamryllin.

The merchant listened without expression. Only when Marlen was done did Master Gelvan say, almost conversationally, "It is well for you that the faith of Galicia prohibits me from the sin of murder. Something you Ellenicans would have done well to adopt."

Marlen could have told him that the idea of a middle-aged merchant killing a swordsman of Humbreleigh was a joke, and in poor taste at that. But in assessing this man, who had taken a threat to his life with such composure, he did not. Instead he rose to his feet, bared his teeth in a smile. "On the contrary, merchant," said Marlen. "Killing is all too rare a pleasure as it is."

WHEN he stumbled out of the merchant's house moments later, Marlen knew he would not be returning to the *Ring and Flagon,* at least not yet. His steps took him away from the broad streets of the city center, from the roses and the jasmine and honeysuckle that seemed to spring up around the smooth white stone in such abundance.

It was a dark warren of streets into which he ventured now, where rickety structures blocked the sun. Most were of wood, a danger if a fire were to break out in the city, as one indeed had a century earlier. It was here, in streets such as these, that corpses had lately been discovered, their blood drained. At last he came to a house with no door, where he was free to enter and ascend the creaking stairs, two at a time.

She opened the door for him immediately. Her full lips curled in a satisfied smile—or triumphant, he thought, which made him angry. Coils of dark hair framed her wide cheekbones, spilled over her half-exposed breasts. "I knew you would be back," she said.

He slapped her face.

Reeling and laughing at the same time, Marilla drew Marlen into the room, kicked the door shut. Her kiss was warm and urgent and sharp with her teeth. When she drew back, he saw the red imprint of his hand on her skin. She was milky white as a demon-woman, he thought, not for the first time.

Marilla's nails dug into his neck. "Show me you still have it in you," she murmured.

And for a long time after that, he did.

IT was like Marlen to disappear for a day—sometimes even days at a time—but his vanishing so close to the contest irritated Darien. While they enjoyed maintaining the illusion that they did not practice, the truth was they had played together most nights since arriving in Tamryllin. And to be sure, they sounded perfect. But never had it mattered so much.

He was sitting in the *Ring and Flagon,* ignoring the tumult of excited poets around him.

Marlen was probably drowning his sorrows in Marilla right now. Why he had sorrows at all was another story. Ever since the ball, Marlen's typical nonchalance had seemed strained, on the verge of snapping like a worn harp string. Darien could hardly blame Hassen Styr and the others for being fed up with him. Even at the best of times, Marlen was more feared than he was popular.

It was then he noticed a newcomer. He waved. "Lin!" he called. "That *is* your name, right?"

The room fell silent a moment, conversations halted midsentence, and people strove to see who had merited the attention of Darien Aldemoor. When they saw it was a ragged boy, they suspected a joke and deliberately turned away, as if to deny Darien the satisfaction of diverting them.

Lin approached his table with wary eyes. "You have my name right," she said. "Naturally I know yours."

"Naturally," he said with a smile. Her expression did not change. "Sit," he said. "Tell me about your day. You're the only person here who's not likely to bore me to death."

"You are charming," said Lin. "But I can't imagine why I'd be more interesting than the other . . . fine gentlemen here."

"You think I am trying to charm you," said Darien. "Well—perhaps you're right. Take care of this one for me," he added, having stopped one of the tavern maids.

"Or get me drunk," said Lin with a raised eyebrow as the girl departed. "It's a rare experience for me that a man would have an interest in doing either of those things. Are you perhaps acting on some sort of dare? Find out if the cross-dressing woman wants men . . . and if so, how badly?"

For once Darien was shocked into silence, if only for a moment. Then he said, "One day—perhaps tonight, after you've drunk enough—you will tell me what has caused you to have such an abysmal opinion of men."

"The abyss, my lord Aldemoor," Lin said crisply. "There, I told you, and stone sober." She took the offered cup from the barmaid who had returned.

To break the tension—wondering at its source—Darien said, "Dear woman, I wanted only to congratulate you on your performance at the ball."

She nodded. Again her eyebrow arched as she said, "That love ballad that you sang. I thought it very—evocative. You seemed to be directing it to someone in particular."

"You think so?"

"I do," she said. "What are your intentions, Darien? You can have anything, anyone. But this one—this one doesn't have the defenses you are used to."

Darien felt a sharp retort on his tongue, bit it back. She looked solemn, no hostility that he could see. She hadn't looked half bad in a dress. And then it occurred to him to wonder. "Who are you, Lin?"

She shook her head. "You're avoiding my question."

"All right." Darien ran a hand through his hair. "My intentions are honorable. I swear it on my harp. I suppose I am glad that someone is looking out for—for her. But there is no need."

Head tilted to one side, she eyed him critically. "I think you are telling the truth. I hope so. I was to give Rianna lessons in poetry. Because I am a woman. Ironic, isn't it?"

"Why ironic—because you're so determined to not be a woman?"

Instead of answering, Lin's gaze turned upon Darien's ring. The stone was dark in the shadows. "Yours is the emerald," she said. "Among other things, you are the trickster. Luck and chaos follow you, twin sisters, and do your bidding." Her eyes rose to meet his again. "I suppose she could do worse."

A WARM evening breeze was threading between the shutters, making the candle dance. Marlen felt it like a caress as he stretched full-length on the small bed.

Marilla had wrapped herself in a blanket and was tending the fire, boiling water for tea. He watched her, taking in the grace of her movements, the way she flicked her hair over one shoulder.

She let the blanket drop as she returned to bed; it had only been for protection from errant sparks. She didn't like pain *that* much, apparently.

They lay that way awhile, not touching. Sometimes, he was unable even to look at her afterward. Tonight he could look, but wouldn't touch. Not yet.

"The masque is tomorrow night," she said.

Marlen stretched lazily. "Yes. Are you saying that so I'll ask you to go with me?"

She shrugged a white shoulder. "If you don't, someone else will."

That would once have worked on him, but Marlen had outgrown the possessive rages that had been his wont. He had given women cause to fear him, at times like that. Then he had met Marilla and such rages seemed beside the point. If he ever lost his temper with her, she'd laugh and urge him on. Even if he killed her.

It was strange, to be sure of that. If he allowed himself to think of it, it made him wonder who he was. Marlen had never thought of himself as a cruel man, or a violent one. He had a temper, that was all.

"What are you doing to me," he said aloud.

Though she could not possibly have known what he was thinking, Marilla smiled, catlike, as if she did. "Does it matter?" she said. "You'll get rid of me soon. You think you can't claw your way up, with scum from the gutter weighing you down."

Marlen's eyes widened. Then he smiled back. "You have an appallingly sharp mind for a common woman," he said, and moved in for a kiss.

She dodged him easily. "There's no need, you know." Her tone was calm, idle, but her eyes were intent on his face. "You can have your fancy mistresses and even a wife—sweet and pure and wealthy. All that and I can still be there, in the shadows."

"Always in the shadows," said Marlen, almost to himself. A painful memory threatened to overtake him, but he would not allow it. With a finger he traced the length of her, rib cage to hip, and down. She lay perfectly still. "I thought I'd go to the masque as a snake," he murmured in her ear. "And you as its charmer."

She smiled and allowed him to move closer this time, to begin their dance again. Outside, laughter echoed in the streets as people began to leave their chosen haunts and head for home. A breath of wind swept out the candle, and Marlen decided—his last coherent thought for a while—that he liked it better that way; utterly dark.

* * *

As night deepened, the mood at the *Ring and Flagon* had grown quiet. Men now huddled in groups, speaking in hushed voices. A drunk young poet strummed his harp in the corner, mumbling a song he could barely seem to remember. Sprawled on the floor with legs outstretched, harp cradled in his lap, he was hardly a picture of Academy pride. He kept stopping to consider the next word, his expression pained, before hesitantly proceeding. *"And it was a time of . . . sorrow,"* he sang, eyes unfocused.

Lin would have been irritated beyond words, had she not been tipsy herself. One drink had led to another—she didn't feel like returning to the empty room at the inn, and Darien apparently had his own reasons for staying. She had admitted, early on, that she had never been drunk; the confession seemed to delight him, as if he regarded it as a challenge. And meanwhile, he kept her entertained with stories of his and Marlen Humbreleigh's time on the road, complete with lords' daughters seduced along the way. It made sense that consummate poets like the two of them lived a ballad of their own.

"So why are you so gloomy tonight?" he finally asked.

Usually she would have dodged the question. But right now the prospect of dodging called for more effort than she could muster. "Leander Keyen—you know, my partner—he left me."

Darien shook his head vehemently. "Now that," he said, "that is an outrage."

She had to laugh. Darien laughed, too, and raised his cup with a flourish. "There was some story of the two of you," he said. "You had something to do with Valanir Ocune?"

She nodded. "He got us into the ball. Now, looking back, I don't know why. But he didn't tell us who he was."

Darien was watching her. "Marlen told me he saw you and Valanir go into the garden," he said. "So . . . what was that like?"

Perhaps it should not have made her angry—she could never quite trust her instincts, knowing their origin. She said, "I hope that isn't the only reason you wanted to talk to me."

"Nonsense," said Darien. "I was bored."

She exhaled sharply, letting out anger along with her breath. "It wasn't like anything," she said. "We just talked. I only guessed who he was just before his performance."

"And now he's in prison," Darien said, shaking his head.

The lamps had died to a spectral glow, deepening all the shadows. Soon it would be dawn, and she and Darien would part ways, perhaps never speak again. Lin had a sudden premonition of hundreds, thousands of nights just like this one: identical doors opening from the same long corridor, on and on, the tired inns and the drunken songs and people chance-met on the road, only to vanish by sunrise. All this to continue until it ended, or until she herself ended the agony of that long walk down the hall.

Her hands tightened on the table. "He's in prison, probably even being tortured. And here we are—*drinking*."

Darien shrugged. "What else can we do?"

Lin stood up. "I'll tell you." She leaned across the table. "I'm going to find the real one. Or try to find it."

"It?"

"The Silver Branch. The Path. Just as Edrien Letrell did."

For once, Darien was at a loss for words. Then he shook his head. "Well. I really did get you drunk."

Lin straightened, looked down at him from all the height a well-bred posture and worn boots could bestow. "That was the message of Valanir's song," she said. "That we have all forgotten our true purpose."

"You're not even properly a poet," Darien pointed out.

For that, there was no answer. Lin turned to leave.

"It's dark out there," Darien said unnecessarily. "I'll walk you home."

He had heard her sing, and now told her she was not a poet. She ignored him, turning on her heel and out the door into the night.

It was quiet in the streets at this hour. The paper lanterns strung between trees in anticipation of the fair were unlit, bobbing in the breeze.

Lin had a hand on her knife, but still the figure in the alleyway was too quick; before she could move, an arm like steel clenched her arms at her sides.

Close to her ear, a breath, and then a voice that said, "I've been looking for you."

CHAPTER
8

A GIBBOUS moon hung white against the sky, over a sea of lanterns strung from trees and darkened shopfronts: red and yellow, blue and green. The perfume of night-blooming jasmine seemed at one with the sounds of laughter and music, which grew louder as they approached together, hand in hand. Dancing light indicated fires. She wondered if his hand tightened in hers because the laughter worried him as it did her. They had grown up so much alike, it was probable that he had never done this before, either.

But when Rianna turned to look at Ned, she could not read his expression; he had already gamely donned his mask. It was black and silver, and nowhere near as splendid as the one he had given her. So she was to be Irine to his prince; it was decided. Quicksilver and cool, a water spirit with a deeply buried heart.

Perhaps he saw her thus, Rianna thought. Perhaps he thought he had only to keep diving to find her heart. Not knowing she had already given it away.

"We don't have to do this," she said gently, noting that he was fingering the hilt of his sword. This was something new as well—she had never known him to wear a sword before. Darien wore one too, but with such careless ease she barely noticed it. Ned seemed to coordinate his movements around his gingerly, as though it were a gimp leg.

In the distance, the pounding of a drum had begun. The singing that rose to accompany it, high and ululating, like nothing she had heard before. She could hear waves, too, as they approached the harbor.

"Do you doubt I can protect you?" he said, forcing an edge into his voice.

She shook her head. "Ned. There is only merriment here." She squeezed his hand. "Come—let's go toward the music." There was a chance that she'd see Darien tonight—if she could recognize him.

"First put on your mask," said Ned, with a smile. It looked uncomfortable, as he did with every aspect of himself tonight: his hand in hers, the mask, the sword. She wanted to hug him and tell him that everything would be all right.

Except it wouldn't, so instead she simply acquiesced, tying the glittering thing over her face.

"There," said Ned. "I wouldn't know you."

She smiled, felt her cheekbones squeeze against papier-mâché, not knowing how else to respond.

"Let's go toward the music," he said, and tugged her hand, guiding her in the direction of the lights and drums.

FROM here he could smell the sea. Out on black water speckled with the light of lanterns, the pleasure barges of the nobility loomed like sea creatures from another world. The music that flowed from their lighted windows was genteel, soothing.

Boring, Darien Aldemoor thought, and smiled widely in the darkness, knowing it would look eerie with his mask. While members of the courtly families, masks raised delicately to their eyes, floated through the paces of formal dances, the city around them exploded with abandon. The men would sneak off later for their slice of the action, Darien was sure. Even the ones with ladyloves or wives.

He and Hassen Styr were lounging by the water, pleasantly warmed with drink, their harps on confident display. Hassen's mask was of the god Thalion—gold on one side, black on the other. The gold half of the mask caught the fitful light of the fires, while the dark half vanished, making it seem that he had only half a face.

Masks of the Three were the most common at the Midsummer Masque, a reminder that the festival had roots in their worship. The mask of Kiara was black edged with silver, that of Estarre pure gold. And their aspects came together in Thalion, their brother in some tales, their lover in others. And sometimes both.

Darien had preferred a mask painted in a rainbow of diamond-shaped colors—red, green, blue, purple, gold. *The court jester,* was what the woman who sold it to him had called it.

Darien didn't know about that—he liked the colors. And he thought it was reminiscent of the six-colored cloak, forbidden to all but the Court Poet. His own private subversion of custom.

Marlen had never returned to the *Ring and Flagon.* It was strange, but Darien was determined to ignore the issue. He and Hassen had taken to the streets after sundown, though the main attraction of the masque was off-limits for Darien. Unless he allowed himself to be charmed by one of the masked women here, put aside his worries for a night.

But that seemed wrong, especially when he knew Rianna would never understand. It was more work than he'd anticipated—forbidden love. No wonder such lovers in all the songs were so depressed.

Around them, people were whirling like butterflies to the rhythm of drums, masks catching the light. Darien found himself watching the women, their motions causing loosened hair to writhe, the ties of their gowns unfastened far more than was decent, leaving pale skin exposed to the firelight. The Temple of the Three had attempted to place sanctions on the garb and behavior of this night, but with the anonymity of masks came unaccustomed courage against the edicts of the clergy. Particularly since most of the palace guards were out enjoying themselves as well.

It was truly unfair.

"I can't understand why a man of your quite considerable stature has so little confidence with the ladies," Darien said to Hassen, mostly to distract himself, his head and shoulders tipped back over the rails by the water. "I mean, I'm stuck in limbo with a girl I can't have yet—what's your excuse?"

"I have no need to make excuses to you, lordling," Hassen growled.

"You can claim to be heir to Aldemoor, if that would help," Darien said with a grin. "I don't plan to be there often." Indeed he had not been there since midwinter, and had regretted it then: his sisters had hinted that it was time for him to marry and take on the duties of an only son. His mother, in bidding farewell to him, had cried.

Coming to himself, Darien realized that Hassen had not responded, and glanced over at the other man. He appeared to be hesitating, struggling to find the right words, though with the mask it was hard to tell. At last Hassen said, almost too quietly to hear over the din of drums and shouts, "There was someone. I thought I'd have forgotten her by now."

"Ah." Darien was taken aback. This was a night for laughter. "Look," he said, rooting for a way to divert his friend. He found a pebble on the ground by his feet. "You see that lamp out on the water? I'm going to hit it with this rock."

"You can't be serious," said Hassen.

"Watch," said Darien. Coiling back his arm, Darien shot it forward and let the pebble fly. It hit the lamp square in the center, tearing the paper to expose the flame within. Soundlessly, the pebble then vanished into the deeps.

"Showoff," said Hassen, but he seemed to relax. Darien smiled to himself. Now the night could begin.

A COTERIE of Sirian dancers, dark-skinned and lithe, were flowing through the complex forms of a dance, set to the rhythm of drumbeats. Never had Rianna Gelvan seen dancers from the east; Ned recognized them from a trip he had taken with his father. She was fascinated by the way bright scarves wafted around their limbs in time to the drums, the controlled abandon of the dance. Every single one of them beautiful.

"They're practicing for the fair," Ned said in her ear. "That's where some troupes get commissions, sometimes even from royalty."

Rianna nodded absently, more stirred than she wanted to let on by the pounding rhythm, the wild dance.

The two drummers rocked from side to side in frenzied unison as they pounded rawhide stretched over wood. Strange large masks concealed their whole faces, forehead to chin. One mask was black, its empty mouth turned up in a raucous grin, while the other was white, contorted in a howl of anguish. As they rocked, the players' necks strained upward and back until their tendons protruded like twisted rope. Their splayed fingers revealed a single jewel on the third finger of their right hands—Academy rings.

A flash alerted Rianna to jugglers casually tossing flaming firebrands to one another, ignoring the hooting and shouts of spectators.

The drums were a dull thud in her blood and bones, slow and then fast, as if they mimicked and then controlled the beat of her heart. Tricking her blood into doing their bidding.

She didn't know whether she was excited or afraid. *If only Darien were here.*

Two women with nearly exposed breasts accosted them. "What a lovely mask," said one, a blonde in the gold mask of Estarre. She half-threw herself toward Ned, long painted nails nearly grazing his face. "What do I have to do for you to buy me one just like it?"

Ned jumped back as if burned. "Move on," he said, sounding strangled. Rianna became aware of the familiar, contradictory feelings of affection and annoyance. She imagined tearing free of him, running into the crowds and throwing herself into the assaulting tempo of the drums, its pounding bearing her away.

"I'm sorry you saw that," said Ned. "Your father . . ."

"Never wanted me here," said Rianna, trying to suppress her irritation. "You must have had a job convincing him." And then realized what she had said, and what it could mean. What if this excursion was intended as a prelude? Would he suddenly kneel here in the street, amid the dancers and the fire jugglers and the drunken celebrants, and ask for her hand?

"I think I'm getting a headache," Rianna said suddenly. She felt that in some obscure way she had been tricked; she wanted to tear off the ridiculously costly mask.

But that was when she felt a stabbing pain in her scalp. A voice behind her said, "Such lovely hair."

Rianna gasped, "Get off," and spun around, tugging her hair free of the grasping hand. Ned had moved closer to her, grabbing her arm protectively.

Confronting them was a tall woman with white skin and black curls that tumbled to her bare shoulders. Her mask a dark red. "Can I have this one?" she said, and spread her lips in a smile. "We could ask her to join us."

A tall man came up beside her. Rianna noticed for the first time that the red velvet collar at the woman's throat was attached to a leash, which this man held in a casual grip. She didn't know whether to be fascinated or somehow, for no discernible reason, embarrassed.

"Sorry, Marilla," said the man with slightly slurred speech. His mask was green and gold, and in the shape of a serpent's head. "This one's taken, and you know it. I told you Rianna Gelvan is Darien's wench."

Rianna felt her heart accelerate. "Who are you? Get away from me."

But now Ned stood between them, sword drawn in the flickering light.

"No, Ned," Rianna cried. "They have me confused with someone else. It's nothing."

"He called you by name," Ned said through his teeth. "Go on, whoever you are," he urged the man, whom Rianna now recognized. Too late, she noticed his harp and the red stone of his Academy ring. "I see you have a blade," Ned continued. "Draw it, and we'll settle this here."

Marlen Humbreleigh inclined his head, looking puzzled, as if he didn't know where he was. It was an odd look for a snake. Then he began to laugh. It was not a brief laugh of calculated mockery. Helpless with mirth, hands clamped to his ribs, he had to draw breath more than once. Then he looked down the length of Ned's blade, and that set him off again.

Ned had gone white. "What ails you, sir?" he demanded. "Is this the form your cowardice takes?"

Finally, Marlen succeeded at containing himself. Marilla had snuggled up to his arm. "Not cowardice," said Marlen. "What you are looking at, Sir Stick, is mercy. I'm in no mood to kill a defenseless boy."

"Oh," said Marilla. "Not even for *me*?"

Marlen shrugged. "Sorry, love," he said. "You're a terrible influence, but I seem to have some shreds of a conscience left. Stay back," he added when Ned advanced toward him. "You know that if you attack me, you will force me to draw my weapon . . . and then to injure you, or worse."

"Then so be it," said Ned. "No one insults my lady's honor."

Marlen looked as if he might begin to laugh again. "My dear boy, she is too good for you and always will be. No amount of waving that thing around will change the fact."

Rianna didn't know what would have happened in that moment, if a masked boy had not appeared, wedged himself between the two men. A harp was belted to his waist. "Stop this at once," he said.

"And who are you?" Marlen asked with amusement.

"Someone who knows how to use this knife," said the boy, holding up a slender blade. Even amid her panic, Rianna noticed he wore no ring. "And your lady's little neck is in my sights."

"Please," said Marlen. "Talk like that around Marilla, you'll never get rid of her."

The boy turned to Ned, ignoring Marlen now, and said, "I won't allow you to do this." And this time Rianna recognized Lin's voice. She spoke gently, a steadying hand on Ned's shoulder. "Marlen Humbreleigh is one of the finest swordsmen in the kingdom—this is known."

"Rianna—" he said. It came out like a plea.

"Your life is worth more than this," said Lin. "Go."

But Marlen turned away first, giving the leash a peremptory tug. "Let's go, Marilla. This drama becomes wearisome. Boy—my advice is to find a woman who wants you."

Ignoring the tug of the leash, Marilla advanced on Ned. She trailed her fingertips on his cheek. Her chin nearly grazed his collarbone, she stood so close. "Such a pity," she said, in a lilting chant like a child's song. "Your blood would have been poured out—out—out— on the ground."

Ned stood rooted to the spot, eyes wide. Rianna reached out to touch him, and he recoiled from her. She thought he might be about to weep, but the mask made it hard to tell.

"Come," said Marlen, and pulled the woman away. But they could still hear her laughter, ringing above the other sounds of the masque, even after the pair had vanished into the shifting crowds.

Rianna fumbled at the string buried in her hair and pulled off the mask, felt the cool air on her face. "Lin . . . what are you doing here?" she said. "How did you—all these people—how did everyone know who I was?"

Lin shook her head. "You don't yet know what you are, lady," she said. "You could never blend into a crowd."

Rianna didn't know how to respond to that. She said, "I thought you didn't have a harp."

"I don't," said Lin. Now Rianna saw that there was a man with her, wearing a mask of Thalion. "It's his."

The man was shaking his head. "What did I say, about not attracting attention?"

Lin laughed. "You may have said that, but I have never met a poet who didn't want to be noticed. And you are no exception."

Rianna watched as they moved to stand beside each other with the formality of a ritual long-established. Lin took the harp in both hands, cradling it reverently as if it were a holy relic.

"Alas, you are probably right about that," said the man.

Beneath the words, they were communicating with their eyes,

Rianna thought. Both stood absolutely still for a moment, and then the man nodded, a slow dip of his chin. Lin began to pluck the harp. The melody seemed familiar to Rianna, but she couldn't have said why. It started softly, picking up speed as Lin's fingers danced across the strings. But it was only when the man began to sing that Rianna realized who this must be. And what he risked—what both of them were risking—in singing this particular song.

> *Who will sing for my city?*
> *Where the great ones are gone . . .*

She buried her head in Ned's shoulder; it had all become too much. He stood, immobile, as other bystanders gathered quietly around the two players, drawn as if in a trance. As one, they let the music wash over them, just in this one moment before the dawn—just this one night.

CHAPTER
9

"*I'VE been looking for you,*" he'd said that night outside the *Ring and Flagon,* releasing her arms so she could turn to face him. She knew him at once. "Don't," he said worriedly, and Lin realized she was about to cry. She saw his right arm was bound in a sling.

"I—we *all* thought—" she stammered.

"Inside," said Valanir Ocune. "Follow me."

"I have your ring."

"I know," he said, and let her help him put it on. "I thank you for that. But now I need you to come with me." And then held out his good hand to her.

Closing her eyes a moment, Lin took his hand. It all could have been taking place in a dream; that was how likely any of it seemed to Lin. Valanir Ocune had been looking for her, and now wanted her to come with him. She would do whatever he wanted, of course. Knowing that made her feel foolish and too vulnerable; she knew it was banal, silly, to see a mere man in this way.

In her head, she heard Rayen mocking, *He wants something, perhaps your gold,* and bowed her head as if beneath a weight. But she let Valanir lead her, kept a tentative hold of his hand.

He walked with a slight limp, she saw. She slowed her pace to match his as he led her through backstreets. At this hour, the only people they were likely to meet would be unsavory, or Ladybirds pa-trolling. Lin drew her knife as they plunged deeper into the warren of Tamryllin's alleyways.

At last they reached a ramshackle inn. After some quiet words with the innkeeper, Valanir led her upstairs. The innkeeper had given him a lamp to light their way, to set on the floor and throw weary beams of light on the plank walls. The room was nearly bare.

"Please, sit," said Valanir, indicating the bed.

Lin did, and was relieved when he sprawled on the floor. At least, most of what she felt was relief. *Even here and under these circumstances, a gentleman,* she thought with a slight smile.

"I could sing of that smile," said the Seer in a low voice, startling her. Though it was difficult to read his face in the faint lamplight, his eyes were intent. "What secrets are you hiding? Have you already re-covered from the shock of seeing me here, alive?"

"No recovery is necessary," she said, carefully. It was hard to speak without emotion. "Not from this."

"Only you know," said Valanir. Now she could see that some of his face was a little darker, in the half-light, than it ought to have been; she guessed there were bruises. "Nickon Gerrard will not want word of my escape getting out."

"Escape?"

"I have friends in the palace still," said Valanir. "That is all I may tell you. But the first day . . . I am fortunate to have other friends in Tamryllin as well, visitors from Kahishi. One is a healer. He set my arm. It gave Nickon pleasure to break the arm I use for playing. But he'll be *extremely* disappointed not to have done more."

"You mean . . ."

"I mean my head would likely have been on display in the Court Plaza, before long," said Valanir Ocune with no change to his tone. "An example to other poets who might have contemplated rebellion. After I'd been tortured, of course. My blood used for something perverse."

"I don't understand," she said slowly, after the shock of his words had dissipated. *What secrets are you hiding?* he had asked. Did he know her identity, and had for that reason sought her out? "What do you want with me, Valanir Ocune?" It came out sounding more harsh than she had intended.

He sighed. "So now we come to it," he said. "I had hoped to dally a bit, perhaps discuss nuances in the songs of Edrien Letrell. But if you must . . ."

She realized that he was smiling. "I'm sorry," she said. "It is only that I thought perhaps—perhaps you sought me because you knew who I am. That I am an Amaristoth."

"No," he said, without hesitation. "If anything that might have been a deterrent. But I know that you are not like your family. I can only imagine how it was to grow up in that house. I knew your mother."

A lump rose in Lin's throat, as if his words tapped one of the weak pressure points of her body that could be used against her in a fight. "You did."

Now Valanir's smile had a wolfish quality. "She did not like my music."

This was a road she would explore with him sometime, or hoped to. But it was not to talk of her family that they were hiding in this room.

She said, "Tell me why I'm here." A breeze from the window creaked open the shutters; Lin gratefully drew it in. Less than an hour earlier she had been nearly drunk, keeping lonely company with Darien Aldemoor. Now her senses were sharply awake.

Valanir shifted his position on the floor. "What do you know," he said, "of the legend of Davyd Dreamweaver?"

This was not what she had been expecting. "Just what the songs say," she said. "That he was a great Seer centuries ago. That because of him, the enchantments of poets are gone."

"The songs do not quite do justice to the history," said Valanir. "And the history, well . . . that is something that would not be approved these days."

Lin's eyes narrowed. "What sort of *history* would cause you to risk your life?"

Valanir nodded, as if he expected the question. When he spoke again, he sounded weary. "I told you of the Red Death," said Valanir. "It is a plague that has not been seen in Eivar since the time of Davyd."

"I know," said Lin. "After what you told me . . . after what you did . . . I had resolved to find the Path myself."

Valanir's eyes flickered, unmistakably surprised, which gave her a small measure of satisfaction. "You did? You are . . . not what I expected."

Lin was silent, unsure what to make of this.

"You understood, then, some of what I was trying to tell you," said Valanir. "But for the rest, I must reach back to the beginning. You know that once the Seers wielded powerful magics, and stood allied with the Crown. But the relationship between Crown and Academy was never easy, with each grudging the authority of the other. And then came King Eldgest, he that we now call the Iron Hand. He longed to destroy the Seers' powers once and for all, seeing them— indeed, rightly—as a threat to the absolute rule he desired. But he did not dare move against the Academy: the power of the Seers was great, and they were popular among the people. So Eldgest did not act, but he watched."

"And what did he see?"

"He saw the Academy undo itself. With the most dark and forbidden of all magics."

"Blood divination," said Lin, remembering.

"You know the tale," said Valanir. "Through the years, there had always been renegade poets who practiced enchantments with mortal blood. These were soon rooted out by the Academy masters and executed. But in the time of Davyd Dreamweaver, a coterie of Seers were practicing the darkest arts in the halls of the Academy itself, in secret. They fed their magic with the blood of innocents that they kidnapped from nearby villages. They were sworn to an oath of secrecy: in the heart of the Academy, no one knew who was friend or foe.

"In the end, Davyd gathered those few Seers that he trusted most, and a battle of magics raged in the halls of the Academy itself. That day, many of the finest poets were slain, yet the Order of the Red

Knife—as they called themselves—was at last dispersed. But the deeper harm was done: the people of Eivar, learning of this horror, turned against the Academy. The Academy itself was weak after suffering so many losses. It was then that King Eldgest saw his chance, and you know what followed."

Lin did know. If she shut her eyes a moment, she could recall the voice that had once conjured the story for her. "The king's guards stormed the Academy and captured its students and adepts, who had already been depleted and weakened in battle," she said, quoting from memory. "And then Eldgest began . . . to torture them."

Valanir's tone was steel again. "He told Davyd that until the enchantments of Seers were gone for good, he would mutilate one man for every hour. And he began to make good on his word."

"So Davyd had no choice."

"He certainly didn't think he did. What happened then is unclear: some have said that he prayed to the gods for aid—the ones worshipped here in the time of Eldgest, before the Three. Others say that he used all his own powers to perform one last act of destruction.

"We don't know, but the end result was the same: that night there was a storm that raged until dawn. And the next morning . . . a poet could recite a song, a rite, to no effect. Whatever enchantments the Seers had possessed were gone. A word was a word, no more.

"Davyd, it is said, left Eivar after that and did not return."

Sometime during his story, Lin had noticed how intense was the silence outside; the hush of night had deepened over Tamryllin. Just as Valanir reached his conclusion, moonlight began to steal between the shutters. An aura of silver light surrounded the Seer, as it had the night of the Gelvan ball. With a difference now: the light surrounding his face was no longer a pale glow but a coruscating rainbow of colors. Lin gasped.

Valanir touched his face above the eye. "You didn't see it in the dark," he said. "One of the gifts I received at the castle—from the hand of Court Poet Gerrard himself. My mark is broken."

"How?"

"Quite easily," said Valanir. "One stroke of a knife does it." He must have seen her expression, for he added, "Don't worry. It doesn't affect what I do."

Lin was shocked, even as she knew he had barely escaped a fate far worse. "He would break the mark of a Seer . . . of Valanir Ocune."

"To Nickon Gerrard, that is nothing," said Valanir. "Do you not see, Lin? It is blood divination that brings the Red Death to Eivar. Not right away, not with one rite, or even two . . . but after years. Once a poet has engaged in it many times, it is not his power to control anymore. A dark spirit rides him. In Kahishi they call such a spirit *laylan*—the night. A man consumed by the night *must* kill."

The blood always drained, she recalled now. "But the Court Poet? Why would a man like him do such a thing?"

"He was not always Court Poet," said the Seer. "And now . . . now there is no why. I believe it is not *him* anymore doing this. After many years, that is what happens."

"Can't we just kill him?" she said. She was thinking, *One arrow through the heart . . . or the throat. Like a rabid wolf.*

He laughed, but it was without mirth. "So in some way, at least, you are your mother's daughter. No, Lin Amaristoth. If I thought Nick could be killed, with the *laylan* riding him, I would give my life to do it. It's . . . it is my responsibility."

When Lin looked questioningly at him, Valanir went on. "When we were Academy students together, Nick and I were intrigued by the idea of blood divination. We would cut ourselves, and each other." He extended his left arm to her, the sleeve rolled up. "Here you can see one of the times I let him cut me. It never faded." Even in the dim light, Lin saw the purple line of a scar up the length of his arm.

"That could have killed you."

"We were fifteen," he said. "Idiots. We knew we were best of our year. Impatient to become great, we sought to touch real power. We never got there . . . but when Nick decided to pursue his own path, we could no longer be friends. I suppose . . . I suppose the fault lies with me, that I didn't kill him then, or tell someone at the Academy. At the time I didn't know what I do now. And I never truly thought . . . that he would kill."

"You trusted him."

"I discovered who he was too late. I thought, at heart, he was still the person I knew. I imagine you know what that is like, don't you, Kimbralin."

She shook her head. "It's just Lin," she said, allowing herself a tone of reproof. Even with him. She could sense that every word he chose was deliberate. He had used her real name deliberately.

She had seen the Court Poet for herself: a man of dignity, intelligence in his dark eyes. She could not see such a man possessed by any spirit. "How do you know, though?" she asked. "Maybe he gave it up before he ever hurt anyone, as you did. Maybe it is someone else doing these killings."

Valanir rose from the floor to stand before her where she sat. "Take my hand and close your eyes," he said. Then he smiled as she stared at him, unmoving. "You're suspicious. As if you could not make short work of me with that dagger, if you chose."

Still reluctant, Lin took one of Valanir's hands in hers. "Stabbing the world's most celebrated Seer is not one of my ambitions," she said. She tried to keep her tone nonchalant. "At least, not without cause."

"A relief," he said. "Close your eyes."

Lin did, though her heart beat fast. He could not know how difficult it was, what he asked of her. Even Valanir Ocune, it seemed, could not read her heart.

In the silence that followed, she heard his breath, regular and relaxed. And then began to sing, so softly that it was barely above the sound of breathing.

Lin felt a plunging in her stomach, as if she were about to be sick or fall from a great height.

Candles were everywhere. The first detail Lin saw. They flickered in brass sconces, illuminating bare walls of stone. No windows, no draperies. Stone and flame, no more. Candles also danced a quiet circle at the center of the room, where a man stood alone. His back was to her, but she saw that he was tall, with silver in his dark hair.

And then somehow she was facing him . . . though Lin had a sense that she wasn't actually in this room. Nickon Gerrard wore his six-colored cloak. He was singing.

Before him, at the center of the circle of candles, stood a strange table of stone, encased in delicate carved shapes the color of bone. A concave bowl was cut deep into the stone surface.

That was when Lin realized two things. The table was an altar. And it was fashioned of bones, with stone at its heart. She saw that cavernous eyes peered from its base, from skulls. Human skulls.

As she watched, Lord Gerrard dipped his fingers into the bowl at the center of the altar. His fingers came up red. With care, the Court Poet applied his fingertips around his eyes, creating a half mask of blood.

Bile rose in her throat. She shut her eyes. But when she did, the song of Nickon Gerrard abruptly stopped. All was silence, but for the hiss of a guttering candle. Suddenly terrified, Lin opened her eyes again. She saw that the man at the center of the room had changed, even as the mask remained. Now he was younger, his body compact instead of tall. And he was looking directly at Lin with pleased recognition.

Rayen Amaristoth smiled; the red mask dripped down his cheeks. In a caressing voice familiar to Lin as her own he said, "Soon, my love."

The moment Lin found herself back in the room at the inn, sitting across from Valanir Ocune, she threw a punch at the Seer. He blocked it with his good arm, but she immediately swung again, hitting him this time in the chest. He stumbled back, caught himself on the bed for balance. "*How* could you do that?" she barked. "How did you do it—and why?"

"Kimbralin—"

Her fists clenched hard. "*You will call me Lin.*"

He nodded, sank onto the bed. She continued to stand over him. Her fury and shock had turned to a coldness. She had not trusted him, exactly, but neither had she been prepared for a betrayal this deep. *But then, when were you ever prepared?* That mocking voice again.

"What did you see?" Valanir asked at last.

"You mean to tell me you don't know?"

"The power I used is not directly in my control," said Valanir. "One of its flaws, to be sure. My dear, I don't know what you saw, but I didn't intend to hurt you. I would never want to do that."

Lin clutched her head with both hands. "All right," she said. "I . . . I'm sorry. Are you all right?"

"I'll be fine," he said wryly. "Perhaps I should have warned you. The enchantment, I suppose we'll call it, can be unpredictable."

"But we don't have the enchantments . . ."

"Not in Eivar, no," said Valanir. "But every land possesses its own magics. In Kahishi, the magicians of the sultan's court have their own power. As a young graduate, I journeyed to Majdara to study with the court magicians—hoping to find a key to our enchantments there. I thought if we could not access the enchantments of Eivar directly, I might be able to come at them sideways."

"That's why you took up residence in the sultan's court," said Lin. "Everyone assumes it's because of your enmity with Lord Gerrard."

Valanir smiled. "It was convenient that they think so. And so I was able to show you a vision, though I myself could neither see nor shape it. Your mind shaped what you saw."

"A hazardous approach," Lin said. "Yet that seldom stops you. You got yourself imprisoned, Valanir, for a song?"

The mark around the Seer's eye burned strong, even broken as it was. "For a beginning," he said.

WORD was all over the city: Valanir Ocune was alive and performing throughout the masque. Or no, it was not Valanir; for if it were him, wouldn't he play his own harp? But it was someone who sounded like him, singing his infamous song.

The Ladybirds were searching for the renegade poet, but naturally he was masked like everyone else that night.

Ned Alterra and Rianna Gelvan stumbled through the dark together, leaving the clangor of the celebrations behind. All she wanted to do was go home. And find Darien, which in her mind was equivalent to finding shelter. He would know what to do.

Valanir Ocune and Lin had made themselves scarce, vanishing just before the guards arrived. Aside from Valanir's harp, there was little to distinguish them; the masks they wore were those of the gods. Valanir's upturned face had shone gold by firelight, his mouth twisted in pathos that he had not displayed at the ball.

It was that image that stayed with Rianna as they left the crowds, heading for Ned's family carriage, which awaited them. The driver had had to miss the masque, Rianna realized. That seemed unfair.

The interior of the carriage was painted with murals dedicated to the gods and ornamented with gilding. Seated beside Ned, Rianna stared down at the magnificent mask now resting in her lap.

Ned did not signal to the driver to go. When she looked up at him, she saw that he was no longer clenched in on himself. He looked almost relaxed.

"We should talk," he said finally. Outside, they could hear the calls and laughter of the crowds they had left behind. And the music.

Rianna is Darien's wench.

"Should we?" said Rianna.

She hadn't wanted it to end like this, with him so hurt. *And how did you expect it to end?*

"I'm not worthy of you," said Ned. "I've always known that. I had hoped to become so, over time."

"What that horrid man said—"

"—Was right," said Ned. "I don't know who he was, or how he knew you. Perhaps he did mistake you for someone else. But of that one thing, at least, I know he was speaking the truth."

Tears were on Rianna's face. What she had wanted was happening.

Here in this carriage, one inconvenient problem resolved. She thought she might cry forever.

"Would you deny it?" Ned said. "Will you say that you love me, that you see yourself happy with me for years to come?"

Rianna buried her face in her hands. She did not know how long she pressed her eyes into that blackness. But he was waiting, so at last she said, "I can't." And realized she owed him a direct glance now, and looked up.

Ned took her hand. There was an elegant formality in the gesture, coming from a man whose movements were rarely elegant. He seemed strangely at peace. "Rianna Gelvan," he said, "I hereby free you of our betrothal, until the end of days." He fell back in his seat. "I love you. Now let's go home."

THEY left masks littered behind them as they went: that was part of the plan. Each time they changed their masks, it was one less clue for the Ladybirds to follow. Valanir wore his cloak draped over one arm to conceal the bandaging that might have made him conspicuous. Lin's fingers ached from playing so much. They were being hunted, there was no doubt of that. But on a night like this, amid the chaos, there was a chance they could escape.

And it was worthwhile in the end, either way. After tonight, she would be alone again, unmoored. She concentrated on this moment, here, with the firelight and revelry and Valanir's voice carrying above the crowds, enspelling them to silence. Her music buoyed his singing, twining with his voice. A dance they did together, over and over again.

Valanir's eyes, rimmed by a mask, watching her as she played.

I don't want this night to end, Lin thought during one of those times, and closed her eyes, the better to become more absorbed in her playing. The Academy taught that the most sublime music came from an abnegation of self.

Once as they took shelter, she thought of a song she loved, by a more obscure poet of centuries past.

I will ride horses like wind
I will warm my hands at fires
I will savor darkened wines
I will not think of the road's end.

It hardly seemed as if any time had passed when Valanir drew her nearer the water and behind the pier and said, "We should rest now. And then there is only one more thing to do."

"We are done playing?" she asked. Feeling relief for her aching hands, but also sadness. As she had anticipated.

He was gazing out at the water. The waves crashed a gentle counterpoint to the fading festivities. It was so late, even the most energetic revelers were starting for home—or taverns, or the beds of strangers.

That was a part Lin knew too well about these festivals. Rayen Amaristoth would come home from Tamryllin every year with new tales about his pleasures at the Midsummer Fair, his prowess with women and girls who—Lin thought—ought to have known better. His tastes were specific: Rayen favored women whose hair matched the icewine that was a specialty of the vineyards of the north. He was first and foremost a hunter. Such women were his prey in the summer months, much as the white wolf was in winter.

Their mother had liked to draw the details of such encounters from him, plying him with drink. And then, after it had all been drawn out in inexhaustible detail, down to the last sigh of surrender—she would suddenly slap the cup from his lips, splattering the yellow-gold wine across the floor, and they both would laugh.

It was a ritual that Lin only half understood, and she was bound to sit and bear witness, though it made her feel as if maggots writhed on her skin. After Kalinda Amaristoth was killed in a hunting accident, Rayen continued the tradition, telling his tales to Lin over a bottle of wine, or several. But with a difference: the gleam of contempt in his eyes, the rage behind his smile.

What made him so angry? Lin never knew, but when she thought of his anger, it ran alongside the memory of her mother's laugh, of sensual lips stained with the blood of fresh meat after a kill.

Valanir's voice—her guide all this evening—roused Lin from her thoughts. His eyes distant as he said, "Out in the villages, they are doing much more wild things tonight. I remember." He was silent a moment, and then, "We can't let a night like this pass without paying tribute. I'll buy you a drink."

And so again, she followed him, noting as they went that they were passing many taverns. She was careful to step over suspicious-looking puddles.

Soon she realized where they were going. "You . . ." she murmured, with a half shake of her head.

"Yes?" He did not stop walking.

"I doubt we're heading to the most popular of the poets' taverns just for a *drink*."

"Well, maybe I also want to hear what they're saying," he conceded. "Tonight I can disguise myself without exciting suspicion. It's convenient."

The *Ring and Flagon* was as busy as if it were dinnertime on any other evening. More, perhaps. The only difference was the masks, which most of the poets still wore, to honor the libations of the night. Most of the poets sat near the center, around Darien Aldemoor, who was unmistakable even in his multicolored mask.

"What does this mean?" one of the poets sitting at Darien's feet asked anxiously.

"Friends, it seems Valanir Ocune or a clever impostor is loose among us," said Darien. "And you'd never guess his age; his voice is fit as ever. To him!" He raised his mug. The surrounding poets echoed him, raising their mugs in unison.

In their corner, Valanir grinned to himself. "Rapscallion," he said. "Rarely have I been subject to such an irreverent toast."

"The cost of eavesdropping," Lin said dryly.

A much taller man rose to his feet. Hassen Styr, Lin recalled. "That is all very well, Darien," said Hassen. "But why would the greatest poet of our age risk his life in this way?"

Darien shrugged. "I don't know," he said. "We don't even know it was him."

"But if it was?" Hassen persisted. He was the only man not wearing a mask. "It is the same message as before—this time to all of Tamryllin. That our prize is worthless. That perhaps even the Academy—"

"Don't say it," said Darien. "You are a good man, Hassen Styr. Don't endanger yourself with heresies."

"Hasn't there been enough damage done?" This from a man on the outskirts: a familiar voice. Lin's heart caught.

Leander Keyen had risen, holding his mug. He seemed unsteady on his feet. "What good are these conversations," he said loudly. "Are you really saying you don't want to win? Or are you trying to put the rest of us off, leaving you with less competition?"

Lin felt Valanir's hand on her wrist before she knew what she was doing. She realized that she had stood up, that some eyes had even shifted toward her as she did so. She collapsed back onto her bench. "He is such a fool," she murmured.

"He is," said Valanir, but from his mouth it sounded less forgiving.

She shrugged helplessly. "I just . . . can't bear it."

"Lady, he cut you from his life," Valanir said. "Learn to let those who wish to go—go. And be glad of it."

Darien had begun to speak again, turning to Hassen, as if Leander were not there at all. "Do you think it's the Path that Valanir Ocune means for us to seek? Like Edrien Letrell?"

Hassen spread his hands. "I don't know. Maybe he's crazy. None of us knows."

The door crashed open, and a tall man in a serpent mask staggered in. He collapsed into a chair, mouth stretched in a sickly grin.

Valanir Ocune and Lin looked at one another. *Marlen.* They rose quietly and began to make their way to the back of the room. If Marlen saw them, he would recognize them. He had seen too much to do otherwise.

"What did I miss?" he slurred.

They never heard the answer to that. Completing a circuitous route about the room, the fugitive and his accomplice dodged through the door, leaving the poets of Tamryllin behind.

* * *

NEARLY everyone was asleep by the time Darien had a chance to corner Marlen alone. He practically had to drag him to their room and fling him onto the bed. "Where were you?" Darien demanded. His anxiety was compounded by Marlen's face, which was vulnerable in a way he'd never seen.

"Making a devil's bargain," said Marlen. "And with a devil, for that matter."

Darien's stomach churned. "What is wrong with you, Marlen? Whatever it is, we can fix it together."

"Too late for that," said Marlen, rubbing his face as if to massage pain from it. "No one can fix it. I sold you out. You're out of the contest, Darien."

Candlelight was the only illumination in that room; the moon had retreated behind clouds. Darien wondered if this were but a dimly lit dream. "Explain," he said. He marveled at his own voice, its calm.

"I can't tell you how I did it—sorry about that," said Marlen. "If I did, you might get it reversed somehow, and I can't allow that, obviously. Anyway, I thought I'd give you this opportunity to—to kill me. Before tomorrow." He drew his sword, so prized, and flung it to the floor. He stood now with his arms extended at his sides. "Go ahead."

"You're drunk," said Darien. "And you disgust me more than I ever thought possible."

"Words," said Marlen, showing his teeth. "What care I for words? Only a blade is real. And here I am giving you this chance."

"I still believe in words," said Darien. "It is, after all, what we do. Though you—I don't know what you do anymore."

"You don't need the Branch, Darien," said Marlen, his face once more an unavoidable window into his feelings. For once, Darien would have preferred him to have none. "You will succeed, just by being you. I—that is not how it is for me. I had to do this."

Darien felt as if the room were tilting under him. "I'm leaving," he said, his voice tight around his words. "When I come back, I want you gone. And don't imagine that this can stand, Marlen—no one is keeping me from the contest. Only, instead of winning with me, you will lose against me. That I promise you."

Without waiting for a response, Darien left the room, stumbled down the inn stairs. By now, the common room was nearly empty. He was alone.

IN the predawn light, they nearly staggered with fatigue through the city streets. It was at the gate north of the palace that they stopped and at last removed their masks. Lin smiled, feeling the air against her face like a blessing. It was good to smile.

I will not think of the road's end.

"So you are leaving," she said.

"I am," said Valanir Ocune. "As are you. After the contest?"

She nodded. "There's one thing left for me to do. Before I go."

"Don't stay too long," he said, sounding serious. "You may be in danger here. When you go—make for the Academy Isle. Any way you can. Take this." In her palm he pressed something sharp and cold. Lin opened her hand and saw a brass key.

"The Path . . ."

"I can't tell you more than that," he said. "I wish I could. But one thing I can say. You may have wondered why it was you I sought, of all the poets in Tamryllin."

Lin avoided his eyes. She felt the chill of dawn keenly, and set her shoulders against it. "I thought . . . because I'm not properly a poet. With nothing at stake."

"No." A forceful negation that made her glance up. "You risked your life with me, played until your hands were nearly bloodied, and all the while believing—that? I regret that. I regret it very much." He took one of her hands in his good hand. "I should have told you, Lin Amaristoth. Of portals between this world and the Otherworld, and the dimensions between. The hallways of doors. Behind one of the most crucial of those doors, I saw you."

"You saw me." Unexpectedly she was blinking back tears. "That's not possible."

"I swear it," he said. "There is a road ahead for you that I cannot see, but it matters."

"And you?" She tried to smile. "Where does your road lead, Valanir Ocune?"

"I will be working to influence events from afar," he said. "We will meet again soon, if the gods are kind." He gave her hand one last squeeze. "Keep safe," he said, and turned to go. For a moment she watched as he shuffled toward the gate, exaggerating his limp, humming to himself as if he were an eccentric old traveler. His hood drawn up around his face.

Turning away, Lin set out to retrace her steps to the city center. Her shadow skimmed the paving stones as daylight grew. The perfect quiet was beginning to break; another day. *It matters,* he had said. Could such a thing be true?

Lin thought of how the night had been filled with music, and hoped the melodies would echo down that long hall, all the days of her life.

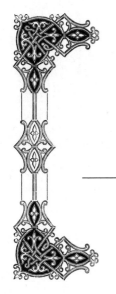

PART II

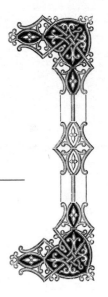

CHAPTER
10

FOR the first time in her life, Rianna was seated in her father's study. She knew it only as a room he reserved for business, for dealing with people related to his affairs in trade and commerce—in other words, with men. It was a side of his life that she rarely saw: the neat rows of leather-bound ledgers on the shelves behind him, the books of his expansive library. These he'd always allowed her to borrow, one at a time.

A tapestry hung on the back wall, depicting a scene from the creation of the world. Thalion and Estarre danced in a meadow against the backdrop of mountains and a waterfall. Kiara in the far corner, pale, clad in dark robes, hand raised in the ancient sign of warding against calamity.

For it was said that Kiara had opposed the creation of the world and of humanity in particular. Knowing the evil they would bring.

Rianna looked across the desk at her father, who was waiting for her response. Waiting with unusual patience, she thought.

"*Avan,*" she said at last. "We both . . . we just decided it wasn't right. That's all."

Her father was absently fingering the fabric of his cloak. He was dressed for the fair and contest, where he would preside as one of the judges. "Forgive me, love," he said, "but I doubt very much that this was Ned's initiative. He cares very much for you."

"It was," she said. "It was when he realized that . . . that I don't feel that way about him." She stared down at her hands.

Master Gelvan now leaned back in his chair. "Ah." His face was unreadable. Then he smiled, briefly. "I wish you had told me you intended to be so strong-willed," he said. "I would have explained to you that this marriage is important."

"Is it . . . is it money?"

"No," said her father. "Do you think I would sell my daughter? That is, of course, what they say about us. But Ned's family was always different. They did not take such a view of Galicians. And they love you."

Rianna shook her head helplessly. "I'm sorry, *Avan*."

"I needed this marriage," said Master Gelvan, "to protect you."

Suddenly her father was on his feet. With brisk strides, he reached the door and threw it open. The hallway was empty. "Good," he said, and closed the door again. "I've become fearful lately, I suppose. Suddenly suspecting even our servants." He sat again. "I will need wine for this, I think," he said. "Do you want something to drink, sweetheart?"

"No," said Rianna, with more conviction than was necessary. He was starting to unnerve her. Yet he seemed calm, his hand steady as he poured red wine from a crystal decanter.

"I don't understand," Rianna prodded him. "Are you trying to convince me to marry Ned by . . . frightening me? Why would I need protection?"

"Well, there's no chance of you marrying Ned anytime soon," said her father, turning a stern gaze on her. "He's gone."

"Gone?"

"For a time," he amended, relenting. "Ned asked his father to send him on one of his ships, in a trade voyage east. It is dangerous . . . I fear for the boy. His heart was always sterling quality, but his skill with weapons—rather less so."

"He just didn't have practice," Rianna said quickly. The memory of Ned drawing his sword on her behalf, brandishing it so clumsily, served as a vivid reproach.

"Whatever the case. He will be gone for a time. So here we are. And it's not the only thing to complicate my plans." He looked so worn, she thought—frighteningly so. Her father had always been someone she could rely upon. A strong presence, even though they did not often speak. "Rianna, I'm sorry I don't talk to you more about your mother."

Rianna opened her mouth, closed it again. She was too confused now even to speak.

"I know," he said. "You wonder why I'd raise that now. You are a sensible girl."

They sat quietly a moment. The wind chimes outside were stirred, a soft and fading melody. A sound from her earliest memory, but in recent days, it seemed to have become a part of her past more and more, and thus a source of inexplicable sadness.

Darien was the present, she reminded herself, whatever else happened from here. Whatever else, however precious, might be lost.

At last her father spoke. "Do you know how she died?"

She stared. He was breaking so many rules today. Discussing her marriage with her, as though it were her choice. Seating her in the study. Offering her wine. And now, most strangely, raising the specter of death.

"She was ill?" said Rianna. It was something she had learned from overhearing whispers, growing up. From servants, from guests. Her mother had died when she was small. From that time, Rianna remembered nothing; her earliest memories of nurturing were of her old nurse, who now lived in a little house at the outskirts of Tamryllin. Master Gelvan did not believe in the practice of having nurses stay on all their lives. That was a perverse Ellenican practice, he maintained, not for a Gelvan.

"A sickness that struck quickly, with immediate results," said her father, his voice hollow. "The doctor was a friend. He confided to me that he believed it was poison."

Rianna opened her mouth, then shut it again. No words would

come. That swiftly, she had passed the threshold from one era of her life to another. Acutely aware in that moment that it was happening.

"For years I wondered who would have done such a thing, and why," her father was saying. "I knew better than to involve the authorities. At court, your mother was loathed for betraying her family by marrying a Galician. If anyone was to investigate, it had to be me."

Rianna swallowed. *"Avan,* is this to do with Dane Beylint?"

He stared. "How do you know about that?"

"I . . . heard you talking," she said. "When I couldn't sleep."

He shook his head. "I hadn't meant for you to know about that . . . to frighten you. But if I am telling you everything . . . Through the years, I have done all the things a merchant can do to gain the king's favor. You know this. It was to gain access at court, to see—and to overhear. Your mother was . . . she was doing things I didn't know about, very much in secret. She was in some sort of plot involving the most powerful players at court. And one man in particular."

"She never told you?" Rianna demanded, feeling the beginnings of anger.

"Never," said Master Gelvan, expressionless.

Rianna's fists closed as she thought of it. Her father betrayed by a city that never regarded him as an equal, and—it turned out—even by his own wife. "Who was the man?"

He hesitated only a moment. Then: "The Court Poet. Nickon Gerrard. For years I've studied him . . . cultivating sources at court, and elsewhere in the city. So far I've reason to believe your mother's death was not the only one he is linked to. Dane Beylint is only the latest. What I can't seem to uncover is why."

Rianna had involuntarily pressed a hand to her head as if to steady it. "The *Court Poet.*"

"I know it is hard to believe," he said. "I have come to think he is a great danger to the city. Perhaps to the country, given his power. There are—disturbing rumors . . ." He trailed off.

"Yes?" She could not imagine anything more disturbing than what he had already told her.

"Well, you know Nickon Gerrard has announced changes to the

contest since it was held twelve years ago. Very odd changes, like introducing a flask of sacred wine and a song in which all the entrants must take part before the contest begins. It sounds harmless, but it also recalls . . . other practices. That, together with the recent killings, have made me wonder . . ."

"Wonder what?"

He sighed. Then he drank all the wine in his cup. "He's planning something for that day," said Master Gelvan. "That much we know."

TWELVE years ago to the day, the last contest of the Silver Branch had preceded Tamryllin's great annual Midsummer Fair. It was a time when crowds spilled beyond the confines of the enormous Court Plaza into adjoining streets and alleyways, for the most anticipated competition in years. Lin had heard the tales but had never thought to be here herself, seated on the flagstones of the plaza, saving a space from which to see the platform that had been erected for that day, hard by the gates of the palace.

From the crenellations of the palace walls hung the brightly colored pennons of Tamryllin's aristocratic families, sponsors of the event. The cloths trailed lifeless in the summer heat. Adjoining the platform were benches, cordoned from the rest of the plaza by a length of silken rope: spaces reserved for those who could pay.

Twelve years ago, someone had won, but in time his memory had faded. Even Lin, for all her obsessive studies of Academy lore, had forgotten his name. It was the man who had won before him who had remained etched in public awareness—the man who was to rise to power as one of the most influential Court Poets in history. Nickon Gerrard had not only assumed the position; he had elevated it to unprecedented levels. He had the king's ear in ways no one else did—or so it was said. Lin, who had heard it confirmed by her family, believed it.

In the city, the Court Plaza was a historic source of pride, flanked on all sides by some of the most ancient and famed of its architectural façades. Dominating the west side, up a flight of polished white stairs was the Eldest Sanctuary, temple to the Three, built more than a thousand years ago. Fronted with pillars taller than trees, the temple attracted pilgrims from across the country and beyond. Its façade was deliberately positioned to catch the full onslaught of light at sunrise, dazzling to mortal eyes.

Loftily gazing to the temple from across the plaza was the palace, a newer and more gilded structure of many towers rising behind wrought iron gates. The royal family and their retinue would be watching from their balcony, protected by spearmen on all sides.

Lin was no longer alone; many more were arriving to claim a place on the flagstones. Soon it would be flooded, and she would have no space to breathe. Soon enough.

It was strange to be here, when for so long she had planned to be on that platform. Supporting Leander with her words and voice.

She had briefly entertained the idea of leaving before the contest but knew she needed to witness this. Leander had been a friend to her. It meant something, as much as the gods and the power of music meant something in the world.

It was not as if the fair didn't offer other attractions. While the contest for the Silver Branch had become the main event of the fair for poets, it could not overshadow what was for most its central function: commerce. For a week after the contest, Tamryllin would be awash in trade goods, both exotic and practical. Spices from Kahishi—cinnamon and ginger and, most dear of all, pepper—would exhale their fragrances into the air, drawing customers who would be faced with glowering guards whose task was to protect the goods at any cost.

There were carpets, woven painstakingly by hand and trundled from the far reaches of the deserts to the south. Bales of wool from northern Eivar, silks of varying textures from the lands of the farthest east. And then there were the ventures that thrived on specialized items: handicrafts of wood, of silver and gold; costly and rarely seen items like silver-backed mirrors and glass delicate as the petals of a rose. The finest gold-stringed harps would be on display to dazzle the poorer Academy students. Blacksmiths would present their finest work of the year, their swords and daggers, shields and coats of armor; and those who made a name for themselves might end up filling an order for a lord before the week was out, or even the king himself.

The stands for all of these had been erected, and tomorrow would be overflowing with colors, textures, and smells. The air would abound with the staccato intonations of bargaining; the plaintive calls of traders with wares to sell; harp music, drumbeats, and laughter. What had begun with the abandon and ferocity of the masque would reach a pinnacle of excitement with the contest and then relax into an event patrolled by the Royal Guard and attended by nobility of the highest ranks.

Lin knew all this from Rayen's tales, told to their mother by the fire late at night. She recalled all that her brother had said about the upcoming contest, for of course he had friends at court who knew. It would be different from the last one, with changes instituted by Court Poet Gerrard himself—Lin suspected self-aggrandizing changes to highlight his importance. A ceremonial cask of wine stored seven years in the Eldest Sanctuary, in the most sacred of its chambers, would be presented to the Court Poet. Nickon Gerrard would drink the consecrated wine, and then he and the poets would sing, a piece that seemed of ancient origin, which Lin had looked up in the archives of the Vassilian library. In recent years, new words had been affixed to the melody; it was now a tribute to the Three. The Court Poet was said to have noted, piously, that there had previously not been enough of a godly presence at the contest. In this way would some of the last vestiges of the Academy's heretical, pre-Ellenican origins be shed.

Not long ago, Rayen had been her only bridge to the world. It was only since her escape that Lin understood the extent to which she'd been imprisoned in Vassilian, knowing nothing of life but what he had chosen to share with her.

Lin recalled the vision with Valanir: Rayen and a mask of blood. *Soon, my love.*

Well did she remember how it had felt to be afraid, more horrible even than the reality of what happened when he did succeed in cornering her, with loyal servants to help wrest away her knives. She remembered, too, the salt taste of her own blood in her mouth, the sickening feeling of spitting out a pebbly tooth. The one time he had touched her face, for usually he was careful to keep it intact, to serve as an unblemished canvas for cosmetics that might attract a suitable spouse.

Not that it would be hard to find someone, he always pointed out. Even with her looks, there were the Amaristoth fortune and name.

Well, not anymore, she thought with an inward grin. Rayen would have to find some other way to expand the family estates. She wondered, not for the first time, if her disappearance had caused him much embarrassment among his peers, signifying his inability to keep even one wayward female in line.

She certainly hoped so.

And with that thought, Lin circled back to the idea that had haunted her for weeks: that it was likely that Rayen was in the audience here, in this square. That he had come to Tamryllin for the fair, as he did most years. If she and Leander had performed together as originally planned, they had agreed she would keep her hood raised. Here, among thousands of people, she blended easily, but there was always a risk. Lin felt for the hilt of the knife in her sleeve, stroked the smooth leather. If it did come to a fight, she was ready.

FROM the stands they had a dizzying view of the crowds that filled the Court Plaza. Her hair swept up in a severe knot, a film of frosty lace concealing her neck and chest, Rianna felt she had gone into hiding—within full view of thousands, yet still somehow unknown.

You will speak of this to no one, her father had said, just before she had crossed the threshold of his study with her new knowledge. Wondering where and how it would fit into her life—or perhaps change nothing at all.

Darien, she thought. More than ever, she needed his help to sort through the immensity of all that had happened.

Soon he would come out to take his place on the platform and compete for a poet's highest honor. *We're the best,* he had told her, as calmly as if observing that the summer was hot or that the roses in her father's garden smelled sweet. It wasn't a particular source of pride for Darien, she realized. Just something he knew.

In the stands were the people who mattered in Tamryllin—many of them judges in this contest. Rianna wondered why her father had consented to be a judge, when he cared nothing for music. But the next moment she thought she knew: his participation was, in some way, related to the preeminence of Nickon Gerrard in this contest. Master Gelvan would have to be involved. Another way to be near the man he was watching.

"I saw Callum slip a note to you at the ball," she had said to him that morning in the study. "What was it?"

Master Gelvan had pursed his lips, for a moment nonplussed. At last he sighed. "I can't think of a reason not to tell you," he said. "Shortly before his death, Master Beylint sent a note to the palace. I wasn't able to recover it, but we did get the note sent to him in response. He was to have a private dinner with Lord Gerrard. With no guards present."

For some reason this answer made Rianna feel light-headed. "I don't understand," she said, her voice thin and strange in her ears. "Why would the Court Poet be killing people?"

"That is a question I have long sought to answer," said her father. "I knew Nickon Gerrard when he was a bitter lad doing everything in his power—*everything*—to surpass Valanir Ocune. I knew his family as a boy, cleaned their mansion every week. You can be sure it pleases him now to keep me by him, imagining that I am his servile creature. His pet Galician, whose wife knew—something. That is what I think, Rianna: she discovered something he wanted secret."

Words like cold fingers, closing around her heart on a summer morning. And for the rest of that day, they had stayed.

Still she felt a flutter of excitement when a horn sounded and a procession of Academy graduates, attired humbly in grey robes, marched onto the stage. Now a pipe had joined the horn to trill a tune as they assumed their places, each with a hood shadowing his face. It was beginning.

Nickon Gerrard came forward, clad in his six-colored cloak, his harp at his side. For the first time, Rianna noticed a crystal decanter of wine and a golden goblet, gem-encrusted, on a small table. The consecration. Lord Gerrard had decreed that without it, the contest would be a meaningless rite, without sanctity before the gods.

Could this man have killed her mother? It seemed an absurdity. And yet.

Tearing her eyes away from him, she studied the hooded men, wondering which of them was Darien Aldemoor.

It was at that moment, as Nickon Gerrard reached for the decanter, that something bright flashed through the air, straight toward him.

The next moment saw the decanter leap from the table even as the Court Poet's fingers brushed it. Wine pulsed from the spout like a bleeding wound and was gone.

The sacred wine.

A voice was calling out, high above the crowds. "Lord Gerrard! Over here!"

A voice she would know in any place, any street of any city in the world. But this time, her heart did not leap at the sound. Now it was of a piece with the strangeness and growing horror of that day.

She could see him, standing on a rooftop in the distance. Waving his arms in mockery. Sunlight glittered in starry points across the strings of his harp.

"That man sang for us, didn't he," said her father, oddly calm.

Rianna swallowed hard. Her voice, low and controlled, seemed to be coming from a distance, from someone else. "Yes, *Avan*," she said. "He did."

CHAPTER 11

THE night before, Darien had stumbled out of the *Ring and Flagon* and into the waning moonlight. His only thought to put as much distance as possible between himself and Marlen, and the place where words he had never thought to hear had been spoken.

A long friendship come crashing down.

Darien realized he was still clutching his mask, despite all that happened. *The court jester,* the woman had said. He let it slip from his fingers to the cobblestones. One of many masks discarded that night.

If he were honest with himself—Darien thought, dodging one of the last processions of merrymakers into the shadows of a blind alley—a part of him had always been on the alert. Half-expecting something like this.

I hoped the music would cure him, he thought, lost in a whirl of shock and the odd, internal logic of fatigue. For, of course, what did that mean? Music was no cure for anything.

He took a rickety flight of steps to the rooftops; a shortcut he and his friend had shared many times. From here—where chimneys marched in uneven formation—the city of Tamryllin blanketed the horizon, white towers rising into mist and out again, to the stars. *Stabbing the sky.* The walls of the imperial palace flowing in harmony with the curve of the hillsides. And then, the sea.

A glancing line of brightness joined sea and sky: the first signs of daybreak. A light, Darien often thought, that was itself like music. At the end of long nights in his stone cubicle in the Tower of the Winds, after he had wrestled with pen and parchment for hours by candlelight, Darien had often gone out to cliffs on Academy Isle that overlooked the sea to the east. Sunrise, to him, had become associated with a song completed—a new thread in the tapestry that was his life's work, luminous in that moment.

Just now, Darien had no desire to watch the sun rise.

Another flight of steps down, and he was back in the streets. But this time, he didn't know where he was. The featureless grey of dawn and a killing weariness worked to confuse him, though he knew he could not be far from where he had started. He was still in the old district, where marble gave art to each slope, every winding passageway and soaring arch. But details were shadowy in this half-light between night and sunrise, grey melding with grey.

Just when Darien thought himself truly lost, a light swam into his vision, blurred as if through fog. And in contrast to the grey all around, this light had a golden cast, verging on red.

Soon Darien could see an arch of pure light that as he drew near, became a building just ahead. Closer still, and sharper details emerged: the arch, which was the doorway, was half-concealed by a red curtain hanging within the threshold. Beyond, Darien saw the curve of a low, circular table, where a candle flame trembled in scarlet glass, throwing darts of light across the surface of polished wood. A rich, sweet aroma met Darien's nostrils as he approached, beckoning him closer still. He saw letters carved in the stone above the arch, their knotted shapes forming no language that he knew.

The curtain in the doorway was of finely woven cotton, light to the touch as Darien flicked it aside. Feathery smoke met his eyes and nose, and that smell, sharp even in its sweetness.

It was a room without windows, hung with draperies of red and thread of gold. A series of tables, low to the ground, receded into the shadowed interior, ringed with cushions of many colors. Low-hanging brass lamps filled the room with a flickering glow.

Darien's attention was at once drawn to the man who sat alone at one of the tables, the only person in the room. His swarthy complexion would have marked him a Kahishian even if not for his garb, loose-fitting and bright in the lamplight. His head was swathed in a turban, and a closely trimmed beard outlined prominent cheekbones. Near his elbow rested a steaming cup.

"*Salem,*" the man said, and then smiled at Darien's confusion. "Be welcome," he said. "I was not expecting a guest, half an hour to sunrise."

"I don't know what I'm doing here," said Darien.

"You followed the light, perhaps," the man replied, his voice deep as the shadows that puddled around them both. "You have the look of a man who has traveled a long time."

Darien shook his head, too tired to explain.

The seated man took a sip of his drink and yawned, seeming to have already forgotten that Darien was in the room. He was smoking a serpentine pipe attached to a brass urn on the floor. Pale blue smoke drifted upward to mingle with smoke from the cup. Darien suddenly felt as if he could sleep for a long time, on the floor of this smoke-filled cave of a room.

"May I sit?" he said.

The Kahishian inclined his head slightly, a gold earring set with rubies catching the light. "If you wish."

Darien sank into one of the cushions at a table near the Kahishian. It was a relief to take the weight off his legs, to rest his harp in his lap. The strap was beginning to chafe his shoulder, a sign that he had been wearing it too long.

"*Khave?*" the man said to him.

Darien blinked. "Sorry?"

In answer, the Kahishian raised his cup.

"Oh. Please," said Darien. He had no idea what he was agreeing to, but it had a good smell.

The man got up and vanished behind the draperies at the back of the room. He emerged moments later with a blue earthenware cup that steamed even more than his own. Brown-flecked foam swam at the top and threatened to overspill the sides. Darien took the cup from him cautiously and nursed it in his hands. He thanked the Kahishian, who returned to his seat.

After a moment Darien ventured, "Do many people . . . like me . . . come here?"

"I see you are a player," said the man. "Or no, what do you call it . . . a poet? No, we get few of your kind here. Few Eivarians know of this place, or care to know." He smiled thinly. "It is no matter. I opened this place only because it reminds me of home."

"You have another business?"

The other man nodded but did not elaborate. He seemed to be contemplating the ceiling, where an impressive collection of smoke rings formed a bluish haze. Darien sipped his drink. Despite the sweet smell, it was bitter, with the consistency of mud. Yet he felt compelled to drink more, to savor the strange flavor on his tongue. So much of tonight had become strange.

Darien said, almost to himself, "I don't know where to go. I was supposed to play . . . today, I suppose it is. Yes. Today."

"And your plans have changed?"

"My closest friend betrayed me."

The other man smiled. "Ah. Something you would not have planned."

"Not exactly."

A silence stretched between them. The Kahishian puffed his pipe, produced a smoke ring the size of his own head. It hung suspended a moment, before gently dissolving into a fine trail of blue.

Darien warmed his hands against the sides of the ceramic cup, stared into the smoke that curled from its brim. "I ought to have known," he said. "Marlen told me—he once told me that his father advised him to poison me, while we were at the Academy. For the good of his career. He refused, but it cost him. I know it cost him."

He remembered: entering their room at the Academy after their return from the winter holidays and Marlen already there, seated on the windowsill, one long leg outstretched above the floor. He refused to meet Darien's eyes, but soon Darien saw what initially had been turned away from his sight: a gash in Marlen's face from forehead to jaw. "He says you will ruin me," Marlen said. "That I will always be in your shadow."

And even Darien, who women quipped had an answer for everything, had no answer for his friend in that moment.

And yet, if I had said the right thing that day—if I had told him that there is no shadow, that we are one in all that we do—would that have prevented this?

To this day, a silvery line curved down the side of Marlen's face. What good were words, when permanent testimony was stamped on the flesh?

"There was a poet here last night," the Kahishian said in a thoughtful tone, as if he had not heard. "Older than you. I remember him because he has come here before over the years. He speaks our language. Always he would have a tale to tell."

Darien never could have said why he had a suspicion in that moment. He asked, "Did this poet wear a pale gemstone on his right hand?"

The Kahishian's eyes met his through the smoke, and for a moment Darien wondered if he knew more than he was telling. "Yes," he said. "A pale stone with a heart like fire."

"A moon opal," Darien said. "So Valanir Ocune was here."

"He told me it might be the last time," said the Kahishian. "That he would likely lose his life in his search for the Path."

"The Path," said Darien, half-rising from his chair. "He said that? Did he explain what he meant by it?"

The Kahishian remained expressionless. With toneless finality he said, "I can tell you only one other thing, Darien Aldemoor. In the court of our king—may he reign eternally in light—the astrologers have seen a red star rising above the white towers of Tamryllin. A sign of great bloodshed and darkness. It has already begun."

"A red star," Darien said. A realization dawned on him. "How did you know my name?"

The Kahishian smiled, a gleam like metal in the shadows. "You ask the wrong questions."

And then the room was gone; the Kahishian was gone. It was deep night, and Darien was lost among stately ornamental trees. Fresh breeze on his cheek, scent of jasmine. Nearby a fountain, splashing softly, the water that pooled in the basin striated with white moonlight. Darien felt his legs suddenly unsteady. He was in a walled garden beside one of the elegant residences of Tamryllin. From here he could see its lightless windows, the sloping roof. Overhead a crescent moon rode the sky.

Wait . . .

Wrong, wrong phase of the moon.

And then he saw: the figure of a man stretched on the grass, spread-eagled. Tree shadows flitted across him as he lay still. Boot toes pointed up at the sky.

Darien drew closer, saw the man's neck was split in a mess of black. His bearded face a frozen mask, eyes like glass. Frozen forever.

A sound behind Darien made him swing around, sword out. Master Gelvan stood among the trees, watching him. He looked sad. "I lost her because of this, you know."

"What?" Darien said. "No."

"Seven bodies found in Tamryllin . . . but that is only a beginning," said Rianna's father. His eyes fixed on Darien's with unnerving solemnity. "You'll see."

It was day, and he was on a city street. A market filled with the calls of people ambling between storefronts and stalls. Darien had to jump to avoid an oncoming cart. The horses reared, and Darien was too stunned to apologize to the cursing driver. Giving shade to the blazing street were unfamiliar trees, drooping with red flowers the size of melons. Their petals littered the ground and raised an overpowering sweet scent in the boiling air.

Just then, a young woman near Darien lost her balance and crumpled at the knees. Without thinking, Darien swerved to catch her around the waist, as people around them turned to stare. She was limp in his arms. Darien turned her over to see her face, what had gone wrong. Her eyes had sprouted vicious red like the flowers, but darker.

Much darker. Petals surrounding blue eyes gone wide and blank. A scream caught in his throat.

Nearby a small boy buckled and fell, the same red tears on his face. As more people in the street began dropping to the ground, a cry of terror spread as if with one voice, but could have been hundreds of separate screams. The cart that had so narrowly missed Darien started to careen wildly down the street. More screams marked its progress, though whether from horror of the disease or of the crazed horses was hard to tell.

Scent of flowers. So large and red.

Now he remembered. *Sarmanca.*

It was night again and he was back in the garden amid the quieter scents of Tamryllin. Master Gelvan was still there. So was the corpse of Master Beylint, prone on the ground beside the standing man as if it were his own shadow.

"We don't have much time," said Rianna's father. "At the contest, Darien—the wine is key."

"The wine?"

"The sacred wine. You must destroy it."

"Destroy it?" said Darien. "Why?"

A wind picked up, stirred the merchant's hair around his face. He looked almost young in the pale light. "His power is trapped in the White City. The ceremony would change all that. You see?"

"The White City," Darien echoed. No one called it that, outside songs.

And in that moment the man before him changed. Still grey-haired, a harp at his side. He was draped in a dark cloak. Eyes an intense blue even in darkness. He said, "I found the Path, and unspeakable sorrow there." His words twined with the hushed music of falling water.

Darien stared. *"Edrien."*

"You see," said the man.

And then he was gone; the garden was gone.

Now it was almost entirely dark, moonlight fighting through a thick cover of trees. Their branches spread full and high overhead, while masses of pines blocked out the world. A wood, somewhere. Darien gripped his upper arms, his teeth clenched. The bite in the air was like winter.

Destroy it. A whisper on the wind.

And then he saw that a figure—small, slight—knelt on the ground, arms oddly outstretched over a boulder, forehead pressed against the stone. It was a strange position, and even stranger that the figure was entirely still. Remembering the dead man in the garden, the woman in Sarmanca, Darien approached with dread like a fist in his throat.

As if sensing his approach, the figure turned its head. Lin. Her eyelids drooped as if in sleep. Her oddly outstretched arms, he now saw, were dripping blood. Darien gasped, saw that a neat wound had been cut in each wrist. A gleam in the corner of his eye—a knife, lying on the ground as if cast aside.

Lin smiled when she saw him, sleepily. "Darien," she said. "Did I do well?"

HE woke to sunlight glaring into his eyes, a hard bump sticking in his back. The next moment, he realized he was lying sprawled in the street and immediately jumped up. Then he saw that his harp had been tangled up under one arm, safe, not stolen, and he gasped with relief.

Darien looked around, bewildered. He didn't recall leaving the Kahishian establishment, and certainly not lying down in the street. Yet his instrument was untouched, and his money pouch—which had been digging into his back—was still heavy.

Now that it was day, he could get his bearings: he was in a cul de sac in one of the old districts. Nearby he recognized the arched door-way of the Kahishian's tavern. He could see now that it was cut into a wall beneath a much larger building. Double doors now blocked the arch, the steel reinforcements clouded with rust.

Darien knocked at the door. Only silence. He grabbed ahold of the door and wrenched the handle. The shriek of metal grating against metal made him clamp his teeth, and dust billowed in his face. The door would only open part of the way, sealed as it was from the inside by a rusted bolt chain. Within, the room was dark. Sunlight that angled inside fell on piles of rags, broken furniture. The hangings that Darien remembered, the tables—none of it was there. A giant cobweb was strung between the broken legs of an overturned chair.

Darien fell back, letting the doors collapse together again with a clang. For the next hour, he hunted for the remembered doorway in the surrounding streets but couldn't find any door that resembled the one he had just left. It couldn't have been a dream—his sleeve was stained dark brown, and when he held it to his nostrils, the bittersweet odor was unmistakable.

He remembered something. Doubling back, he returned to the door. There had been a sign carved above the archway in foreign characters, no doubt in Kahishian. The sign was still there—he recognized its rectangular shape. But now it was smooth stone, with only traces of lettering that had long since faded away.

Destroy it.

Darien shivered even though it was day now, and warm, in Tamryllin of the waking world.

WHEN he came to Marilla that morning he hated himself for his weakness as well as all the other reasons he could have had, by then, to hate himself. He had vowed the night before that he would never see her again, yet here he was just hours later. Vile as she was, Marilla knew him. She knew him better even than Darien had. If Darien had known him better, Marlen reflected, he would never have been his friend.

She had once been a lady's maid, he knew, and later on a prostitute. He gathered that a large part of her appeal was an ability to mimic the manner and graces of a lady, for those who fantasized about liaisons with nobility. It was ironic: Marlen wanted her for her savagery. For the way she hurt him without compunction, with guiltless abandon. And of course, the way she reacted when he hurt her back. He hadn't intended to make her privy to his plans, believing her an ignorant prostitute with no place in his affairs, even though she had never charged him for their nights together. But the day before, seeing her preening before the cracked mirror above her washstand with his leash around her neck, he had changed his mind. He could not have said why.

She was full of energy that morning. It amazed him; he had a headache so fierce it would be a wonder if he could sing today at all.

"Sit down," she said. "I'll rub your head."

"You?" Marlen said. "This isn't a ploy to get me to expose my neck?"

Marilla laughed gaily and shoved him into a chair. She was disconcertingly strong. "You're no use to me hungover."

That was probably as near to tenderness as she was capable, Marlen mused. "We made a mess of things last night, my dear," he said as she caressed his temples.

"Oh, the boy will be the better for it," she said dismissively. "Men with illusions are so . . . unattractive. Though sweet."

"That's not what I meant," he said. "I might have revealed Darien to Rianna's father. With all that I'm taking from Darien, I wanted to leave him at least that—at least her."

He felt her pause in her ministrations, as if considering. Then the rubbing resumed, and she said, "It will be well. The masque is a wild time. The boy will not trust his own ears, come morning."

"Do you think that was Valanir last night?"

"Perhaps," said Marilla. "More interesting, though, was the woman who was with him. His lover, perhaps?"

Marlen stiffened. "Woman? Are you sure?"

"Certainly," she said. "Why?"

He didn't answer for some moments as he considered. There was only one woman he knew of who went about dressed as a boy and possessed the skills of a trained poet, and that same woman had been on intimate terms with Valanir the night of the Gelvan ball. If she had aided him, that would of course make her his accomplice.

"I think I may know who she is," he said at last.

"Oh, good," said Marilla, and leaned forward with a dazzling smile. "When you win the contest, I'm sure that's something Court Poet Gerrard would want to know."

WHAT had once been home seemed strange now. Darien paused on the stair inside the *Ring and Flagon*, lingering to absorb this odd new feeling. He had run up this staircase so many times in the past months that he knew where the faults were, where it creaked. Yet now it was someone else's staircase, and he felt himself an interloper, an exile.

The place was nearly empty, as most had left to prepare for the contest, or to grab their places on the stones of the Court Plaza.

But Darien knew there was one person who would still be here. He could hear him in a room upstairs, practicing scales, his voice building and building and then falling to an impossible depth.

Yet the door was flung open after Darien's first knock, as if his friend had been waiting—as no doubt he had. Seeing Darien, Hassen's face went slack with disbelief. "You look . . ." Hassen began.

Darien leaned back against the wall beside the door. He laughed a little. "I pray you, don't tell me how I look."

"Come in then, come in."

It was a room Hassen shared with several others, but none were there now. Darien sank into one of the hard chairs.

"So what happened?"

"What happened." Darien shook his head. "Let me see. Well, you know about the court order I came back to this morning. *'No participation in the contest—on pain of severe punishment.'* So I thought I'd explore my options—my connections. But Master Gelvan refused to see me. Or was 'indisposed'—what does that even mean? So I went to the court's offices. Do you know what they told me? That there is a list of poets who are permitted to participate in the contest. And I am not on the list."

Hassen looked blank. "A *list*. How has it come to this?"

"Exactly." Years of writing, of studying lore from the most ancient texts, as well as from the men who had been selected to pass on that knowledge. Years of knowing—beyond any doubt—that his destiny was to do more.

"Listen," said Darien. "I have a plan. And it's important—it's important that you *not* be involved, or know about it."

Hassen snorted. "You just told me."

"I'm serious, Hassen. It could be dangerous for you to know more. But—there is one thing I need you to do."

"I don't like any of this talk." Hassen planted himself in front of Darien's chair, a towering, glaring bulk. "Are you thinking of acting against the court? You may as well fall on your sword right now and get it over with."

"Dying is the last thing I want." Darien pressed a paper into Hassen's hand. "Take this and listen to me."

THE *Ring and Flagon* had been like a home to Darien Aldemoor, as it was for many poets getting their start in the world. He knew with bone-deep certainty that he might never be able to return—yet with the memories the place carried for him now, perhaps that was for the best.

It was not in Darien's nature to be nostalgic, but he wondered if for the rest of his life his mind would circle back to the brightness of the past year, searching for the fault line that had gradually fissured deeper and wider without his knowing.

In his mind, it had already begun to be words set to music. But for that there was no time.

He knew he had a choice. He could vanish quietly away, taking his dreams with him. Marlen had beaten him this round, but there would be other opportunities in years to come.

Darien didn't like the idea of doing anything quietly, and he certainly didn't like the idea of vanishing. Never in his life had he felt so strongly that he was choosing a path—bypassing green meadows for the knife's edge of a cliff, or a dark wood.

It was a simple plan—inevitable since he had constructed it within just a few hours. He first visited the home of a friend he knew, one who happened to owe him a favor. There he made an acquisition, for a fee, and concealed it in his cloak. This was the first—and most easily accomplished—part of his plan.

As Darien approached the streets leading to the Court Plaza, he noticed that others were on their way, no doubt to reserve themselves spaces with a good view of the stage.

Darien smiled. He did enjoy a good performance.

He chose the house carefully: it belonged to a lord for whom he had sung many times. The family was summering in his northern estates, he knew, for they had told him. They abhorred the crowds that accompanied the fair. And there was no escaping those crowds if they remained at home, for their house faced onto the Court Plaza. A magnificent location, they asserted, at any other time of the year.

There would still be guests there today, Darien knew, by the windows and on the balcony. Friends of the family who would watch the contest from their privileged height while nibbling tiny sandwiches and sipping aged wine. So much the better: if any of the servants caught sight of Darien, he could claim that he, too, was a guest. *I represent House Aldemoor,* Darien imagined saying, tilting his nose toward the sky. *I am so bloody special.*

He realized he was giddy with excitement, made an effort to calm himself. Giddiness would not be an asset in the next few hours.

Flaunting his harp and ring, Darien had no trouble gaining entry to the home, blending with the guests as they filed up the stairs to the topmost floor. He reflected that under other circumstances, he would have been thrilled to snare such a coveted spot, and would have boasted of it afterward to his friends—and enemies.

Yet now it was only a means to an end. While the guests congregated on the balcony—more than one woman eyeing Darien, for he had made several conquests in just such a setting, where the wives were bored and idle—he slipped away to an adjoining chamber, where it was quiet. And where he could climb onto the windowsill and from there, pull himself up along the outer wall and onto the red tiled roof. It was dangerous, but he found a flat surface where he could drop into a sitting position. *Now to wait.*

From this height, the crowds were a dark sea, and the palace and temple joined by the Court Plaza all the more splendid. Darien could see gilded detail on the palace towers and light through the stained glass of the temple windows nearest the roof. Wonders that had been crafted to pay tribute to the grandeur of gods or royalty, whether any man could see them or not.

And he could see the cordoned area of seats, where Rianna and her father would be. For the first time since he'd begun this enterprise, Darien felt a pang of remorse. She would, justifiably, want to kill him for this.

It was windy up here, warm as a breath that ruffled Darien's hair and filled him with a kind of peace. Lulled by the wind and the distant hum of the crowd, Darien let his mind linger on memories.

They had met in the spring, at a party in Master Gelvan's home. It was a moment entirely unlooked-for; Darien was not interested at the time in any entanglements past a night or two. That spring he had pleasantly drifted through the pick of Tamryllin's wealthier women, and some common ones, too. It was precisely in such a manner that he had procured the honor of playing at one of Master Gelvan's dinners: an older, generous paramour had made the connection for him. Darien still recalled her fondly.

He and Marlen had been singing a duet together, a piece of comic raillery with a dark heart, such as Marlen enjoyed most. They took pleasure in discomfiting Eivarian high society with skewed versions of its cherished ideals, and knew—a bit contemptuously—that their audience found guilty enjoyment in them too.

As they sang, Darien caught sight of Rianna Gelvan, wide-eyed and curious. She seemed preternaturally solemn, as if regarding them from a distance. Their music interested her, but it did not touch her.

When they were done, Darien did not yield the floor to another musician, as had been the plan. Instead, after conferring hurriedly with Marlen, he began to sing again. This song in traditional meter and melody; a tale of a heroic man-at-arms and his love. One of his earliest songs, glowing with the idealism he had brought to the halls of the Academy when still a boy.

Sensing his purpose, Marlen had withdrawn to stand a bit behind Darien, playing the soft refrain but contributing no vocals, letting him sing alone. And Darien was not even sure what he'd intended until he raised his eyes, briefly, and saw Rianna's face, saw a flush in her cheeks and her eyes fixed upon him with a glow he had seen before, many times. But never had it meant to him what it did now.

For such beauty I would destroy my life
Much as a god may unmake the world.

He had sung those words with his eyes trained on her face, drinking in the ivory perfection of her skin and the gold of her hair. And then lowered them again to his harp, an unmistakable quickening in his heart. As if all the brightness of the year, his and Marlen's year of freedom, had been arrowing in the end, unexpectedly, toward this.

Afterward they had met in the garden, in moonlight, within the shadows of a moon-white cherry tree. There had been no need to plan it; they both had seen the other moving toward those shadows and knew it was for the same purpose.

Darien did not touch her that night; they only talked. But he had known even then that his course was changing and that from now on, Rianna Gelvan would be a part of it, however improbable that might seem.

And now, on a rooftop at the Midsummer contest when he ought to have been on the stage, he was about to change his course yet again. But still that course, somehow, would be with her—of that he was determined. The triumph of his quest and their love would someday make the greatest song ever sung, a story to be told again and again. Darien would not be like the dry old men who had taught him the lore of poetry; like Valanir Ocune, like Edrien Letrell, he would first live what he was destined to create.

The grey-robed figures were gathering on the platform. Darien felt grim watching them. His own robe still lay folded in a chest in his old room at the *Ring and Flagon*. He had never worn it, and now perhaps never would.

From his cloak, he brought out his new acquisition. That summer Darien had written a poem for a craftsman he'd befriended, a birthday gift for the man's wife. He was thus able to acquire today, at minimal cost, a small crossbow and arrows. It was a device exquisite in its compactness as a toy. But the arrows were steel-tipped: no toy at all.

He had always had a talent for the bow. It was true he had not practiced in a long time; and it was also true that he would have only one shot now, two at most. *I must be mad,* he thought. And yet. There was something in the feel of the bow and the set of his shoulders as he drew that felt *right,* like the crescendo to a song.

Destroy it.

Nickon Gerrard paced with majestic solemnity down the length of the platform, passing each of the robed contestants, at last arriving at the flagon of sacred wine.

With a prayer and a peculiar lightness in his heart, Darien let the arrow fly.

CHAPTER
12

A GASP rippled through the Court Plaza; all eyes focused upward at the roof where a figure stood outlined darkly against the sky. Though he was no bigger than her thumbnail from this distance, Lin knew him at once by his voice.

"Lord Gerrard! Over here!"

Her heart thudded with shock and a deep sadness. *No, no Darien,* she thought. *I liked you.*

And she thought also of Rianna Gelvan and the multiple knife edges of heartbreak.

Darien Aldemoor had flung his arms wide, like a street performer announcing his next act. "Friends, I have been betrayed," he called, and his strong, trained voice soared to fill the perimeter of the square. "I, Darien Aldemoor, have been cast out of the contest for one reason only: my former friend, Marlen Humbreleigh—whom you see before you today—could not bear to share the honor of victory with me."

Nickon Gerrard was busy during this: with an imperious gesture, he commanded the guards to ascend the roof. They began to force their way through the crowds.

"If a man's ambition can so corrupt the contest," continued Darien, "then it is not sanctified before the gods. And while my friend's greed is largely to blame, the real fault lies with the court, who have made our art a mockery."

Now audible gasps were filling the plaza. In Tamryllin, a man who said such words had thrown away his life. Though in truth he had already done that from the moment the wine was desecrated.

A tall man onstage came forward, flung back his hood. Marlen Humbreleigh stood smiling, shook his head. "It grieves me that you were cut from the contest, Darien," he called. "But to place the blame on me is unseemly, don't you think?"

The guards were halfway across the plaza, Lin saw. It would not be long now.

"It's all right, Marlen," Darien flung back, his voice ringing with bright clarity across the vastness of the plaza. "I forgive you. I forgive you for the weak and power-hungry man you are. Here, then, is my message to you."

His harp cradled tenderly in his arms, Darien was still a moment, as if there were not palace guards bearing down upon him. He plucked the strings, and the tune that streamed from them was not surprising; it was, Lin thought, an inevitability. She had played it so many times.

> *No matter the color*
> *of the branch—silver, copper or gold,*
> *there is one surety:*
> *It is false. It is false.*

When he stopped, the silence in the square was disturbed only by the harrying of the guards and by the birds calling as they wheeled indifferently overhead. Darien approached the edge of the rooftop, and for an instant Lin was afraid he would jump. Like a bird spreading its wings, he stretched out his arms above the transfixed spectators as if to bestow a benediction upon them all. When next he spoke, his voice held a kind of wonder. "I had a dream last night that turned out to be no dream, after all. Now I believe the Path is real." More stridently he called, "You go ahead and win the false branch, Marlen, my dear friend. I am going to find Edrien's Path, and the real Branch. And who will be the greater poet then?"

The guards had reached the house now, Lin saw, her throat choked with anxiety. *What is he waiting for? Is he truly a fool?*

Marlen was still smiling. "Find it," he said, an arm outflung gracefully, "and I will kneel at your feet."

"Done!" Darien said gaily. "Until that day, then; wish me luck. Oh, and the rest of you—enjoy the fair!"

He dashed from the edge of the roof and out of sight, just as the guards advanced on the door of the house and kicked it open.

Very often in her life—and especially in the depths of that winter a year ago when she had wandered the dark forests alone, expecting to meet her death—Lin had found it difficult to believe, to truly believe in the existence of any divinity. Growing up with a mother who was mad . . . *For really, isn't that what it was? The truth of it?* . . . a father bound entirely in his wife's shadow, a brother who ruled Lin with his fists and boots . . . if she believed in any power, it was in her mother's contorted idea of Estarre, the huntress, pitiless and cruel and concerned only with rewarding the strong.

Only when Lin found love, for so brief a time, did she begin to feel that perhaps the divine was present in her life. It was then that she opened herself to belief in Kiara, who was protectress of poets, among other things, and saw in the trembling beauty of the forests surrounding Vassilian a hint of transcendence, a curtain thinly concealing eternity. The frosty air, the mountains, the falcon wheeling with a lonely cry that resounded for what seemed an endless time—all of it took on a larger significance, and at last the rote lessons of the Temple she had been taught all her life seemed to cohere. As if it had been an incomprehensible code and at last she had the key.

When she lost that key, she lost it all. The pale beauty of Kiara then seemed as cruel, as unreachable as the fire of Estarre. But still she nurtured a hope that was not quite faith, nor was it disaffection. She lit a candle in the Temple the day of the ball because she had hoped, for her and Leander's sakes, that there was power in such things. Unlikely as it seemed.

The image of Darien vanishing from the roof and out of sight, the guards in pursuit, prompted Lin to do what she usually did not do: she prayed. *Kiara keep him safe,* she murmured. *Kiara, Thalion, Estarre . . . please keep him from harm.*

She could recognize the courage of what he had done, and what it meant for all poets. Even for her.

Afterward it was difficult to concentrate on the contest. The performance of Marlen Humbreleigh was flawless, of course: he had sung a comedic refrain that still disturbed, a technique that he and Darien Aldemoor had made popular. No one laughed. When his victory was announced, only a smattering of people applauded, and not for long.

Second place was awarded to a small, sour-looking man named Piet Abarda, whom Lin vaguely remembered seeing at the *Ring and Flagon.* The prize was a jeweled copper buckle that he threaded onto his belt. When Piet gripped both hips and strategically posed so the buckle caught the sunlight, his head flung back, the audience applauded with unusual energy, as if unleashing all that they had kept pent up from Marlen. Piet grinned then, with visible pride, and Nickon Gerrard had to prod him to leave the stage.

But the real reason Lin had come, the only thing that had drawn her to secure a place for endless hours in the sun, was the dispirited-looking man that no one noticed now.

Leander Keyen's material had been strong—none knew that better than she did—but he had fumbled one of the chords, and that had thrown the rest of his performance off-kilter. He had not managed to recover from the mistake. It was what she had always feared—that his anxiety would get the best of him.

She could feel nothing but sadness. He had abandoned Lin, but first he had saved her. She did not forget.

THE place for a Poet is on the Mountain, the wind in his face. Unexpectedly, his thoughts had turned to this, one of his Masters' favorite platitudes, as he emerged from a luxurious carriage into the haze of honeysuckle scent and moonlight. Yet it occurred to Marlen that his place had lately been in rooms and that it was in rooms where the path of his life took shape time and again. Shaped by Marilla, by Master Gelvan, and now—just now—by Nickon Gerrard, the Court Poet himself, as he ushered Marlen with breathtaking solicitude into his palace suite.

No mountain, this, with its velvet-covered couches and graceful hardwood table, the deep carpet with its strands of many colors. Yet to Marlen—who was jaded to velvet and carpets—more precious than these were the books: shelves upon shelves of leather-bound treasure. Legends, myths, and discourses upon the meaning and theory behind them. For legends were considered by some to be symbolic tales whose meanings were veiled by descriptions of enchantments. Lord Gerrard apparently subscribed to this relatively modern thought and lined his shelves with the evidence thereof.

Marlen had been drinking, and the excitement of victory pulsed through him. This was the highest point of his life so far. Bought at a steep price, but it was too late for regrets. The parties and congratulations showered upon him by fellow poets and aristocratic benefactors were a concoction stronger than any drug.

Now it was nearly midnight, yet Court Poet Gerrard had chosen this time to invite Marlen to his private rooms. "Wine?" he asked Marlen, removing the stopper from a decanter. The glistening of rubies seemed to wink at Marlen from behind the thick glass, and he could not help but accept. *No wine more potent than this night*, he thought as he swirled his glass. Stirrings of a song.

He remembered one of his first lessons as a spindle-legged fifteen-year-old, when he and Darien had sat jabbing one another with their elbows, sharp with youth, whenever the Masters' backs were turned. When they had learned of the sanctity of composing songs by night; for enchantments, they were taught, must come in darkness. Each boy was assigned a tiny cell with a desk, each cell carved into the rock of the mountainside. A candle lit the angular gloom of each. The windows faced out upon ocean and cliff rock; the murmur of water and the call of seabirds the only sounds.

Marlen had hated those exercises at first, the enforced quiet and the loneliness. Yet as time went on, they became a part of him. And now, long after they were over, he saw how the nights of composition—thoughts running from mind to pen to parchment in the solitary glow of candlelight—had been the only moments in his life when he felt at peace. When he had been able somehow, through the alchemy of darkness and the flow of words, to submerge his need, the terrors that lurked in the recesses of his mind like sea creatures deep underwater. Invisible but nonetheless continually, terribly present.

Cutting into his reverie with the deftness of a knife, Nickon Gerrard said, "I had looked forward to meeting you ever since your impressive performance, Marlen. But that can be no surprise to you. My interest in new blood is surely no secret."

Marlen sat back in his chair. It was surprisingly comfortable for all its angles and carvings, but he did not let himself relax. It was true that he had won the Branch, but he could still go wrong. This man, who would name a successor in his lifetime, held the key to Marlen's future in his smooth hands. So Marlen said, more cautiously than was his wont, "I am honored, my Lord Gerrard. I hope that I shall be so fortunate as to continue to meet your expectations."

"Meet, and exceed them perhaps," the older man said, and laughed.

His heart beating faster, Marlen said, "I am delighted to be of service in any manner that I can."

Nickon Gerrard's smile in the dim room was a bright flash of perfect ivory teeth. And then he spoke, with the quiet intensity that Marlen remembered from all the other times he had heard the man speak. Even he was stilled by the power of Nickon Gerrard's voice. He listened in a bit of a daze, trying to assimilate what was being said yet feeling as if the words were slipping past, quicksilver and gleaming as fish in a stream. The goblet of wine lay forgotten in his hands.

Just as he was about to leave, he poured all the contents down his throat in one gulp. It was the only move he allowed himself that lacked composure. Otherwise, he was dimly aware of having conducted himself with his habitual poise and calm. Lord Gerrard's eyes could surely not pierce Marlen's breastbone to see the frantic heartbeat beneath, Seer or no Seer.

The place for a Poet is on the Mountain. The words whispered after Marlen on the night breeze as he drifted down the main streets. He had been offered a carriage home but had declined. Too many enclosures of velvet and silk and deceit hemming him in, and it was too late now to turn back. He didn't want to turn back, but neither did he want to continue down the only path Nickon Gerrard had left open for him.

The Mountain. One of the cleverer students—Piet, perhaps?—had suggested a different interpretation. To be on the Mountain in the path of the wind was to experience hardship. The Master had nodded slowly to this as if half-asleep, Marlen remembered, or as if he had been waiting for exactly this suggestion from one of the students. Eyes half-shut, he had pronounced, in a voice that Marlen could still remember: *Those of you whose hearts are wrung for blood, drop by drop, will return with tales to tell.*

Morbid old men on the edge of the final sleep, dreaming of chill winds and heart's blood in the cavernous embrace of the Academy halls. Marlen had respected their superior knowledge and applied himself with grim discipline to his assignments, but he had never aspired to be one of them. Or anything like.

Perhaps that was why he had chosen this gilded path, which held no hardship at all.

He realized that he was making his way toward Marilla's lodgings. After only a moment's hesitation, he made an abrupt turn back the way he had come and through a side street that would lead, ultimately, to his inn. He knew what Marilla would say when he told her what Lord Gerrard had asked of him . . . asked, or ordered. And Marlen knew that he would be committed to his purpose, to the upward climb he had set for himself. But tonight, at least, he would not tell her. The wheel of betrayal could rest on the brink of this night, for tomorrow and ever after, it would be tumbling on, and down.

LATE that night she found him in the seedy inn they had shared, deep in his cups. Lin had known Leander would not be at the *Ring and Flagon,* where undoubtedly the winners were being celebrated at that moment. But how she knew he would return to the seedy inn they had once shared—well, maybe that only made sense, and had nothing to do with any bond between them. In any case, there he was, deep in his cups, and she felt a twinge of guilt that she had not arrived sooner. It was by now very late.

When his eyes met hers, they clouded over even more than before. "Come to gloat, have you."

She came up behind him and began to knead his shoulders with her hands. He had always liked that. "Of course," she said. "Without me, you'd have never messed up those chords."

"Lin." It was somewhere between a sob and a sigh. She was silent. Slumping in his chair, he leaned against her arm like a child. Anywhere else, they would have attracted stares, but in this place and at this time of the night, the inn was nearly empty.

It seemed that a long time passed before he looked up. "Don't you hate me?"

"No," she said. She reached out and smoothed his hair as she had once been wont to do. "Always, even after you left, I've wanted you to win."

Leander closed his eyes. When he spoke again, his voice was barely above a whisper. "Who are you, really?"

For a long time, Lin did not answer, and both their breaths seemed to stretch in a quiet duet in the space of silence that she allowed to grow. Night had filled this room as the light faded from the dusty overhanging lamps. There were people scattered here and there, but they were quiet, and the dark isolated each in their own pool of flame-flickering shadow. Finally, Lin bent close to Leander's ear, knowing what she risked even as she allowed her lips to shape the words. "Kimbralin Amaristoth."

Leander pulled back almost violently and stared up into her face. He shook his head. "The one who disappeared. Of course."

She set a hand to his mouth. "You must tell no one, Leander. My brother might be in the city."

Mention of Rayen seemed to usher him into the room like a specter. She remembered the last time she had seen him and his parting gift to her. The bones of her wrist still ached sometimes. Yet she had been able to play the harp all the night of the masque with Valanir Ocune—Rayen had not succeeded in taking that away.

Leander had meanwhile taken her hand in his, and without losing his grip, rose to his feet. She found herself noting that he had not used her hand to help himself to stand; for some reason that mattered. It was the old Leander back again, the one who had taught her to take care of herself on the road, who had helped her put flesh back on her bones in winter. Whose melodies poured forth with the carefree pleasure that he took in everything, or had, before the shadow of competition intruded. He met her eyes and she could see the questions forming there. But he only said, "Thank you for telling me, Lin. For trusting me."

"Leander, you're going to be fine," she said. "No one remembers mistakes made at the contest. And after the Gelvan ball—"

"Hush," he said, and leaned in to kiss her full on the mouth.

It had been so long. That was her first thought, even as her body, rigid with surprise, began to tremble. Too many thoughts tumbling in her head like dice in a cup. This was Leander, who had never been attracted to her. And it had been so long. Memories she didn't want, breaking over her in waves like the waves of warmth from him.

Moments or an hour may have passed before she pulled away. She could have loved him once, she knew. If matters had fallen out differently.

His eyes were unfocused and he was smiling. "What is it?"

She reached out and touched the side of his face. "You never wanted me. You want comfort now, and I'm here. And that's not . . . what I want."

"Why are you so sure that that's all it is?" he said, looking hurt.

"I think it is. And I . . . can't. Though I will always be indebted to you."

"Lin, what are you saying?" She could see the beginning of sadness or anger in his eyes.

"I'm leaving the city," she said. "I've started to think the Path of Edrien Letrell might exist and I want to find it myself."

His face fell, and she could see disappointment—possibly even disgust—stamped on his face. "That's lunacy."

"Maybe," she said. "But that's what I'm doing." She rose up on tip-toe and kissed his cheek. It was cool as marble to her lips. "Try to think well of me," she said, before she remembered where she had last heard the words spoken.

Leander sat down heavily. "Farewell, Lin."

"Is that it?" she said. "Is that going to be all?"

He looked up with a flat gaze. Then he looked away from her, straight ahead, as if she had already gone. She felt a rush of anger. Perhaps Valanir had been right.

"Farewell, then," she said. The last thing to keep her in Tamryllin was done. It was time.

CHAPTER
13

THE night held voices that called to him, beckoning just beyond the rim of the light cast by his candle. By his elbow, pinpoints of flame gleamed from the delicately curled leaves of the Branch. Marlen had thought that to have it close might prove comforting. Yet instead its shine was curiously cold. It was an object, no more. He could melt it down if he chose.

He sat at the great desk within his study, in his new apartments near the palace. Marlen had not slept alone since he was a child and had never had so many rooms to call his own. It was a great honor, he knew. The rooms, with high ceilings and long windows that let in great strips of moonlight, seemed cavernous in their silence.

Writing by candlelight recalled his school days, a time whose purity Marlen now vainly sought to recapture. The song that had seemed to scintillate within his mind with such clarity on the night of his victory now seemed a frail, evasive thing, a pale moth flapping beyond his reach. He thrust his parchment aside and took up one of the books he had purchased that day at the fair. Its wooden covers and yellowed pages showed age. He flipped through it with as much care as he could muster.

What does he know? he thought feverishly, combing the hair back from his eyes with his fingers. *How could he think to undertake such a thing, unless he knows something that I do not?*

The book read like nonsense to him: divination and portals and rites. He was familiar with the ideas but had not seriously read up on such dusty concepts in some time. In here might lie the key to what Darien was thinking, where he planned to go. It was still inconceivable to him that Darien Aldemoor would go gallivanting off after a legend. Not the man that he knew. Yet thus had he promised before all the city of Tamryllin. And had vanished thereafter, despite Marlen's best efforts to find him for Nickon Gerrard.

For that was the price that was expected of him, the only path to the summit of which he had dreamed for so long.

"You will command a modest detachment of the castle guard," Lord Gerrard had told a bewildered Marlen the night before. "The king wishes that the future Court Poet prove his loyalty thus. It is known that Darien was your friend. A friend now turned renegade."

"I already betrayed him," Marlen said with a forced smile. "Surely that proves that we are no longer friends."

"You betrayed him, if you will forgive me, in a rather petty way," said Nickon Gerrard. "You ruined his career for your own advantage. You must now prove you are willing to take measures to punish him for his offense against the Crown." He leaned forward then, and his eyes bore into Marlen's. "There is more, of course. With the position of Court Poet comes a great deal of power. I wish to see if you are capable of exercising power."

Marlen's mind had been thrown into chaos by this. Now in the more coherent state of a day later, he felt a measure of fury. *What of my art?* he thought. *What has* this *to do with it?* He resisted a suddenly powerful urge to tear the book in his hands to shreds.

The Court Poet had had more to say before he allowed Marlen to take his leave. "It is quite dangerous for the sentiments expressed by Valanir Ocune, and now by Darien Aldemoor, to become widespread. It could mean a reopening of certain doors that must remain closed, for the safety of the realm."

Reopening of doors. What did Nickon Gerrard mean? All the

legends, all the lore of enchantments that Marlen had dutifully swallowed in his history lessons at the Academy . . . that was all myth, and no more. So what did the Court Poet intend to convey, if he did not mean that there was some truth to them after all?

It was not his prerogative to question, of course. He had only to find Darien, and his future position as Court Poet would be guaranteed. Already a message was making its way to the estates of Humbreleigh, notifying his family of his victory. It was no small thing for a youngest son to win the Silver Branch, certainly no small thing to be given command of a detachment of the king's guard. Even Lord Humbreleigh must acknowledge the truth of that.

And to hell with him if he doesn't, Marlen thought. That old gargoyle had determined Marlen's course for too long. The search for Darien would be the last unscrupulous act he would permit himself. Afterward, he would start over. Perhaps even manage to manipulate events in such a way as to save Darien's life, if nothing else. He had not seen Marilla since the day of the contest, and he did not intend to. She and his father clustered together in Marlen's mind, a concentrated patch of blackness that signified the shadow in his own heart. He could still avoid that shadow, once he had finished doing what he must do. There was still time.

CHAPTER
14

NEARLY one month into their journey, the flames of summer were at a low ebb. There was bite in the air; a new urgency drove the winds in the hillside grasses where Darien Aldemoor and Hassen Styr made camp at night. Cutting through fields to stay off the main road, their rings and harps concealed, they had made their way past Tamryllin and into the outlying farmlands. Various homesteads took them on for days at a time to work the fields in exchange for a hot meal and shelter in the barn at night. It was a long journey traveling in this roundabout manner, the only way to thwart pursuers.

Ruddy and golden apples were coming into season. Darien recalled harvest celebrations in Aldemoor. Every year they made a feast, cooked with the harvest offerings. He would be sorry to miss it this year. He wondered if they would be thinking of him—if news had traveled to them yet from the capital.

It was likely that the king's guards had already paid them a visit, though surely Nickon Gerrard must have known that Darien was not such a fool as to flee to the arms of his mother.

If Hassen thought of his own family as the days went by, he gave no sign.

Their mission was to reach the mountains in one piece. What would happen when they got there was not something Darien liked to dwell on, knowing that he did not—as yet—have anything that could be said to resemble a plan. Edrien Letrell had intimated that the Path lay somewhere in the mountains to the northeast, but scores of his contemporaries had sought it there and failed.

But Darien had dreamed of a Kahishian with tidings of Valanir Ocune, if it had been a dream.

For every man a different road, the song went. *For every poet, a road eternal.* A past Seer, nameless now, had made this observation many turns of the sun before Darien was born; yet Darien had always instinctively felt the truth of it. In practical terms, it was the fate of every poet to wander, whether on the king's highway, rutted wagon paths, or forest trails bestrewn with leaves and stones. It was true that once a poet attained the rank of Seer, he might be installed in the home of a noble family to instruct its scions in branches of knowledge common and esoteric, as well as provide entertainment. But so few poets achieved that rank that most could only hope to wander or, failing that, relinquish their art and become scriveners or clerks, marry and have children. That was, in the end, the life most of them chose. Contentment and a memory of dreams beside the winter fire.

Never for Darien that road. He and Marlen were different from the other Academy students, and they had been drawn to one another as if by a whispering of blood to blood. Marlen had chosen to befriend Darien when lads from more prestigious houses had sought out the young lordling of Humbreleigh. Darien always knew better than to feel gratified: they were of a kind, and Darien proudly cherished the name of Aldemoor, minor as it was. With his fame, he would instill it in the common tongue beside the names of Ocune and Letrell.

The road he and Hassen traversed resembled the one he and Marlen had known in a different time. The road was the road, regardless of its form. They had cut through forest and onto dirt paths where only the occasional farmhouse could be seen, and they had stopped for supplies and hot baths in hamlets so small they had no name. They dared not sing for coin, for that would mark them; their harps they had swathed in muslin and stored away in packs they carried, their Academy rings on leather thongs around their necks.

When they labored shirtless in the fields, their rings were carefully secreted in the packs. The sun beat on their necks, and Darien was not built for manual labor as Hassen was, but the food at the end of the day was always hearty, and in his mind Darien was composing a song about the rigors of such work. The blue eyes of a farmer's daughter shyly blinking up and then away from him was a verse; the ripple of wind in the wheat fields another. When he swung the farmer's young boy in circles and sang a silly song—a boy like he had once been, lithe and laughing—Darien sensed that there was a pattern to everything, even this; an unrelenting cycle larger than himself, larger even than the endeavor that had led him to abandon his former life. Whether or not they succeeded, a farmhouse would most likely remain here, and the boy would grow into a man and out of the memory of two strangers who had once worked his father's field for a handful of days. All these moments danced briefly around them on the summer winds and then away.

Hassen Styr made a quiet companion. Darien found it difficult to get used to this at first, being accustomed to the exchanges he had shared for so many years with Marlen Humbreleigh; the dagger wit they had tossed back and forth, spinning and dancing for the sheer pleasure of it, never flinching from its sharp edge.

He asked me to kill him. That haunted Darien. *All the years that I knew him, and then this.*

On one of the nights that they were forced to bed down in the forest, they had stayed up talking for some time.

"I can't say that I saw it coming," said Hassen. "But he was never quite with us, Darien. You never saw it." He clenched a large fist. "I'd have killed him for you. Pity I wasn't there."

Darien found himself regretting that he had told Hassen about that. Marlen's eyes so full of self-loathing . . . and so weak. His friend, who had always been strong, proud, and a match for him. "You wouldn't want that on your conscience," he said. He had never told Hassen of his dream and didn't think it would be well received if he did: the man was ruthlessly rational.

But he was more than a rational man; Hassen was also a formidable talent who would most likely have won second place at the contest had he not chosen to follow Darien. Like a bolt of poison, Darien recalled Marlen's contempt for Hassen's fiery temper and apparent lack of subtlety, and then it angered him that the thought had even crossed his mind.

Perhaps it was guilt that spurred Darien to ask Hassen now, after weeks on the road and in the dark of night, "Are you sorry you decided to come with me?"

A short silence. Then Hassen said, his voice even and calm, "I was sorry the moment I dropped my grey cloak and ran from the stage. I was sorry when I found you and knew what I meant to do. This isn't how I planned things, but at the same time . . . it's the right thing, I think. It doesn't matter if I'm sorry or not."

Darien glanced away as if to hide his thoughts, even though it was dark. He was tempted to tell Hassen about the *khave* house, the corpse of Master Beylint, the vision of Sarmanca. He knew he would sound like a madman if he did.

Hassen followed him, and that was a responsibility. Heeding the call of a more-than-dream, Darien followed Valanir Ocune, who in turn seemed to be following Edrien Letrell.

Yet Edrien Letrell had followed no one.

The stars were clear tonight, a sea of gems in which Darien could easily lose himself before sleep. But a chill that was too much at the core of him to be from the autumnal winds was teasing his bones. It was too late, he thought, to have it wrong. He let sleep take him away, and would awaken in the morning renewed, washed clean of doubts.

THE house was too quiet. That was the sense Rianna had every day since Lin had gone. Darien was gone, and Ned, and now Lin; and making everything worse was that Rianna's father was distant, lost in a world of his own. Strange people came to the house in a hurry under cover of darkness and departed just as swiftly; and Rianna was strongly discouraged from meeting the visitors, even from catching a glimpse of them.

Only once during the interminable last month of summer did her father speak to her about anything of substance, when he said, "I am thinking of our leaving early for the south this year. Would you like that?"

"I don't know," she said listlessly. "*Avan*, what is happening? I don't understand."

"Nothing is happening, love," he said, and forced a smile. If she had needed any indication that something was wrong, it was this; yet when she tried to draw him out, he smiled with greater cheer and told her to practice her embroidery. Furious, Rianna stalked out and sought the one outlet she had. It was her dagger, and the rocks that she lifted every day in the garden, watching with surprise and interest as the muscles in her arms became taut and grew.

Her blade darted in weary repetitions, an echo of her thought patterns. She felt fury with her father, with Darien, with Lin, even with Ned. The stabbing thrust Lin had taught her matched Rianna's mood; she practiced it, over and over again. Her wrist ached at the end of the day, and she bathed it in warm water and vinegar. She read books of poetry, though they had lately begun to stoke her fury. It was all very well for these poets, who wandered off to have adventures and then could string them to words, to music. Anything she might write would be formless, a creature of rage and stormcloud. No music there.

Do I have your leave to keep on clinging to a dream of you?

A note the tall, kindly poet named Hassen had delivered to Rianna in the hours following the contest. The last words Darien had written her before he vanished from her life, perhaps forever. *Dreams are no use to me*, she wanted to tell him. When she lay in bed at night, sleepless, she would speak to him in her mind. *I am tired of dreaming.*

THE act of buying a drink was not as simple as it had once been. If anyone had thought to ask Marlen Humbreleigh how his life had changed since his victory, it was this development that he would likely have cited, with accustomed dryness. When he entered the *Ring and*

Flagon, all conversation died. He felt himself watched by a roomful of suspicious eyes.

They would no doubt have been talking of the recent arrest of a young poet who had written a song praising Darien Aldemoor as an example for all poets. Naturally, the song had not received official approvals, yet for weeks it was a furtive staple at parties where poets were in attendance.

Within a week of his arrest, the offending poet had publicly recanted in the Court Plaza, looking small and shamefaced in the company of a detachment of king's guards. Everyone knew why he had recanted: it was that, or be given the choice between flaying or the galloping horses that had greeted such offenders in the past. The only reason he'd even had such a choice, Marlen thought, was that Nickon Gerrard was wary of allowing the young poet to become a symbol for an uprising. He was subsequently released, his fingernails pared to the quick so that he could no longer strum the harp at his side. No one was surprised when he vanished soon after.

The song of a certain Piet Abarda became famous following this incident: a clever satire that mocked the rash contrivances of young upstarts and then subtly questioned, at the end, whether true conviction was what was needed here. No one had ever thought of Piet as an idealist, and this reinvention of his character increased his popularity. And inevitably, in the depths of night at tavern tables across the city, over drinks and through tabak fumes, the contrast was drawn between this idealism and the crass ambition of Marlen Humbreleigh, who had sold both his friend and his soul in pursuit of power.

This particular detail may have chafed at Marlen more than anything—that the little weasel had managed to convince the masses that he was somehow noble. Marlen knew better, of course, but no one would ask his opinion.

In fact no one would ask Marlen anything, or talk to him at all. The only people he conversed with, it seemed, were the useless guards he had been assigned to command and Nickon Gerrard, who lately had begun to express his disappointment with Marlen for failing at so simple a task as finding two men on the run.

The idiot guards had already made a false arrest, dragging a terrified blond man into Marlen's presence after two days of mistreatment on the road. The event had caused Marlen to be satirized by poets throughout the city as a cruel authoritarian who was overfond of arresting innocent men—or pig farmers, as this particular man turned out to be. An unfortunate detail.

Maintaining his usual air, Marlen strode to the counter to order a whisky. He noticed that Piet Abarda and his new hangers-on congregated in the corner, watching him with sneers on their faces. There was strength in numbers, Marlen thought; any of these paltry men on his own would never have dared to look at Marlen with such an expression, or even to look him in the eye. They were all cowards, he thought, and felt his accustomed weariness harden into anger. Though in truth, the anger was always there; he felt it bubbling beneath the surface of everything he said and did.

In his last meeting with Nickon Gerrard, in particular, it had been difficult to control. The old man had accused him of not working hard enough to find Darien Aldemoor and had even begun to complain about Valanir Ocune as well. As if Marlen was responsible for every poet who had ever committed a crime in this damnable city.

The threat had been blunt: if Marlen failed to provide Lord Gerrard with new tidings within the week, he would be turned out of the new apartments and replaced with someone more capable.

Marlen's mood was no better after overhearing—no one had told him, of course—that the latest popular song was a fable about a minstrel fox heroically outwitting an evil, greedy snake. It did not take much imagination to guess who the fox and the snake were. Worst of all, the song had passed the official approval process because the censors had not detected the symbolism, and now it was too late to ban it from the books; it had spread too far.

Marlen thought that was probably only the officially stated reason: Nickon Gerrard, that knife-boned sadist, probably enjoyed the joke at Marlen's expense.

It did occur to Marlen that alone as he was in the echoing rooms of his luxurious apartments, ostracized by those who had once been friends, he might be losing his capacity to judge between a sane thought and a delusion.

By day, he inspected maps and gave orders to the guards. By night, he scoured the books and papers at his disposal, searching for clues to the location of the Path. He had already posted guards in the main mountain pass, though he doubted Darien would go there. The Path was somewhere in the mountains, but to say that was somewhat akin to saying that the needle was in the haystack. So how could Darien have dared tear off in that direction, unless he knew more?

Unless it is a red herring, Marlen thought feverishly, downing his whisky in an instant. *Unless this is all just to make a fool of me.*

One thing was certain, whether Darien was pursuing the Path or not: the other poets believed he was. Some had even begun forming bands claiming that they, too, would seek the Path as Darien had. Marlen wanted to dismiss them all as madmen, but he knew Lord Gerrard was watching—and was displeased.

He had one week.

He became aware of another man beside him, a familiar voice ordering from the bartender. Marlen looked up and saw Leander Keyen. The other man's eyes met his, then quickly darted away, but it was too late.

"You are going to decide you don't want a drink after all," Marlen said conversationally. "You are going to leave now, and I will follow to make sure you do as I say."

Leander's face was grey. He turned to face the door, like a condemned man facing the gallows. "What do you want?"

"I think you know," said Marlen, feeling very much like a snake in that instant, hearing the silken quality of his own voice. "You are going to tell me everything."

THE next evening, Darien and Hassen made camp on a hilltop overlooking the midland town of Eirne. They were only a short distance now from the forest that ran for miles north; an ocean of great trees that broke against the gleaming walls of the mountains and fell back.

The two of them shared bread as the sun set, watching it transform the valley and town below into splendor. They were silent now, though on occasion they had sung together in the late summer nights. Darien enjoyed singing with Hassen—his own voice was a silvery tenor while Hassen's was deep as an underground river; the two of them harmonized well. Almost as well as Darien and Marlen once had.

They sat and chewed in silence, stretching their legs in the sere grass of the burnt hillside and gazing out into the spreading dark. Tiny points of light were starting to appear from the town below. Darien longed to descend and explore the life there, the color and smells of people. And of course he itched to perform to an adoring crowd, an experience that had been denied them these past weeks. It was torment of a unique sort, forbidding Darien to sing for an audience. Hassen didn't seem to mind, but to Darien the reaction of people who heard him—their rapt attention, their laughter and even tears—mattered as much as the act itself.

"Maybe no one would recognize us," he said wistfully.

Hassen shot him a baleful look. "Don't start. Eirne is a miserable backwater anyway. They'd have no appreciation of your work."

Darien smiled. "Your estimation of my work is flattering, but I can think of several shamefully crude pieces that they would appreciate very much."

An hour later, it was fully dark and they were ready to sleep. Hassen seemed pensive. Darien felt a little guilty that the man shared his peril, though it had been his own choice and not at Darien's urging. At least, not really.

Then Darien squinted and said, "What's going on down there?"

At the base of the hill where it pooled into a valley and just before the town walls, he could make out the figures of men carrying torches. And something large and black and vertical looming over them like a great tree.

Hassen joined Darien by the edge of the hill. "Looks like they are building a bonfire."

They looked at each other, at a loss. Just then, the first flames burst upward from the valley. As they watched, bright orange tongues licked the night and caught on what appeared to be a mountainous pile of dry branches. Soon the individual flames had coalesced in a tower of fire. So massive was it that even from their height on the hilltop, Darien and Hassen could hear the simmering hiss of the flames. Darien thought it was as if someone sought to rip the dark of the night apart.

"What *are* they doing?" Hassen said, worried now.

"Wait," Darien said. "Listen." A strange calm had settled over him. And with that, paradoxically, the beginnings of an excitement that he could neither define nor explain. From a distance, he thought he could hear his grandmother telling him a tale. Her voice a whisper now borne upward by the voices that were drifting up toward them from the valley. The rise and fall of a chant, plain and sad and wild. A tune Darien knew well and at the same time had never heard before in his life.

"What is that?" Hassen said in a hushed voice.

Darien listened a moment longer. The tune spun circles now, collected harmonies, and lilted up and down without finding resolution. It had no resolution. Tongues of fire clawed at the sky, shooting sprays of sparks that fell to earth and died.

"If I am not mistaken," Darien whispered, "it is one of the old rites of our land brought back."

"Rites?"

Darien wanted to tell Hassen to lower his voice but knew that the impulse stemmed from an irrational awe that had no basis in anything that he himself believed. At least, so he thought. The aching purity of the voices tugged at his heart, but then what else could be expected of him, with the way he felt about music?

"I had thought it a discontinued practice," said Darien. "Maybe here in the hill country . . . I don't know." He was silent, absorbing the music and the reaching glory of the fire. He looked up at the sky as if expecting a change there, but the stars and quarter moon drifted undisturbed as ever. He said, "At one time it was believed that the fires of midsummer must be . . . invoked to lay to rest the flames and herald the harvest time. The singing . . . that is part of the old enchantments. Or so it is said."

"You don't believe in any of that, do you?" Hassen said sharply. "What would be the purpose of such enchantments? To allow the summer to pass? It does so every year without our guidance."

"I know," said Darien. "Of course you're right. I can't explain it. I didn't think anyone still believed . . ."

"I'm a fine one to talk, though," said Hassen. "Setting out to find an enchanted portal but scoffing at enchantments. Ah." He shook his head. "Darien, sometimes I think I ought to have been a lawyer like my father."

Darien laughed and rose to his feet. "Perhaps. It would have been less complicated, but think of the fun you'd have missed." He could not take his eyes off the fire in the valley. "I must see who's down there. If anything, just to hear the music better."

"Darien," Hassen said, and Darien felt he could hear if not see his eyebrows drawing together in disapproval.

Darien lifted a hand. "No one will know who I am. You yourself said this place is a backwater. They've probably never even heard of me, if that's possible." He grinned.

"Well, I'm coming with you then," said Hassen. "In case it turns out that sacrificing the first person to approach them to the flames is another tidbit of these old rites."

"Actually, I think that sounds familiar," Darien said, and laughed when he saw Hassen shake his head in the moonlight.

The singing grew louder as they made their way down the hillside, and Darien began to see the figures of men outlined in the glow of the bonfire. There were fifteen, twenty men in all; it was hard to gauge in the uncertain light. Despite their number, each man stood with a distance of several paces around him, his long shadow unbroken by the shadow of another, as if each man sang alone. But their intertwining harmonies gave the lie to that impression: this had clearly been rehearsed. And as he and Hassen drew near, the truth dawned on Darien, and how obvious it had been all along. These men were trained in music. Academy-trained, in fact.

And now that he knew this, it grew stranger still. For what did Academy-trained poets have to do with rites in a grassy valley by night? Darien had been expecting villagers. Not his own kind.

None turned at their approach. Their song rippled unbroken into the night, blending with the hiss and murmur of the flames. Now that they were close, Darien could feel the heat on his face, and the fire seemed impossibly high.

He had an idea. Darien waited for his moment and when it came, began to sing. His voice blended seamlessly with the other voices, a new harmony that added a layer to the whole, yet could have been there all along. Hassen nudged him with a nervous grunt, but Darien shook his head and continued to sing. Now the other singers were turning to look at him curiously, surely guessing that he was one of their own. None intervened. They let him sing, and Darien felt strangely peaceful here among his own, singing a tune he didn't know for a purpose that eluded him. Perhaps there was no purpose, and these men simply wished to honor midsummer in the old way.

At last it was done, and the song allowed to fade into silence. One of the men stepped forward to feed more wood to the flames. A shower of sparks forced the men who stood nearer the flames to step back. Darien had had a chance to look around as he was singing, and he noticed that most of these men appeared to be well into their middle years, which explained why he recognized none of them. Men his own age or a bit younger, he would have been more likely to know.

One of the poets approached Darien and Hassen, a tall man with a shock of unruly dark hair and stubbled cheeks. His clothing was the worse for wear, but the harp at his side and the gold ring on his right hand confirmed Darien's guess. When he spoke, his voice was almost as deep as Hassen's own. "Who are you?"

"Poets like yourself," Darien answered. "We couldn't resist joining you when we heard the music."

The other man's face remained impassive. "Where then are your rings?"

Hassen tugged at Darien's arm. "It matters not if you believe us," he said. "We have nothing to prove. We were only passing by and shall be on our way."

"Hold on," said Darien, shaking off his friend's arm. He parted the neckline of his tunic and lifted the ring that hung there for the man to see. "The ring," he said. "It is an uncertain road we take, and so prefer to wear them thus. A precaution."

"The road of every poet is uncertain," said the other man dismissively, and from the poets surrounding him there was a general murmur of agreement.

"Be that as it may," Darien persisted, "why do you do this now? I had thought it was a ceremony long dead."

"Not dead," said the dark-haired man. "Only forgotten. Like so many things that should not have been forgotten. Haven't you heard?"

Darien was taken aback by the abruptness of that. "Heard?"

"We are doing what needs to be done to recover the enchantments that were lost and reach the Path," said the man.

Darien tried not to gape, letting Hassen ask, "The Path?"

"The Path to the Otherworld, once found by Edrien Letrell," said the man patiently. Firelight glinted in his eyes, and Darien could see there were streaks of silver in his hair. "Can it be that you have not heard? We are Seekers. We follow Darien Aldemoor."

IT had been so simple. The poet was not of the disposition to withstand pain for any length of time, and the information Marlen Humbreleigh wanted had slid out of him like oil. Still, Marlen had not been able to resist battering the man as he lay on the tiled floor of Marlen's front room. The cries made it worse; they were like an intoxicant. For days, Marlen had felt a rage building in him that he'd had to suppress as he groveled and glided from one artificial blandishment to another. And all that rage had now found its focus. *Darien,* he thought as his fist made contact yet again. Leander screamed. *Always the lucky one. Even now.*

By this time the words Marlen had wanted had long since left Leander's lips. He shouted them again from where he lay, broken and bleeding, as if perhaps Marlen hadn't heard them the first time. *"Kimbralin Amaristoth!"*

A rush of disgust had overtaken Marlen, and that, too, he turned outward as he took rough hold of the man and threw him out on the street. It was done.

The implications of these new facts had only begun to filter into his mind, so clouded was it in a red haze of fury and gratification. *Amaristoth.* Her brother was here in the city. He had glimpsed Rayen at the fair. He would no doubt be happy to hear that his sister was alive and, though ugly as ever, quite well. And only a few weeks' journey ahead of him by foot.

Marlen rubbed his fist, which ached. There was blood on the heretofore pristine tiles of his floor. Moans outside . . . Leander, lying there, or a passing animal? He didn't want to know.

When at last he stepped outside the house, the poet was gone. It was very late, and the moon rode high. A quiet night, not another soul stirring abroad that he could see. There was only him, and the shadow that dogged his steps, and the moon overhead.

He knew the way as if it were to the place where he was born, or as if sinews in his body had been stretched along this path and he only followed them back now, to reclaim what was his. He heard the call of a nightbird from a tree, and a second cry out in answer. There was a world beyond his just out of reach, a night world of gleam-eyed cats and the rustle of dark wings, of shadows that stirred under the moon. He was among them now.

When he knocked at the door, she opened it immediately, her eyes coolly surveying him as if he had been expected all along. Her hair hung in a thick black rope down her back, leaving bare the lines of her fragile face. "So it's you," she said.

Marlen grabbed her upper arms. He tightened his fingers until he could almost feel bone. "I need you," he said. "I'll never leave you again."

Marilla smiled up at him. "Come in," she said, and touched his cheek. When she drew back her hand, Marlen was shocked and sickened to see that red stained her finger where she had touched him. She examined it, smiling widely. "You *have* been busy tonight," she said, and sucked the finger, lingering at it with her eyes on his. Marlen felt his mouth go dry. It had been a long time.

She shrugged off his grip as if it were nothing and pulled him inside. "So very busy," she said, smiling again. "But I hope you've saved some for me."

THAT night Darien could not seem to fall asleep. Long after Hassen's audible breaths indicated that he was in the realm of dreams, Darien was still staring up into a sky aswirl with constellations. The Rider, the Longship, the Great Tree: quiet glitter amid the scattered clouds. Darien clasped his hands beneath his head to cushion it. After a bone-wearying day of tramping the hills in the burning sun, there was no reason he should be wakeful now. Except.

The fire, the group chanting, and its aftermath had opened a well of dread within him. Or perhaps *dread* was the wrong word. Unease. *We follow Darien Aldemoor,* Algur had said. The poet who had told them who the Seekers were and what they sought to do. A whole movement inexorably rippling throughout Darien's own community, and he unaware of it until tonight. And it was *him* they claimed to be following!

"How do you follow Darien?" Darien had asked Algur cautiously, as the other poets stood in silence all around them. They seemed to answer to Algur, as if he were their leader. It made sense: he was an imposing man, and handsome, with a voice that sounded as if it could drive deep to the core of the earth. "Do you know where he is?"

Algur shook his head. "Darien Aldemoor was ever known as wily and clever, as Edrien Letrell was in his day. That he is journeying to the mountains is certain, but that is all."

"How then do you follow him?" Hassen said. Darien didn't need to look at him to see that he was as disturbed by this turn of events as himself was.

Algur drew back a little, as if this was a private matter for him, and in the firelight his face was angled black. "We seek what it is he seeks, and in reviving the ancient enchantments we hope to find it. All across Eivar, fires like this one burn tonight. The Seekers are abroad."

By now it was obvious that Darien could not reveal his identity to this man. He wasn't sure what Algur would do—idolize him, abduct him, or both. "It is a worthy quest," he said. "Alas, my companion and I are not made for such lofty ideals." He was careful to keep his voice devoid of irony. "We shall leave you to your quest, and wish you much luck."

Algur had nodded and turned away with brusque indifference. Darien and Hassen had silently departed, with Darien turning only once to look back at the flames. The surrounding men were staring into the fire they had built as if a tale or a prophecy were painted there, but Darien saw only a riot of color and light and felt the crushing heat on his skin.

And now, trying to sleep, he recalled that fire and the impassioned spirits around it, even now keeping vigil over the remaining flames at the base of this hill where he lay. The singing . . . he could still hear it, as if that fretwork of voices was a solid thing that hung now in the night air with nowhere to go. Voices, weaving in and out, just beyond the edge of the Otherworld they so desperately sought to reach.

The very edge.

He was in the Academy again, in a corridor very like the ones he had spent so much of his youth traversing as he made his way from one lesson to another. Only then, he had always been trailed by a posse of friends and admirers, their laughter and talk the rhythm by which he lived his days. Now emptiness ahead and behind, and silence. Many doors that all looked alike, doors that he passed knowing somehow that they were not for him. *But which is it, then?*

At last he came to a door that although the same as the others, hung partly ajar. *A sign,* he thought to himself, and pushed the door open the rest of the way. He almost collided with a masked Rianna Gelvan, who stood in a white gown, her hair a drift of gold around her face and down her back. It made him ache to see her, even in a dream. "My Snow Queen," he said, and touched her hair.

Her eyes behind the mask seemed full of sorrow. "My love," she said. "You have to come back."

"I can't," he said. "I'm sorry, my dear one. Not yet." He reached to clasp her waist and the sensation was surprisingly real: he could feel the texture of the fabric and, through it, the warmth of her skin. *Like no other dream,* he thought dazedly, and lifted the white sparkling mask from her face.

And now it was Marilla who smiled back at him, her blue eyes agleam. "A kiss?" she purred.

Darien cursed and pushed her roughly away. She laughed as she fell into the arms of Marlen, who stood in the shadows, where he had been all along. "You never learn," he said. With his free hand, Marlen held out the white mask to Darien. It looked frail and trivial in his hand. "We have ever created our own dreams," he said. "This dream is yours."

This dream is yours. Darien stared at the mask, uncomprehending. Conscious more than anything else of bitter disappointment and the hurt of seeing Marlen again. "I don't want it," he said coldly.

Marlen raised an eyebrow. "Are you sure?"

And Marilla added in a singsong tone, her head tilted back on Marlen's shoulder, "Queen of ice and snow and dream, do you renounce her now?" She laughed again.

Darien turned and slammed the door shut, cutting off the laugh. No one followed. Silence reigned once again in the corridor.

He walked faster now, wishing the dream at an end and himself awake. Sorrow in his heart like a squeezing sensation in his chest. Rianna's eyes becoming Marilla's eyes. His lost love still lost, and by his own doing. But even if he were not being pursued, he could not yet go back. Something drew him, something that he could sense more strongly here than in the waking hours of the day. He had about convinced himself that he had undertaken this journey only for the fame, if not for the satisfaction of thwarting Marlen and amusing himself along the way. But here . . . Here he heard the voices again of the men who had been singing by the fire that night. The unearthly quality of the melody as it spiraled in the air, which even now seemed to follow him in the corridor. This strange and familiar corridor of his dreams.

"*One song and many,*" a voice said. Darien turned and saw that a man stood in the corridor. He wore a harp at his side, a moon opal shining palely on the ring that adorned his hand. Valanir Ocune.

"First Edrien Letrell, now you," said Darien.

"So you've seen the visions."

"Dreams," said Darien.

"No," said Valanir. "You must have a vital part in all this, Darien Aldemoor, given what's been happening."

"In all what? What is going on?"

"Lin Amaristoth will tell you," said Valanir. "You must work together to avert the dark that is coming."

"A red star rising," Darien recalled.

"Yes."

Darien shook his head. "Are you saying what I saw . . . Sarmanca. That wasn't a dream?"

"You did well, Darien. Destroying the sacred wine has hindered Nickon Gerrard, if only for a little time. It's why he can use portals only within the city walls, for now. And it's why he can't pursue you himself . . . not yet. You stopped him from expanding his powers—he needed as many poets as possible gathered together to accomplish that."

"This is all beyond me," said Darien. "It seems far beyond any poet . . . especially one not a Seer."

"And what do you think a Seer truly is, Darien . . . or is meant to be?" Valanir Ocune extended his hand, indicating another door.

"Through there is where you must go. Be shielded from ill winds, young singer. This will not be the first portal to open for you, nor the last."

The Seer was gone the next moment. Darien paused only an instant to wonder at this. The lifting of many voices still tingled in his mind. He grasped the handle to the door that Valanir had indicated and unhesitatingly pushed it open.

DARIEN lay flat on his back, gazing up at the stars again. But now there were torches, and someone was bending over him, looking incredulously into his face. It took a moment for Darien to make sense of what he was seeing.

Then with an effort, he smiled. "Hallo, Lin."

CHAPTER
15

FIRST light was breaking over the bare hillside, grasses gently waving in a dawn breeze. So weary were they both by this time that they clasped hands, for balance, as they trudged up the hill. Hassen watched them come, his hands on his hips, shaking his head. When he deemed them within earshot he called out, "Do I want to know?"

Lin waved to him. "Hallo, Hassen Styr," she called back. Her heart lifted when she saw him smile. She had always liked him. And she'd had a long, lonely road up to this point, with smiles few and far between.

"No sooner do I go to sleep than this character goes off to get drunk in a village tavern and some floozy seduces him," said Hassen. He was still smiling.

Lin smiled back. "It was surprisingly easy."

Darien gave a martyred sigh. "Why must you assume the worst of me? The truth is, rather, that Valanir Ocune sent me into Eirne. As I was sleeping."

Before Hassen could send him tumbling down the hill with a well-placed punch, Darien went on to tell of his dream, of waking to see Lin bending over him. She said, "I could swear that he appeared out of nowhere—I almost tripped over him. The street was well-lit." Lin hesitated, not wanting to lose Hassen's goodwill by seeming insane. "I think . . . I think Valanir meant for us to find each other."

"And why would that be?" Hassen asked. "With no offense intended, lady—your company would be delightful. But that's hardly a concern of Valanir Ocune."

Unable to stand any longer—she had not slept all that night—Lin dropped into a cross-legged position in the grass. The two men dropped beside her. In the stillness before sunrise, there was no sound but the breeze.

"We seek the same thing," Lin said. "Valanir advised me to begin my search on Academy Isle. And he gave me this." She had noticed that engraved on the key was an ornate knot: the mark of the Seers.

"What does it open?" asked Hassen.

"I don't know," said Lin. "I think it might have been important to him that I discover that for myself. Or that we discover it, since he has brought us together."

"And why do you seek the enchantments?" Hassen asked. "Meaning no disrespect, of course."

"It is a fair question," Lin said. Quickly she recounted to the two men all that Valanir had told her about Nickon Gerrard.

"You mean to say Lord Gerrard is a murderer," said Darien. "I can't even pretend to be surprised."

"A dark spirit rides him," said Lin. "He can't be killed. His use of blood divination all these years has brought a darkness to Eivar. It's begun already, in the south."

"What's begun?" asked Hassen.

Lin avoided his eyes. They both seemed so buoyant, and she brought these tidings to ruin it. "The Red Death," she said. "And other disasters, besides. But that plague hasn't been seen since—"

"Since Davyd Dreamweaver. The Order of the Red Knife. Of course," said Darien. His face changed. "I know it seems crazy, Hassen . . . I'm not usually inclined to believe these things, either."

Hassen was shaking his head. "Lady, how do we know any of this is true? Forgive me, but it's all . . . it's all rather far-fetched. We don't even have proof that Nickon Gerrard is committing the terrible crime you suggest."

"Do you doubt Valanir Ocune?" Lin said. "Do you think for anything less he would have risked capture, and his life?"

"There's that," said Darien. "But here is one thing we know beyond doubt: last night I went to sleep on this hill, which is an hour's journey by foot from Eirne, and when I awoke I was lying in the village street just as Lin turned the corner."

The three of them were quiet a moment. The sun was climbing from beyond the hills, bathing the grasses in its light.

Finally Hassen said, "So you're telling me that what we do now is . . . for all of Eivar? Perhaps the world?"

Darien suddenly grinned. "Looks that way."

Hassen sighed. "What I wouldn't give for a drink."

"Likewise," Darien said. "Meanwhile, I'm hankering to see what we're going to unlock with that key of yours, Lin. That is, if Hassen approves of these new developments."

"You mean, do I approve of Lin traveling with us?" Hassen said. "You ought to be grateful: one more day alone with you and I might have throttled you in your sleep."

"So that's settled then," said Darien.

"There is one more thing that is not settled," said Lin. Her heart had begun to beat fast. "This is important," she said, unnecessarily, wishing not to continue.

"Go on," said Hassen. Lin wondered if she imagined the compassion she saw in his eyes.

Lin drew a breath and exhaled slowly, willing her heart to calm itself. "I owe it to you—if we are to travel together—to tell you that my full name is Kimbralin Amaristoth, and that my brother, an experienced hunter, is searching for me."

"*You* are Kimbralin Amaristoth?" Darien was incredulous. "Oh my."

Hassen looked blank. "I'm sorry—who's Amaristoth?"

"Only the most notorious family this side of the mountains," said Darien. "Marlen used to say that even his father was wary of Kalinda

Amaristoth and drew a breath of relief when he heard of her death. Wait, that would be your mother, right? I'm sorry," he said to Lin.

She smiled thinly. "Quite all right," she said. "I had a similar reaction."

"And your brother," said Hassen. "What happens if he finds you?"

"Nothing that has not happened before." She meant it lightly, but it did not come out that way. She was disconcerted to see comprehension in his eyes.

"Then I hope he does find us," Hassen said, "so I can avenge you."

"It would not be—simple, to do that," said Lin. "But I'm grateful for your words."

"Come, come," Darien said, smiling but impatient. "Sleep now, and then we go. West this time."

"To the Academy," said Hassen.

"Yes," said Darien. The wind had picked up and blew his hair, which had grown shaggy, about his face. Despite his fatigue and the new, strange things they now knew, he looked exhilarated. "We're going home."

SHE was collapsed against the garden wall, gasping for breath. "Still too weak," said the man behind her, and she gritted her teeth. As if she didn't know that her arms trembled like harp strings, that her chest heaved uncontrollably. Rianna Gelvan no longer felt the autumn chill that had laid bare the ornamental garden trees and withered the rose hedges.

Rayen Amaristoth laid a hand on her arm. "It's difficult to build up the strength," he said. "It means daily practice, nothing less."

"I know," Rianna replied. "And why not? I have nothing else to do." Then she regretted her words, not wanting to seem to him like a petulant child. If he had such thoughts, he gave no sign. His dark hair and eyes were so much like those of his sister. But while Lin could blend into shadows, Rayen Amaristoth was a striking presence.

During his earlier visits, she had kept away from him, mindful of her loyalties to Lin. When Lord Amaristoth had first begun calling on her father, for business purposes, she had been struck by the timing of it. It was not unusual for Master Gelvan to receive partners in his home. Even less unusual for it to happen at the time of the fair, when so many of the aristocracy and mercantile class descended on Tamryllin. But of course, this was different. She remembered Lin's words, her flat tone not quite a mask for emotion. *My brother is looking for me.*

At first, she succeeded in avoiding him. It was when he found her practicing with her dagger in the garden that the lessons had begun. She had been wearing an old pair of her father's trousers and a tunic, her lips pursed in concentration. Repeating the thrust and parry that Lin had shown her, the only moves she knew.

"A woman of hidden talents," said a voice.

Rianna had spun to see Rayen in the shadow of a rowan tree that had begun to turn crimson with the season. He was clad in dark blue that contrasted with his pale skin, his lips curved in a half smile.

She had not gotten a good look at him until now, and it threw her off balance. That, and her awareness that she was not groomed as she usually wanted to be when in the presence of anyone other than her father. Her hair had been carelessly pinned up and was escaping in wild tendrils around her face.

"Where did you learn to do that?" Rayen asked. "Though your technique is—you'll forgive me, lady—rather basic, there is something in your style that is of the north. It reminds me of home."

Rianna's mouth went dry. *It reminds me of home.* "I—had a fencing master for a short time," she said. "There wasn't time for me to learn much from him. He had to leave."

"Well, he didn't stay long enough to show you how to perfect your parry," he said. "May I?"

Caught off guard, Rianna nodded. Rayen came up behind her and held her wrist cupped in his hand. Gently he guided her arm around, down, in a motion reminiscent of the Sirian dancers she had seen the night of the masque.

"Now practice it with me," he instructed. He kept his hold on her arm, correcting her when she wandered off course. "And naturally," he added, "you must stay lower, much lower than that. You would do well to practice squats and lunges in addition to bladework."

"I see," Rianna said, a bit stiffly. She was relieved when he disengaged and moved aside.

"It interests me that you want to learn," said Rayen. "It's not what I would expect of a woman of your origins."

"You mean, a Galician woman?" Rianna asked with narrowed eyes.

"No," said Rayen, and laughed. "I suppose I mean any woman not of the north. I have never known any woman with the fierceness, the technique of my sister, for example. She is a northern woman to her bones."

"Your sister," said Rianna. Her pulse had quickened slightly. "You mean, the one who disappeared?"

Rayen looked startled. She explained, "We received the painting last year. She's beautiful." He continued to be silent. Rianna was afraid she had betrayed her knowledge of Lin's secret. "It must be so difficult for you," she offered. "I'm sorry."

Finally, he nodded. "It is difficult, yes," he said. "Sometimes more than I would have thought possible. Thank you—thank you for that." He paused, seemed to be thinking something over. Then he said, hesitantly, "You know, I intend to be in the city for a time. Perhaps, if you like, I can instruct you in the art of daggers? Since it seems to be an area of interest for you."

"I'm betrothed, you know."

"Are you?" Rayen said. "Your father had mentioned that your betrothal to Ned Alterra was—dissolved."

Rianna's brow furrowed. And then, unbidden, her eyes filled with tears.

"There now," said Rayen. His tone was gentle. "There is someone else, isn't there? Someone you can't talk about to your father?"

Rianna's eyes widened. She could hear the blood pulsing in her ears.

"It's all right," said Rayen. "I understand. Your man, whoever he is, must consider himself luckier than anyone in the world. And must himself be exceptional."

Rianna nodded emphatically, forced out a weak, "Yes."

Now Rayen gifted her with a full smile. "Rianna," he said, "in the north we know how to conceal our hearts behind walls of stone. Sometimes we know this too well. But that is just a long way of telling you that your secret is safe—I will tell no one. And," he went on, his face becoming earnest, "I would still be happy to teach you."

She had thought that if Rayen could guide her in her purpose, so much the better. She wasn't sure she understood why she felt such passion now to learn the dagger, but thought perhaps she had finally seen that to be weak was to be left in the shelter of garden walls while the strong went forth on adventures—leaving the weak behind. And her father, she thought. He had regarded her as a chess piece, to guard and protect—in his plans, she had no will of her own.

Rianna knew that was unfair, but she was quietly furious with him nonetheless. She submerged her rage in the cut and thrust of her lessons with Rayen, in the burning of every muscle with fatigue. At the dinner table she was often unkempt, for she sometimes did not bathe and change until just before bed. Though Master Gelvan seemed to eye her with concern at times, he otherwise did not comment. Or he would ask, "How go the lessons, my dear?"

Normally he would have disapproved, she thought, and wondered what had changed. Was it that he thought she might need this skill one day—or was he coldly weighing his options now that Ned Alterra was gone, hoping she might take to Rayen Amaristoth? She was not thinking clearly, she knew—on some days, she could impute devious motives to anyone, even her father.

Rayen, for his part, was impressed, albeit bemused, by her ferocity, and guided her in channeling it through practiced technique.

"I know," he said one day, straightening during a lesson to look at her. "You want to carve through that tree over there with your fingernails. You want to pummel it until your knuckles bleed. Don't you?"

Rianna's breath was coming hard. "How do you know?" she forced out between breaths.

Rayen looked sad. "I know too much about anger," he said. "Let's leave it at that."

"What good would getting bloody knuckles do me?" Rianna demanded. "What can I do?"

"There isn't really anything you can do," said Rayen. "But I promise you that if you are patient and learn the technique—there is no shortcut to that—you will find that your energy will be turned more and more to your skill and less to your rage. At least, that is how it is with me."

He dropped to a seated position on a garden bench, and motioned for Rianna to sit by him. She did, at a careful distance. Her hair had come loose from its ties and fell in a tangled mass around her face. She wondered what Darien would think if he could see her now, with the sweat and the knotted hair and her father's cast-off clothes. *Would I still be the Snow Queen of his heart?*

"All my life, rage has been my enemy," said Rayen. He was not looking at Rianna, gazing at and yet seemingly beyond the garden wall. "The only way I could escape it, prevent myself from harming others, was by retreating into the black forests surrounding our home. Of course, they were not really black, but in those moments I felt they were—cold, dark, deep, a place to get lost. I would lose myself there for days, hunting prey as if I had no other purpose. . . ." He trailed off.

"This garden is a poor substitute for the forests of your home," said Rianna. "I cannot get lost."

"And you are a woman," said Rayen. "Remember, that makes you even more vulnerable."

"I know," said Rianna, and thought that this, too, was both an immovable truth and perhaps the most enraging thing of all.

"But you have spirit," said Rayen, and now he was looking at her. In his eyes, Rianna saw something that both thrilled her and made her deeply uneasy, and she turned away from his gaze. "You have strength, Rianna Gelvan. I see it in your determination . . . even in your anger."

She kept her eyes averted, and after a moment he rose. "I will see you at dinner," he said, and went back to the house. Rianna remained seated on the bench, her arms wrapped around herself, until the chill of twilight made it impossible to stay in the garden anymore.

THEY had been on the road nearly a week when a town perched on a hill came into view. In the course of those days, the autumn winds had become fierce on the high hills, whipping their hair and penetrating clothing to skin. That day, icy sheets of rain drummed down on the hillsides, and the travelers were fortunate to find leaky shelter in an abandoned hut. Wrapping themselves tightly in cloaks, they fixed their sights on the town as if it were a beacon, and tantalizing images of warm rooms, beds, and hot food tormented their waking thoughts.

Or so Darien described his sensations, and it seemed from his irritated grunt of a response that Hassen grudgingly agreed with him. Lin was less susceptible to such thoughts—the cold was familiar to her, and she had not eaten cooked food more than a handful of times in all the past year. Her soft fur-lined cloak—Leander's long-ago gift to her—was like a comforting embrace all through the chill days and nights.

Secretly, Lin was happy. She knew that Darien and Hassen were worried about king's guards and the Path, so she kept her irrational feelings to herself. She knew they could be arrested at any time.

But right now, she was with two men whom she liked, and was on the road with a definite purpose. For weeks following her departure from Tamryllin, Lin had felt as if she fought to keep nightmares at bay. Days had been wearying, and the nights she had huddled and tried to sleep, listening to the wind. Now she had the friendly bickering of the two men to enliven her days, and at night sometimes Darien could be coaxed—or tricked—into a conversation.

He had a good heart, she thought, and knew he would have been horrified if he had known she thought so. Removed from Marlen, he seemed loose in his moorings, as if the foundations of his identity were now a question he turned ceaselessly in his mind. But it was with curiosity and wonder that he did so, it seemed to her. For all that he and Marlen had traveled far together, there was still more within Darien to unlock on his own. At nights, sometimes the three of them would sing or create new songs on the spot.

"Lady Amaristoth," said Darien with an exaggerated bow, breaking into her thoughts.

"What is it? And don't call me that."

"We seem to have entered your kingdom—so to speak. Can you tell us what town that is up ahead?"

Lin sighed. Hassen returned her gaze with a sympathetic roll of his eyes. "It's Dynmar," she said. "By all accounts a terrible backwater. They do have a reputation for some decent smithies and tailors. Is that what you wanted to know?"

"Well, that and the average eye color," Darien said blandly. "On the other hand, Dynmar does have the distinction of being the town nearest the mountains. Which makes it our last civilized stop in—a long while."

"That depends what you mean by 'civilized,'" grumbled Hassen.

"Didn't you know—sheep innards are a delicacy," Lin said innocently, and he laughed.

THE town was quiet, as might be expected at midday in a place on the edge of desolate mountains. The narrow streets were so empty that the wind seemed to chase itself around their sharp corners, whistling as it went.

"The edge of the world," Lin mused aloud as they turned a corner onto a street where they could see the grey slopes of the mountains rising just beyond the town walls. "It's been more than a year since I was this far north."

"This calls for a drink," said Hassen.

They found the town's only tavern on the main square. Here the mood was more lively despite the early hour: the seats were crowded and a space cleared for a group of musicians to perform. Lin immediately noted their rings. While two of the players strummed their harps in harmony, the rest sang together in unison. They were all young, and at the sight of them, Darien cursed softly and drew up the hood of his cloak. Hassen followed suit.

"These men would know us," he said, sinking in his seat and holding his mug of beer close to his face.

"Do you hear what they're singing?" Lin said suddenly. She did not know whether to be amused or horrified.

It was a ballad that followed the traditional structure, and it told of a trickster hero—a fox—who with his courage and cunning had outwitted the cruel snake. Various details, such as the ability of the fox to sing and play a harp, had drawn Lin's attention immediately. The fox had gone on to seek liberation for the other foxes by setting out on a quest, accompanied by a loyal companion.

"His *hound*?" Hassen hissed. "His *faithful* hound?"

"It doesn't even make sense," Darien said. "Why would the hound care about liberating the other foxes?"

"Darien, you do see what this is, don't you?" said Lin. It was clear that Hassen certainly did. "You're a legend."

"These boys," Darien whispered, "are complete idiots. I knew them when they were getting poor marks at the Academy."

"Well, I'll just have to take comfort in that, I suppose," Hassen muttered. He gulped down his beer a bit too quickly.

When the song was done, and the snake defeated for good and all, Lin approached the singers. Hassen had tried to hold her back, but she argued that they were highly unlikely to recognize her. And they would have news from the city.

"Greetings," she said to them. "Have you come from Tamryllin?"

"Yes, of course," said one, a blond poet with wide eyes. "We were at the contest. We saw it all."

"So what are you doing in this place?" Lin asked. "I'd have thought poets like yourselves would be out seeing the world."

"We're doing more than that," said another boy, dark-haired and arrogant. "Have you no idea what has been happening in this past month? We are Seekers."

"Right," said Lin. Darien had told her of this phenomenon, though she had been tempted to dismiss it as his bragging. But Hassen had confirmed that there was, indeed, a movement of poets styling themselves Seekers and claiming to follow Darien Aldemoor in his quest for the Path. "This must be your last stop before the mountains, then," she said. "Truly I wish you luck."

They nodded to her gravely. Lin thought it was just as well that these young men were all too preoccupied with their quest—and themselves—to ask for her name.

"We will encounter dangers on the way, of course," said the blond boy. "King's guards have been combing even the outlying towns for signs of resistance. And in the city it is worse. One poet was nearly executed, and another brutally beaten by Marlen Humbreleigh."

"Who was beaten?" Lin demanded. Yet there was a sinking in her heart even before she heard the answer, as if she had suspected all along. She mumbled something to the young men and staggered back to Darien and Hassen, nearly tripping as she went.

"It's my fault," she muttered.

"Surely not," said Hassen. "What happened?"

Quickly, she told him. Over his shoulder, she could see the blood drain from Darien's face. "Marlen wouldn't do something like that," he said slowly. It sounded as if he were trying to convince himself.

Mercifully, Hassen was silent. With his capable arms, he enfolded Lin and allowed her to bury her face in his shoulder.

"I think we should find a room," said Darien, and left them hurriedly.

"He saved my life," Lin whispered into Hassen's shoulder.

He sighed. "I am sorry."

She stayed in the room after that, while Darien and Hassen went to the market for supplies. Lin was grateful to both of them for letting her be, for allowing her to retreat into herself. She sank into the bed that they would share that night and stared at her hands.

It was possible that Leander's beating had had nothing to do with her. It was possible that he had suddenly become an idealist and decided to defy the authorities in a way that had put him in Marlen's sights.

But knowing him as she did, Lin very much doubted that. Since she'd gone, Marlen had had time to mull the events of the masque, had likely given thought to the identity of Valanir Ocune's accomplice.

The two men returned to the room to set down the goods they had bought—dried meat and oatcakes and apples. And then, after she declined to come, they went downstairs for dinner.

It was dark by the time Darien returned to the room, alone. "Hassen wanted to get some air," he said. "He said we shouldn't wait up for him." Darien sighed and began to untie his shirt. "He's worried about you, you know."

"There is no need for worry," she said. "I hope he will not be too bothered by that song."

"Those idiots," said Darien. "Well. Good night."

When Lin awoke, the room was dark, save for moonlight that shafted into the room and across the floor. She had been dreaming, something that involved a knife and blood and the mountains, and she was grateful to find it all a dream. Until the memory of the news from Tamryllin hit her again.

Kiara. You have turned your face from me.

She turned around and looked across to where Darien slept. Then another moment, and she rolled out of bed and into her trousers, threw on her cloak. Arming herself in the various ways she had, the knives under her pillow transferred to her sleeve and boots. She thought of waking Darien, but decided against it. Maybe she would find Hassen Styr down in the common room. They would laugh about this in the morning, how she had risen and dressed so frantically.

He should have been back by now. It was so late.

She felt as if someone had shaken her awake and now summoned her to descend the stairs. But that couldn't be right.

She would find Hassen downstairs, probably; that's what her instincts were most likely telling her.

Lin drew her knife and concealed it in the folds of her cloak as she stepped into the hallway.

16

THE hall was quiet, and the shadows did not seem to hold surprises. Still she made her way cautiously, step by soft step. The doors to other rooms, which were few, remained closed. The only sound Lin could hear was her own fluttering breath, and she shut her lips to quiet that, too.

The stairwell was faintly illumined by light from the common room. As she stepped carefully down the rickety stairs, Lin could hear voices.

"I saw him," she heard one say. A young, dreamy voice, as if it came from someone only half-awake. "The night of the fires, when I slept. I saw him finely clad as he had never been in life."

Lin peered around the corner. As her eyes adjusted to the dimness, she saw a group huddled at one of the tables. The dying flame of a lantern was the only source of light, and it was cold; the fire had died to red embers. Shadows of the men, long and wavering, danced on the wall with more life than they themselves showed.

"I saw my father, who passed on last year," said another voice, equally dreamy. "He spoke of the many regrets he had. I played him a song."

Then a new voice, unmistakably awake, said, "A friend approaches."

To her shock, they all turned to stare at Lin, their heads moving in unison like machinery. Their faces featureless in the night.

"You are a friend?" one asked.

Catching her breath, Lin said, "I am no man's enemy."

Again, the voice that had announced her approach spoke. "Join us here," he said, in a tone resonant and commanding.

"Thank you," she said, "but I'm in a hurry."

"Sit with us a moment," he said, and Lin felt compelled to draw near.

"Who are you?" she said. In the constant shift of light and shadow, his face, too, seemed to shift, so that one moment she thought she was seeing a very young man and the next, an older one. It was impossible to tell from his voice which it could be.

"We are Seekers," said another of the men, and by now Lin's eyes had adjusted enough to see that this one was young. He might even have been one of the poets who had been singing that evening— who had given her the news of Leander. "No doubt you have heard of us."

"I have," Lin said wearily. She looked past him at the man who had bidden her to approach. "And who are you?" she said again.

As if in response to her words, moonlight from the window softly touched his brow, and around his right eye an intricate knot of color caught the light. But the mark was slashed through, the light splitting into many colors, as it ought not to have done.

"You know me well," he said, and now his voice drew her back to the memory of a summer night in Tamryllin.

Lin's breath caught. "You." Now she could see his eyes even in the darkness—that unmistakable green.

"I am not really here," he said, and sounded regretful. "This is no more than a dream for you—and for me. The portal will join us here for all too short a time."

"Why, then?" Lin asked, keeping her voice even with an effort. The night was too strange; she felt cold and frightened, and the man she would once have expected to allay her fears was now somehow inextricably a part of them.

Valanir stood. She saw that the moonlight passed through him gently, as if he were translucent, or a dream. He motioned to the younger men that surrounded him at the table. "Depart," he said. Without a word and as one man they rose and marched to the door. Together and in silence, they filed out into the night. The last man carefully shut the door behind him.

Valanir smiled. "I can only do a few useful things," he said, "but I have a particular fondness for that one." His smile faded abruptly. "I will keep this quick. The guards have Hassen Styr. I am sorry."

Lin shook her head. "No, no, no," she heard herself say, her hands gripping her head.

"I can delay the guards only a little time," said Valanir. "You *must* leave tonight."

"Can't you help him?" Lin demanded. "You are Valanir Ocune. Isn't there something you can do?"

No sound but the pop and hiss of embers in the grate, as Valanir Ocune, his face weighted with sadness, bowed his head. His eyes closed for a moment. "The powers that I would need—those we seek—are still beyond my reach," he said. "For this—and for everything, Lin Amaristoth—for all of this I am truly sorry."

She reached out to him, tried to catch hold of his hand. Her fingers passed through his translucent ones, and she felt nothing, there was nothing there of him. It was all illusion.

Yet there was his voice, and in the case of Valanir Ocune perhaps that was something nonetheless. "Forgive me," he said. "And please save yourselves. So much depends on you."

"Too much," she said. "You should be here."

"I am doing what I can," said Valanir. "But I believe now more than ever in the vision I had of you."

Lin shook her head. Tears stung in her eyes. "I once thought that in music I might find some way to—give shape and meaning to—all the horrible things," she said haltingly, feeling her way through the thought as if it were a darkened wood. "But I've begun to think it's not enough."

Valanir looked sad. "For as long as you live," he said, "it won't be."

They were the last words she heard him say before his image faded to the palest outlines and then was gone. His harp took longest to vanish, its graceful curves flashing farewell in the dark.

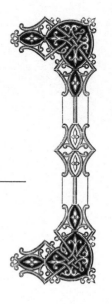

PART III

CHAPTER
17

MARLEN woke to find his face pressed against a scroll on his desk. His head swam with runes and archaic characters, those in his head and those that loomed large before his eyes in faded ink. Wearily, he lifted his head and saw that Marilla was watching him. While he slept the sun had set. She could have been a spirit of temptation appearing at his side, her bare throat and face a glimmer of white against her hair.

She watched him come awake. Then she spoke, voice rich with mockery. "I had not known Lord Gerrard's chosen was such a diligent scholar," she said, and edged closer to him. Now—whether he wanted to or not—he could inhale the heady spice of her scent. "I had thought, rather, that he was supposed to be finding a certain man."

"Damn you," he said blearily. "That's what this is about. If I can figure out where Darien is going, it makes more sense than tramping around the country." She continued to watch him. Shrugging, Marlen stretched and yawned with luxurious thoroughness. *To hell with her.* "Besides, I have fifty guardsmen doing that."

"And the Seekers?"

"Damn the Seekers," he said. "Those lunatics have naught to do with me."

"I'll wager," Marilla said, "that Nickon Gerrard would say otherwise."

Marlen shook his head, unwilling to advance further into that discussion. For it was true: Court Poet Gerrard was furious about the Seekers, considered Marlen to be partly responsible for their swelling numbers. Of course, that was one thing Nickon Gerrard was good at: blaming Marlen for the ills that were clearly his own fault. If the Court Poet had not stirred up resentment with his draconian treatment of poets, the Seekers would not be so popular. That was, at least, what Marlen thought, but he kept his opinions to himself. With everyone but Marilla, that is; there was little he did not tell her.

He allowed her access to his apartments. It seemed to make sense. At first he had offered her lodgings with him, a spontaneous gesture that he had not really thought through. That had been when he was at the nadir of his despair, before loneliness had become as habitual as meals and sleep. But Marilla would have none of it—she wanted her own apartments. With his prodigious allowance Marlen had procured for her just that, moving her out of the squalor of her former accommodations.

"You'll be my lady," said Marlen on the day he installed her in her new home, hiring her a maid. "You let me know if you need anything—anything at all. I only have one condition. There's to be no whoring."

Marilla had laughed and stroked his face with unaccustomed tenderness. On the few occasions when she touched him gently it almost sprung open a well of grief in him. Fortunately, the occurrences were rare. "You are wise," she had said. "A man of your stature must not be seen consorting with a whore."

Smiling back, Marlen had caught up her hand and bitten her fingertips. "Smart girl. I know you'll make me proud."

And she had, standing by him despite public opinion, offering suggestions in the cool, careless way she had, as if it made no difference. Yet he knew better. If anything, that was the one thing Marilla *did* care about: his success. Not for his sake—he would never be naive enough to suppose that. She was the well-fed cat curled at his feet, her every desire catered to. She dressed like a lady now, in silks and brocade, jacquard and damask. Marlen gifted her with a necklace of rubies, the red of blood and his desire. The plumes of rare birds curved from hats nestled in the complex weave of her hair. Her maid attended to her hair every morning, he had learned after paying an early visit one day. Before he met her, he had not known much about the way women lived, their lives outside of bed and night music. But even in her daily tasks Marilla seemed exotic to him, a creature he could feed and shelter but never cage, never tame. He would not have wanted to try.

It had been months now since Darien Aldemoor's disappearance, and the city was restive with tensions. Marilla came to be recognized on the streets as Marlen Humbreleigh's lover and was accorded the same contempt and fear that was accorded him. Rather than being fazed by this, Marilla seemed to relish the antagonism, carrying herself with regal contempt for others in turn. She paraded about the city in her new finery, impudently flashing jewels, and the ice of her eyes discouraged any attitude but deference. *She was once a whore,* it was whispered, but that only served to add a dimension of wonder to her reputation, and a layer of boldness to Marlen's. Amid their hatred they still admired him. It was evident in the way people would watch him when he passed, as if unable to tear their eyes away. Marlen took some satisfaction in that, at least.

But the self-proclaimed Seekers *were* a headache, with their songs that skirted the edge of outright treason without being explicit enough to present grounds for arrest. Piet Abarda in particular had proved a master of the art of subversion, weaving songs so complex in their symbolism and yet so easily interpreted that Marlen was impressed despite himself. Marlen found himself thinking that Piet might have even been competition for Darien and him in the contest, if he were more handsome. And taller.

Had Piet Abarda been less conspicuous in the public eye, Marlen would have sent him the way of Leander Keyen long ago: a little physical intimidation, a little rearrangement of his facial features (which would only have been an improvement), and the little weasel would have scurried out of Tamryllin with his tail and whiskers in a twitch. Unfortunately, his fame had caught on in the city like wildfire in sere grass—and, with it, his popularity. Worse, there were aristocrats who acted as his patrons, soliciting his performances at their parties and balls. The same people who had fled in terror during the arrest of Valanir Ocune, lest their names be linked in some way with his, now applauded and smiled at Piet's clever and near-treasonous allegories.

As the poets became more crafty, they became bolder as well. The events of the past two months had hardened them even as it had made them more cautious: no one had forgotten the poet who had been a hairbreadth away from execution, but the episode had induced them to be more circumspect in their rebellion. A group of enterprising Seekers had built a vast bonfire just outside the city walls at the end of summer, constructing an elaborate chorus of melodies that it was said had been sung by poets in ancient times. Masses of people had gone out to gawk at the spectacle.

Marlen recalled having particularly odd dreams that night, though he could not recall them now; the few images that remained were entwined in his memory with the odor of burning. Later he had heard that groups of Seekers scattered throughout Eivar had kept vigil by similar bonfires. A night of strangeness, it was thought of now. A rite that was, according to the men themselves, intended to reawaken enchantments long thought dead.

Marlen continued to study scrolls and books for answers. These he borrowed from Nickon Gerrard, who had given him the run of his extensive library. Hated or not, there were definitely advantages to being in Marlen's position. And when he was not researching, Marlen was composing new songs, recognizing in them a note of melancholy that his work had never before possessed. These he sang in the court of the king, before nobles who had reason to curry his favor; it was no surprise, then, that whatever he wrote was met with enthusiastic applause.

He loathed them all. *The place for a bard is on the Mountain,* his teacher had said. Buffeted by dour winds, alone.

So gradually, Marlen had begun to detach himself from the place he had once so desperately embraced. What did it matter, in the end? Darien would ultimately outdo him, find the Silver Branch that would be the true article, the one that would never tarnish and prove him a poet above all others. Darien would prove conclusively, and for all the world to see, that Marlen was his inferior. The moon to his blinding sun.

Studying the scrolls now, Marlen sighed at the blur the symbols had become, between candlelight and his fatigue. After a while the act of deciphering the text became so automatic that he forgot to pay attention to the words themselves. Marilla had meanwhile returned with a glass of wine in her hand. "Is that how you plan to spend the rest of tonight?" she said. "Reading?"

Marlen glared at her. "You have a better idea?"

"When I met you, you were one to take action," she said, swirling the wine in her glass. It was almost the same shade of red as her dress. "Scholars are half men, eunuchs too afraid to come out from their books and *live*."

He barked a laugh. "With an opinion like that, I'd wonder why you took up with me in the first place," he said. "What do you think an Academy graduate *is*?"

"A eunuch?" she said innocently.

He was around the table and by her in one smooth motion. Her eyes had grown blank, watching him. Marlen took hold of the ruby necklace around her neck, clasped the strand tight, and pulled. The jewels tugged at her skin—almost cutting into it, but not quite. "It was my scholarship that got me here," Marlen said. "That got you *these*."

"That's right," she said softly.

For a moment Marlen thought she was agreeing with him; then he realized what in truth she really meant. He flung the necklace back against her neck and flung himself away from her, seized with an impulse to ram his fist into a wood-paneled wall. Or her. But that would give her what she wanted, and he was in no mood for that.

"You are magnificent when you're angry," Marilla breathed behind him.

Marlen whirled on her. "Just a moment ago, you said you disdain scholars because they do not live. Do *you* want to live?"

"Of course," she said, smiling. Coming forward, she caressed his cheek with her long nails. Not tenderness—rather, it was in the way of a spider with its gossamer-wrapped prey, injecting sweet poison before the bite. "And live and live . . . until it's over."

He shuddered away. It was suddenly too tempting, and that frightened him. Her madness, to which he had thought himself accustomed, made her in that moment incomprehensible. "You're insane," he said. "You know that, don't you?"

She stuck out her lip in mimicry of a pouting child. "Now would be a terrible time for you to become banal," she said. Then as if to soften the words—as if they needed softening, ludicrous as they were—she kissed his cheek. "I'll be off, then. Have a lovely time with your . . . books."

Nights passed in this fashion. Marlen had the maddening sense that somewhere amid the arcane scribbling was the solution to his predicament. The tales were not ordered in any way that made sense to him, probably because until fairly recently, nothing had been written down. Well did he know, as every first-year Academy student knew, that in the past all knowledge had been memorized by the poets. Tradition still dictated that poets be subject to a rigorous program of memorization, but the students knew full well that what they memorized was recorded in books. Marlen didn't even want to think about what he would have had to learn by heart, had he lived several hundred years earlier. Though with that exclusive knowledge, he thought, had come power that was unknown among poets of today. The king had depended upon the learning of Seers.

So Marlen plowed diligently through the musty scrolls—by daylight streaming through the windows of his study and by candlelight long after the sun had set—wading through historical anecdotes of Academy Masters and kings of centuries past. Accounts of enchantments began to spring up in Marlen's research. He found himself smiling occasionally, if rather tiredly, at what he considered the more outlandish tales. He read of one Seer who had inflicted a plague of canker sores on a nobleman as punishment for failing to provide him adequate hospitality—"adequate" in this case meaning every ridiculous thing the Seer could possibly wish for.

It was no wonder that they had not taught this nonsense at the Academy. Certainly the Masters had alluded—with what seemed now like deliberate vagueness—to the enchantments that had once been. The mark of the Seer was frequently referred to as the last of these, with only the Masters knowing its mysteries.

So what did the Seekers know, when they spoke of resurrecting old enchantments? Marlen didn't see how they could know more than he did; yet they clearly possessed a confidence that he lacked. Accounts of Edrien Letrell's journey were all second- or third- or even fourth-hand; there was no indication that any one could be relied upon. The only primary source was Edrien's own song about it, and that was so laden with images and symbolism that it was of no help to Marlen. Unsurprisingly, it had not been popular even in its day.

There was one verse from Edrien's song of the Path that lingered in Marlen's mind:

> *Guides on the Path are not of the living—*
> *a balm and a wound, both*
> *to the heart that remembers.*

He wondered. Was the Path haunted with spirits of the dead?

At last Marlen decided that there was only one way, an obvious way, to find out what the Seekers knew. He came to this decision one evening hunched over his desk, his eyes scraped raw from too much reading. Marilla had not visited that day. Come to think of it, she had not visited him at all lately. Marlen rose with an effort and ran a hand through his hair. He would have to make himself presentable before he went out. He realized that he couldn't remember the last time he had left the apartments, or seen the sun.

Stepping out an hour later, Marlen thought there was nothing quite so good as the cool air. Each city turn seemed renewed by his absence, and mercifully, no one he passed seemed to recognize him. In contrast to what he had striven for all these years, he now longed for anonymity: to blend into the tree shadows that even now cradled his own shadow, disappear.

When he entered the *Ring and Flagon,* he was lucky; Piet was already there. Marlen well remembered the days—just recently—when Piet Abarda had been respected for his ability among most Academy students but otherwise barely tolerated; his puniness and pettiness had always worked against him. Marlen had thought him a weakling who toed the line out of fear, but as it turned out, he had toed the line because it had worked to his advantage. Piet Abarda had, perhaps, had a father much like Marlen Humbreleigh's own, someone who had tailored his instruction to Piet's size. And so Marlen and Darien and everyone else had underestimated the man.

Now Piet was surrounded by a crowd of admirers, poets and young women. Women. Before this, Piet could not have made a girl look at him if he had stood on his head. *If Darien could see this,* Marlen thought disgustedly. Piet now claimed to have been a great friend to Darien Aldemoor. It was truly sickening.

The weasel was expounding on something or other as Marlen approached, his admirers listening eagerly. All that changed when one of them, a young poet, caught sight of Marlen and nudged his friend. Instantly all eyes were on him, and Piet fell silent. As he watched Marlen come forward, there was a trace of his old smirk on his lips. He said, "Is there something I can do for an old friend?"

"So many things," said Marlen. "Disposing of this rabble would be a start."

Piet smiled. "Ever a friend to the people." He addressed his followers, "Go. He won't dare harm me here."

One poet—they all looked the same to Marlen, earnest and firm-jawed—said, "With respect, my lord, there's no telling what he might do."

Piet's smile widened indulgently. Marlen had to restrain himself from gaping. *My lord? What has happened here?* "Those of you who are concerned may watch from the far corner," said Piet. "But remember, act only in gravest necessity. Anyone who lifts a hand against this man risks his own death."

Marlen could feel their hatred now. As a group they retreated to the corner to keep watch, ostensibly to prevent him from choking the life out of their rodent leader. He wouldn't even have needed a sword to dispose of him, Marlen reflected, though he would not have wanted to sully his heirloom blade in any case. Once they had dispersed, Marlen said, still feeling their eyes on him, "Your friends don't seem to like me much." He sat on the bench across from Piet, turning so he could stretch his legs. It felt good to be back, even like this.

Piet shrugged. "Darien was even more popular than we realized," he said. "They've taken your betrayal of him rather hard."

"I imagine you're a great comfort to them," said Marlen. "Let's skip the games, Piet. We both know what's going on, even if these idiots don't. Honestly, I'm impressed with your strategy. You really surprised me."

"I'm quite sure that I did," said Piet. "All those years, you think I didn't know of the contempt you and Darien held for me? But I knew, Marlen, that a time would come when you would regret it."

"Yes, yes," said Marlen, unexpectedly amused. "Look, I'm just intrigued now by your Seekers. Really."

Piet raised an eyebrow. "Intrigued."

"Yes," said Marlen. "You say that there are enchantments . . . ?"

"Oh . . . that." Piet looked behind him, but his admirers were out of range of hearing. Still, he lowered his voice as he said, smirking a little, "It keeps them in line."

"You mean . . . you don't believe in it." Marlen had never considered this possibility.

Piet laughed. "Why, do you?"

"There's no need to lie to me," Marlen said patiently. "I ask only out of curiosity."

"I don't fear you, Marlen," said Piet, "and therefore have no reason to lie to you. I am quite honestly amused to see you barking up this tree. Marlen Humbreleigh, pursuer of spirits."

Marlen rose to his feet. "That has a ring to it that I actually like," he said, and turned to go. *Another dead end.*

He considered attempting to expose Piet as a fraud, but only for a moment. The man was too clever. He *could* still be lying, and concealing the information Marlen now sought. But his derisive laugh had seemed genuine, as had his surprise.

The moon was out by the time he reached Marilla's apartments. He wondered if she'd been angered by his absence. It was strange, actually, that he had not heard from her.

Marlen noticed that her windows were dark. When he tried the door, it was locked. He entered with his own key, but it was only to confirm what he already had guessed: she was not there. Sighing and suddenly feeling more tired than he had in a while, Marlen dug deep into Marilla's luxurious bed without even removing his boots. The softness that enveloped him washed away all thought, save one: *What does Darien know?*

IT was when autumn harvest was at its peak, on a day when the trees flared like torches in the streets of Tamryllin, that Marlen was informed by a palace guard that Hassen Styr had been captured and was now in the capital. It had happened in Dynmar. Darien Aldemoor had, unfortunately, escaped. Nickon Gerrard now summoned Marlen immediately, to be present for the interrogation.

Marlen guarded his features as he took in the news. He knew he was expected to feel triumph, but instead a curious numbness had settled over him. Against his better judgment and despite Hassen's obvious distaste for Marlen, Marlen liked the man. He had a blunt honesty that Marlen had respected, even as he had been wary of its force; a club beside the slender daggers he and Darien and Piet were wont to use.

When Marlen arrived at the palace, Court Poet Gerrard sent him down alone as a prelude, instructing him to obtain whatever information he could. Marlen had to remind himself, before he entered the room where the prisoner was held, that Hassen had brought this upon himself. He thought, *Have I not also brought this upon myself?* And then: *It is my prison, too.*

Marilla, he knew, would have scorned such thoughts. She would have reminded him that he had freely entered into this mazelike game, that such games were necessary if he was to achieve what he desired. *Would you have preferred to share the glory, be the shadow to his light?* she had said once.

Steeling himself, he entered the dungeon. Hassen was a hunched shadow on the floor behind an iron grille. The stench was nearly unbearable, and Marlen felt stirrings of anger on behalf of a man who did not deserve this humiliation. He was glad that it was dark, that he could not see the other man's wounds. Never one to be sickened by blood, Marlen still had no wish to know the extent of Hassen's mistreatment.

"Hassen, it's me," he said with an effort.

Hassen stirred, grunting as if awakening from a dream. "What is that?" His voice was hoarse; Marlen wondered if he was being given enough water. "Methinks I heard a mouse. Or is it a snake?"

Marlen gritted his teeth. "Hassen, Lord Gerrard will be here soon. I suggest you tell us everything you know, and then some."

From the darkness beyond the grille came a snarl of a laugh. "You *would* suggest that. Or else you'll kill me, I suppose."

"He will," said Marlen. "But not before he's exercised every torment he can devise. I know the man. I am telling you this for your own sake. You *will* break in the end; it's best if you give up now."

"I'm surprised," said Hassen. "I'd have thought you'd enjoy seeing me crushed beneath the thumb of your . . . protector. Is he good in bed, or do you speak of these torments from experience?"

Marlen had forgotten how Hassen could grate on his nerves. "Listen," he hissed, coming closer to the grille so that the other man would hear him even in a whisper. "I've told Nickon Gerrard that you're an idiot, Darien's pawn. Now is your chance to redeem yourself. Act as if you had no mind of your own, and there's a chance he will let you go free when this is done."

A moment. Even in the dark, Marlen could see that Hassen Styr had turned his back to him, to face the cracked and dripping wall. "I don't betray my friends," he said. "I have no more to say to you, Humbreleigh."

Each word sank into Marlen like a crossbow bolt. But Hassen's anger hardened him. If the fool would not listen, there was nothing more that he could do.

He was about to say as much, when Nickon Gerrard swept into the dungeon. Marlen glanced over his shoulder at the man who had been his master these many months. His heart faltered. He had become accustomed to thinking of the Court Poet as an irritating old man, for so he was much of the time. But it was a different man who had entered the palace dungeon. In a room lit only by torches, he seemed to glow from within with the silver of trapped moonlight. Sparks of torchlight danced in his eyes. Strangest of all, though, he had seemed to have grown in height, until even Marlen felt small beside him.

Marlen resisted the urge to take a step back, and hoped that his feelings were not written plain on his face. To think he had considered killing this man. He now realized it might not have been so easy as he had supposed.

"You will reveal yourself to me, Hassen Styr," said Nickon Gerrard, coming to stand beside Marlen. Marlen felt a tingling on his skin, now that the man stood this close, as if the light that seemed to emanate from him was a tangible thing. He lifted his hands, and a silver glow was between them. "Whether by your own will or by magic. I assure you, you will not like the second way."

Marlen found his voice. "It's all real, then," he said. "You've known all along."

Lord Gerrard waved an imperious hand, silencing him. Hassen spat at the Court Poet's feet. "Do your worst."

Nickon Gerrard's expression froze, as if in concentration. He extended his hands and the coalescing light toward the bars of Hassen's cell. The light glided from his hands, grew brighter, and surrounded Hassen's head in what looked like a coronet of shining steel.

And as Hassen began to scream, Marlen Humbreleigh ran for the door. He didn't know what was going to happen. All he knew was that he had to flee the stench and darkness of this room, or the madness he had battled for months—perhaps for years—would overtake him here beneath the earth, well beyond the reach of the sun or moon.

CHAPTER
18

THE days Rayen Amaristoth spent visiting the Gelvan home would be tinged with unreality to Rianna when she recalled them later. Each was similar to the next: after his meetings with her father had ended, she would meet him in the garden in her father's old clothes, her hair tied back, the dagger in her hand.

He would greet her with the same smile each time, extend his arm as if escorting her to a dance. Lightly, she would take his arm and smile back. In the course of this time she felt herself changing. Her smile began to come more readily, and one day she realized she was laughing again. Yet she knew it would be a mistake to think too much about what was happening, so she didn't. She let him guide her in the exertions of their lessons each day, and afterward they would sit companionably on the garden bench, and speak of his life and her dreams.

He told her of the violent death of his mother, and how he had gone slightly mad after. There was pain in his voice when he told the tale, though he seemed to try to make light of it, even laugh at the absurdity of his behavior. "When you live in a place like Vassilian, where the winters are long and dark and you are indoors much of the time, it is easy to think that your life—your family—is the whole world," he said. "Poor Lin, it must have been worse for her—I, at least, was free to travel when the roads were clear."

Despite his words, Rianna thought she saw a deep torment in his eyes. It was difficult not to reach out and touch his hand in moments like that. His fingers were long and delicate and looked as if they would be deft in all manner of things.

During those weeks she had dreams that she tried not to think of, after.

It came to an end one day in the middle of autumn, when the winds in the garden were chillier than usual. Rianna wore a dark velvet cloak over her father's shirt and trousers. She could see in Rayen's eyes, when he looked at her, that he appreciated the contrast of the velvet against her skin and hair, even though he said nothing of it. She felt almost as if she were guilty of something to have noticed it at all.

"There is something I must tell you," Rayen said. They were sitting with only a few inches between them on the garden bench, carefully apart.

Rianna looked up into his face, her lips parted slightly. Half-afraid and half-anticipating what he would say.

"I'm afraid it's not good," he went on. "I'm leaving. I've just been informed where my sister is. She is in danger."

"Danger?" Rianna said sharply.

Rayen glanced around the garden, as if to ensure that there were no listeners crouched in the ornamental hedges and trees. "If I tell you something extremely sensitive—can you keep it secret?"

Rianna nodded.

"I've known for some time that my sister was here in the city during the fair," said Rayen. "Marlen Humbreleigh found out this information and passed it on to me. But it was fairly useless unless I knew where she had gone. Which I found out today."

"How?"

Rayen's face was very solemn. "Now comes the part that you must keep in the darkest corners of your heart. It's dangerous knowledge, given the politics here. Can you do that?"

She nodded again.

"The palace guards found Darien Aldemoor's companion, Hassen Styr, in the town of Dynmar. Just today, Court Poet Gerrard met with me to tell me the findings of his interrogation. Hassen revealed that my sister joined with Darien and Hassen and was with them in Dynmar. Strangely, though, they are not heading to the mountains in the northeast as everyone had thought. They are going west, for reasons that even Nickon Gerrard cannot fathom."

Rianna found her voice. "I know Hassen," she said harshly. "He would never betray his friends."

Rayen looked surprised. "You knew him? I have heard he is a good man and a stalwart friend. But the Court Poet has methods we can only imagine."

Rianna turned away, her hands twisting in her lap.

"I am sorry, Rianna," said Rayen. "I didn't anticipate this news being so difficult for you. Is he the man you love?"

Rianna shook her head. "Stop. I mean, no, he isn't. But I still don't see why you have to go running after your sister. To hear you tell it, she can more than protect herself."

"Up to a point," he said. "But she cannot take on the full might of the king's guard. I must find her before they do, or I fear that even my word will not be enough to save her."

"Aren't you a hunter?" Rianna said. "Lord Gerrard only told you so you'll lead him to her—to them."

Rayen's eyes flickered with surprise. "You are clever. But my dear, so am I. Nickon Gerrard may imagine that I am playing his game, but I am an Amaristoth." He rose. "When . . . all this . . . is at an end, I do have hopes of seeing you again. I've enjoyed this time very much." He kissed her hand. She nearly flinched. "Perhaps I'll even be here in time for your wedding," he added, gently now.

Rianna forced a smile, but it soon collapsed. She was thinking about Hassen Styr. About Darien on the run, on the verge of being found and captured.

"Unlikely," she said. "Good-bye, Rayen."

She turned away her face even before he stood.

*　*　*

HER father found her there, hugging herself against the cold, after it felt as if hours had passed. In truth, the sun had hardly moved; it was a crisp morning, with golden, copper, and ruby foliage blazing on the garden trees.

Master Gelvan surprised her by sitting beside her on the garden bench. "May I join you?"

She reluctantly turned to face him, tangled hair blowing about her face. "What is it?" For the first time in a while, she noted the deepened lines in his face, the knifelike creases between his brows. That his blond hair had more streaks of grey in it than she remembered. She didn't want to notice, but she did.

"I would have to be blind," he said, "not to see that there has been a change in you since the summer. You are more dear to me than anything in the world, and I worry."

She shrugged, and her eyes dropped under his gaze. "What sort of change?"

"Is it Lord Amaristoth?" he said. "Did he—did he try anything with you?"

"Of course not," she said, trying to sound reassuring. "He was kind to me." It was not exactly how she felt about Rayen's visit, but she could not have put her feelings into words in any case—and she knew she did not want to articulate them to her father.

"I am sure he was interested," he said. "I was surprised, actually, that you were not. You seemed to enjoy spending time with him."

"He taught me daggers," she said. "That was kind of him. And yes, I did—I liked his company. Of course."

"Rianna-li," he said, using an endearment that reminded her of being ten, or younger, curled up with a book by the fire while the world had beckoned, mysteriously and invitingly, just outside the windowpane. "I am starting to think you are hiding something from me. And it grieves me to think that this is so—that I have made you feel that you must hide things from me."

A crow gave a harsh cry in the branches above their heads; its shadow fluttered over them. Even after the bird had flapped away, over the garden wall, its call echoed for a long time.

In that time, Rianna had come to a decision. She said, "At one of your parties in the spring, I met a poet and began seeing him in secret. Nothing—nothing happened, *Avan* . . . we had hoped to be married."

Master Gelvan drew a breath, and let it out raggedly. He looked away from her for a moment, as if to get his bearings. "Married?" he said at last, his tone flat. "Who is he?"

It was too late to turn back, Rianna knew, though it was not too late to lie. But no longer did she feel like that child who had been so enthralled in the world of tales, excited about what lay ahead at the next bend of the road. Right now she felt almost as if she and her father were equals. "It was Darien Aldemoor," she said. "We thought that once he won the Silver Branch, you would consent to our marriage."

In the same monotone, her father asked, "Has he been in contact with you?"

Rianna shook her head. She was surprised to find herself calm. "I don't know if he's alive," she said. "And I know there's a good chance that he soon won't be."

What Master Gelvan said next was the last thing she would have expected him to say. "Oh, my dear," he said, and suddenly held her tightly. Stunned, Rianna was rigid in his arms. "My dear," he said again. "I am so sorry. I wish now that you had told me."

"Why?"

"Because I might have been able to stop—all this—from happening."

"What do you mean?"

Sighing, Master Gelvan pulled away. "That's not important now. Now what I must figure out is what to do."

"What to do?"

"Yes. If you love this man—if that is what will make you happy—then we must find him before Nickon Gerrard does. Perhaps send the two of you to Kahishi, until this blows over."

"I don't understand," she said. "I thought you'd be angry."

He looked searchingly into her face. "You say that he did not do anything inappropriate," he said sternly.

"We . . . kissed," she confessed, feeling childish again.

"He meant for you to marry."

"Yes," she said. "The plan was that after the contest, he would ask your permission."

He sighed. "Of course, I am worried that you are in love with a poet. They are a volatile breed—everyone knows that. But I met Darien, and I know he comes of a respectable family. I admit, it would have been hard to convince me before he won the contest . . . but all that seems unimportant now. Give me a little time today, and we will devise a plan."

True to his word, sometime later her father summoned her to his study. She had bathed and changed into her accustomed clothing—it now seemed silly to have been dressing as a boy, as though she had been trying to make a point. Like a rebellious girl, which she was not.

She had told him about Rayen's tidings: that the last place Darien was known to have been was Dynmar.

"I have a wagonful of oranges that are due to go north at dawn tomorrow," said Master Gelvan, busily shuffling papers on his desk. "I just wasn't planning on going *with* the oranges. As it is, it will have to be done in secret. There is a compartment in the wagon where I can conceal myself. I will let it get around that we went south, just to throw off the scent. Meanwhile, *you* will go south—I will just have to arrange an escort. That will take a day. I hate to lose so much time."

"But how can you go alone?" Rianna said. "It will be dangerous."

"You don't know your *Avan,* to ask that question," he said. "There, hand me the wine. Let's drink to the success of our journeys."

Just then, there was a knock at the door. It was the maid, her eyes wide and her gait unsteady; she seemed to almost fall into the room. "Master," she gasped.

"What is it?" he said sharply, but that was when they all heard a heavy clatter outside the door.

Rianna grabbed Master Gelvan's arm. "What's happening?"

What she saw in his eyes was resignation. "Don't be afraid, my love," he said. "I am so sorry. Remember the door. Go directly to Ned's family—they will protect you."

The next moment, the guards were in the room, a flurry of black and red. They surrounded Master Gelvan and held him fast. Four of them, gripping the merchant with gauntleted hands. One pressed the tip of a spear to his throat.

"Why could I not protect you," Rianna heard herself say, despairing.

One of the guards detached himself from the group to approach her. "Mistress Gelvan, you will be held in this house under guard until such a time as the Crown sees fit to release you."

"You touch her," said Master Gelvan conversationally, "and I have ways of ensuring that you die horribly."

A Ladybird clubbed him on the side of the head with a sword hilt. Nonetheless, Rianna thought his eyes locked with hers just before his head fell back and he was dragged away.

19

FOR months he had dreamed of home, even when he was awake: the scents of jasmine and honeysuckle that were the essence of Tamryllin in midsummer, graceful white palaces by a sapphire harbor, harp music melancholy and joyous on the breeze. Perhaps it had all been so luminous in his memory, thought Ned Alterra, because that was what happened when you left home. And he had left when Tamryllin was at the peak of its splendor: in midsummer, during the fair.

Not so when he returned. The honeysuckle and jasmine had faded and died, the trees beginning to lose their leaves. There was beauty in the autumn colors on the trees, but Ned thought it was overwhelmed by the vastness of the grey sky, which blended in a ghostly way with the white palace towers. Where he'd been, the sky was a turquoise like he'd never seen, the light always golden and warm. In the eastern cities beyond the Blood Sea, the domed architecture and alien tongue, the labyrinthine tunnels from which some men never returned, had all seemed impossibly strange.

Yet now, tossing in his silken bedclothes night after night, amid more pillows than any one man could need, it was home that was strange. His nights were restless, haunted by dreams of a foreign sky and in a bed that no longer felt like his own. Even his body no longer felt like his own.

Ned's father had placed him on a ship that seemed unlikely to encounter dangers, destined as it was for the ports of Marabag, a coastal city only a few days distant. They would journey by caravan through Kahishi to the port where the ship was docked, and from there set sail. Ned's father had various agreements with the Kahishians that permitted this. There would be very little danger. He would learn the responsibilities inherent in trading and the skills it took to sail a ship. He would assist the captain, who had been given strict instructions about the young lord's safety.

Ned realized that he was stroking the ropy line of the scar on his thigh; a back and forth caress as if it were a pet serpent. It was only by accident that the sabre had missed the vein, sparing Ned's life. That was one thing he had learned in his first weeks overseas: the gods were fickle, operating without reason—or perhaps did not exist at all.

Heretical thoughts for which a man might pay with his life, but thankfully no one could see into his mind. If they could, they would have seen much worse things.

Now that he was back, Ned's father wanted him to resume his old life: to continue learning to mind the estate, to marry someone worthy of the family name. To Lord Alterra, Ned's flight overseas had been an aberration, an act the lord had opposed but had been nearly powerless to prevent.

"Rianna's feelings might have changed," said Ned's father upon his return. "Why don't you go to her?"

Ned didn't answer. He had never told his father what had happened on the night of the masque. A night that he thought would be etched in his brain for always, no matter how many oceans he might cross.

He turned away from his father, toward the window that looked out upon the shaded courtyards. The fountain that graced its center was replete with carved figures from myth. When Ned and Rianna had been very young—perhaps five and six—they had incurred the wrath of their elders by climbing the fountain as it was running, soaking themselves and hauling themselves up by the heads of stone creatures. Rianna had reached the top first, squealing with delight at her own naughtiness and her ascendancy over a boy.

The memory made Ned smile a little. He hadn't thought of that day in a long time.

"You know, Rayen Amaristoth has been visiting their home," Lord Alterra persisted, directing his remarks at Ned's back.

"I've heard," said Ned wearily. "The gossip has been relentless." His mother and sister had made certain he knew that the handsome and wealthy Lord Amaristoth was wooing Rianna even at that moment. They had meant for it to spur Ned to action—as though some action of his could change her heart.

"I don't think Rianna is one to be won over by a man's wealth or family," said Ned at last. "If Rayen Amaristoth can win her heart, it will mean that he—that he deserves her."

His father made an impatient noise. "In any case, Master Gelvan wants to speak with you," he said. "Perhaps bring you to your senses— I don't know. I told him, of course, that you would see him."

Ned had always liked Master Gelvan, had in fact considered him the best possible potential father-in-law. And it had always been clear that the merchant liked Ned in turn and even seemed to see past his clumsiness. In some ways, Ned felt more at ease with Master Gelvan than he did with his own father.

Ned was unprepared for how haggard Master Gelvan looked on the day he received Ned in his study, but the merchant waved away his concerns. He said, "You, on the other hand, look to be at the peak of health, which pleases me greatly. Like everyone else, I was worried you would not return."

"In truth, I am thinking of going back," Ned said. He had not realized it, not fully, until he spoke now.

Master Gelvan looked pained. "I know you are aware of the dangers, more so even than I," he said. "I suppose nothing I can say will convince you otherwise. Except this: I have always seen you as a man of extraordinary promise. It would grieve me to see that promise lost to an eastern disease or gutted on the deck of some ship." The man's eyes were piercing. "Don't let my daughter's feelings dictate your sense of yourself."

"There was a reason you wanted to see me?"

Master Gelvan sighed. "Yes, of course," he said. "You have changed, you know. I suppose that's to be expected. I hope you'll forgive what will sound like a presumption on my part."

Ned smiled slightly. "No more presumptuous, I'm sure, than was my intent to wed the most beautiful girl in Tamryllin," he said. "Go on."

Master Gelvan hesitated. He said, "It is about her, actually. I need your assurance that if something happens to me, you will protect her. I had hoped it would be as a husband, but if not—I hope you will recall the friendship the two of you once shared, and honor that."

"Master Gelvan, are you ill?"

The merchant shook his head. "No, it's nothing like that," he said. "Can you promise me that you will protect her?"

"There is no need to extract such a promise from me," said Ned. "I would never let harm come to your daughter. If I go overseas again, I will make my father aware of your concerns. He sees her almost as his own daughter."

"I know," said Master Gelvan. "Truly, I thank you." His hand trembled slightly as he reached for his wine.

Ned said, "Can you tell me what is going on?"

Master Gelvan smiled. "I'm afraid not, young lord," he said. "Suffice to say that very old ghosts might be coming to claim me, rather sooner than I had expected or planned." He shook his head. "Well. I suppose you have heard that Rayen Amaristoth has been calling on us. I am sure the rumors have been—colorful."

Ned shrugged and took a sip of his own wine. Struggling to keep his tone casual, he said, "Do you have news for me, Master Gelvan?"

The merchant leaned back in his chair. "He set his sights on her, I think," he said. "But she's rebuffed his advances."

"How do you know that?" asked Ned, relieved in spite of himself.

"He told me," said Master Gelvan. "And then he said a strange thing. He said that to have a chance at winning Rianna's hand, he'd first need to learn to play the harp."

"What do you think he meant by that?"

"Well," said Master Gelvan, looking embarrassed, "by then we'd both been drinking a bit. I actually have no idea what he meant." He rose, reaching out a hand. "Ned. You will come see me again?"

"Of course," Ned replied, gripping the older man's hand firmly. As he left the house, he was grateful that Rianna was nowhere to be seen, nor was Rayen Amaristoth. In his mind he was bidding farewell to the merchant's house, which he had once nearly thought of as a home. He thought again of unfamiliar shores, of twisted streets in distant cities. Where none of his memories lived.

SMOKE was drifting around his head as he sat back in his chair, in one of the more popular taverns of Tamryllin. He had gotten into the habit of smoking during the voyage—having been mocked by the men, at first, for not knowing which end of the pipe was which—and now Ned found he needed a smoke when his thoughts threatened to overwhelm him. He had bought his first pipe at a bazaar in Ankora, a bustling, colorful city where he had felt pale and foreign, and weakened by the wound in his leg.

His hood shadowing his face, Ned covertly watched the people around him. He never used to patronize taverns—his mother would have disapproved. But she would also disapprove of his smoking. And in truth, the neat gardens and bright rooms of his parents' home had begun to infuriate him. The tidy murmurings of his mother and sister had about the same weight in the world as gnats. He was exhausted by them. The disappointment in his father's eyes when he looked at Ned these days . . . it was best to be away.

And just now, since meeting with Master Gelvan, there was much to think about.

He would first need to learn to play the harp, Master Gelvan had said. A joke of Rayen Amaristoth's that did not make any sense, actually.

But another voice was deeply engraved in Ned's mind: *Rianna is Darien's wench.*

For months, Ned had discounted Marlen Humbreleigh's remark, found ways to ignore it. Rianna had seemed so confused, Marlen clearly drunk. But now the name Darien Aldemoor was famed in Tamryllin; everyone spoke of the renegade poet.

Rayen's joke made sense if Rianna was, indeed, Darien's wench. And if Rayen somehow knew about it.

Without finishing his drink, Ned abruptly left the tavern. There was only one way to find out what he needed to know. The first step was easy: after some inquiries, he found himself in one of the wealthier districts. The façade of the building he came to was imposing, and Ned felt a chill. He became more aware of the sword at his hip, though he knew that he was, as yet, unskilled.

The woman who opened the door at his knock looked familiar. Coils of dark hair hung loose to her shoulders, and she wore a gown of red satin that looked as if it was meant for the boudoir. Ned wondered if she was a whore, and his pulse quickened slightly.

"My name is Lord Alterra," said Ned. "I am here to see Lord Humbreleigh."

"Come in," she said in tones that were clipped, well bred. She did not wear face paint, and her dignified tread as he followed her did not bring to mind a whore.

Ned's companions in the voyage had been well versed in the brothels of the east—particularly the costly ones, where the women were rumored to know all the secrets of a man's body. Ned had avoided the brothels, had never in his life found release with any woman, a fact he was careful not to divulge to his companions. But in the company of sailors, he had seen many of their whores, costly and cheap. It gave him a strange twinge, that there were women willing to be used in that way. Seeing them had stirred an excitement in him that made him feel ugly, as ugly as he had felt when he was with Rianna and found himself overpowered with thoughts that he knew would have disgusted her. Ned had lain awake at nights wrestling with those thoughts, willing himself to be different.

Sometimes he thought the ugliness inside him was what had kept him from being handsome, that the poison could not help but seep to the surface.

And so he had been willing to vanish into the far east if that was what it took to escape his feelings, the terrible knowledge of what he was. He had abandoned his father's crew after learning enough skills to get himself hired onto another ship on his own merits, rather than in his father's name. And the ship he chose was that of an adventurer captain, a man as reckless with his life and the lives of his crew as Ned was with his own. He was, in his way, quite mad. They took to each other right away.

In the end, Ned had been one of the few survivors of that voyage. His desire to vanish into the east had nearly been fulfilled.

Yet now Ned was beginning to realize that even when he had expected to die on eastern waters, he had still had hope, though so deeply concealed that he had not known it was there. A hope that perhaps, just perhaps, Rianna might feel differently when he returned with tales to tell. When she saw that he had been willing to risk losing her, if it meant proving himself to her first. It was the reason he had held back from the temptations of the eastern cities; he had been saving himself for his love—in case.

He had been an idiot. It only remained to discover just how much of one.

Meanwhile, the woman had stopped in her tracks, turned to face him. She had brought him to a room with high ceilings and tall windows hung with sumptuous dark velvet. One end of the room was dominated by a massive desk, and it pained Ned's sense of order to see the papers and books piled haphazardly in mounds atop it, utterly obscuring its surface.

"I am Marilla," she said. "I believe we have met."

"Have we?"

Now she smiled, a cruel smile that showed all her teeth, and he recognized her immediately. "You seem different," she purred. "There is no longer that cowed look in your eyes."

"You are no different," he said. He felt a surge of disgust for this woman who had, he recalled, expressed a desire to see his blood spilled on the ground. "You are as ill-mannered and odd as ever. Is Marlen Humbreleigh here?"

"He's not," she said. "But I think I can help you with your problem."

"My problem," Ned repeated. He was beginning to regret that he had come here, into the lair of a disturbed man and his bizarre consort. Marlen, it was said, was dangerous and prone to fits of rage, especially in recent months. Ned had even heard, in whispers amid the tavern smoke, that he had beaten a fellow poet nearly to death, without provocation.

"You want to know if what Marlen said on the night of the masque was true," she said. Her eyes were intent on his, and he realized she was moving closer. He could smell the rich exposing scent she wore. Involuntarily, Ned's thoughts turned to smooth skin, to secret places where he could sink, irrevocably. Sink and lose himself.

He backed away a step. "I am beginning to think I will never know," he said, and detested the bitterness in his own voice. "Why should I trust either of you?"

"You're right—Marlen would lie to you," she said. "He would tell you that he was simply drunk, and that Darien never touched your Rianna Gelvan. In the depths of his heart, he desperately wants to see himself as someone who would not betray a friend—in spite of overwhelming evidence to the contrary."

Ned thought he was prepared, yet a rush of nausea welled up from the pit of his stomach. "You are saying—that he did touch her."

"I think you will find that if you think back, you will know the answer for yourself," Marilla said. "The little girl, Lord Alterra, never saw what you are. But I do."

"And what am I?"

Marilla touched her nails to his cheek, as she had done once before. They were long, and painted a deep crimson that was almost black. "She never saw the violence in you," she said. "The rage that is—isn't it?—aching to burst free."

Ned broke away. "You're mad."

She laughed. "Go then—Marlen will be returning soon, and would not be pleased to find you here," she said. "But you are welcome any-time to visit me." She told him an address.

"I suppose I could visit you," said Ned. "But I'd sooner be hanged."

He turned and left the room, heading for the front door, but not before he heard her laugh. It was a sound that had rung in his ears on the night of the masque after his cowardice was exposed, had seemed to pursue him all the rest of that night. Now it filled him with revulsion and sadness and yet also, unexpectedly, recognition.

THAT evening, as Ned sat and smoked—this time in a different tavern—he mulled the events of the day. Marilla had been right—thinking back on his memories of the summer, he realized that, all along, there had been something strange in Rianna's behavior. She had never been enthusiastic about the idea of their marrying, but it was only in the summer that she had seemed to become acutely unhappy when he was near, almost tearful. Her heart heavy with guilt, he supposed. No doubt she had thought *poor Ned* many times in the course of those weeks.

But Ned had carried on in ignorance, knowing himself to be inadequate but still hoping—hoping. Until the night of the masque, when he had finally realized that all the ways he had attempted to be what Rianna wanted were exactly wrong. He had striven to show her how much she meant, how willing he was to do the slightest thing. That night he had realized that none of that behavior could conceal what he was.

But now that he knew she had loved Darien at that time, he could also see how unappealing his clumsy attempts must have seemed in comparison to a graceful, charming adventurer. And more than that—to a mind that continually crested the heights of music and art, leaped and teased and induced ecstasies so close, so very close to the ecstasies of shared love.

How much she meant.

He could never have put it into words. He had no songs for her. *The violence in you.* What had the woman meant by that? Ned didn't think he was violent. He didn't think he could even have summoned the impulse to harm Darien Aldemoor, his rival, if given the chance. It didn't make sense to him, as no act of violence on his part would have caused Rianna to love Darien any less, or Ned any more.

He could not fault her for her feelings. For years, he had refused to look honestly at himself and had presumed where he'd had no right.

Around him, the tavern was a bustle of people laughing, drinking, and smoking. And unavoidably, there were poets playing a song about love and erotic passion. Their favorite subject. Tavern patrons thumped the table in time with a ballad about a clever tinker who charms his way into the bed of a princess. It was a bawdy, tasteless song that, Ned thought, had nothing at all to do with real love.

It was too late at night to do anything but go home, but he could not bear the thought. He wandered the streets aimlessly, in the direction of the Court Plaza.

Or not aimlessly, not really.

When Ned came to the door, he knocked. When there was no answer, he noted the light inside and tried the door. It opened immediately. Stepping inside the house, Ned closed and bolted the door behind him. In case.

He had a thought then that perhaps Marilla was even more devious than he'd supposed; that this was some sadistic scheme to pit him against Marlen, get Ned spitted on that heirloom sword for good. And it would work. He was more experienced now, but still no match for Marlen Humbreleigh.

Ned smiled grimly. If that had been her plan, then the girl was perceptive: she knew a dead man when she saw one.

The first floor of the apartments were quiet. Ned took to the stairs, making no effort to silence his steps. Whatever happened now—if it all ended here—then so much the better. He was tired.

But he found her alone, which in a way he feared even more. She was sitting on her bed with her back to him. It was bare, covered only by a fall of long black hair.

She turned her head to look him in the eye. "I thought you would come," she said. Rising so he could see that indeed, she wore nothing, she turned to face him, stretched out her arms in an oddly ceremonial gesture. Or even vulnerable, which Ned had not expected. Her breasts were round and firm, her legs very long. She said, "Shall we begin our lesson?"

Here was one way, he thought then, to finally disappear.

"I'm leaving Tamryllin," he told her, hoarsely. It seemed important that she know.

Her lips curled. "Oh, good," she said. "Then neither of us shall sorrow."

A WEEK passed, and then another. Ned thought Marilla was not even a woman, that she was some sort of demon, but still he could not leave. She had been right about the violence in him—too, too right, and many times since that first night she had driven him to prove it. Ned knew that if he waited too long, winter would freeze the mountain passes, and he would be barred from traveling to Kahishi and the eastern ports. It was time to leave. And yet every day he found his way back to that house, to the bed that contained a universe.

Sometimes he imagined, when she turned away from him and slept, that the hair that brushed against his chest was golden instead of black. That her cries had been in a different voice, one that he had known all his life. And then, even though he knew that such thoughts were shameful, all he could feel was black loss hollowing out his heart.

But he also felt, losing himself in her, that he had been saved.

Once, after a particularly brutal night, she kissed him full on the lips almost as if with love. She said, "There is no one like you."

How, then, could he leave?

TWO weeks later news reached the Alterra household: that earlier that same month, Master Gelvan had been arrested by Ladybirds, taken into custody by the Court Poet himself, who had ordered the affair kept quiet. But the arrest of such an important figure could not stay secret for long.

Worse, infinitely worse, was that Rianna had vanished.

"What does that mean?" Ned had demanded of his father. "How does a girl just disappear?"

"She was being kept under house arrest," said Lord Alterra, looking shaken. "That is all I know. The guards confined her to the house for the night—and the next day, she was gone. They have scoured the house for her—and apparently discovered an altar to the Unnamed God and books of forbidden texts. On top of what Master Gelvan is already charged with—and that is secret—they will doubtless add heresy to the list of crimes."

Ned shook his head as if that might clear it of the confusion that had flooded him. "Can you get him out?" he asked. "Can you use your influence?"

Lord Alterra looked more bent and old than Ned had ever seen him look. He said, "Even we cannot circumvent the will of the Court Poet, Ned. His power at court is absolute."

"What of Rayen Amaristoth? Where was *he* during all of this?"

His father's eyes were keen now. "Have you not heard? Nickon Gerrard ferreted out that Darien Aldemoor was spotted in the northern town of Dynmar with Rayen's runaway sister. Lord Amaristoth left immediately—just before the arrest."

Dynmar. If Rianna had heard Darien Aldemoor was there, perhaps that would have been her destination? It would all depend how much she was in Lord Amaristoth's confidence.

He had been courting her, Ned reminded himself. In those situations, did a man not reveal everything?

THAT day Marilla could see, the moment he entered the house, that something was wrong. "What is it?" she said sharply.

It was hard to meet her eyes, but when he did, he saw that they were hard and glassy as ever. For some reason, that did not comfort him.

"I told you I am leaving the city," he said. "I think you know why I need to go now."

"I heard the little girl ran away," she assented, with a shrug. "But where will you go?"

"You know that, too," he said, though he could not be sure. But even though they never spoke of Marlen—he was no more than an unseen presence and threat—Ned had never forgot for a moment whose creature Marilla truly was.

He thought he saw her lips turn down, just for a flicker of an instant. "You are so clever," she said. "So it's to be Dynmar, then."

"I think so."

"She may not have gone there, you know."

"I know," said Ned. For the first time, he was gentle with her: he took her hand in his. "You will always mean something to me."

She smiled and withdrew her hand gracefully. "Then you are as much a fool as ever."

"True," he agreed, and stood. There seemed no more to be said, and there was very little time. He wanted to be angry at Rianna, for running off into a world that was far more dangerous than she knew, but it was not in him to be angry just then. Ned left the house that had been his obsession for a time, that had changed him so much. And he wondered if the sadness living in him since he returned home would be a constant companion now.

CHAPTER
20

MARLEN awoke to sunlight and the vertical blackness of a figure in the midst of it. Groaning, he lifted his head from the desk, even as the voice intruded on his dreaming once again.

"What *is* it, Marilla?" he said. As his eyes adjusted, her face no longer seemed black against the sun. Her curls brushed his face as she bent over him, her nails cold and smooth against his cheek as claws. As he gained consciousness, another thought occurred to him. "And where have you been lately, anyway?" She could at least *pretend* to love him, if she wished to keep enjoying his generosity.

Marilla brushed his forehead with her lips. "Out and about. As you must be today, if you are not to miss important events."

He shook his head. His mind was only now catching up to his body, the memories rushing back to him. "You know what's happened?"

"I know the version that has been put about in the streets," said Marilla. "The proclamation and the announcement of a public funeral. Which you of course know nothing about."

"Funeral?"

"For Hassen Styr," said Marilla. "Apparently, Darien Aldemoor killed him."

Marlen jumped to his feet. "Show me the proclamation."

"It's in the Court Plaza," Marilla said. Her uptilted chin and trailing skirts gave her a regal appearance as she swept toward the door. "Come see."

He had no choice but to follow her, though he resented that she couldn't just tell him what the proclamation said. Was it more jewels she wanted—had he outlived his use for her? The thought made his fists clench, aroused his fury and his desire simultaneously. And then he thought: *Playing into her hands. She has trained me well, it seems.* The anger drained from him. If he had allowed her to cause anger and lust to run together in his mind, he had only himself to blame. And what difference did it make? Perhaps she had corrupted him, but he had been flawed from the beginning, metal damaged already in the crucible.

The proclamation hung at the palace gates. It announced the discovery of Hassen Styr's body. He had been slain with a knife to the throat, Marlen read. As no blood was found, it was assumed that Darien Aldemoor had killed Hassen in one of the darkest of the old magics: divination by blood.

Divination by blood. This stopped Marlen dead for a moment, his head swimming. He had read of this. A practice employed only by a few, usually with the blood of animals. Some used their own blood. To slay another human—or a *mortal,* as the texts spoke of it—in the practice of divination was the darkest possible venture into the art, punishable by death. He had thought it a legend. *Along with the rest,* he thought. He had thought it all a legend. *And would that it were.*

He continued to read. There would be an official funeral held for Hassen today, since the Crown saw him as the victim of a larger terror to the land. The reward for Darien Aldemoor's capture, alive or dead, had been doubled.

So many thoughts jostled one another in Marlen's head. No one had given any thought to blood divination until Nickon Gerrard had made it a matter of public speculation today. Now he had simultaneously made Darien Aldemoor a monster—the advantage of that being obvious—and publicized an obscure, discontinued rite. What he had to benefit from that last, Marlen could not be sure.

He thought of Piet Abarda's derision when Marlen had questioned him about the enchantments. *It keeps them in line,* had been his words. Even he would be forced to rethink his position, now that the possibility the enchantments were real had been dragged out in the open.

Marlen turned away from Marilla and began walking back to his apartments. He needed to think. She did not follow, nor did she call out to him.

Absorbed in his thoughts, Marlen retreated from the sunlight into the house. Although he had not eaten yet, he poured himself a glass of wine. *When you want to know why,* his father had once said, *look at the consequences.*

The consequences here would be twofold. The first was easy: all the Seekers would now be tainted with Darien Aldemoor's alleged crime; they would be perceived as potential murderers themselves. They after all claimed to follow Darien Aldemoor, to seek the enchantments of ancient days. How far will they follow him, people would wonder now, and which enchantments will they resurrect? It could go so far, Marlen thought, as to cause the people to beg the Crown's protection from these criminals. The Crown would be only too glad to oblige.

As for the second . . . Marlen thought, *Was it really necessary to mention blood divination?* To claim that Darien had murdered his companion would already have turned the tide of public opinion against him and against the Seekers who claimed to follow him. To raise the specter of a long-dead practice was to risk its resurrection in the flesh. Nickon Gerrard must have known this.

Marlen stirred in his chair. He would be expected to attend the funeral. He concentrated on his need to bathe, shave, and have his servant brush down his good clothes. As long as he thought of that, he would not think of Hassen Styr bloodless white in a casket, a black gash in his throat.

"Marlen." Marilla was back, unexpectedly.

He lifted his head with an effort. "What is it?"

As always she spoke without emotion, but she approached with unaccustomed speed. She circled him until he was forced to look at her, to meet her eyes. "I heard a rumor today," she said. "That the Red Death is in the south. In Sarmanca. That by winter it will have reached Tamryllin."

"The Red Death?" Marlen shook his head. "Isn't that another legend?"

"They say it's blood divination that brings the Red Death," said Marilla. "That it was Darien."

WHITENESS engulfed their boat on the still mirror of the bay. Since dawn the fog had been growing, and the chill air hung like a blanket. The only sound was the splash of oars in the white-reflected water, churning it in flashes of silver and green.

Lin sat near the prow, staring out into the fog. Her dark hair curled and wafted around her neck. A thin line split the skin between her brows, as though in her mind she struggled with something. She was swathed in her black cloak, her face floating above it like a waning moon against night.

Darien looked away; he didn't want to look at her, even though she was all he had just now.

The oarsman was silent; it was not in his trade to make conversation. His family had lived on the shore since the days of the earliest kings; and in the years since, each of the eldest sons bore the sacred duty of ferrying poets across the waters of the bay.

Darien remembered mornings after he and Marlen Humbreleigh had sneaked into Dynmar for the women and drink, returning on the ferry, singing as loudly as they could—sometimes still sodden drunk. Occasionally other students had joined them in their mischief, Hassen Styr and Piet Abarda among them. Naturally Piet was always angry by the end of the excursion, always vowing by the time they reached the boat the next morning that he would never accompany them again. Usually it was due to some insult from Marlen, Darien recalled. Lounging in the boat, Marlen and Darien would sing, and joke, and boast about their conquests of the night, while the other poets laughed enviously and Piet sat hunched and glowering. And then they would reach the Isle and the masters would berate them for their disobedience, punish them with dinners of biscuits and roots for a week.

Marlen and Darien always agreed it had been worth it. Especially since they could usually charm the cook into giving them meat scraps on the sly.

It was not the task of the ferryman to determine if a poet was worthy of entering the Academy Isle. He only determined if the man was in fact a poet: in order to ride the ferry, a poet must show his harp and ring. Darien had foreseen this difficulty before he and Lin had reached the man's cottage, had instructed Lin brusquely, "We'll say you're my servant."

"A female servant?" said Lin. Her hair was longer and wilder by now, almost to her shoulders.

"He won't notice that you're a girl. Trust me." He let a bit of nastiness drip into his tone, even though he knew she didn't deserve it.

It had been his choice to abandon his friend. He knew that. When Lin had rushed into the room that night and told him what had befallen Hassen Styr, Darien had jumped from the bed and scrambled for the door, his sword already half-drawn. He knew where the town hall was, where the guards would be keeping Hassen.

"Darien, *think* about this," Lin had cried, catching his arm. "It's a death sentence for you if you attack them."

"And for Hassen if I don't," he said. "My gods, Lin. Are you such a coward?"

He tore out the door of the inn and ran in the direction of the town hall. He could hear the light patter of Lin's pursuing him, see her shadow by his side in the predawn light. Through the twisted streets they ran, and Darien knew that what he did was folly. They ran in silence until they reached the town hall. It was modest like the rest of the town, a squat wooden structure with only a clock tower to distinguish it.

Yet even before they came to it, Darien saw the guards, their black armor smoothly shining against the red livery they wore. Catching his breath, Darien stared at them from behind a hay bale. There were at least fifteen.

"There will be more inside," Lin breathed, speaking for the first time.

"I know that," Darien hissed back. "Maybe you don't know there is such a thing as honor—for men, at least."

In the dimness he could still see her close her eyes, briefly. She had drawn her knife. "Do you think I care if I die?" she said, her eyes like dark caverns when they met his. "I loved him too, Darien. What can we do?"

There behind the hay bale Darien felt as if something sharp had punctured him, draining all the air out of his lungs in one gust. He collapsed to the ground, breathing hard and deep as if he might vomit. When Lin touched his arm, he flung her off so roughly she nearly fell over.

They journeyed in silence in the days that followed. Lin seemed to see the violence in his eyes, and to understand. She approached him only when she had a specific question. As the days went by and they were by turns rained on and buffeted by winds, she looked more and more bedraggled and sad, yet he could not reach out to her. It was all he could do not to sit down on the ground somewhere in the midst of the northern forests, and weep.

He was following me, he thought, and it was like a refrain, a lyric carried by cold voices on the wind.

Hassen Styr is worth ten of me, Darien thought. *Where are we now?*

There was no way now but forward. He could certainly not run back, into the arms of Marlen and Nickon Gerrard.

It was during one of the nights in the forest, hunched over a small fire as the wind howled that Darien said, "I'll kill him." It was in a flat, dead tone that he didn't recognize. Not the voice of a man who sang playful songs to crowds and ballads to a gold-tressed merchant's daughter.

Lin eyed him. "Who?"

"Who do you think?" Darien said. "You're not stupid, are you?"

"I'm still with you," she said. "So to be honest, I'm not sure."

Darien had glared at her but did not reply. He knew he was being far too hard on her, yet could not seem to stop himself.

But now in the blanketing silence of the bay—it was so quiet Darien could hear his own breath in his ears, thought he even heard the slow thrum of his pulse—he felt his resentment evaporate, to be replaced with a vast tiredness. It was said that a man crossing water left his past behind on the shore. It was true that with every stroke of the oars, he felt the quietness around him enter his soul.

"Did you ever think you'd be coming here?" he said to Lin Amaristoth. Across the length of the boat, he extended the question like an offering. It was as near to an apology as he could imagine getting just then.

She looked surprised, almost pitifully glad that he had spoken. But still wary—he could see that, too. He remembered his first impression of Lin—that something had happened to her once. "I didn't think so, no," she said. "I never expected to leave my parents' home, except to be married."

Darien tried to imagine a life like that. He had spent most of his life unfettered, whether it was running in the fields with the village children, or wandering with Marlen Humbreleigh on every road they cared to explore. Into every township, every castle, every bed.

Lin tightened the cloak around her, gazing away again toward the fog. "My mother was mad," she said. "I don't think I realized it, until recently. Maybe it wasn't my fault that I turned out this way. Maybe it wasn't even Rayen's fault that he is what he is."

And what are you? Darien thought. Something he had never considered in their time together.

As if she could hear his thoughts, Lin looked him in the eye and said, "You don't know me. But that's all right."

"I was just thinking that there doesn't seem to be anything wrong with you," said Darien. "Only that you seem unhappy."

Lin smiled at him, but looked as if she might weep. He glanced away; he couldn't bear that sort of look right now. It swept him back to thoughts of Hassen, and the pain and rage that accompanied them. If he could, Darien wanted to leave those feelings on the shore. At least for now.

Darien noticed then that he could hear birds—the calls of seagulls and owls intermingled. The next moment, he saw the dark cliffs of the isle rearing through the mist. He had never before seen the entry to the Isle as something intimidating, but now he could see how it might be.

"Now whatever happens," he said, "let me do the talking."

Lin was silent, looking out at the water and the cliffs ahead.

As their boat glided toward shore, grey-robed figures came into view. They stood as if carved from rock, their faces shadowed by cowls, and watched the boat as it proceeded through the glassy waters.

Darien expelled a long-drawn breath, said a bit wonderingly, "Well. I've never received such a welcome."

"Are you sure that's what it is?" said Lin. Her speech was slow and relaxed, as if the calmness of the water had at last worked its effects on her.

Darien shrugged. "I know these men," he said, with more conviction than he felt. It had, after all, been nearly two years since he had left Academy Isle for the last time.

She nodded, but said nothing. When the boat reached the shore, they tumbled out silently, with only a quick word of thanks to the boatman, who did not look their way.

As one, in smooth formation, the robed figures advanced to meet them. And then surrounded them in a circle, five men in all. Most had beards of grey or silver-white.

Then the one who led, whose beard was pure white, lowered his hood to reveal his face. With skin that was sandpapery and pale, and blue eyes sunk deep in their sockets, Darien thought he looked older than ever. And tired.

Darien inclined his head respectfully. "Archmaster Myre," he said. "It is an honor to be in your presence again."

In a voice unexpectedly deep for such a fragile throat—a voice Darien knew well—the man who had been High Master of the Academy for decades said, "Darien Aldemoor. You are a hunted man."

Darien forced a laugh. "Master," he said. "You're not usually given to stating the obvious."

The High Master did not smile. "Come with us," he said. "Both of you."

Even as he spoke, the men surrounding them began to move in the direction of the grey towers that rose above the trees. Darien and Lin fell into step with them. Darien was keenly aware of the figures that followed them behind and beside, as if escorting criminals to their cell. He wondered whose faces lay behind the cowls, for he knew them all as well as he did his own family. In some ways, even more.

The castle courtyard was quiet and had not changed in the years since Darien had gone. A statue still dominated its center, of a king upon a throne, and at his feet a poet strumming a harp, head uplifted in song. In his student days, Darien had aspired to become that poet, for there was no honor higher than playing in the presence of the king.

It was only now that Darien noted the subservient position of the poet, sitting at the king's feet. He wondered if it was a statue of King Eldgest, imposed upon the Academy courtyard in a gesture of dominance. For the first time, alongside his pride in being an Academy graduate, Darien understood that this place—which he had alternately regarded as a sanctuary and a prison, depending on his mood—lay in the shadow of greater powers. For the first time, he realized that it may not have been safe to come here, to the place he had once regarded as a haven from the world.

Shadowless and still under an overcast sky, the courtyard seemed a desolate place; Darien felt something like loss tug at his heart.

He stole a sidelong glance at Lin, who was trudging at his side. Her face was expressionless.

There was no one in the vestibule of the castle. Archmaster Myre led them to a chamber that adjoined it. It was a room with a long oak table, benches lining its sides. They were followed by all the men, who each flung back his cowl as he sat. Now Darien could see their faces— some he remembered as friendly, others not; but all were Archmasters, the highest rank of instructor at the Academy. One in particular, Archmaster Hendin, had nearly been a friend, though Darien's standing as a student had made a true friendship impossible. Hendin's brown eyes were creased with what looked like worry. When Darien tried to meet his gaze, Hendin glanced quickly away.

Archmaster Myre spoke. "Sit down, Darien Aldemoor. Lady Kimbralin."

Without showing any surprise, Lin sat on one of the benches. Darien followed her. He said, "How do you know who she is?"

A silence. Lin spoke. "Darien," she said, "didn't you notice that the Masters who met us outside did not ask who I was?"

"We received word from Lord Amaristoth." Archmaster Lian, speaking for the first time. Well did Darien remember those gravel tones and the cold authority they held, directing a much younger Darien to reposition his hands on his harp again, again, and again. "A brother's instinct, perhaps, told him you might come this way. We were instructed to send word to him if you did."

Lin held out her thin arms, palms up; a gesture of surrender. "Masters, I am in your hands." Her chin was lifted, and Darien found himself surprised at her composure.

Archmaster Myre's masklike features did not change. "What is it you seek here?" he said then, his eyes turning toward Darien, and Darien felt then exactly as he once had as a student: fidgety, inclined to be rebellious. To charm his way out of a scrape only to allow his sense of mischief to get him into another one almost immediately. It was as if nothing had changed.

Darien tried to remind himself that he was no longer a recalcitrant student. "You have surely heard that I seek the Path," he said. "I wish to search the archives for information that might be relevant. A few days is all I ask, and then we shall be on our way again."

The old man's brow furrowed; Darien did not know if it was with anger or something else, some response engendered by mention of this most treasured of their legends. At last the High Master spoke, his voice heavy as if weighted with every one of his years. "You waste your time, children," he said. "For hundreds of years, others have tried to make sense of Edrien Letrell's writings, to find the Path with the information we have here. And some of our finest scrolls were— requisitioned, by the Court Poet. You will find nothing here to help you."

Darien held the other man's gaze. "Nonetheless," he said. He could almost feel the coiled tension in Lin at his side. *The key*, he thought. The one thing they had that might give the lie to the High Master's words.

Archmaster Myre's expression grew dark; he was silent. Darien's gaze slid to the other men, their features slack with careful neutrality. Immovable sentinels, they were, recorders of events. When his eyes locked with those of Archmaster Hendin, the other man looked away. It would not go well for Darien if Hendin seemed to favor him. Darien understood.

A new voice, faintly melodious, threading into the silence. "As I understand it," Lin said, and all eyes turned to her. "It is the right of every Academy graduate to have access to the archives. Darien Aldemoor has earned his ring; therefore, he has that right."

Archmaster Myre's face grew darker still; Darien resisted the impulse to glare at Lin. She had to know it was already an insult that she was here, a woman in this castle. Silence should have been her only recourse under those circumstances.

Archmaster Lian spoke again. "And what is a woman doing, quoting our laws?"

Lin said, "I was tutored by one of your own, one Alyndell Renn. Had I been born a boy, it would have been my wish to attend the Academy; hence I commissioned Master Renn to teach me all that he knew." She spoke evenly, appearing more in her element now than Darien could remember her being.

"He acted against our laws," Archmaster Myre said grimly.

"I know," said Lin. "But however wrong it is that I know those laws, still they stand."

"I have no need to be instructed in our codes by a woman, however highly born," said the High Master. He looked at Darien, said, "Do you have any idea what you've started? Our graduates have begun resurrecting ancient rites, in *your* name. Rites best left alone."

"How does that hurt you?" Darien asked.

The old man's lips thinned. "You cannot imagine the havoc it has created. Something is stirring, awakening with the acts of these men. There is no telling what they may unleash in their ignorance."

"Then perhaps," Darien said, "it is best if I find the Path and put an end to it all."

"Once men have tasted power, they will not stop," said Myre. "And besides, you will not find it. Cease to speak foolishness here."

"Will you deny him his right?" Lin said again. As if she did not notice the ring of hostile eyes trained on her.

Myre wheeled on her as if in fury, but to Darien's surprise said, "I will not. I cannot. His ring grants him a right that I cannot take from him."

Not a flicker of emotion crossed her face. Darien said hastily, "I thank you, Archmaster Myre."

The High Master did not turn from his regard of the small woman seated on the bench. "You, however . . ." he went on. "You have no rights here to speak of."

Lin bowed her head. "As I said, Master, I am in your hands."

A glint in the old man's frost-blue eyes: emotion, or a trick of the light? This was a man who, for more than forty years, had never left Academy Isle, never even set foot on the planks of the ferry. The laws of the Academy were most severe upon its most powerful.

"You," continued the High Master, "will remain here for so long as Darien Aldemoor does, provided that you abide by our rules. You shall not have access to the library. You shall not converse with the students. And you will apparel yourself as befits a woman."

Relief flooded Lin's face. "Agreed."

"We have had guests in the past," said Archmaster Myre. "Nobility.

I shall let it get out that we have noble guests here, a lord and lady. We have apparel, left behind by one noblewoman, that may fit the Lady Kimbralin."

"You are generous," said Lin. "I thank you."

"My dealings with your family over the years have not been numerous," said the old man. "But they have one and all been . . . memorable. Your parents taught you well, Kimbralin Amaristoth."

Lin bent her head in a polite nod. "I thank you, Archmaster Myre," she said. "No doubt they did."

CHILL that evening, deep inside her. It may have been the ocean winds that wended through the narrow casement. Lin drew Leander's fur cloak about herself, for comfort as well as for warmth. From here she could see mountains, not the sea, but she could hear the sighing of the waves. The mountains piled up impenetrably black against the blue-black of the sky.

This is where Alyn was. All the tales he had told her of his days in the Academy, all the lessons; she had carried them within her the way an oyster carries the resplendent agony of a pearl in its shell. And now the tales were given shape, faces bestowed on anonymous old men. He had told her of Archmaster Myre; she'd had some idea what to expect.

What became of you, Alyn? It felt like a betrayal of self to wonder, but still she did. Was he among the Seekers, or had he done as she suspected, taken flight across the border, where the wrath of Rayen Amaristoth would not find him? It was hard to imagine him one of these blank-eyed men who claimed to follow Darien. But in the end—as it had turned out—she had not known him at all well.

Just as she had not known Leander Keyen very well, either. A flaw in her character, or in theirs? Or simply the nature of things? A surface, she reflected, exists for so many reasons, concealment only one. For it may also serve to protect, from others and from oneself. And perhaps, in an unexpected twist, to protect others from oneself.

For perhaps if she had never known of Alyn's lie, she would not have run. None of Rayen's pummelings over the years, none of the threats, had had the same effect as that simple unveiling of the truth.

The door opened, illuminating the room briefly, revealing two narrow beds, a washstand, a chair. They had the same amenities that were given to students. Darien closed the door and flung himself down on his bed with a sigh.

Lin said, "No luck?"

Darien groaned. "I remember now why I never spent more time than I had to in the library. Did you know there is a book about the Academy sewage system? Lays it all out quite nicely, with plenty of four-syllable words."

She could not help but laugh. "An important topic, I suppose."

"Easy for you to laugh," he grumbled. "Resting here while I do all the work."

"Confined to a drafty room without distraction," she pointed out. "I'd much rather do the work, as you put it." She rolled her eyes, then relented. "There," she said, motioning to the chair. "They left a tray of supper for you. I've had mine. And we're invited to dine with the High Master tomorrow evening."

"Splendid," Darien mumbled into his pillow. "Dry bread and an even drier invitation."

"I'm excited," Lin said wryly. "I'll have a chance to leave this room. I was told that exploration of the castle was . . . discouraged."

"I'll say," said Darien. "They're afraid you'll seduce the students. Can't have that sort of thing." He pulled himself up, rested his forehead in his hands. For all his talk, he was clearly spent. "I saw no sign of a locked door, nowhere to use the key. It would have been nice, wouldn't it, if Valanir Ocune had seen fit to explain himself."

"I suspect that Archmaster Myre is right," said Lin. "Though there is much that the books may tell us, others before us have had access to the Academy library and found nothing. The answer *must* lie with the key."

"I agree," said Darien. "I'll keep looking." He looked at her from under weary eyelids. "Thank you, by the way. For your help today."

Lin shrugged. In the old days, she knew, they would have garroted a woman who had learned their secrets. She had known the risk she took, had banked on the times being different . . . and on the Academy, now in a diminished state, fearing the wrath of House Amaristoth.

"Maybe Hassen is all right," Darien said, almost to himself.

Lin turned back to the window to hide her face. She wanted to reach out to him, and she knew he would hate her for it. She let silence drift between them, the sound of distant waves.

CHAPTER
22

AT dawn he left her sleeping, and still bleary-eyed made his way to the kitchens, where he knew the cook would give him an early breakfast, for old time's sake. From there he would return to the library, a cavern of books and scrolls that seemed to stretch for miles beneath the island's rock.

He already hated it: inching through stack after musty stack of tomes, unrolling fragile scrolls that whiffed dust into his nose, made him sneeze. Darien had never been one for books. It came to him—so natural and painful a thought—that Marlen had been better at this sort of thing. Or perhaps, simply more driven, goaded by the sting of his father's taunts.

How did I not see?

As he clambered down the narrow, winding stairs, Darien remembered a spring day years before in this castle. He had entered the room that he and Marlen shared, and his friend had been sitting, slack-jawed, legs outstretched, on the mantel beside the window. It was Marlen's first day back from a long visit home. Darien had said, "Just what I knew this room was missing. A gargoyle."

Marlen turned his head toward him, shaggy dark hair dangling about his ears. Both hair and shadow conspired to hide his face. "So happy you missed me."

"So how was it?" said Darien, sensing an awkwardness.

A short silence, then: "Charming," said Marlen. "I told my father I was the best student, except for you. Do you know what he said?"

"Go ahead."

"First," said Marlen, "he said I was weak for allowing anyone else to be equal to me. Then, once he had wearied of that theme, he suggested that I poison you. One, two drops in your wine at dinner, and no one else the wiser. Who would suspect your dearest friend?"

Darien kept his face expressionless. "Well, now I can see where you get your direct approach to problems," he said. "What was your response?"

Marlen smiled then. It was a smile that Darien would always remember, especially when he watched his friend in the act of seducing wide-eyed girls. Half-wondering if he should warn them.

For the first time Marlen faced Darien full-on, the shadows falling away. He said, "I told him I have more reasons to kill him."

He turned away, but not before Darien had seen the crusted red slash that crossed his friend's face from cheek to jaw. It took many weeks to heal. Now, remembering that day years later, Darien thought perhaps it never had. Marlen Humbreleigh carried a scar with him and within him and Darien had mistaken it for worldliness, for humor. He had joined Marlen in mocking the weaker students, the ones inept with irony. People like Lin's partner, Darien thought, who was no match for their games . . . their ferocity.

She had told him what had befallen Leander Keyen. He remembered now.

AT breakfast, Darien had allowed himself an hour to reminisce with the cook about old times. The only woman generally permitted in the castle, she was portly and middle-aged, her husband the head of the household staff. Like most women, she had always had a soft spot for Darien, always feared Marlen Humbreleigh just a little. She clucked sympathetically at Darien's story and gave him an extra cake for his pains. It tasted as he remembered: honey, cloves, and ginger.

She still smelled like onions, garlic, and sage; her kitchen was still warm and rich with smells both enticing and foul, herbs and raw meat and animal's innards thrown away as waste. He told her that he loved her, and she shooed him away with her wooden spoon.

The smells of the kitchens followed Darien as he descended deeper into the heart of the castle and toward its most subterranean chambers. He wondered why they chose to keep the books so far down, but he was grateful; this way, he could escape where it was quiet. Otherwise the sounds of the Academy aroused memories that distracted and saddened him. Echoing down the hall, a chorus of song; a class practicing with a traditional lay Darien knew well. The ageless solemnity of their voices catching in his heart like an arrow. Darien retreated down the stairs, and down.

He had been researching many areas of ancient practice, discovering scraps of lore. His teachers had mentioned portals only in passing, and none seemed to know how they were opened. As it turned out, the world was riddled with portals: some of these led to the Otherworld and its manifold dimensions, others to a place between—which was commonly experienced as a dream.

Darien read an account of a poet who in a dream had dined with a giant king and a host of eldritch servants at the king's table. He had feasted upon meat slathered in a thick red sauce and drunk many goblets of ale. And come morning when he awoke from his dream he was sated, dizzy, and red sauce stained his shirt.

The man with the *khave*, Darien remembered, grim. The dream that had led to Lin. He would have been willing to bet his own harp that on those two occasions he had passed through a portal, into the between-state the books described. But the ways to do that were few. And the deeper one sought to penetrate—to the Otherworld itself—the higher the price to be paid.

Darien scanned the story for some possible insight. Before his adventure with the portal, the poet had been a guest in a noble household and entertained his host with a song he had written about the kingdom of the giants. And that same night he had found himself in the gilded and massive great halls of the giant king, at the opulent abundance of a table laden with dishes of meats, pheasant, capon, duck. And of course, great quantities of ale and a wine that burned like sweet fire when the poet tasted it from his gem-encrusted goblet.

The giant congratulated him as they dined, saying, *"You carry my fame to all the world."* The feast was his reward.

But that was a tale, one that could easily have been invented by a poet and taken for history at a much later date. Such things happened. The book was replete with questionable material, superstitions and myths, the likes of which Darien had not heard since his grandmother died. She, who had been the first to urge him to become a poet. She had believed them all.

One phrase the books repeated often, until it was nearly a refrain: *There is much that we cannot know.*

Darien leaned back in his chair—stout wood and hard beneath him—and closed his eyes. He inhaled the thick odor of vellum and for a moment could understand why some might find it comforting: all the centuries that had passed, and still all this was here; would be here, by the blessing of Kiara, until world's end. The candle danced, enlivened by his breath. One other student worked at a table some distance from him, but each table was surrounded by a barrier, creating the illusion of privacy. It certainly served to make Darien feel isolated. He thought of Lin and then, inevitably, of Hassen and Marlen. So many more losses than gains.

Much that we cannot know.

"It must be recorded, for posterity!" an aged, fretful voice. Darien opened his eyes. He saw two men standing in the shadow of the stacks. One was small-boned, handsome but getting on in years, with extra weight around the middle. His hair was greying at the temples; his face struck Darien as profoundly weary.

The other man, the one who had spoken, was older, painfully thin, also bearded. Both men wore Academy rings.

"There is no reason for anything to be recorded, Tyler," said the tired-looking man. "It is just as well if no one ever finds it again."

That was when Darien noticed the gemstone on the man's ring. A moon opal.

The other man balled his hands into fists. "Edrien. What has happened to you?"

Edrien smiled, and for a moment looked less tired and more mischievous. "Every man must have his secrets."

Tyler's face was drooping in a frown, and when he spoke again his voice was nearly a whisper. "Don't you understand," he said. "You found the thing . . . the *one* thing that gives meaning to . . . all this." A wave of his hand took in the library and somehow seemed to include the entire castle, the Isle . . . and perhaps beyond that. "And now you mean to keep it to yourself."

"My friend," Edrien said, "there is meaning in all of this, and there is none at all. What I have seen—where I have been—it changes nothing. I have nothing, Tyler—only a silver branch, and that I took for a memory. A memory I do not even want. It is useless now." He turned away, as if he could not bear to look at the other man, or did not want him to see his face. "Can't you understand? We pay a price for everything."

"Edrien, is it true what people say?" Tyler said. "Is it true that you had a chance to bring the enchantments back?"

And suddenly Edrien looked neither old nor tired. His face hardened. "And where did you hear that?"

"Never mind," said Tyler, unmoved. "Is it true?"

Blue eyes simmering with anger, Edrien said, "I did not tell such a thing to a living soul. And I intend to never speak of it."

"You mean to conceal knowledge that Seers have been desperate to find, for centuries?"

"I do," said Edrien. He was calm now. "And what's more, it will die with me."

DARIEN awoke to find that his head was tipped back, straining his neck with a stabbing pain. Cursing, he straightened. The men were gone. So was the student who had been there earlier. He was alone, his breath the only sound in all that room. He was glad to see his candle still burned, much nearer the base now. Darien sighed and stretched. He wished Lin could assist him—she would thrive in the company of these deadly tomes. In contrast, Darien felt quite ready for his dinner and never wanted to see another book again in his life.

When he reached their room, it was empty. Lin had left a note on the back of their dinner invitation. *See you in the dining room.*

By the time Darien reached the masters' dining room, he was weary and ravenous. Still, he was alert enough to be surprised that the dinner was only for himself, Lin Amaristoth, and Archmaster Myre; nor was he too hungry to notice that the woman who stood with her hands resting on the back of a chair as she conversed with the Archmaster was a different Lin.

The dark blue velvet bodice of the dress she wore had been tailored to her frame, bringing out what slight figure she had. Brocade of blue and silver swelled from her waist and struck the floor in a rustling cascade. A dainty collarbone showed where the bodice left it exposed. She had washed her hair, and it curled softly around her ears from a plumed velvet cap of the same fabric as the bodice.

She seemed to be talking animatedly, though with composure, to the Archmaster, but fell silent when Darien entered. In her face he thought he detected vulnerability as she awaited his verdict, tacit or otherwise.

Darien found his voice. "Lady Kimbralin," he said, and bowed. "You look lovely."

Lin dropped her eyes. "You are kind to say so."

"So tell me, Archmaster," said Darien, "does that dress really belong to a noblewoman who was visiting and inexplicably left it behind, or does the High Master enjoy more privileges than I'm aware of?"

"Darien," said Lin sharply.

Archmaster Myre lifted his chin. His comportment was majestic as he seated himself at the head of the table. "I see you have not changed, Darien Aldemoor," he said. "I have done you a good turn, and you repay me with insult. It is no wonder that you have been brought to this pass, is it?"

Darien's first impulse was to return the thrust with a riposte of his own. Then he knew such behavior for the folly that it was. "I apologize, Archmaster Myre," he said. "It has been a wearying day, but that is no excuse."

"It is not," said the High Master.

Lin said, "I implore your forgiveness on Darien's behalf, Archmaster Myre. We have recently lost a friend."

Darien stared at her, for a moment angry that she would invoke Hassen for the sake of smoothing over a quarrel. Then he thought, *She only says what is true. Even I am not usually so much the fool.* He bowed his head.

"I will accept your apology, Lady Kimbralin," said the High Master. "Though I suspect your manners are superior to those of your companion—he has no doubt learned rough ways in the stews of Tamryllin and on the road. For your sake I will let this pass."

Old bastard, Darien thought. "I thank you," he said shortly, and was relieved when the food was brought in moments later.

As he shoveled mouthfuls of meat and vegetables into his mouth, Darien stole a glance at the girl across from him, who ate more demurely and with evidence of gentle upbringing. He marveled at the fact that this was the same girl he had gotten drunk in a tavern not long ago.

"Darien, Archmaster Myre and I were discussing the recent events in Tamryllin," said Lin, as their knives rattled against their plates. "The High Master has sensed that for some time now, Nickon Gerrard has been meddling with dark powers. But it is still secret among all but the innermost circle of the masters. There would be chaos and panic, otherwise."

"All Seers bear the same mark, and this binds us together forever after," said Archmaster Myre. "Even when a mark is broken, as in the case of Valanir Ocune, it cannot be undone."

Lin looked startled. "How did you know Valanir Ocune's mark was broken?"

The High Master's mouth crinkled slightly in what was not quite a smile. "Lady Amaristoth, think a moment. We are all connected—thus we felt it. All the Seers, of whom there are very few in these days.

Some twenty, most of them in Eivar, the rest scattered in the wide world."

"Does that mean you can tell what Court Poet Gerrard is doing?" Lin asked.

Archmaster Myre shook his head. "The connection is faint. We are made aware of it mostly in ways I cannot explain. And in dreams. But in ancient days, when our powers were real, a cadre of Seers joined together could be a terrible force."

"If that could happen again," Lin said slowly, "the enchantments brought back . . . doesn't that mean the Crown may once again see the Academy as a threat to be crushed?"

Archmaster Myre's pale eyes were unblinking. Darien noticed that he had barely touched his food. "She is quick," said the old man to Darien. "It is well that at least one of you is."

Lin said, "Archmaster Myre, Valanir Ocune has told us that Nickon Gerrard's use of forbidden magics is bringing a darkness to the world. The Red Death, and worse."

He closed his eyes. "I know."

"You mean he has told you?"

Now his eyes opened, trained coldly on her. "I mean in my darkest dreams I have seen it."

They completed the meal in silence. Darien thought Lin looked pale with worry. Yet she had carried the conversation until this point— had in some ways known how to communicate with Archmaster Myre better than Darien had.

It had been a mistake to imagine he knew her remotely well.

And Rianna Gelvan, how well did he know her?

It was with a new sense of disquiet that Darien followed Lin back to their room that night.

She wasted no time when the door shut behind them. "Did you find anything?" she asked. The room was dark, but for the glow cast by a candelabra set in the wall. Four candles, light playing softly on her face, the sleek velvet of the gown.

Darien rubbed his face and sat on his bed with a sigh. "Nothing important," he admitted. "Some bits about portals. And I had a strange dream when I . . ."

"Fell asleep?" Lin said dryly.

"You've got me there." In his mind he had been going over it since the library. "It may have been more than a dream, though I didn't think so right away." He recounted to her the exchange he had seen, or dreamed, between Edrien Letrell and the man named Tyler. "It is interesting," he said at last. "But even if it was not just a dream, I don't see how it helps us."

"Nor I," she said. "I'll give some thought to it during the endless time I seem to have these days, to think. Can you smuggle books to me?" She pulled off the velvet cap, ran a hand through the short waves of her hair.

"I suppose I could," said Darien. "But I don't see how we're to get anywhere this way."

"I know," said Lin. "If we could only figure out where to use the key. It has the Seers' mark upon it; it must be of this place." In the half-light he could see her mouth set in a thin line. "Damned Valanir Ocune." Businesslike, she began to unlace her bodice. Darien realized that he was staring. Turning away quickly, he had to smile; they had shared a room more than once, there was no reason it should be different now. A change of clothing should not make such a difference.

A song was forming in his head; only the merest outline, not yet the words. *My lady* . . . Pluck of a string, two strings against a backdrop of silence. A melancholy air. *My lady.*

He thought of Rianna Gelvan and how sweetly remote she had always been. The walls of the garden protecting her.

He glanced over his shoulder at Lin. She had changed into a knee-length shift that he had not seen before, lace-edged and clean. Another remnant of the mysterious noblewoman. She had bony knees and angular skinny calves, like a colt. "Lin."

She turned, and again he saw that vulnerability around the chin and eyes. "Yes?"

He inclined his head to indicate the bundle beside his bed—his harp, left sealed in its wrappings since he had left Tamryllin. "Do you mind if I play?"

She looked surprised. "Not at all."

In the silence of night, the sound of the sea made gentle music. The shape of the harp in his hands, the smooth warmth of the wood, was like returning to the embrace of a lost love. Darien sighed, his chin resting against the frame of the instrument he loved so well. It had been too long. A part of him had all this time been missing.

It was a private moment in a way, and he wished he was alone. Then he thought perhaps it did not matter. In her own way, Lin might understand. He felt her hungry gaze on him, his instrument. She wanted a harp more than anything, he realized. Perhaps when all this was over . . . His mind had trouble forming an image of how the end of all this would look. But he would be pleased if it happened to include Lin Amaristoth hale and smiling for once, and wearing a harp of her own.

"What shall I play?" he asked the air. One string, two strings in the silence; a song coming to him there in that moment, the waves singing melancholy counterpoint. It was the sound of all that had befallen him in the past months: the loss of one friend to betrayal, another lost because of him. Love waiting in the luminous city that had cast him out. And through it all, the songs. They had haunted him throughout this strange journey, sleeping and waking, begging to be written and released. He had a duty to transmute his losses, his grief, into the music that now danced through him.

"My lady," he sang, a new tune formed here from the night and candleflame, from the vulnerability in Lin's eyes and his memories of this place. "Swift the river flows, and with it all my hopes. My lady," he sang, and then found the line that had been eluding him, that his heart had been searching for all through their long journey. "Never shall we see such times again."

Lin echoed him, a sweet and unexpected harmony. "Never shall we see," her voice wavered, "such times again."

Knowledge came to him, diverting him a moment, though his fingers did not cease their playing. Not a surprise, rather of a weave with the fabric of the night itself. "You've had your own losses," he said. "I'm sorry."

She said, "Please keep singing."

New words and verses coming to him, a part of his brain storing it all away to be written later—written and rewritten until it was perfect. He sang now not only for himself, but for her. Candleflame, eyes dark with thoughts he could not read. A night in a tavern that seemed so long ago. Strange powers bringing them together, in dreams, toward an end he could not see. A ruthless tide had swept them both from all that they had known and loved.

It seemed a long time when at last he stopped. His mouth and throat were dry; his fingers ached. He looked over at the next bed and saw she lay stretched atop her coverlets, asleep. The neckline of the shift had slipped down to expose the pale skin of her chest, her small breasts still hidden. Darien set his harp carefully beside the bed. He rose, stretched to relieve his stiffened limbs, flexed his fingers. He came to the next bed and lifted Lin gently, and as she protested, eyes still closed, he slipped the coverlets from beneath her and covered her to the chin. She sighed when he set her down, snuggled into the thin pillow. Murmured a name, not his, too softly for him to hear.

HE walked down a dark hall, a candle in his hand. Doors before him: one, two, three—all of them shut. Trapped within the labyrinth of the corridors, a gust of wind was keening. *Not so easy to leave as it is to get here,* Darien thought. And the next moment wondered why.

The last thing he remembered was lying down to sleep. And now here he was. The symbols carved in the walls, reminiscent of the Seer's mark, were familiar to him. He was in the Academy, then, but could have been anywhere in the castle for all that he could tell in this dark.

All that remained to him, then, was to decide which way to go.

And then someone was with him; Darien could sense a new presence in the stillness of the hall. He turned sharply, candle raised. A tall, broad figure emerged from the shadows into the tremulous light.

Darien almost dropped the candle. "Hassen," he said hoarsely. "Are you . . . ?"

The big man put a finger to his lips. "Quiet now," he said. "Follow me." When Darien tried to speak again, to protest, Hassen Styr said with annoyance, "Darien, think. This is a dream." He strode to the second door, opened it, and vanished within.

Falling silent, Darien followed.

Torches burned here, illuminating a long, magnificent room. The high ceiling was decorated with intricate, arching scrollwork and carvings that cast strange shadows. Darien knew right away where he was. Down the center of the room stood marble pedestals, chin-high, in vertical rows. Atop each pedestal, a harp. They were in the Hall of Harps, where the instruments of the most celebrated poets throughout history were preserved and displayed. Where on a high dais before all, the Silver Branch cast its own light.

Hassen was standing by the door, watching Darien.

"Why did you bring me here?" said Darien. Not knowing what else to say. *This is a dream*, the man had said.

"I didn't," Hassen said. "I am only a vehicle here. You willed the powers to show you something, and here you are. You know, then, what you must do."

"But I don't," Darien muttered. He began walking between the pillars. Tried to focus, though the presence of Hassen unsettled him. Many harps here, even the one that had belonged to the founder of the Academy. Some truly exquisite pieces, as one would expect; gracefully carved willow wood polished to a brilliant sheen. Strings that Darien could only guess were of gold. He was tempted to touch them but knew that it was forbidden, and even he who rebelled at most rules found himself willing to respect that one.

And then he came to the harp of Edrien Letrell. It was weatherbeaten, though its owner had obviously shown it much care. There were nicks in the wood and most of the strings showed wear.

There was a quote etched into this pillar, just below the pedestal. Darien recognized it from one of Edrien's songs. *Sweet sings the wind by the shore. My heart finds peace here, beneath the great oak of my home.*

"I think I understand," Darien breathed. Even a breath seemed too loud in this room.

"There's a novelty," said Hassen Styr with the dryness Darien remembered. Darien turned, surprised, but his friend had vanished as suddenly as he had appeared.

I never had a chance to apologize, Darien realized. And in that moment, at least, his new discovery did not seem to matter.

"I'M not going to the library today," Darien told Lin the next morning. "I'm going outside. Want to come with me?"

Lin was already half into a dress, plainer than the one she had worn last night. It was still pretty, though—white with tiny pink flowers embroidered into it. Catching his eye, she wrinkled her nose and said, "Don't stare. I hate this dress." She shrugged her arm through a ruffled sleeve. "And yes, of course I'll come with you. I'd go to the gates of the Underworld by now if someone asked. But may I ask why?"

Quickly he recounted the dream of the night before, avoiding her eyes during the telling, focusing on his bootlaces as he fastened them. He didn't like to talk about it, but neither did he want to keep it a secret from her.

Lin sighed. He knew what she was thinking, and it irritated him. *He was my friend,* he thought. She had simply appropriated Hassen for several days, and it made her think her grief could be equal to his.

She said, "I'm sorry, Darien. I know it must be much harder for you than it is for me."

Thrown off-balance, Darien said, "That's all right," and finished lacing his boots.

He allowed her to pass before him as they left the room; it had been too long since he had had anything to do with a woman. Daylight was not kind to Lin, making her pale skin look sallow and her brown hair mousy rather than alluringly dark. But the bodice of her dress cinched in her waist attractively enough, and she did have hips, at least. Darien would take what he could get in this dismal, womanless castle. Such had been his philosophy during his days as a student, as well, though he had learned quickly enough that the prettier girls in the nearby village were as likely to be soft for him as the plain ones. Another reason, perhaps, that Piet had hated him.

It was without much of a strain on his memory that Darien led them to the great oak by the shore. It was a historic tree, and a popular haunt for lovelorn poets, dreaming away their sorrows under its boughs by the crystalline stillness of the bay. And of course, writing a song about it later.

"What do you expect to find here?" Lin asked.

Darien shook his head. "My lady, I have no idea." Then an idea occurred to him. A rock nestled within the base of the tree, and Darien knew it was exactly the sort of place where he himself would have hidden something. "Help me move this rock," he said.

Lin grasped one end of it as he took hold of the other, and together they wrenched it free. Lin inspected the tree as Darien rolled the rock away. He saw she was staring at the leaves and dirt that were clumped within the hole, stopping it up. "I suppose this wasn't the best idea," he said, looking from his own dirt-stained hands to Lin's soiled white dress.

"Don't be sure of that just yet," she said, and began to rake away the leaves and dirt with her fingers. But the dirt was thickly caked, so that she was forced to get a sharp stone to shovel it away.

"Want me to help there?" Darien said.

"The dress is ruined anyway," she said, and continued on. There was a feeling of rightness to all of it, Darien suddenly thought, as if he had dreamed this all before and knew the outcome. Her slight figure by the tree, kneeling in dirt, was something he seemed to remember. So Darien was not surprised when he heard a thump, just as Lin gasped and, in the next moment, lifted a small metal box from the base of the tree. A steel lock with the mark of the Academy clamped it shut.

"It's almost too easy," she said.

"Easier still," Darien said, "if that key of yours fits the lock."

Lin reached into her pouch and with dirtied fingers pulled out Valanir's key.

CHAPTER

23

IT was like something in a dream when the key clicked easily in the
lock and the box popped open without prompting. In later days,
Darien could not have said what he had expected it to contain. But
he could remember feeling no sense of surprise when what emerged
was a collection of old scrolls. This was, after all, the Academy. The
parchment crackled like flame as he unrolled it, and Darien could
almost imagine that it whispered secrets.

He set them back into the box and tightened the lid. "We had better take these to our room before someone notices us here."

Stumbling in their haste, they made their way back along the shore
to the castle. Darien experienced a moment of anxiety when they entered the courtyard, the box clutched to his chest, but they did not
meet anyone there, or on the stairs to their room.

They spread the sheets of parchment on his bed. The ink was
faded, the lines curled in a rounded, elaborate hand. Darien began to
read it aloud before he realized what it was, and stopped. They were
verses.

"There's a note here at the end," Lin said. *"These being the verses
which I used to enter the Otherworld. All but the final verse, which I have
kept to the grave, that no one will follow my path and pay a price that is
far too high."*

"*A price,*" Darien read, "*that I could not pay.*" It ended there, signed with the initial *E*. Darien grimaced. "He left us all but the last verse. What good is that?"

"He didn't mean for it to do us good," Lin said patiently. "He did not want anyone else to discover the Path."

"Yet he came up with—all these." Darien indicated the verses spread before them. "He somehow knew how to summon that portal."

Lin nodded. "We can't know how they came to him," she said. "But perhaps it was very like the way these scrolls have come to us."

"*There is much that we cannot know,*" Darien quoted with a sigh. "I'm growing tired of hearing that. It seems as if we're no better off now than when we started."

"There's more here," said Lin, gesturing at the pages that remained. "These look newer than Edrien's verses, and they're in a different hand." She began to read the headers of each. "*Rite of Enchainment . . . Rite of Joining . . . Rite of—*" She swallowed.

"*Of Summoning the Dead,*" Darien finished for her. "This seems very forbidden indeed."

"Some of it," said Lin. "Some may not be . . . just lost. I believe I know what these are. Valanir Ocune told me he and Nickon Gerrard worked to transcribe some of the old magics from encoded texts. Valanir must have hidden them here."

"That must be why he didn't tell you what the key was for," Darien said, feeling grim. "He couldn't risk such a secret coming out to the Court Poet under torture. I'm guessing he enchanted himself to silence."

Lin ran a hand through her hair and grimaced. "And all this time, I was irritated with him. Of course."

"Glad I could put an end to *that* lover's quarrel," said Darien.

"I think I'll go for a walk," said Lin, without changing expression. She rose and left before he could think of a reply. From the window, the air had turned chilly even though it was afternoon, the rough winds abated.

* * *

ALL that day, Darien felt the nagging sensation that he had done something wrong. It pursued him through his tedious exploration of the library, which, as usual, yielded crumbs of information that fell just short of being useful. *Damn Lin,* he thought. Damn the girl's touchiness, her moods. He couldn't help it if he was unable to be sensitive to her all the damn time.

More than ever, he missed Hassen, who would simply have punched him and gotten it over with.

He was in my dream, Darien mused. *Maybe that's a good sign.*

Her granite eyes and flat tone had made him uncomfortable. Most women reproached, or cried; even that was better. Then again, those were usually women Darien had seduced, who felt that he had a duty toward them. Darien was proud that in his long career with women, he had made many more laugh than cry.

It occurred to him that he had promised Rianna he would write her, an idea that now seemed like bridging one world to another. What would he tell her? *I have seen things you would not believe.* Exhilaration warring with the knowledge that, regardless of the thrill of what he had glimpsed—the world outside his world that he had touched—the price had already been far too high.

Unsurprisingly, he found nothing on the last verse of the song Edrien Letrell had composed to enter the Otherworld. He leafed through works by Edrien that had been scrivened just before the poet's death but found nothing that looked like a detached verse, let alone one the culmination of possibly the most powerful song ever written.

It will die with me, the Seer had said.

HE returned to the room that evening after an extended visit to the kitchen, full of a warm glow of well-being brought on by the combined powers of adoration and good food. The cook had fed him a kingly meal after he had sung some silly songs for her. At the end, he took some bread and meat for Lin, in case she had not yet had her supper. Perhaps his obvious thoughtfulness would be noted, and she would put aside her grievance. It had been such a harmless comment, after all.

Stars were kindled in the dimming sky by the time Darien arrived at the room. Lin was standing by the window, looking out into that sky and the mountains. In the gloaming her white dress seemed to beckon eerily, like the mast of a ship at sea.

Sucking in his breath, Darien resolved to swallow his pride. "Lin, I really am sorry," he said. Resisting the urge to add: *Be reasonable.*

Without turning, she said, "What do you have against me, Darien?"

A good question, when it came to that. He had still thought to blame her for abandoning Hassen, but could not. In his heart he knew that had he gone after his friend, neither of them would be here. "Nothing," Darien said. "I'm just a bastard. Not a good excuse, but I hope you'll forgive me." He cleared his throat. "Afraid I didn't find anything that interesting today. How was your walk?"

She was silent, still not turning to look at him. Darien came up behind her and touched her shoulder, gingerly. She turned to face him then, and there were tears on her face.

"What is it?" he said, suppressing his first instinct, which was to draw back in alarm.

She shrugged and looked away.

"Is this about that poet you mentioned in our meeting with the masters?" Darien said, pressing. "What was the name? Alyndell?"

Lin dashed away the tears and refused to answer. Darien noticed for the first time, even in the fading light, that black dirt had stained the front of her bodice and skirt. But of course—she had practically waded through dirt to retrieve Valanir's worthless box for them.

"You should change," he said, indicating the bodice and skirt, where stains marred the white, the sweet feminine embroidery.

She laughed without merriment. "Indeed."

"I'll turn around," said Darien. "I'll look away, and you'll change, and you'll tell me what happened to you. Why you ran away."

"Why should I tell you?"

"Why not tell someone?" True to his word, he sat on his bed with his back to her.

"You'll mock me," she said, sounding tired.

"No," he said. "I won't."

He heard a rustling—the sound of her unlacing the bodice. She said, "He was my tutor. I was expected to be educated to some degree, you see. It's required of a lady."

"So I've heard," Darien said equably. "And you fell in love with him."

"We shared a bed for a season." She had not spoken of this recently; he could hear it in her voice. Perhaps ever. "Rayen didn't know. With our parents dead, Rayen was my guardian until I was to be wed. He had a number of suitors in mind and wanted time to judge the merits of them all. Or he liked having me around to torment—I'm not sure."

"Torment?"

A brief silence, then, "I have a scar from one of those times."

He had seen it, a white line slashed across her left palm.

"You must have known he would find out," Darien said.

The tiredness had returned to her voice. "Alyn had promised we would run away together when . . . when the time was right. Instead . . ."

"Rayen found you together?"

"No . . . no, not that. Though that would have amused him." She swallowed, said, "He found out, because I was soon with child. The moment he saw me taking sick one day, he knew. He knew right away." A pause, then, "In a way, we know each other so well." He heard a rustling again, the sharp report of the wardrobe swinging shut. "You can turn around."

Darien did. She was clad now in the lace-edged shift she had worn to sleep the night before. Lowering herself onto her bed, hair tousled, pale legs and feet exposed to moonlight, she looked like a very young girl. He had never asked her age.

"So let me guess," Darien said. "This Alyn was a coward and ran away, rather than face the consequences."

"No," she said. "I would have understood that, though. But, apparently, Rayen knew him better than I did. He gave Alyn a choice:

my hand, with me disinherited from the Amaristoth holdings. Or gold."

"And he took the gold," Darien guessed.

She bowed her head.

"And the child?" he said. It almost pained him to ask.

Lin looked up to meet his eyes. "Beaten out of me." In the silence, she spoke again. "I knew then what a fool I'd been, in any case. Believing that a beautiful man could love . . . someone like me."

Darien was starting to regret he had urged her to talk about this. "Hush," he said. "That's nonsense."

Lin shook her head. She held up a hand, as if to forestall him. "Please," she said. Her arms were wrapped around her stomach. "It is such a sordid little tale. And it becomes so clear, when I tell it, what a fool I was."

"The fool was this Alyndell character," said Darien. "Because if I ever meet him, I promise you, I'll kill him for you."

A moment of silence. Lin laughed.

"You don't think I could do it?"

She was grinning, a heartening sight to him now. It was very dark now, but for the moonlight. "I'm sure you could," she said. "Alyn was common-born, didn't know one end of a sword from another. But while it's dear of you to offer to avenge me, I'm fairly sure he fled the country. He vanished the day he accepted his gold, probably fearing Rayen would come after him. Which he probably would have, for sport. Hunt-the-poet. It would have been his style." In uttering the idiot man's name, her smile had faded. Her voice seemed to go on with effort, as if stretching a skein of wool as far as it would go and then stretching it some more. It was a desire, he saw, to make light of this pain, to consign it to the past. He saw that she had not succeeded, not yet.

There are some things that a poet knows.

"Lie down," he ordered.

"Why?" Lin said, instantly suspicious.

"Don't be silly," said Darien. "You're safe with me."

She quirked a half smile. "All right."

"Get under the covers," Darien instructed. He meanwhile released his harp from its wrappings. Cradling it in his arms, he sat on the floor beside Lin's bed. "I'll sing you a bedtime story," he said, and strummed lightly. The familiar movements, the music in that stillness, filling him with peace. A tune from his childhood that he remembered and loved, albeit with a measure of sadness now.

Her face was soft in the moonlight. She closed her eyes.

SHE had thought of Alyn all that day, strolling along the shore and picking her way over the roots of trees young and old. He had told her so much of this place. She had begged him to teach her the ways of poets, everything he knew. There had not been time, of course, for everything, but there was much that she did know. They had had a year.

She had felt him with her the night of the Midsummer Ball. Alyn had schooled her for such occasions, in the formalities that a poet must know. All but the most secret ceremonies, such as how a poet must conduct himself while receiving the mark of a Seer. That, she realized, he probably had not known himself. After meeting so many poets, Lin now knew that handsome as Alyn had been, his voice liquid silver, he was by no means among the best the Academy had produced. It was likely that he would never become a Seer.

So he had sought to ease his future with a marriage vastly above his station, and when that failed, simply the gold. And who could blame him?

And it had been so easy. She had made it easy. *Liquid silver.* It had been summer; he had first taken her in the forest to the sounds of awakening birdsong in the pines.

"You should thank me," Rayen had said, weeks after Alyn had gone, when she still lay recovering from the loss of the child. She had incurred three broken ribs and assorted bruises from Rayen's concentrated pummeling.

Lin remembered: lying motionless in the bed, her thoughts, mercifully, still too much a blur of pain to focus on any one thing. Even

Rayen's face, familiar to her as her own, a mirage that floated in and out of her field of vision. For so long she had lied to him, lived apart from him in a world of happiness of her own, that now he seemed almost a stranger.

"I saved you from an adventurer who wanted nothing but your gold," Rayen had said. At the time, the words had not fully penetrated, but her mind had stored them away for later. Repeated them many times since. "And you, poor filly, thought he wanted what's between your legs."

She had screwed her eyes shut then, she remembered, as if by not seeing him she could will him into nonexistence.

He continued relentlessly, his voice like silk. The same voice she could imagine him using to seduce his yellow-haired paramours. "Don't ever make that mistake, pet," he said. "The next time you think such a thing possible, look in the mirror. I'll have a new one made, full-length, of finest silver-backed glass, if that is what it takes to save our fortune. I don't want to be throwing any more gold away on useless lovers. Or physicians." He sucked in his breath and let it go, what he did when mildly exasperated. "I'll have to bribe this one to keep silent, on top of his fee. No one would want used goods."

Weeks later, when she had recovered the use of her limbs, Lin ran. Imagining, then, that death was not far off. But for the warmth of Leander's cloak and his words, that might have turned out to be true: a debt she owed her former partner that she would probably never have a chance to repay. In any case, so much had been marred between them: their trust broken, and his body, because of her.

But the portal was real. Edrien had found it, had summoned it with his song. That was one thing that had not been marred. The Path was real.

That was the last clear thought that passed through her mind as she lay wrapped in the strands of Darien's song. His sung words echoing from the stones, backed by the strains of ocean waves. *You're safe with me*, he had said to her. She let herself drift, trusting that—trusting his music.

* * *

SHE was clad in a dark velvet dress, diamonds woven into her long hair. The bedroom she stood in was familiar—too familiar. From the window, a forest encased in ice that glimmered as if to echo the dead stones in her hair. *Not here*, Lin thought in a panic. *Please not here.*

But when the door opened, it was not Rayen who stepped through. "Do not fear," said Valanir Ocune. "I don't know why the portal chose this place . . . perhaps it was in your thoughts tonight."

"Valanir," she said with a sigh, and her fists unclenched themselves. She hated the weight of the dress, the way the boning of the corset cut short every breath. She was attired as if for a ball, some occasion where she would be presented before the nobility like a prize mare, praised over cool gold wine—disingenuously, and for all the wrong things.

"You found the scrolls," he said. "We must talk. There isn't much time."

Lin noticed that the Seer was solid here, not transparent as he had been at the inn in Dynmar.

"You and Nickon Gerrard were thorough in your work," she said. "But the thirteenth verse—"

"Is lost," said Valanir. "But Lin, you have it in you. This I know. Or you *will* have it in you, when all is as it is destined to be."

"Your visions are incomplete, *Erisen*," she said, turning away from him. "Else perhaps we could have saved Hassen Styr." Spires of frosted pine outside the window glittered a thousand memories, few of them good.

"You're angry with me."

"I don't know how to trust you," said Lin.

"His fate will forever be on my conscience," said Valanir. "You must believe that."

She turned to look at him again. "Very well," she said. "Speak. What have you to tell me?"

"I can't be sure of this, mind," said Valanir Ocune. "But I believe— based on my research, and the visions I have had with the aid of

Kahishian magic—that the key to the thirteenth verse is in the Tower of the Winds. There is some—transformation there, that awaits you."

"The Tower of the Winds," she said. "The place where songs are made."

"Night after night, for hundreds of years, poets have sat each in a stone-carved cell and created verse," said Valanir.

"Each by light of a single candle," said Lin, recalling her own efforts to re-create that experience for herself, in this very room. She looked to her bed, saw that the blankets were still tumbled upon it, as if she had only just risen from a night of dark dreams.

"Yes," said Valanir. "Think of it—for centuries, poets and Seers calling forth their songs from the night. By now there is a sacredness to the place. If a temple of worship for the Seers existed, it would be the Tower. If I am right, reciting the twelve verses there will open the portal."

"I will need Darien's help," Lin mused. "The Masters would never allow it."

"You must do it tonight," said Valanir. "The stars are positioned in our favor. Once you have opened the portal, I will sense it, and join with you. You won't be alone."

"You make it sound so simple," said Lin.

"Hardly," said Valanir. "We already lost a good man. I pray we will not lose more." He took a step toward Lin, let his hand drift in her hair. "Whatever happens tonight, Lin . . . you have done well."

She caught his hand in a firm grip. "Valanir, if you want me to trust you, explain this: how can it be that *I* am the one in your vision? I am no one."

He regarded her hand a moment. "You are someone," he said. "I don't know how or why. But I fully expect before long, you will show me. Show all of us."

Lin woke with a start to someone pounding on the door.

DARIEN saw Lin had drifted into sleep when a sharp knock at the door brought both of them scrambling to their feet. Wide-eyed, Lin drew the coverlet about herself as Darien opened the door. It was Darien's old teacher, Archmaster Hendin, looking solemn. Darien gripped the old man's arm. "What is it?" A tightness in his stomach. Nothing short of an emergency could bring the old man to their door at such an hour as this.

"I'm sorry, Darien," the man said. "We've received word from Tamryllin. Hassen Styr is dead."

Dimly, Darien heard Lin choke behind him. "No," he heard himself say dully. So useless. All he could think was that all the world had hung suspended in the moment before the Master had spoken, and was now altered irrevocably. The night and its blanketing peace stolen away.

"There is more." Lin's voice behind him. "Isn't there, Archmaster Hendin?"

Darien recalled in that instant that the Archmaster had been Hassen's teacher. He saw then what he had been too shocked to see before: tears in the old man's eyes. "Yes," said the Archmaster. "Yes, there is more. It is being put about that—that you killed him, Darien. To work enchantments with his blood."

"Enchantments with his blood," Darien repeated, dazed.

"Yes," said Archmaster Hendin. "Blood divination, the oldest and darkest of the enchantments. Lord Gerrard is saying that you've attempted it."

"This is—this is much bigger than the original charges," said Lin. "Darien, he must think you're very dangerous. It must mean we're close."

Darien closed his eyes. "What matters that?" he said through his teeth. "They killed Hassen. *He* did."

"It matters," the old man said, "because it appears the Court Poet believes you might find the Path. And will stop at nothing to prevent your finding it."

Darien nodded, taking this in. "Then it's simple," he said. "We must stop at nothing to find it."

Lin tripped toward him, her feet tangling in the concealing blankets. "Darien, Hassen knew where we were going," she said. "They might have got it out of him. They might be on their way here right now."

Darien found himself moving very quickly, yet smoothly, as if through water. He shoved her, hard, so she had to catch herself on a chair to keep from falling. "Don't ever say something like that again," he said. "Hassen was my friend, and he was no traitor."

"Darien!" Archmaster Hendin said. He shook his head. With an abrupt turn, he departed the room.

Lin turned away, too. "I'm getting dressed," she said. Her voice reedlike, as if someone held a knife to her windpipe. Then she turned back to him, met his gaze steadily. "If you are wise, you will ready yourself to leave," she said. "Not for my sake. For theirs." She inclined her head in the direction of the doorway and the departing Archmaster.

"Very well," said Darien. It was sinking in, along with Hassen's death, what he had done. "Lin—I should not have done that. I'm sorry."

She turned away without answering. Not troubling to warn him before she grasped the hem of her shift and flipped it over her head, as if he were not in the room. He caught sight of a bony back and hips before he turned away.

"I had a dream of Valanir Ocune," she said as she dressed. "We need to get to the Tower of the Winds. You must take me there."

"I really am sorry," he said.

"Shut up, please," said Lin. "This is important. He believes that with the verses in the Tower, we can open the way to the Path. And now there is very little time."

Darien nodded. "Let's be off, then."

Lin strode to the door and opened it. And was instantly seized by the wrist by what felt like a steel clamp. With a shout, Lin drew her dagger and slashed at what had to be a hand. She heard a strangled cry in the shadows of the hallway as her arm was released, and then Darien was beside her in the doorway, sword drawn. Lin saw the glimmer of steel in the moonlight that streamed into the corridor, a face that contorted in pain above the shining path of Darien's sword. He withdrew it immediately, reeling back. A body tumbled to the floor with a crash, armored and liveried in the red and black of the king's guard. Blood was already puddling beneath the corpse and sinking between the stones of the tiled floor.

They stared at each other in shock.

Lin breathed, finally, "They're here."

Darien seized her arm and together they ran down the corridor. Pulled beside him, trying to keep up, Lin forced out, "What are you doing? They'll be everywhere."

"Not where we're going," said Darien. She stared at him. He returned her gaze with a wild grin. "To be honest," he said, "I'm a little offended that they only sent one to get us. But there will be"—he caught his breath—"more downstairs."

At that moment, he plunged down a stairway that had materialized before them. "Then why are we going downstairs?" Lin demanded.

He didn't answer, and she had no choice but to follow, trying to move quickly without taking a tumble down the treacherously smooth, narrow steps. They seemed to descend forever, skimming past three floors and descending still lower, until at last the moon was lost and they were plunged in darkness. But she could hear a metallic commotion in the halls upstairs. "Where are we going?"

"Hush," he said. "They might hear us. Trust me."

At last they reached the end of the staircase. Torches burned here, and in their light, Lin could see no other stairs. The walls here did not appear to be cut stone, but living rock as in a cave. It occurred to Lin that they had reached the deepest part of the castle.

Her heart fluttering, she said, "Where are we, Darien?"

As if in answer, two robed figures emerged into the light. Students, both of them must have been, for they were young; but in their eyes Lin could see some measure of age and acquired wisdom. Not beginning students, then, but men who had learned the ways and secrets of this place, or some of them.

"Good morrow," Darien said pleasantly. "My companion and I seek passage." He held up his ring, still attached to its thong about his neck.

"You may pass," said one of the men. "But a woman may not set foot on the planks of these boats. You know the laws."

"To be honest," Darien said, his voice still smooth, "I don't give a damn about the laws. I'll slit your throat if you try to stop her coming with me." He raised his blade. The blood of the guardsman shone slick in the dim light. "I've already killed a man tonight."

The men stood still and silent, as if his words had possessed the power, like that of Davyd Dreamweaver, to turn them to figurines of stone. At last one of them said, "Break this law, and a curse will fall upon you."

Lin felt a thrill of foreboding. In this place beneath the earth, one could believe such things were true. In a night already soaked with death—of Hassen, of the guard they had killed.

Darien seemed to feel it too; he shivered slightly. He said, "So be it, then."

Gripping Lin's arm, Darien strode past them without another word. She followed, not sure whether to laugh or weep. It was wrong: Darien was a soul of light and music—not murder, not blood. His smile at the students had seemed bloodstained to her.

They came to a portcullis, beyond which the torches revealed dark, still water. An underground entrance to the lake. Darien silently worked the mechanism that raised the portcullis as Lin lowered herself into the boat. He joined her moments later, looking tired.

"So much for the Tower," he said. "So much for the Path. So much for all of that."

"Would you have killed those boys?" she said as they each grasped an oar.

He shook his head. "There was no need."

"The curse . . ."

"It's probably nonsense," said Darien, rubbing his eyes. Ahead was enough moonlight to see the black outline of the banks upon the water. He said, "If I had left you behind, they would have taken you."

"I know," Lin said quietly. No more was spoken between them as they rowed. They had lost the night's peace, the song that had been cut off so abruptly. Everything they had worked for had come to this: shadows on black water. It seemed to her that Hassen Styr was a presence in the boat, as if they rowed him to the Underworld. Or as if there was still something more, something they did not yet know of, to be done.

CHAPTER
24

A TINY new cut, like the prick of a needle, had blossomed on the joint of her left thumb. Raw, red skin had already cracked over Rianna's knuckles; blood oozed thinly into the grey water where she plunged each dish.

The sleeves of the man's shirt she wore were rolled up to the elbow, her arms and elbows also beginning to show signs of red and cracking. She gritted her teeth against the burning sensation that had come to seem almost commonplace. The first few days, she had paused occasionally to gape at the destruction of her smooth skin, only to be reprimanded for "mooning."

Irma had done her a favor by taking her on, and would certainly not let her forget it. The busty, sharp-eyed innkeeper had wasted no time assessing Rianna as useless, but said she felt sorry for her. She had been fooled not a whit by the masculine guise, yanking off Rianna's cap that first day to crow over the tumble of long gold hair, dulled and dusty with a week's worth of travel. An animal's mane, the innkeeper said, was better cared for.

A week had passed since that humiliating day, and Rianna was becoming accustomed to the grinding mindless rhythm that dishwashing entailed. It was constant: there was no surcease of plates and bowls and tankards and pots that needed to be rinsed or scoured. She stood hour after hour by a tub filled to the brim with water afloat with pearly suds, soap that was relentless both on the dirt and on her skin. At first she had been disgusted at the thought of scraping plates and bowls with half-eaten remains of mash and bones, and even more disgusted at the thought of plunging her own hands into a tub with them hour after hour. But by now, disgust seemed like a luxury, and her prevailing feeling, throughout the day, was the longing simply to sit and rest her legs. She was given three meals of bread and cheese a day, and she looked forward to each not for the food but for the simple act of sitting. But she dared not complain—one wrong word to Irma, early on, had taught her that. The woman had struck her on the behind with her spoon, as if she were a child, and barked that she'd be out the door if another word was spoken.

Hating Irma as she did, Rianna did realize that she had been fortunate. Matters had taken a turn for the worse soon after her flight from Tamryllin: the wagon driver had discovered her within hours— stowed within the secret compartment beneath the crates of oranges— and demanded a fee in return for the continued journey, and his silence.

Soon after the contest, Master Gelvan had taken Rianna aside, showing her the secret exit from the kitchen out into the garden he'd built shortly after the death of his wife. In case of need. He had refused to explain what that meant. Now Rianna could only wonder if her father had foreseen, or at least had some intuition of, his own arrest.

The fee the wagon driver demanded was exorbitant, costing Rianna all the coin she had taken from her father's stores. But they had been in the midst of windswept hills that stretched for miles in all directions, and he had threatened to throw her out right there. Rianna still had nightmares about all that emptiness, of being lost in it. She had paid him.

She could not tell him that she was Master Gelvan's daughter, not with the merchant in prison. At least she hoped he was alive, in prison. But that was one of the thoughts she avoided.

So she had sat beside him right above the horses as the wagon lurched and jounced, and the driver—whose job was a lonely one— regaled her with tales of his drinking exploits in various villages, and of his strapping sons and daughters. Once, perhaps when he had tired of the sound of his own voice, he had said, "You're a quiet one, aren't you?" Rianna shrugged. Too many words and he might guess that she was a girl. It was the beginning of a regret that she would come to know well: the necessity for caution, even when need was strong. She wanted to confess everything, to this man who claimed to have children of his own. But something held her back. Maybe it was that he had been willing to extort money from a thin boy or leave him to the mercy of the road, or maybe she had learned—perhaps from Marlen Humbreleigh's betrayal—the deadly consequences of trust.

With barely any money and no idea what to do next, Rianna had asked the wagon driver to direct her to Dynmar's inn. There she had found out that she could not afford to buy even the most modest of the meals, let alone lodging, and it could perhaps be considered luck that Irma had discerned her horror and taken an interest. Within moments, Rianna was hustled into the kitchen and set to work, with the promise of food, lodgings, and a tiny wage for each day ringing in her ears. Her life of a serene house and wind chimes was a dream washed away. Her days were simple, reduced, as if viewed through a keyhole: she washed dishes from dawn to dusk and slept—or tried to sleep—on a thin pallet on the floor of the kitchen. A kitchen boy slept there too, on a pallet nearby, and tended the fire. He and Rianna did not speak much, but she was grateful that he let her alone.

Irma wasted no time telling Rianna that she would have been eaten alive if left to herself on the streets of Dynmar. Seeing the sorts of men who blustered into the inn every day for food and especially drink, the quick and battered lives they led, Rianna realized this was true. The dawn she had once loved to watch break over the rooftops of Tamryllin, which had seemed a renewal of hope, she now realized was nothing more than the mechanism of a returning sun that had no care for the people on earth or their dreams. It was all withering away: the promise of love she had shared with Darien Aldemoor, the image she had entertained of herself—only half-consciously—as the remote and immaculate Snow Queen. The image she had seen reflected in Darien's eyes. Now she was a kitchen maid, lower even than a kitchen maid, with her once-smooth skin turned scaly red and her muscles aching all over, all day. And all for the purpose of earning passage back to Tamryllin, which she no longer felt was home. She would be a fugitive when she returned and forced to seek protection with Ned Alterra's family. Ned, she knew, would not begrudge her; but she thought it cruel to him nonetheless.

But now, seeing what it meant to be in a strange town alone, Rianna knew she had no chance of finding Darien Aldemoor on her own. It had been an idiot plan. And sometimes, amid the perpetual motion and fatigue and ache in her legs, she felt a pang of fury at her lost love. *You left me,* she thought, addressing his handsome face in her mind's eye.

"Too slow, Leya," the cook barked at her. Rianna had given her middle name when asked. "We need more tankards, and we don't need them now. We needed them an hour ago."

"Then I'll stop washing plates, and then we won't have enough of those," Rianna retorted.

Quicker than Rianna could see it coming, the cook boxed her ear. Rianna reeled back, wet hands clasped to her head to halt the rattling pain. It didn't work.

"Don't ever backtalk me," said the older woman. "Or I'll see to it that you're out on the street—yes, no matter what Irma says. We don't need an overly pretty, uppity dishwasher here. You're here only because Irma has a soft heart, and for no other reason. I'd as soon get someone who knows her place, like the last one did before she fell pregnant."

The humiliation was worse than the pain, as it had been when Irma had slapped her with a spoon. Rianna could do no more than avert her face to conceal her flush, the sudden stinging tears that she would not shed. Not with everyone watching.

The serving girls had taken in this scene with avid interest. She had seen the hostility in their eyes from the moment Irma had released her hair from its cap, even though she wore it bound in a knot ever since. These were girls whose matted hair had never been cared for as Rianna's was, whose meager diets had never allowed for the shine she took for granted. There was a world behind the world she knew; she had not known it until now.

One thing sustained her. Her face became a cold mask as she thought, *Soon I will be quit of this life*. Her eyes slid to the woman who had berated her moments earlier, mechanically chopping meat and humming tunelessly. Rianna looked away, thought, *You, you will stay in it forever*.

Plenty of heroines from the stories she knew so well had fallen upon hard times, had had to work for their bread. There was no shame in that. If she could keep in mind those tales, she could yet maintain her pride. *I will come out of this,* she thought. The copper a day that she earned from dishwashing she hid each evening inside the pallet upon which she slept. Thirty coppers would earn her passage to Tamryllin. And perhaps when she returned, she would discover that it had all been a mistake: Master Gelvan had done nothing wrong.

If this new life had taught her anything, it was that pride was sometimes an obstacle to survival. She could afford to put it aside, at least for a time.

One thing she would not compromise upon, and that was cleanliness. The heroines of tales, she was sure, did not smell like stale sweat or have black ridges under their fingernails. Rianna had learned to bathe before dawn, drawing the water herself and warming it on the kitchen fire. Otherwise, the serving girls and the cook would crowd about and make lewd comments about her body, how well-fed she looked.

"Does that look to you," one of the serving women smirked, "like someone who has ever known a man's touch? Maybe we should introduce her to some of the boys." She meant the regular customers, who pinched the bottoms of the serving girls black and blue and groped under their bodices with dirty hands. Rianna was not often enough in the common room to observe for herself—she kept closely to the kitchen—but she heard the tales.

"A little doll," another woman mocked as Rianna hastily covered herself, biting her lip almost hard enough to draw blood.

Soon I will be quit of this life. Two weeks meant fourteen coppers, which meant that she needed sixteen more. Sixteen days. And today it was nearly dusk, and so fifteen. Very soon.

Another seven days had passed—another seven coppers—when it happened again. One of the larger girls, with a leering laugh, said as Rianna was bathing, "Maybe we should introduce her to the boys," and made a lewd gesture. Rianna said, "Do that, and I'll cut off his manhood and cook it for your dinner." And even as the girl recoiled, surprised, Rianna went on with, "That would get rid of some of the diseases you could get from eating cock—though it's too late for you, isn't it?"

It was known that the girl was given to pleasuring the inn's customers for extra coin. She reddened and turned away, muttering imprecations.

One of the other girls said, "You're not going to get away with that, Leya," before they left her to bathe alone.

No longer the Snow Queen, she thought, imagining what her father or Darien would think if they had heard her filthy words—weapons obtained from the enemy. If she kept her thoughts steered away from those she loved, she could survive, using whatever weapons came to hand.

THEY came for her that night—five of them. Two held her legs, one twisted her arms behind her back, one stopped her mouth with a rag. That left the fifth, who wielded shears, with a laugh Rianna knew. She struggled in the silence and dark. But for the one laugh, it happened quietly. The shears made short work of Rianna's hair, but the girl who used them took her time, until Rianna felt the cold blades on her scalp. Scraping off anything that remained.

When it was done, they tossed her hair in the hearth, beside which the kitchen boy either still slept or made every pretense of it.

After they'd gone she lay shivering so hard her teeth rattled. Tears channeled silently down her face in the dark. She thought of running away. Then she thought of the perils of Dynmar and the money she needed and knew there was nowhere to go.

There was nothing left of her now. Each gold coil that had snaked to the floor was a piece of her story falling away, Leya the kitchen maid replacing Rianna Gelvan at the last. And kitchen maids had no prominent part in any tale. She was no heroine, then, but a cipher, and had been so all along.

When Irma saw her the next day, she said, "I see. It may be for the best." Rianna even understood. Now she was one of them. While the other girls avoided her gaze from then on, they no longer seemed hostile. A girl named Bella helped Rianna tie a rag around her head that first morning, to conceal her shame. Drained and sad-eyed, Bella seemed to have few opinions, but she did say, "They should not have done that." Rianna took to sleeping with her knife close at hand, but no one disturbed her nights again.

In the days that followed, she was consumed with a feverish energy. Each day was no more than a number. She ignored the women who had attacked her; they were nothing, less than nothing. She gave no thought to her father's face, to Ned's hurt; she did not even think of Darien. She thought only in numbers: six more days. Five. Four.

It was when she had three more days that she first saw Rayen Amaristoth in the inn's common room. Shocked, Rianna retreated to the kitchen. He had not seen her, and even if he had—she doubted he would know her. She had no mirror here, but she knew she was hideous. Her shirt was nearly in tatters, and holes had worn through her trousers at the knees. Only three more days, and she would earn her own freedom; there was no need to allow the handsome Rayen Amaristoth, who once had attempted to woo her, to see her reduced to this.

So from then on, Rianna was even more zealous than she had been previously about avoiding the common room, leaving the kitchen only at dawn and in deep night to draw water from the well. Her efforts were successful: she did not see Rayen again.

One more day. She awoke joyful and with a sense that perhaps she had been wrong; there could still be a story left for her. She had survived a month of purest misery, had at last reached her goal. She could even believe that when she returned to Tamryllin, it would all have been a misunderstanding, and Master Gelvan would be waiting for her at the house. "*I was so worried,*" she could imagine him saying. Of course it had all been a mistake.

But two things happened on that day. The first was that the kitchen boy had finally wearied of his duties and fled the inn, leaving them without a kitchen boy to keep the fire stoked and sweep the ashes from the hearth. The other thing, related to the first, was that he had seen fit to finance his departure by stealing every last copper from inside Rianna's pallet as she slept.

Rianna's first instinct was to leap at the girl who had used the shears on her, grip her around the shoulders, and press her knife against her throat. "My hair not enough for you?" she hissed. "I swear I will spit you on this like a rabbit."

The girl's eyes rolled up in their sockets in her terror; she looked as if she might faint on the spot. "I swear I don't have it," she shrieked. "I swear. I swear. I swear."

Weeping, Rianna shoved her brutally away and jammed the knife into her boot. She had known, really, that the girl had not taken her money. Only the kitchen boy had known where it was, and it was too great a coincidence that both he and her money had vanished at the same time. And while she had entertained fantasies of carving out this girl's eyeballs and feeding them to her—startlingly vivid ones, in fact—the consequences would not be worth the satisfaction.

Rianna's eyes were blinded with tears as she left to draw water. Yet even so, she wondered later if it was truly because she could not see that she found herself stumbling into Rayen Amaristoth and in a shaky voice begging his pardon. For if it had happened because she was blinded, she could have scurried away before he recognized her: so thoroughly had she transformed into Leya the kitchen maid. But she stopped to apologize, aware that he might know her voice. And so the events set in motion that evening were, she was to know for always, her own doing; hers alone.

CHAPTER
25

LATER, Rianna would recall the moments that followed as a muddle of images, and in her memory she could stop each moment short, examine it from all angles. Rayen Amaristoth's face turned toward her with a start, eyes narrowing. A hand rising to his jaw as the realization struck. "Rianna?" he said, the first time she had heard him sound uncertain. His arms fell to his sides.

Yes, it's me, she'd said, her voice sounding hoarse in her own ears.

Such an odd thing to say, she would later think. *It's me.* And she would wonder whether it was an assertion that underneath her present hideousness, she was still Rianna Gelvan . . . or an admission of defeat: *This is what I am now.*

Slender hands gripped her shoulders, steadying her. "Come with me," he said, his voice thick with what sounded like emotion. "Rianna, dear, come with me and tell me what's happened."

She would remember: his hands sliding from her shoulders to take up the yoke that held the buckets she carried, sinews tightening in his forearms. Shouldering her burden. "Take my arm," he instructed. "Stay close to me." She almost laughed, that he sought to protect her now. *It's late for that.* But she was stopped short by the solemnity in his voice, for it reflected back to her how she must look. In contrast, his face seemed more handsome than ever, a mask of perfectly pro-portioned marble like one of the statues in her father's garden.

Rianna would remember the warmth that flooded her in that moment, the relief. And at the same time, a numbness, as if she were herself of stone. "The kitchen will want them," she said.

He nodded. Down the street they wended their way together, with him bearing her burden beside her. She admired the way he did not so much as bend beneath its weight. There had been times, she re-called, when she had thought the bones of her shoulders would break. It was astonishing, really, that one could endure so much, and still not break.

It would linger in her memory, the feel of his muscled arm under her fingers as they walked.

Irma had stared, as had all the girls, and one thing Rianna would not remember later was what she had said to them. Somehow she must have made clear what she'd decided: that she was not returning to the kitchens for a copper a day. Even if it meant letting Rayen see her as this skeletal, hairless version of herself.

He had a room upstairs, all to himself. Only a man of his station could procure such a thing, and so clean. Rianna almost cried at the wonder of it. A bed, a washstand, even a rug slapped against the dingy floorboards. The bed sank beneath her as she sat; she resisted the impulse to curl into a ball amid the blankets.

"You ran away," Rayen said. He sat beside her on the bed in the same way he had once sat beside her on the garden bench—at a care-ful distance.

"I had to. My father was arrested by the king's guard. I don't even know why. Please, Rayen, can you help him?"

"This is serious," said Rayen. "I always suspected your father had—secrets. Rianna, even a lord of Amaristoth carries scant influence with the king."

"It was Nickon Gerrard. I know it was," said Rianna. *But I can't tell you why,* she thought. She didn't know if Rayen would willingly help them if he knew the truth.

His features were still and sorrowful. "All the more so," he said. "But I can shield you until your father stands trial. Perhaps his crime was minor. We can't yet know." He leaned toward her. "But that doesn't explain why you are here, Rianna Gelvan," he said softly. "Why run to the heart of the cruel north? I am sure Ned's family would have taken you in."

Rianna dropped her eyes, confused, and looked down at Rayen's hands where they rested on his knees. Callused, embattled hands that still retained an aristocratic delicacy. His nails were nearly as long as Darien's harpist's nails, and perfectly shaped. "Why here?" he prompted.

Rianna shook her head, unwilling to tell him, yet equally unwilling to lie.

"This is about the man you love, isn't it," Rayen said gently.

Rianna buried her face in her hands. "I'm sorry," she said. And then thought: *Idiot, why would he care? No one would want you now, not unless they were blind.* She didn't realize the tears had come until she felt their wetness against her fingers. She dashed them away, angry at herself for being so weak.

Rayen laid a hand on her arm. The warmth of it and the strength were comforting. Even knowing that he did not want her, that was comforting too—it simplified everything. "I do not cast judgments," he said. "He must be an extraordinary man for you to risk yourself in this way."

"I'm sorry," she said again, but now she met his eyes. Quirking her lip and gesturing downward—a gesture that encompassed all of herself—she said, "Though you can hardly want me now."

He withdrew his hand from her arm, and for a moment she thought he was withdrawing from her. Then he wrapped his arm around her shoulders. Strong and warm. "Dear, hush. You've been through a horror, that's clear. Rest now. I will see you safely home."

And it was thus, encircled in Rayen Amaristoth's arm, her head sliding to his shoulder, that Rianna fell into a deep, exhausted sleep.

I will see you safely home.

So he had said, and when she woke, he began to make good his word. But first, he insisted on buying her clothes.

"I'm a wealthy man, Rianna," he said, overruling her protests. "Some women's garments, hastily fitted, will hardly be the ruin of me. Whereas, you . . ." He smoothed down the rag on her head with a glaze of sadness in his eyes. "You must gather your dignity back to you."

The dresses he procured for her were simple and hastily fitted. She did not think anything could make her happier than the feel of proper clothes against her skin. But she was wrong, for Rayen also bought for her matching snoods of soft velvet to conceal the shame of her stubbled head. She could hardly look pretty without hair, but the snoods were a vast improvement over the rag she had been tying around her head.

RAYEN knew better than to ask more questions about what had brought her to Dynmar, but she could read them in the space of their silences. To divert him she asked, "How is the search for your sister progressing, Rayen?"

It was remarkable, come to think of it, that she could address one of the most powerful men in the country by name. Rianna wondered when she had begun to consider him a friend, how it had happened so quickly.

Such a thought might have never occurred to her, had she not recently been working in the kitchens as Leya the maid. A girl whom such a man would never deign notice, unless it were merely to bed for a bare hour of the night.

Leya the kitchen maid. Rianna Gelvan. Which was she, or was she truly either one?

Rayen sighed as he considered her question. At last he said, "No word yet. I've been asking around all the past week, with no luck."

They were in the room he had rented. It was evening, and Rianna was wearing one of the new dresses and a sleek snood that hid her scalp. One more night they would stay here, Rayen had decided, so she could build up her strength.

"I'm sorry I never told you this, but I did meet Lin, and knew her, if only for a short time," said Rianna. "She did not seem to want to be found."

Rayen nodded. "I know. She would not."

Rianna waited, watching his face and the candle-shadows that flickered across it. For a moment she felt a queer sense of vertigo, as if she hovered now on the edge of a precipice.

Rayen bowed his head. "You must want to know why such a high-born lady as my sister would flee her own home. The truth is . . ." He trailed off. Rianna watched him, and waited. There was something here, she felt—something that was important for her to know. Something that held the key to what was puzzling her about him.

When he saw she was waiting, Rayen went on. "The truth is, I am ashamed to tell you. She—she did have her reasons." He shook his head. "I'm sorry, dear. I cannot tell you."

"It's too private?"

"That," he said. "But mostly . . . it's too ugly."

"I've grown accustomed to ugliness," said Rianna.

Rayen reached out and touched her cheek, tenderly but without desire, as if she were a child. "You think so," he said. "But when I look at you I see—a white rose. Pure and untouched by everything around it, in spite of rain, in spite of the surrounding grime. And I—I will not be the one to sully such loveliness. You are who you are."

"The man I love," Rianna heard herself say, "used to call me his Snow Queen."

Rayen smiled, half wryly. "He saw it, too."

At night he insisted she sleep in the bed, while he curled in blankets on the floor. She felt guilty, but her attempts to apologize only made him laugh. "Dearling, I'm a hunter," he said. "I have slept on the cold ground of the forests in the mountains. Soft blankets in a clean room are more than I need."

The night was thick with silence. Snuggled among the downy pillows, Rianna's mind drifted. *A hunter.* She pictured him in the forest, white-skinned and watchful, knife in hand. The image made her feel protected, safe. Sleep crept over her in no time, as the fire died in the hearth and a patter of autumn rain drummed gently against the closed shutters.

Another day passed, during which, in the course of their conversation, Rianna revealed that she had brought her knife from Tamryllin. She showed it to him now, shyly as if revealing a childish attachment to a toy. "I know I can't use it well, not yet," she said. "But what you taught me—that was better than nothing." Sometimes she caught inflections in her words that were surprisingly rough, a common tongue she had absorbed in the kitchen.

But if Rayen heard a difference, he showed no sign of it. He said, "Show me what you remember." In the next hour—an hour that stretched to two—he demonstrated to her ways to improve her stance, her reflexes, the taut correctness of movement that was necessary in the delicate and implacable dance of combat.

He explained that a knife was different from a sword: it was closer, more intimate. Your hand only inches away from the severed artery, the burst of blood—the life whistling away to stillness. Rayen was clear about this to her, even harsh, though she could see that he meant it for her own good. Perhaps he thought in teaching her this, he was protecting that spark of purity he saw in her, that she herself had imagined was gone. *A white rose,* he'd said. So much like something Darien would say.

But Darien had never pictured her with a knife. He would be surprised, she knew. Saddened, perhaps. The thought awakened an answering sadness in her, but was quickly submerged in the effort of responding to Rayen's instructions. He demanded perfection of her, as if she were a man in his command.

Later, she accompanied him on errands about town. Although he had explained that Dynmar was crucial to his own commerce in the north, she was still surprised that he seemed to know everyone they encountered by name. One and all they bowed to him reverently, said "Lord Amaristoth" as if the name itself were magic.

"There is a great deal of need here," Rayen said. "But truly these people owe me less than they believe. Their independence is what buffers them through hard times. I have always admired that about them."

"Independence?" Rianna had never given thought to such things.

Rayen smiled, as if sensing this. He said, "This part of the world, they don't give a damn about the king or courts. They pay their taxes grudgingly and take pride in the fact that they are almost entirely self-governing. I admire their stubbornness, their pride. They believe the poets of Eivar have their roots here, on this border of the forest and mountains."

Rianna thought of Darien, somewhere in the mountains, and shivered a little.

He brought her along to the shoemaker, to repair her boots. She sat in a corner of the tiny workshop and watched as the shoemaker stitched, and the two men talked. It was soon apparent that Rayen had known this elderly man for years. He had introduced her to the shoemaker as his friend, and though the other man's wizened face showed immediate curiosity, he asked no questions.

"So much like your mother," said the shoemaker appreciatively, in response to one of Rayen's more acid comments. "She always spoke her mind. You'll pardon my saying so, I hope, but I didn't think even a boar with spears for tusks could have finished *her.*"

Rayen laughed. "You need never ask pardon for speaking *your* mind, old friend," he said. "In truth, I agree. It was a shock to all of us—discovering that even we Amaristoth are in fact mortal." His smile faded as he said more quietly, "A terrible shock." Seeing that, Rianna felt annoyance at the shoemaker for raising a painful subject.

Sensing the change of mood, the older man said, "She was a great lady. Always did a lot for us here."

"I hear complaints," said Rayen. "That of late, there has been unrest."

"That's everywhere," said the shoemaker grimly, snipping a stray thread. "That business with the poets in Tamryllin is spreading. Especially now, what with the blood-magic murder."

"What do you mean, it's spreading?" Rayen asked, his eyes intent.

Rianna froze to stillness where she sat.

"Ever since word got out that Darien Aldemoor killed his companion to use his blood for magic . . . well. There's some that believe he's a danger to all of us, and not only for his knife. Rumor from the south is that the Red Death has returned . . . for the first time in hundreds of years. Who can fail to see the connection?"

"People think it is Darien's doing?" asked Rayen.

The shoemaker ceased his work for a moment. He wouldn't meet Rayen's eyes, but for the first time Rianna thought he seemed uneasy. *Jumpy*, her kitchen companions would have said. As if a chill had seeped under his skin. "Darien . . . and these Seekers who claim to follow him," he said. "No doubt they are bringing this upon us."

Rianna swallowed hard, she hoped not loudly. Her stomach was tight with tension. "Surely they don't condone murder," she said. She was recalling her last conversation with Rayen in her father's garden, when he had told her about Hassen Styr's imprisonment. The pieces of a story were snapping together with horrifying clarity. How many, aside from her, knew the truth?

Rayen glanced her way, his gaze impassive. The shoemaker did, too, as he said, "Perhaps they don't *all* condone it, my lady, but if even *some* of them do . . . how are we to know whom to trust? Let's just say," he continued in hardened tones, "that the harp and ring are not welcome in our town as they once were."

Rianna exhaled softly. Just as softly, Rayen said, "A pity." And when he met her eyes again, she thought she saw compassion there.

That evening, Rianna was restless. They would be leaving the next morning for Tamryllin, and she knew it was important to go to bed early and conserve her strength. Even so, she asked Rayen if he would accompany her to the common room before bed.

"Are you sure?" he asked. "It's a rough place."

She smiled at him. "That won't matter," she said, "if you are with me." It was spoken honestly, without flirtation. Yet even so, she blushed.

Rayen smiled back. "I can hardly refuse now."

* * *

IT was strange, she reflected as she rested her hand lightly on Rayen's arm and glanced around, how different a place could seem when you knew you were safe. As a kitchen maid, this same room had seemed to her like a wilderness, teeming with drunken, leering, idle-fingered men. Standing tall now beside her noble companion at the top of the stairs, surveying the scene, Rianna felt regal and at ease. Rayen Amaristoth was more than enough protection for her. And her fine raiment was protection of another kind against stares and jeers; her scalp was concealed by a snood of velvet and lace. Even the regulars would never recognize her now.

Clearing her throat as if trying out a new voice, Rianna said, "Why don't we have a drink, while we're here?"

Rayen seemed to think nothing of it: he guided her to a seat in a corner, where the noise was less invasive. "And what would you have, my lady?"

She frowned. "I suppose . . . wine?" It made her think of her father, and the way he had offered her wine just before his capture. *I will drink to him,* she thought, and closed her eyes a moment, focusing her thoughts in the wisp of a prayer. *Gods watch over him now and always. And Darien. And the soul of dear Hassen Styr. And a plague of purest poison take Nickon Gerrard.*

"Wine it is, then," said Rayen, and called over one of the serving women. As the girl approached, Rianna saw, with a shock, that it was Bella. From the look in the girl's faded blue eyes, she knew Rianna, too. But all she said was, "What will you have, my lord? My lady?"

As Rayen gave his order, Rianna tried to meet the other girl's eyes, but to no avail. By the time she had mustered the courage to say something, Bella had slithered back into the crowd. As she went, Rianna saw a filthy hand shoot out and grasp the flesh of Bella's thigh through her skirt. They had done laundry together many times: Rianna knew that underneath that skirt was a yellowed, stained petticoat that had been washed and wrung a thousand times to a threadbare rag. Her heart clenched and she felt herself lost as if in a swamp, sucking her down; for there was, she knew, more suffering in the world than in the eyes of this girl. There was more than she could ever imagine. She had escaped it all so easily, because of who she was.

And she had wept for the loss of her hair.

Warm pressure on her hand: Rayen had reached out and set his hand over hers, where it rested on the table. "You knew her, I take it."

Rianna glanced up at him through sudden tears. "She was kind to me."

Rayen nodded. "I will give her extra coins when she returns," he said. "I'm afraid that alone cannot rescue her from the life she is in, but perhaps can ease it a little."

Rianna looked down at the table. "She can get a new petticoat," she said dully.

Rayen said nothing, but his hand tightened over hers. She closed her eyes, imagining that the warmth of his hand was flowing into her, warming her. She could get lost in that warmth, and forget for a while about the things she could not change.

A scream tore through her calm. Rianna jumped with a ragged gasp. Rayen Amaristoth sprang to his feet and toward the center of the room, where a large man was holding another man down and brutally ramming his head into a table, over and over again. Before anyone else could intervene, Rayen was already there, in one smooth motion gripping the aggressor's shoulder and throwing him against an unoccupied table, where he crashed and grunted and lay still.

A silence fell, where once there had been a multitude of noises and voices. Serving women froze where they stood, men with tankards upraised stood as if paralyzed, like a scene in a tapestry. All was quiet, marred only by the moans of the injured men. And then Rayen Amaristoth's voice, dangerously soft. "How did this start?"

It was understandable, Rianna thought, even as her heart thumped violently in her chest, that no one particularly wanted to answer. But the men who had been nearest the scene were too conspicuously trying to look uninvolved. For the first time, Rianna noticed, with a rush of excitement, that at least two of them bore harps, and no doubt rings as well.

Rayen collared one of the men nearest the scene. A boy more than a man, with a harp strapped to his chest. "*What happened?*" Rayen said, the ring of authority in his tone unmistakable.

The boy swallowed. "You see—"

Rayen shook him. "Don't waste my time."

"It's about Darien Aldemoor," the boy blurted. "He's been found. Here in Dynmar!"

Now a babble of excited voices arose even as Rayen let go the boy's collar and stood very still, as if lost in thought. Rianna rose to her feet. "How do you know?"

Now Rayen turned to stare at her, he and the boy both. "The townspeople have him in custody, my lady," the boy said respectfully. "Me, I think it's what he deserves. I'm tired of people thinking I'm a murderer because of my harp and ring. He desecrated everything we stand for as poets."

"Idiot," another man sneered. Older, grizzled even, with a harp. "He had power within his grasp. Why not use it?"

The boy lunged. Rayen intervened between them. "No more of that," he said. "Get yourselves out of sight. Whether you support what's happened or not, it is going to become rather unpleasant to be a poet in the coming weeks. You can count on it." He turned to Rianna. "My dear, we should do the same."

"There's something I have to tell you," Rianna said to him as they departed the crowd.

"Not here," Rayen said, and steered her out and upstairs.

She did not waste time when they reached the room. "Darien Aldemoor is the man I love, Rayen," she said. "That's why I came here. I was looking for him."

Only a short silence passed. She could not tell if he was surprised. But that lasted only a moment before his gaze softened and he slid an arm around her. "So that's the secret you've been holding close for so long," he said. "A vagrant poet, and now a fugitive on top of that. My poor Rianna, these past months must have been a nightmare for you."

Whatever she had expected, it had not been this. It would occur to her later that sympathy is disarming even without surprise, but un-

LAST SONG BEFORE NIGHT 289

expected sympathy leaves no defense. "Thank you," was all she could say. She let him embrace her, a firm clasp around the shoulders, chaste and comforting.

At last he stood away from her, and said, "It's simple, then. What we should do."

"What?" she said, resisting the impulse to lean against him for comfort.

He took her hand lightly, as if for a dance. "What do you think?" he said. "We have to get him out."

As it turned out, by *we*, Rayen actually meant only himself . . . he insisted that she remain behind in the safety of the inn. When Rianna protested that she knew something of weaponry now—even if very little—his response startled her. Before she could react, he hugged her close to him, then pulled away quickly as if he feared his own response.

"You are dear," he said. "Very dear and brave. But I will not risk you. If anything happens to me, you are to take this money and go. There's more than enough here to pay for passage." He set a leather pouch on the bed that looked to contain all he carried upon him.

At this talk of something happening to him, Rianna's throat went dry. "Why are you doing this for me?"

He touched her cheek. "The less we speak of that, the better," he said. "Strangely, I seem to be invested in making you happy. Besides," he grinned, "I'm curious to meet the man who has been so fortunate as to steal your heart."

With a mix of excitement and trepidation, she watched him go. On the one hand, Darien was so close. But on the other hand, this man was risking his life for her, for another man who was nothing to him. Who was even, in a way, his rival. *If anything happens to him,* she thought, and let the thought hang there a moment in the deepening night. If anything happened to Rayen, she was responsible.

He had instructed her to sleep, but that was impossible. She curled up in a chair by the window and watched the leisurely passage of the moon. Usually she saw everything by moonlight as imbued with a silver luminescence. Now she saw it as white, cold fingers that drained color from everything they touched. She was alone here. Rayen may not come back, and she might never see Darien again. Hours passed as the moon rose and dipped in the endless sky.

She was standing on a hilltop in that same moonlight, under a black withered tree. All was still, without even the breath of a breeze. But under that tree she saw two figures. One with knife upraised. And one a corpse, blood leaking from a gash in the throat in a stream of black. So black under the moon.

Darien lowered the knife as he looked at her. He said, sadly, "My love. It had to be done."

She awoke to light—Rayen kindling a lamp in the dark room. Relief and a nameless fear flooded Rianna as she awoke.

"Rianna," Rayen said, "I have him."

It was only a dream, Rianna told herself as she turned sharply. She stared a moment, said, "This was the prisoner?"

"It's not Darien?" Rayen asked.

The blond, slender man Rayen had ostensibly rescued spoke up now. "I *told* you I wasn't Darien," he said. "I told everyone. No one will listen."

"It's not Darien," Rianna said flatly. She did not know what she felt. "Why would they have taken you for him?" she asked the young poet, mildly curious now.

"It's the ring, I think," he said with a sigh. "They say Darien Aldemoor's is a green stone . . . so is mine."

"An emerald," Rianna said. She wondered if she had truly awakened; this felt like a dream of another sort.

"Mine's not an emerald," said the poet. "It's a peridot. Idiot townsfolk can't tell the difference between shades of green. At least they didn't take my harp." He turned to Rayen. "I thank you for rescuing me, good sir, and my lady—wherever your man is, he's lucky to be cared for by someone such as you. Of course," he added, "I would expect no less of Darien Aldemoor. Gods preserve his soul."

A contraction in her, hearing this stranger speak so of Darien. She said, calmly enough, "Rayen, will you help this young man reach the gates and away?"

"I shall," Rayen said, and pressed her hand. "And then I will return to you."

"I'm sorry."

Rayen smiled. "I saved an innocent man. That's more than enough good deeds for a night's work. There is no need for you to be sorry." He escorted the young man from the room as Rianna watched, still unsure what she felt and why the terrible dream she'd just had was still with her, a cold hand against her throat.

She was sitting up waiting for Rayen when he returned. "It was no trouble," he told her, and sat down with a sigh. "The townsfolk here know nothing of taking prisoners. They were planning to inflict their own sort of justice on him tomorrow, but the poor boy has been spared that." Rayen began to pull off his boots. "None of it was any trouble, really," he said. "I am only sorry you are disappointed."

Watching him intently—every movement so smooth, unthinkingly graceful—Rianna said, "No. If he is not here, that means . . . maybe that means that he is finding what he wanted to find. I do want that for him, despite everything."

"All the same, I am sorry," said Rayen. "Well. We have a long day ahead of us. We should sleep."

"I don't understand," said Rianna, "why Lin would run away from you." When he was silent, she added, "You have done so much for me."

The room was dimly lit by a single lamp, but even so she could see the way he studied the air in front of him rather than meet her eyes. At last he said, "Rianna, what you see in me . . . it is not the whole truth. Lin was right to run away. I drove her away."

"How?"

A moment of total silence. At this late hour, even the inn was silent; they might have been the only ones awake. At last Rayen said, softly, "I was beating her."

Rianna swallowed. "Beating her." She thought of Lin's slight frame, her hollowed eyes.

"I know," he said, as if he could read the muddle of her thoughts. "There is nothing to say. All I can do now is find her and try to make it up to her, if I can. Give her the share of our inheritance that is hers, at the very least. She deserves more than that, but what can I do?" He ran his hands through his hair, hid his face from her. "What can I do."

Rianna thought he sounded lost, as if for all his decisiveness and commanding manner, he was still a bewildered boy underneath. A boy whose parents had died, she recalled now, when he was very young.

She dared now to approach him, to rest her hand on his arm. He did not move, or lift his head. She said, "You have always been so gentle with me. I don't understand."

He laughed, though it sounded more like a sob, wry and twisted. "Someone like you—as beautiful as you—could never understand," he said. "It is simple enough, I suppose. There was a girl that I loved. Loved very much. She had hair like yours. A smile like yours, though in truth, she was not as beautiful. Soon after my parents died, so did she. One morning she simply—didn't wake up. Gone just like that." He lifted his head now to meet her eyes. His eyes seemed very large, very dark by candlelight. "Some men use grief to fuel their efforts to do good," he said. "I—I retreated into violence. That says something about me, doesn't it?" He shook his head, back and forth. "Poor Lin, with a monster for a brother."

"I don't think you're a monster," said Rianna. She felt a warmth spreading through her, from her hand on his arm to all of her, and she longed to wrap her arms around him. Still she held back, thoughts suspended, her heart a rattling beat in her chest.

Rayen's voice caught in his throat as he said, "Rianna—you make me want to be better."

When they kissed, Rianna felt the tears on his face. Wave after wave of warmth ran through her, so that she felt, when his hands reached for the fastenings of her dress, as if the waves had crashed over her and left her no choice.

* * *

THE first thing she noticed, when she awoke, was the ache that remained of what had been slicing agony the night before, pain like she had never experienced it, at the core of her. She could feel, still, the sliding wet of blood and of him, seeping from her and onto the bedsheets. An irrevocable change, she realized, not for the first time. It had been exciting as well as frightening that night. Now it was simply frightening.

"Rayen?" she called softly.

The room was empty. She saw that at once. All his belongings were gone. Aware now of her nakedness as if it were an injury, Rianna swathed herself in the coverlet and stepped gingerly out of bed. "Rayen?"

The answering silence was louder in her ears than an answer would have been.

There was a note on the chair beside the bed. Her hands felt numb, as if frozen, and trembled as she opened it. She read,

> *And at the end what pleases me most is that you succumbed to me not before, but* after *I told you what I had done. That you gave me love after I revealed myself at my most heinous. That shall ever be my triumph, dear Rianna.*
>
> *However, unfortunately for you, I spoke the truth. That part, at least, was true.*

It was unsigned. But then, there was no need.

A knock at the door. Hardly knowing what she did, Rianna unlocked it, the coverlet slipping from her shoulders and trailing on the floor. If it had been one of the men from downstairs intent on raping her, or an outlaw, she did not think she would have cared.

It was Ned.

CHAPTER

26

CLOUDS obscured the moon the night they escaped Academy Isle; the scissors of low-hanging branches clawed their faces in the dark. But they had one advantage: Lin knew these woods. In this cold, forbidding forest she had returned to her home. In the dark, she reached for Darien's hand and found it, murmuring, "Stay close to me."

He did not object. He was still in shock, she knew, from the news of Hassen, and that he himself had killed a man.

They had set the boat adrift after they disembarked, to frustrate their pursuers for a little time.

A curse will fall upon you. The poet who had uttered those words possessed a deep, resonant voice that had echoed in the caverns beneath the castle. That echoed now in Lin's mind.

When they reached a grove, wind whistling through branches, she said, "We'll stop here for the night."

"How do we know they won't find us here?" Darien said. He was out of breath.

Lin sighed. "We don't. But they're blundering in the dark. They won't move quickly through these trees. We dare not make our way further in this dark, in any case. We could end up going in circles, run right into them."

Darien sank to the ground. "I don't think I can sleep."

"Just as well," said Lin. She drew her knife. "We'll need to be ready for them, in case." She saw that in spite of his cloak, Darien was shivering. "If you like," she said, "we can sit with our backs together, for warmth."

His response was a curt nod. Lin dropped to the ground and sat with her back against his, as she had sometimes done with Alyn—as she had even done with Rayen, when they were on the hunt together. A moment passed as Darien allowed himself to be warmed by the contact, his breath to slow. At last he said, quietly, "What are we going to do now?"

Near as he was, Lin felt powerless to reassure him.

She must have dozed, because when she opened her eyes pale dawn was seeping through the evergreen canopy above. Lin straightened, her hand tightening on the handle of her knife, but all she heard was the chittering of birds. The chill air was rich with the scent of pine and morning dew. Darien was awake and studying one of the pages from Valanir Ocune's box. When she stirred, he glanced at her and said, "Good morning." He sounded weary. "I hope that wasn't your idea of keeping watch."

Lin flushed. "It wasn't." Stretching, she clambered to her feet. Her muscles were cramped and sore. "I'll find us breakfast," she said, "and then we had best keep going."

"What do I do," Darien said dryly, "if the guards come while you're off killing rabbits? Yell a warning?"

"Something like that," she said. "I'll be fast." *Once, I was a hunter,* she thought, an echo of her mother's voice. Here in the woods near home, even the wind seemed to whisper in the tones of those she had known and lost.

"Lin, where do we go now?" Darien said, a note of desperation in his voice. "Guards are swarming the Academy—we can't do what Valanir Ocune bade us do. We can't get to the Path now. And we can't . . . we can't return to Tamryllin."

"Maybe it was never meant for us to find the Path, to recover the enchantments," said Lin. "Maybe Valanir will realize that now, and find another way."

"Or maybe there is no other way," said Darien. "Maybe whatever happens from now on—the darkness, the destruction of our land—will be because we failed."

Lin touched his shoulder, felt it rigid under her fingers. "I'm sorry," she said. She was cold inside. *It will soon be over.* What happened now seemed the logical conclusion to what had begun nearly a year ago, the winter she had fled her home. All that had befallen in between—Leander Keyen, Tamryllin, Valanir Ocune—was a bright interlude of seeming purpose, leading to this moment. Leading to nothing.

In her heart, Lin had always known she was destined for darkness. There was a flaw in her, or in the blood that had gone into her, that no amount of running would escape. No amount of journeying through portals, even with the greatest Seer of their age. But she could feel for Darien Aldemoor, whose life had once seemed like a golden ballad unfolding. That loss, Lin thought, she could grieve.

It was when they halted by a stream to refill their flasks that they saw him. A guardsman, bent over the water for a drink, his horse restive at his side.

Darien was instantly at the man's throat, jumping atop him where he knelt on the ground. Neither of them had time to draw blade, and for some moments there was a struggle in which the guard, not as weary as Darien and perhaps fueled with anger at the death of his comrade the night before, succeeded in pinning Darien to the ground. He was about to draw his sword when Lin was there, her knife pressed against the guard's back. She barked, "Don't move."

Darien scrambled from beneath the man, breathing hard. To Lin, his eyes looked crazed, as if he were in the grip of some fury. Sweat darkened the strands of hair pressed to his forehead. He threw his arm in a stranglehold around the guardsman's throat. "Are you alone?"

The guardsman closed his lips sullenly. Lin prodded him with the blade, though it almost made her ill to do so. This man was only doing what he'd been told to do. Perhaps he even believed that Darien was responsible for Hassen Styr's murder. Still: "Answer him," she commanded. Her mother, she knew, would not have hesitated for a moment.

"The others . . . are close," said their prisoner through his teeth. "They'll find you."

"Then we'll have to keep you as a hostage," said Lin.

Darien shook his head. There was a focused intensity in his eyes as he looked at the man that frightened Lin. "I have a better idea," he said. "Nickon Gerrard wants people to think I'd use one of my own for blood divination? Well, I'll give him another song to sing. I'll use one of his."

"No, Darien," Lin gasped. The guard opened his mouth to scream. Lin thrust her forearm against his mouth, though she felt sick.

"*Think* about it, Lin," he cried. "We don't know where we're going. Only Edrien Letrell knew what to do, and he's dead. And we have a way . . . I know a way to bring him back. To talk to him."

"Darien, listen to yourself," Lin entreated. "There is no way to bring back the dead."

"On the contrary, my dear," he said. "Death is a portal, no more. One of the most final of portals, but just a portal nonetheless. And we have it, right here in these papers left to us by Valanir Ocune. But it takes lifeblood, and the right words. Lin, we are the only ones who might be able to stop the darkness Valanir spoke of. And here we have our chance."

"Fighting dark with more dark?" said Lin. "That makes no sense."

"Just this one time," Darien pleaded. "Once will make no difference, compared to what Nickon Gerrard has been doing for *years*."

"I hope you're right," said Lin. She brought the hilt of her dagger down on the guardsman's head, hard. He crumpled in Darien's arms.

"You killed him?" Darien cried, enraged.

"No," said Lin. "I got him out of the way."

His blade outstretched, he was still, his face uncomprehending.

Lin caught and held his gaze. She herself was not sure of the reason for what she was about to do. Again she recalled what the books said of poets who earned the emerald as their gemstone. *He is the wanderer, light of heart, ever free.* She recalled the night before, when he had brandished a crimsoned blade, that grin she had never seen stretching his face. For an instant and in the torchlight of an underground cavern, she had seen him become someone else. Certainly not the man who had played her a sweet song as she drifted into sleep.

That song, if he does this, will be lost forever. That, and all the rest.

All this flickered in her mind in the space of an instant. So she said only, "You're not meant to shed blood, Darien. I can't see you do this." She took up the page where the instructions for the rite were written, scanned it briefly. "Be ready with the words." Deftly, she slashed each of her wrists. The pain that ran through her, though expected, was a shock. She sank to her knees.

"Lin . . . you idiot!" Darien rasped out, and ran to her.

"You're the idiot," she said. "Make sure you get . . . the blood."

"No," he said, and began to rummage urgently through his pack. "I'm going to bandage your wrists."

"Do that," she murmured, "and I'll cut them again. *Let me do this.*"

He gathered her up as if she were a child; she felt very light in his arms. There were tears in his eyes, she saw, but could hardly credit her own vision just now. "First Hassen, and now you?" he said, and she could hear real anguish there. But she saw him take up the papers in his other hand, and only then allowed herself to close her eyes. She had done her part—it would be left to him to finish what she had begun. This last thing.

DARIEN leaned against a tree. Sunset approached; he could tell by the lengthening of the shadows, the softness of the light. Otherwise there was no view here of the sky, of anything but gradations of quiet dark.

With no one to see, Darien had let himself weep. He wasn't even sure why, whether it was for Hassen, or for Lin, at what he had allowed himself to do to her. Or if it was an accumulation of all these things, made the more wretched by the futility of it all.

Open now the gate, he had recited. *Open here the gate between worlds. Bring forth your darkness to the light.*

A gate between worlds.

Lin's blood, for a story.

Two bodies on the ground: the guardsman, knocked unconscious a second time, draped across the roots of an oak. And Lin Amaristoth, her head pillowed on Darien's jacket, her face so white as to be transparent, violet branches of veins like cracks in her temples and cheeks. The bandages he had made of his one extra shirt were less white.

For what seemed like the hundredth time, he felt her bony, bandaged wrist for a heartbeat. It was hard to feel anything through the cloth, but he thought she was still alive. Had he a mirror, he would have checked for a flutter of breath.

If she had died, would it have worked?

The thought should have tormented him, but instead he found that he didn't care. The guardsman was still at his mercy, and yet . . . insane as Lin's action had been, seeing her slash her own wrists had soured his taste for shedding blood.

He had used her blood. He had bandaged her before she could lose too much, but . . . he had lifted her to a nearby rock, where a crevice ran deep, and he had held her cut wrists over the crevice and allowed it to fill with red.

Bring forth your darkness to the light.

If Lin were to die, he'd be no better than Nickon Gerrard had announced to the world. He would be, in truth, a murderer.

He watched her a moment: the taut face, her mouth a drained curveless line. She would slow him down, he knew. She had planned on dying, on saving him from himself. She had not thought to become an inconvenience.

He lifted her very gently, but even so she groaned when her arms left the ground. He smoothed back her hair and began to advance, slowly, away from their makeshift camp. It was sheer luck that they had not been found just yet, and Darien knew better—by now—than to ever again trust to his luck.

* * *

It took a long time for the dark to arrange itself into shapes. Her arms were heavy and an agony, each one. Although the darkness was absolute, she felt as if she had only just now emerged from a deep cavern beneath the earth and into light. Light and pain. Her mind was reaching back . . . to something she had just seen or touched. She thought she could still hear whispering, fading now with the fading of sleep.

A shape materialized in her range of vision; she felt the warmth of a hand on hers. "Alyn?" she said. And then her mind took a leap, and she laughed. "Oh Darien," she said. "I'm not myself."

He took her hand. He said, "No . . . I think you're the same idiot as always."

"Did it work?"

"No," he said, stroking her hand.

Lin tried to lift her other hand to touch his arm but quickly gave up. The pain was too much. "I'm sorry," she said. "It might be because you didn't let me die."

"Then I don't care."

"I'm sorry," she said again.

Darien snorted. "Lin, you have to stop saying that. Now do you think you can sit up to eat something? I made a stew."

Lin tried to pull herself up and fell back, dizzy. She heard Darien say, quietly, "You lost a lot of blood."

"If you prop me up . . ."

"I'll do that," he said. "I'll feed you. You won't have to do any-thing."

"Darien," she said, and stopped.

"What?"

"Am I going to die? Because I can't imagine you being this kind, otherwise."

He laughed. "My lady, now you've wounded me."

Darien fed the stew to her as she sat against a boulder for support. She felt too weak even to chew and swallow, but he made no com-plaint as she applied herself slowly to each morsel. The meat was what she needed, she knew, to restore herself. When she was finished, she could hardly keep her eyes open. "I'm tired," she said.

Darien helped her back to her bedroll and covered her with a blanket. "Sleep is the best thing."

It was only then that she remembered. "The guards. Darien—don't stay and get caught because of me."

"Lin, it's night, and barely a moon," he said. "They won't find us. I haven't heard a sound all day—they probably lost our trail by now. Sleep."

She wanted to argue, but the fatigue that rolled over her in a black wave was so heavy that she could hardly even struggle beneath its weight. The night disappeared again as true dark closed overhead.

HE was back in the dream, again in the hall with its many doors. Darien remembered what had happened here last time—what he had seen—and felt dread. Last time, Rianna had melted into a laughing, gleam-toothed Marilla in his arms.

Rianna. She had no place in the world where he now found himself. The death of Hassen Styr melded seamlessly in his mind with the sickening *crunch* of his sword through the guardsman's chest. With Lin's blood pooling in a crevice. The dark under trees on a moonless night. So much black he had entered into; she could have no part of it.

More to quiet his nerves than from any intuition, Darien chose a door and slowly pushed it open.

He was awakened by a scream. Darien leaped up, terrified; Lin was sitting up, arms rigid at her sides, a shriek escaping her throat, a long shrill noise that sounded nothing like her. "Lin, what is it?" he cried, and grabbed her shoulders.

In the dark it was difficult to see much of her face. And suddenly her back arched; her body jerked like a marionette, once, twice. "Lin!" he said. She jerked again, out of his arms and onto the ground. Her scream died to a low rattle deep in the throat. And then, as abruptly, was still. Her eyes were open and unblinking, staring at nothing.

The dark around him spun; *surely,* Darien thought dimly, *surely this is a nightmare.* He listened for her breath, but he already knew what he would hear. Her eyes stared and she made no sound. Darien swallowed, tasted bile in his throat. He was going to be sick, here in the forest in endless dark. *Don't leave me here, Lin,* he thought, and was immediately appalled by his own selfishness. He wanted to scream.

It took a moment for Darien to realize that the darkness was lifting—or rather, a light was gathering. As he watched, the light coalesced before him, over Lin's prone shape. It began as a vertical line. As the line of light widened, it seemed to Darien as if the night were a curtain with light behind it that someone now slashed neatly with a knife. He found that he couldn't move, couldn't do anything but watch as the light took shape.

The shape was one he recognized from his dream in the Academy library, yet even without that, he would have guessed who it was. Even without the telltale ring. A figure that flickered, translucent and glowing, clad in folds of shroudlike grey.

The man he'd summoned.

The shade of Edrien Letrell turned its gaze on Darien. Where his eyes should have been—blue-grey and thoughtful, Darien remembered—were dark holes. His face was ravaged, the flesh like rags stretched over bone. His brow contorted with fury.

Darien didn't know what to say, or do. It had seemed so simple this morning—he would raise Edrien Letrell and ask him a few questions. Now that seemed impossibly stupid. How did one address a man who had passed through death?

Very slowly, Lin drew herself up. Darien was about to exclaim for joy when he saw that her eyes were still staring, her movements halting, mechanical. When she spoke, it was in a voice not her own. A man's voice. "How dare you summon me here?"

With an effort, Darien found his voice. "Honored Seer," he began. "I—I have some questions."

"Idiot," said the man's voice from Lin's mouth. It was sibilant with hatred. "I have endured unspeakable pain on account of your . . . curiosity. And you, a bearer of the emerald ring!"

Darien looked down, too ashamed to speak.

Edrien went on, "Then again, perhaps it is because of your damned, meddling nature that you have done this." The gaze turned away from Darien, the tortured face became contemplative. "I had a friend like you. All these many centuries, I still have not found him in the deeps. Though I hear his voice at times, in dreams."

The dead have dreams? Darien was filled with more regret than he had ever thought possible. "If I had known it would cause you pain—any pain," he said, "I would never have summoned you. Please accept my apologies, and help me."

"You want the Path," said Edrien harshly. Lin's face twisted in a smirk. "And you would even use the most forbidden enchantments to find it. That is why you could summon me. Why I *had* to venture here, when blood met moonlight."

"And Lin?" Darien asked. "What's happening to her?"

The shade revealed its teeth, but not in a smile. "You should know," Edrien said. "You killed her."

"I didn't!" Darien said. "I used only some of the blood . . ."

"That would explain why my hold in this sphere is so tenuous," Edrien replied. "I will be freed soon, and go. Another excruciating journey, thanks to you." As if to indicate this impending freedom, his image flickered momentarily, nearly fading to black. "I had it in my hand to return the old enchantments to the world," he said. "Why do you think I didn't?"

"I . . . don't know," said Darien.

"You don't know very much. I won't tell you how I found the Path—I vowed I would tell no one, and I will not. A great Seer in the days of old could have forced the truth from me, I suppose—tortured my shade or somesuch. But frankly, boy, you lack both the power and the skill."

"I wouldn't want to torture you," said Darien. "*Erisen,* our world is in danger if you do not tell us."

A tunneling sound, like a great wind, from the shade. Darien realized it was a sigh. "I should be moved by such words," said Edrien. "I should be moved and yet—it is hard, so hard now, to care about the world." He fell silent. An owl was calling, oblivious to the strangeness of the night.

"You are the only hope we have," said Darien. "Please, *Erisen*."

Again that sigh, like the sound of ocean winds between cliffs. "One thing will I tell you. You must first lose everything." Edrien's voice dropped very low, almost to a whisper. "I did."

He vanished then without a sound. Lin collapsed with a thump. Darien ran to her. To his relief, her eyes focused on his face, and she said his name. But when he embraced her she started, very quietly, to weep. He held her a long time, and she wept for a long time, as night gradually lifted to make way for the dawn.

PART IV

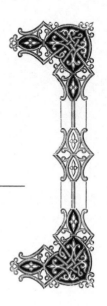

CHAPTER 27

THERE is a path.

Words heard in a dream, in a waft of smoke and an old woman's whisper. In all and none of these. Edrien could no longer remember where he had heard, or how he knew. Perhaps his grandmother, when he was very small, had told him on one of the many occasions she had set him on her knee and regaled him with a story. But that would have been many years ago, indeed, for his grandmother was long since in the ground. And it would not explain, in that case, why he only remembered now.

The mountains were cold this time of year, the trees withered. It was no time to be out wandering. Far better that he return home—he could imagine his mother telling him—lest he fall ill. And now, unlike when his mother had been alive, the cold had a way of settling into his body like an unwelcome guest. Cor would have laughed at him, beckoned him to the fireside of an inn to discuss a new technique in song, or verse. Edrien did not have to close his eyes to imagine it, his highly visual mind trained to recall every detail with ease: Cor's plump face reddened with heat from the fire, the sharp angle of his nose catching its light in a bright thin line, the blue eyes that could see through anything. That could even be cruel, when he wished it.

Thinking of Cor made Edrien's stomach contract, as if he were already ill.

The wind was rising, high-pitched and eerie like a ghost.

What it came down to was that there was no one to tell Edrien Letrell to come in out of the cold, not outside his own memory. *The best I have known,* Cor had said. High praise from an exacting, willful man.

If I could understand, Edrien thought, and stopped. People were approaching, horses. For the first time, he noticed that it grew dark.

"Sing for my supper?" he offered, almost a reflex. He had almost forgotten that he needed to eat. Funny, he had been teased often enough for his expanding girth and love of sweets. Funny to remember that now, in this place.

It seemed to be two families that approached him: two men, two women, and an assortment of thin, dark-haired children. All with eyes deep and dark as the mountains themselves. Edrien had encountered the nomadic people in his travels; he had some experience with them, and some sympathy. He had studied their myths, and in so doing had absorbed their dreams and desires as if into his blood. And there, they had become music. Years ago.

They asked him his name; he introduced himself. Was met with disbelief.

"You surely can't be Edrien Letrell himself?" said one of the women, her voice soft but incredulous.

"Allow me to sing for you," he said, "and if you do not care for it, I promise you my name and reputation shall be as nothing."

"He is about the right age," the other woman mused. "And we can spare the food tonight. There's no harm in it."

One of the men—perhaps her husband—elbowed her roughly. "It is not for you to decide," he said. Edrien noted, not for the first time, that all of the adults had lined faces even though they could hardly be past thirty. A short life and a weary one. "But yes. Just for one night, we will agree upon. For supper and a place to sleep, after."

Edrien thanked them and, sliding to the ground, fell to tuning the strings of his harp. Soon the simple rhythms of the task began to soothe him, and the pain he carried was like a voice singing, now a corridor away, now many miles in the distance, where it became an echo, sorrowful but no longer urgent. Within his hands was the deft sureness of what he knew, and what he could still do now to make a difference.

The men built up a fire, and the women ladled food onto the plates of their menfolk and children. Darkness had overtaken the camp; now only the fire cast light upon them, for even the moon was hidden that night. Edrien found himself withdrawing into shadow. It was only when he began to play that he realized why: he did not want these people, these simple men and women and their children, to see his face.

His hands stroked the strings almost tenderly, to start, but that of course did not last. As with so many things, tenderness was only a beginning, giving way to need and to violence. And on the first chord where tenderness gave way to need, Edrien's voice joined the music of the strings, lifted in a chant that recalled the earliest songs of the people who had wandered these mountains, the songs they had bequeathed, over centuries, to their children. That much, at least, he owed his hosts. But it was a song he had written himself, combining their traditional forms with his own inspiration as a young man. It was one of the songs that had made his name what it was.

The children were talking and laughing at first, but soon Edrien was aware that in addition to the darkness that encircled them, they were ensconced in a breathless silence that only his music filled. But only a part of him was aware, for it had been decades since he had charmed and amazed an audience for the first time; the silence was an homage that was his due. He was Edrien Letrell, in spite of everything, and whatever it might mean. Even if it meant nothing at all.

Then, as if some charm in the night took hold of them, the children jumped up and began to dance. Their parents looked on for a moment; then one of the men seized his wife's hand and spun her along with him nearer the fire. Into the transient and wavering circle of the light.

With stirrings of wonder that he had never thought to feel again,

Edrien watched these thin, tired people transformed into spirits of the mountain by his reaffirmation of their myths and dreams here on the mountainside.

To understand . . .

"You may travel farther with us, if you wish," said one of the men to Edrien in the morning—the same one, he noticed, who had barked at his wife the previous night. And then, later, had led her into the firelit circle for a dance. So many contradictions in life, Edrien sometimes thought his mind could not possibly encompass them all.

"We know now that you are Edrien Letrell, and we are honored to share your company," the man added.

"It is I who will be honored to accompany you," said Edrien. "What is your name?"

"Aram," said the other. "Tonight I will introduce you to everyone in our family. We go south, where there is shelter from the winter winds and food to be had in the neighboring towns. Where are you going?"

Edrien smiled then, the first time since they had met. "I'm not yet sure."

There was a path. He had sung about it many times, but he had never believed it existed. And, indeed, there was no reason to believe that it did, save a vaguely tuned instinct that was little more than a whisper, yet insistent, waking him from dreams he could only barely recall upon awakening. And when awake, a pall hung over his thoughts, for the music was no longer enough, had never *been* enough, and now there was no turning away from that truth. Not when Cor was gone. And Myra.

He had laughed when she had suggested they marry. Had laughed. For what use is a married life to wandering artist such as himself? And what if—he knew this now—what if he wearied of her? He had never admitted that thought even to himself, but now he understood, for as a young man he had wandered half the world and into a great many beds, and marriage would have been the end of that. If he had known how soon Myra would be taken from him, perhaps he would have indulged her. Given himself a memory less bitter than that of the slammed door, the silence. And then, weeks later, news of her death after the onslaught of the great plague of that year.

Many years ago that had been, and Cor had told him the pain would go away. But it still arose when he least expected it. Sometimes all it took was the sound of a woman's voice lifted in song; at other times, the sight of running children and the thought: *what she wanted.* Perhaps Cor had spoken from experience, from a preternatural ability to exorcise his own ghosts with ease. Yet somehow, remembering his friend, Edrien doubted that now.

You thought to be kind, by being cruel, he thought fondly. *Old bastard gone to the Underworld, and I the only one left. Why?*

One of the women came up to him now, offered him water. Her smile was nothing like Myra's, guarded and shy like a wild thing, while Myra had been the essence of cultured life, a winter rose. Yet this woman's smile, the sadness in her eyes, made him think of Myra all the same.

A good memory, the very best. And not always a gift.

The path was through the mountains—this much, he knew. He would find it, or his old blood would freeze and he would die, and few would be left to mourn him. He, thinking of it, did not mourn. He had seen many lands, sampled the courts of kings and sultans; yet he could think of no better end to his days than here, amid the stones of his own land, in search of the one story from his childhood that was perhaps no story, after all, but truth for the poet who sought it out.

Aid me to understand . . .

LIN'S eyes fluttered open. Through the trees she could see the moon, ghostly against the grey of dawn. Curled up in his blanket beside her, Darien's breathing was regular and subdued. His face was wet with her tears, so close had he held her for much of the night.

She would not tell him about her dream, Lin decided there in the dark. Her wrists ached. *If it was a dream.*

CHAPTER
28

THE air where he sat was thick with smoke and smelled faintly of incense. Head bent toward his chest and arms tight at his sides, gazing sightlessly ahead, he would have appeared to an onlooker to have been in a drug-induced trance. Before him on the low table sat a porcelain cup of *khave*, abandoned, congealing. Its smoke had long since ceased to rise.

There were no onlookers. It was nearly dawn, and there was no one else in the *khave* house save himself and its owner. And the Seer had known the owner for many years. Neither man communicated much to the other, but the passage of time—and other events—had shaped a curious bond between them.

Earlier that evening, one of the cityfolk had told of a shooting star spied descending across the sunset. It exploded on the way down. In Eivar, they thought little of such things, with astrology remaining only the tales of country folk, those who were believed to be ignorant. But in the east, the study of the stars was as much in evidence in the royal courts as it was in the villages. A falling star that exploded in its descent portended a disturbance in the world. A disturbance—he himself believed, being of the Academy—that signified contact between the world and some Other.

The opening of a portal.

And so he sat now and reached out with his mind, with all the accumulated knowledge of his art, and searched.

There was blood on the horizon; he could taste it, salt and metal gritty on his tongue. Entire threads of event that tasted of blood. A brief image flashed before him: a heavyset, bearded man lying in a casket, a mortal slash black against the dead white of his neck.

He kept searching and tried to ignore the sensations of guilt and grief that rose within him. Laying them aside, as one would a plowshare in time of war.

And then an image that filled all his senses: the smell of pinewoods, the silvered dark of a moonlit night. A cry of such agony that it broke the night. And beyond this, a voice that whispered one word. A voice Valanir Ocune had never heard before in his life, but nonetheless recognized instantly.

The word was *Myra*.

THE path ahead of him was dark, and he was sweating, even though the night was cold. A jungle of thorny pines clawed at his face. Marlen Humbreleigh cursed as he stumbled over a rock and was nearly sent sprawling to the ground . . . a ground he couldn't see.

That voice. He had to get away from that voice. He wasn't sure what would happen if he didn't, but it promised cold, and a void that stretched an endless black within his mind.

"Wait." A woman's voice behind him. He turned. He saw a small, slender woman with dark hair whipping in the breeze. That was all he could see in the moonlight.

Until she drew a knife. The blade gleamed in her pale hand. "He gave me the key."

It was Lin Amaristoth. He was suddenly close to her. Her eyes loomed large before him, like tunnels, her lips forming words. *"I am the key."*

When he awoke, Marilla was in bed beside him, outstretched on the coverlet. She wore a red satin shift with black lace, a gift from him. Her coils of hair were a river over one shoulder as she watched him. Eyes cold as the void in his dream.

"You were thrashing," she said. Behind her, the draperies were drawn to reveal a whitening sky.

Marlen felt the life seep back into his limbs as he sat up. A dream, he thought. Always, he returned to that wood in his dreams—ever since he was a child. But this time had been different.

Shaking free of the thought, he narrowed his gaze on her. "You," he said. "I didn't know you were here."

She shrugged. "So?"

"I haven't seen you in weeks," he said. "You've been seeing someone else, haven't you?"

"I suppose 'seeing' is one word for it," said Marilla, stretching her white arms languidly. "But not one that I'd expect from a poet."

"Then why are you back?" he asked. "I'll wager he didn't keep you in silks and jewels as I do."

"That, and he seems to have vanished from the city," said Marilla. Her face was expressionless.

"You know I could turn you out in the streets."

"You could," she agreed, and studied the fingernails on her left hand like a leopard surveying its claw.

Marlen wondered why she had told him so readily that she had betrayed him, as she lay in his bed clad only in satin. He wondered if it was a game for her, to see if she could ride the edge of a knife and survive.

But he couldn't find the fury he would once have felt. All the fire had gone out of him . . . when?

"It was amusing while it lasted, but he left in a hurry," Marilla went on, still inspecting one crimson nail. "Probably on account of the girl he loves."

"Girl?"

Now she looked at him, and her grin revealed all her teeth. "Yes," she said. "Rianna Gelvan. Think of it, Marlen. She should be easier to find than Darien, knowing nothing of the world. Capture her, and Darien will come out of hiding. He'll have to."

"Ned Alterra, then," said Marlen. He felt inexpressibly weary. "I suppose that was easy pickings for you. And no doubt I'd find him, if I did Rianna Gelvan. Can it be that I know your mind?"

She kept smiling. "You only wish you did."

He knew that in her way, she might have thought it a gift. Rianna Gelvan, to help him lure Darien to Tamryllin. Ned Alterra, to kill in revenge. Perhaps Marilla wanted that, as punishment for abandoning her? She was right, in truth: he didn't know her mind. He didn't even know his own. She had just revealed a betrayal to him, and he could not care. All his thoughts now were shadowed by the walls of that dungeon, the horror he had witnessed there.

In all of Tamryllin, he was the only one who knew.

Looking bored, as if disappointed by his lack of reaction, Marilla extended her long fingers to him. "This came for you."

Marlen unfolded the message, expecting it to be a summons from the palace. When he saw what it was instead, his blood quickened. "Who brought this?"

"Some hooded man," she said, and sneered. "That's the most excitement I've seen from you in months."

HE was lost in a forest of pillars, malachite and porphyry and marble, arching toward a high ceiling rich with gold. It was massive enough to contain ten of the Court Plaza and was ringed with the sculpted heads of all the kings who had ever ruled in Tamryllin, their flat gazes turned eternally downward as if to keep watch. Though hundreds milled within the walls of the Eldest Sanctuary—priests, pilgrims, and worshippers—the silence was vast as the space. Few spoke above a whisper—and if they did, the articulation was lost in all the vastness, much as a shout would be from the height of a mountain into wind.

Even at noon, the sanctuary was only fitfully illumined by afternoon sunlight that crept through windows far above. It was a place designed to overwhelm, to mystify, favoring shadow over light.

It was with difficulty that Marlen found the place he sought: a bench on the north side of the sanctuary, situated under a painting that depicted the birth of Estarre, emerging a full-figured woman in a gold chariot from the sky. White horses with red eyes and swan's wings pulled the chariot toward the green earth below. White wolves with red eyes ran ahead of the chariot's great wheels, tearing with gory relish at the throats of squat black creatures with claws. The emergence of Estarre into the world had banished a slew of demon spirits. From the start, she was a warrior; the full force of her light killed some, drove others mad.

The man waiting beneath the painting with his large hands on his knees. A hood concealed the upper half of his face, while shadows masked the rest.

"My lord," said the man.

"What did you mean in your message?" said Marlen. "Who are you?"

"No one," said the man. "But once I was servant to a Galician merchant."

"What do you want?" said Marlen. "I can't free him, if that's what this is about."

"The crowds here are bigger today than usual," the man said, as if Marlen hadn't spoken. "Everyone fears the plague. The king has ordered the gates of Sarmanca shut, with no one permitted to go in or out. But still it comes."

Marlen edged closer to the man, hoping his imposing height would make the desired impression. "What do you want?"

The other man tilted his head to look up. Now Marlen could see the eyes in the shadow of the hood, unnervingly intense. "Your master is not a man, Marlen Humbreleigh. He keeps his body alive with a rare magic."

"That's ridiculous," Marlen said at once, though he felt his knees go weak. He thought of Nickon Gerrard's eyes the night he had tortured Hassen.

"See for yourself," said the man. "It happens at first dark of the moon—I swear it. Just use the passageway behind his chambers—you know the one."

"How—"

"No one sees a servant. I've watched you. I know you make it your business to learn what is hidden. That you've used the passageway to spy on your master—perhaps hoping to blackmail him—but saw nothing useful."

"He's not my master," said Marlen.

"You certainly aren't your own," said the man. "Yes, I know you are dangerous," he added as if he had read Marlen's thoughts. "But we are in the Eldest Sanctuary, where blood spilled angers the gods. And I think if you consider, you'll know I have helped you today. Now that Dane Beylint is dead, you and I may be the only ones who know." The man stood. "If he is ever freed, please tell my master—tell Gidyon Gelvan—that Cal did not desert him."

Before Marlen could think of a response, the man began to run, darting around the nearest pillar and into a crowd of worshippers. Marlen stared after the running man but did not follow, and soon he had vanished into the crowd. Marlen had a feeling "Cal," whoever he was, would not remain in Tamryllin.

I know you are not the snake, the man had written in his message. Perhaps it was for that, as much as anything, that Marlen let him go.

ENTERING the palace later that day, Marlen felt as if no one saw him. He had diminished to a cipher, his sword a laughable append-age, a stick he brandished to make himself feel important. Anyone who saw him with Nickon Gerrard would know Marlen was no more than his creature. Marlen may have had the appearance of power, but it was nothing compared to what the Court Poet was capable of.

He stopped a moment to survey the tapestry in the alcove near Nickon Gerrard's quarters. Now its gold-and-silver-threaded loveli-ness struck him more than ever. Davyd Dreamweaver, excising the land of enchantments. A legend, yet as real as was Marlen's own life.

But whereas the Dreamweaver would be remembered as a tragic hero, Marlen had some idea how he himself would be remembered.

He was ushered into Nickon Gerrard's rooms without ceremony. The force of the man's presence shook him like a wind as he entered the room. The Court Poet appeared years younger, his skin radiant, his bearing upright as a tree. Even his clothes seemed to fit him differently, as if they were filled in once again with the muscled shape of his youth.

Nickon Gerrard did not waste time. "I know what you dreamed last night."

Marlen tried to conceal his fear. If Nickon Gerrard knew his dreams, what else did he know?

The Court Poet laughed. "You seem startled," he said. "You have an assignment, Humbreleigh. You haven't found Darien Aldemoor— that displeases me. You fled when I was disciplining a treasonous poet. Here is one last chance to prove you can be of use. I don't think I need tell you your fate if you fail."

With a bow, Marlen cast his eyes down. "I am at your service."

"You want the Path?" Sunlight fell upon Nickon Gerrard's brow, catching the mark of the Seer and silvering his hair. "Lady Amaristoth has been possessed by Edrien Letrell himself. She has the knowledge now. Whether she is aware of it or not."

"Lin," said Marlen. *I am the key.*

The Seer's smile chilled Marlen as if he were back in the dark wood of his dream. "You will go north to retrieve her for me," he said. "Don't imagine you can flee. I will always find you, Marlen Humbreleigh."

"Flee?" said Marlen, flinging back his hair and standing tall. His voice rang so confident in his own ears that he almost convinced himself. "I am to be Court Poet someday, my Lord Gerrard," he said. "For that destiny I will gladly return."

MARLEN began preparations to leave the city. His orders were to journey north, to a village east of Dynmar, and there to seek a man.

How that would lead to Kimbralin Amaristoth, Marlen could only guess.

"I expect you'll take full advantage of my absence," he said coldly when he told Marilla of his trip. It was in his mind that he could dispossess her of everything, let her go. There were other women, even if none so fully grasped the roots of him the way she did.

"I could," Marilla conceded. "There is an alternative, however."

"Which is?"

They were standing in the corridor of his home; she leaned against the wall like a willing victim. "I've always wanted to travel."

Marlen laughed. He couldn't help it. "Are you confessing to an interest that doesn't involve your usual? Because that's just a bit hard to believe."

She shrugged. "Women of my class don't travel much, Marlen," she said with a touch of wryness. For the first time since he had known her, Marlen thought she sounded almost sane. "If you're going to northern Eivar, I'd like to come with you."

Marlen looked at her a moment. She seemed to have dropped her façade, and it unnerved him. Maybe because he'd thought that if one thing in his life was dependable, it was Marilla's utter inability to behave like a human being. "It will be a hard road," he said. "You'll have to keep pace. I won't be able to hire a carriage for you." He thought of something. "Can you ride?"

Marilla smiled. "Yes. My parents were farmers."

"You had parents," said Marlen. "Well that's quite enough surprises for one day."

DARK of the moon came that same week. Marlen Humbreleigh delayed his journey, citing the need for preparations. He knew, though, that it was a risk.

All that day he'd stayed hidden in the castle gardens, knowing the gates would be barred at night. Though he had a little food to sustain him through the day, he could barely eat it, as if his stomach were a knot. He had a story: if anyone questioned his presence among the hedges and flower beds and elaborate fountains, he would hint there was a lady that interested him in the palace. He even had a name—a silly girl, a lord's daughter, who'd made eyes at him when he performed at court. But even that story might not be enough; it would be best to evade questioning altogether.

At nightfall Marlen crept to the tapestry of Davyd Dreamweaver outside the Court Poet's chambers and pushed it aside. The stone protruding from the wall like a small knob looked like a flaw, a curiosity. Until you gripped it and pulled, and the stone turned out to be the handle of a door cut into the wall.

All castles had their secrets—especially those that were very old, and the king's palace in Tamryllin predated Ellenican rule. The Thracian period of a millennium past had bequeathed architecture and relics long since fallen into disrepair. By now Marlen had discovered such doors everywhere in the castle, which seemed to have escaped the notice of its residents. They were a uniformly thick-headed lot, Marlen thought—except Court Poet Gerrard, who was something else entirely.

Glancing around to be certain no one saw, Marlen pulled the door open. He was unnerved by the sound of it in the quiet of night, stone grating against stone. But no one came, and he was able to duck inside and pull it shut after him, praying no one had seen. As his eyes adjusted to the dark, Marlen struck up a flame from tinder and flint. All his previous spy attempts on Nickon Gerrard had been in daylight.

Marshalling his courage, Marlen crept down the dim passage, aware that the night's silence amplified every sound. The passageway led up a flight of stairs, ending in a tiny window that overlooked Lord Gerrard's chambers. From inside the room it would have passed for an air duct. And this passageway led to others, which overlooked other rooms in this wing. A man could spend a lifetime exploring the remains of what the Thracians had left behind in this castle alone.

It was close to midnight now. Within the room was silence, and Marlen wondered if Cal had been sent to test his loyalty—if the Court

Poet would send someone to kill him in the dark. Marlen rested his hand on his sword hilt.

After what seemed like hours, Marlen saw a light. A candle. Then another. He heard movements, a rustling. His mouth suddenly dry, Marlen quieted his breathing, hardly enough to stir a feather.

A new candle was lit. And another. As if Nickon Gerrard needed the entire room to bear witness.

When the Court Poet finally came into view, the first thing Marlen saw was the cloak—the six-colored cloak that Marlen had once coveted more than anything else in his life. It swept from the Court Poet's broad shoulders and swirled about him to debonair effect.

Then Marlen saw the mirror that hung before the Court Poet—finest silver, reflecting every detail. He saw that where Nickon Gerrard's face should have been was a skull, hung with black tendrils of flesh. Only the eyes were alive, whirling with a cold light.

Not a man.

Marlen clamped his hands to his lips. He felt a cold sickness in his stomach all the way down to his knees and then up again, in his throat.

Not here, he bade himself, in frantic silence. He was frozen in place, terrified that the wormlike eyes would catch sight of him in the mirror.

The Court Poet was unstopping a glass bottle of a delicate triangular shape. It was red, its stopper like a false ruby. As Marlen watched, the thing that had been the Court Poet let three drops from the bottle fall onto its black tongue.

The change was nearly immediate: even as the Court Poet stoppered the bottle again, a mask of flesh began gathering across the skull like a mirage of light; and soon it was the handsome face of Nickon Gerrard again, coolly expressionless. He flicked back his cloak in a dramatic gesture, as if preparing to resume a role.

Then suddenly Nickon Gerrard looked directly at the place where Marlen crouched. With calm precision he said, "You know I will find you."

Marlen jumped back. He drew his sword and leaned against the wall, heaving shallow, desperately quiet breaths. Only after a long time did he realize no one was coming for him. As if he were not a threat. Nickon Gerrard didn't care what he knew, secure in the knowledge that Marlen was his.

I will find you.

29

In his short life, Ned Alterra had already faced many things. He had come within a hairbreadth of being flayed alive, for a start—by a pirate of the east with a sense of humor and a blunt knife. If not for considerable luck and the camaraderie of good men, his head would now be perched atop a pike, grinning eternally over the expanse of the Blood Sea. Along with many others.

Ned recalled ships lined entirely with skulls, although worse were the heads that had not yet finished rotting. Sighting one of those ships in the eastern seas induced terror in even the most stalwart men. There was talk of a pirate queen who wore a necklace of snakes and sustained them on a diet of prisoners. The east held dangers undreamed of elsewhere. Ned's fellow crew members, who had come to seek their fortunes from all parts of the world, had made him aware that this was so.

In such places, Ned thought, even the darkest songs caught in one's throat. There was too much else.

Yet he thought he'd rather be anywhere, even battling pirates again for his life, than meet the eyes of the woman who sat across from him, her hands in her lap. Despite her demure manner, she was a girl no longer. His heart had constricted in his chest when she told him, in brief, lifeless sentences, about her month in the kitchens of the inn.

My love, he had wanted to say, and then recalled whose love she was. And after all he had seen, all he had learned in the world of blood beyond their borders, still he wanted to weep.

He did not know how long they sat in silence. There had been a great deal of silence between them in the beginning.

"How is it you?" she had said that first day, staring at him around the door. She was bald; he was not prepared for that. Her shoulders heartbreakingly bare and delicate above the blanket she had wrapped about herself. Then her eyes widened with horror. "Ned, please, go," she said. "Don't look at me."

"Who did this to you?" he demanded, even though he knew.

In the end, Ned had been surprised by how easy it was to find her. Lord Amaristoth's presence in Dynmar was the talk of the tavern, and Ned heard that recently a young girl had come into his care. No one knew who she was and few had actually seen her, save a young seamstress who described her as "sad."

It was child's play from that point on to find the room where the lord was staying. It was also too late.

Though Rianna couldn't talk about what had happened, she did show him the note from Rayen Amaristoth. Ned had felt such an unexpected mix of grief and rage—rage at Rianna, too—that he'd had to leave the room.

When he came back, Rianna was dressed, and looked surprised to see him. "I thought you had gone," she said. There was a dead quality to her voice.

"I know about it all, Rianna," said Ned. "I know you love Darien Aldemoor, and that you gave yourself to Rayen."

Rianna nodded. All the lies she had once relied upon to spare Ned's feelings—those were gone.

"I could never leave you." It was all he could do to keep his voice steady.

"I can't give you what you want," said Rianna Gelvan. "And I'm tired of men wanting things from me. Please go. I can work in the kitchens again until I've paid my way out." There was a grim set to her face that he had never seen before. It was all the more stark now that her face was nearly a skull and her hair was gone. The dark snood she wore was unkind to her face, contrasting with her skin to bring out every line of bone. But that was less unnerving than the ridged bones of her skull, which served to remind Ned how fragile she was. How fragile and fleeting, he thought, were both their lives.

"I know I can never have you," said Ned. "I will help you find Darien Aldemoor."

She eyed him with cold suspicion. "What's in it for you?"

"Rayen Amaristoth is hunting Darien," said Ned. "I expect we'll come upon him. I'll kill him for you."

In a graceful, deliberate motion, Rianna reached into her skirts and drew out a knife. The insignia on its hilt was of Master Gelvan's house, a letter *G* flanked by eagles. Weak sunlight flickered along the blade's edge as she held it up for inspection with this new cold gaze he didn't know. "Only if you let me help."

THEY charted their course that evening. The noise of the tavern provided a distraction, gave them something to look at when they could hardly look one another in the eye.

Rianna thought Ned might try to win her with a gentlemanly manner by pulling out her chair or with other cultured affectations, but he did not. On the contrary, he kept a distance and avoided small talk, which he had never been that adept at in the first place.

Perhaps with the way she looked now, he was having second thoughts about her. That would be convenient. It seemed to her now that beauty was an inconvenience at best.

"We'll have to camp in the woods," Ned was saying. "I'll pick up supplies tomorrow morning."

"Does that mean we'll need a tent?" said Rianna. Her hands clenched in her lap under the table, where he would not see them. She knew Ned would never harm her, and yet.

"No," said Ned. "It's not too cold yet, and if it rains, these forests are full of caves."

"How will we go about looking for him?" she asked. "That's the part that I don't understand."

He nodded. "Well, lucky for us, your man is being hunted by a rather ostentatious character. Everyone in this part of the world knows Lord Amaristoth. Anyone he encounters will remember him."

"But how is *he* searching for Darien?"

Dipping his quill in the inkwell and then blotting it on a rag, Ned touched the pen to a parchment and drew. A shape that resembled half a figure eight emerged from the pen, and then he closed it with a straight line. He drew another line through its center, tipped with a triangle. A bow and arrow. "Rianna, you must bear in mind that the man we are tracking is an experienced hunter," said Ned. "More than experienced. It defines who he is."

Rianna's jaw tightened. "I know."

"I'm not telling you this to upset you," said Ned. There was something different about him, though she couldn't understand quite what it was. All she knew was that in all the time she had seen him that day, she hadn't once been seized with the impulse to reassure him— or to lie to him. *Is that a change in him, or in me?* she wondered. *Have I become cold?*

Ned had developed muscle that made his lank limbs seem more proportionate. He walked with more ease now, rather than as if he half-expected to trip over himself. The tooled leather scabbard at his belt, which had once been an ornamentation, now looked weather-beaten, with shallow slashes in it.

Ned was still speaking; Rianna focused again on his words. He was speaking to her as he would speak to another man, matter-of-factly and without softness. "I'm telling you these things because, in order to accomplish our goal, you have to understand the nature of what we're dealing with."

Next he drew a curved line and connected both ends of the parabola with three straight lines. A harp. "Darien Aldemoor," said Ned. "He may know how to fight, but ultimately he has no power against someone like Rayen. If we manage to find Darien before Rayen does, we will have to be ready to help him defend himself."

"Darien knows how to fight," said Rianna.

Ned looked down at the parchment on the table. "I'm sure," he said. Then he raised his eyes with what seemed like an effort, and his tone became all business again. "I'm sure he does. But he's not an Amaristoth." He cleared his throat. "There's something else you ought to know. Darien is believed to have murdered his companion, Hassen Styr."

"He didn't," said Rianna.

"I wouldn't be helping you find him if I believed he had," said Ned. "I believe the politics of Tamryllin have taken a strange turn. But I thought you should know what is being said, and that if you find Darien, it's unlikely that the two of you can stay in Eivar."

Rianna nodded curtly. "I knew."

And what was Eivar to her? A white, rose-entwined mansion that had been her home. A town where her soul, it seemed, had been devoured and swallowed. The idea of leaving Eivar did not disturb her, but that was not all. It was a freeing idea, as if the world could become new again.

Her soul grow new again, in Darien's arms. There, at least, was something she could still hope for and believe. And once she found Darien, perhaps he would know how to save her father.

"We'll leave tomorrow," said Ned, "unless you are not well. Have you the strength?"

For some reason the question gave her pause. *Strength.* "I don't know," she said. "I mean, I have strength to get up tomorrow and to do what must be done," she added, seeing his concern. "More than that—I don't know."

For the first time Ned touched her. Rianna stiffened slightly, but it was a brotherly touch, his hand on her wrist. "That is all the strength anyone needs," he said.

"But what about pain?" she asked. She couldn't help it; she wanted answers, and Ned, with his new calluses and grim look seemed to have them.

But she was wrong; he shook his head. "I don't know."

CHAPTER 30

TRUE silence was a thing she had never known in her life. Her
father had made a point of shielding Rianna from the noise and the
rudeness of the world—she understood this now, too—and once she'd
have been hard-pressed to think of a place more deeply quiet than the
stately street of their house. But here in the woods, silence was tangible, much like a live thing itself; she was at once awed and tormented
by it. She could not retreat to her father's library and lose herself in a
story. There was no great sounding of bells from the Eldest Sanctuary threading the silence of deepest night. The clatter of the kitchens
that had worn at her mind and body had receded, like a memory
from someone else's life. If not for the stubble of her hair and the
cracked skin of her hands, she would not have believed it had happened to her.

Now there were the pervasive scent of pine, shadows piled upon
shadows from a maze of overhead branches. Amid so much quiet,
Rianna's thoughts echoed in the chambers of her mind as if it were a
dungeon with no door, wall folding into wall of moldering smooth
stone. Nights, the echoes reached into her dreams; she would awaken
in the morning with Rayen's whisper like a knife rasping in her ear.
Yet somehow it was worse to be awake.

There was, of course, Ned, but he didn't speak much. It was as if he sensed that she couldn't bear conversation just now. What could she say? And if she did begin to talk, she feared she might break down and weep. And that, she thought, was enough of that. She was finished with turning to others for sympathy—and especially to men.

In a different frame of mind, the cold might have distracted her. She was well-fitted against the weather—Ned had bought her a cloak and warm undergarments before they had set out—but nonetheless it was getting to the end of autumn, and a chill had begun to gnaw deep in the northern woodlands. At this time of year, the Gelvan home would have been warmed by wood fires, and she and her father would have been preparing for the journey south.

Thoughts of her father were chief among the echoes that tormented her in the woods' stillness. Again and again she saw him collapse, his eyes fixed on hers even after the light had gone from them.

At such times she was most tempted to turn to Ned, to hide her face in his shoulder as she would once have done without even thinking. But that had been before Darien Aldemoor, before the ill-fated betrothal. *Before Rayen Amaristoth,* her thoughts supplied helpfully. *Yes,* she replied within her mind. *Yes, curse you. That, too.*

It was also out of consideration for Ned that she did not turn to him. She knew he loved her, and she knew—now more than ever—that he was a good soul. He did not deserve the pain of false hope. He seemed stronger now, but she knew that could be illusory, that men concealed so much behind façades of strength. Or façades of vulnerability, come to that.

She would not allow her thoughts to go down that road—she would instead think of what remained to be done next. So far, the task of tracking Rayen Amaristoth had proved surprisingly simple. On their last day in Dynmar, she had suggested that they pay a visit to the shoemaker she had met with Rayen, recalling that Rayen had had some remaining items to pick up from him before he was on his way.

Now that she knew his true nature, Rianna marveled that a man such as Rayen Amaristoth had so endeared himself to the common folk. Once she would have taken it for proof of his goodness and generosity. Once, a mere week ago.

Clearly there was an advantage to procuring the loyalty of so many, even the powerless. It was a valuable lesson.

The day they were to set out from Dynmar, she and Ned had entered the workshop at dawn, where the shoemaker was already at work. With Ned keeping a respectful distance behind her, Rianna had greeted the man warmly, but with the reserve of a highborn lady. She knew if she were too friendly, she would lose his respect and excite suspicion.

"So it's the friend of Lord Amaristoth—Lady Leya, wasn't it?" said the shoemaker, looking wary. "He's already left—I'd have thought you'd be with him. Wasn't Lord Amaristoth escorting you to your family?"

Rianna trilled a lighthearted laugh. "He was," she conceded, "but Lord Amaristoth is a man of the world, with many worldly concerns. Thus he appointed me a bodyguard and departed on his own errands. I don't recall where he said he was going . . ."

"Well he was just here a few days ago," said the shoemaker. "I believe he said he was heading toward the village of Korrit. Needed to see to it that his boots would last the journey."

"Of course—Korrit," said Rianna with a nod and a smile, as if the memory were coming back to her. "What such a man would have to do in such a dismal place, I can't imagine."

"Nor I, my lady," said the man. "Were you needing something?"

As they left the shop, Rianna noticed that her hands were shaking. Still she managed to keep her posture erect and to maintain a stately pace, as if they were out for a stroll.

"You're good," said Ned, showing the first sign of humor she had seen in him since his return. "I would never have guessed you were anyone but the cheerful, exceedingly shallow Lady Leya."

She had given him a sharp look, wondering how he could congratulate her, so guilelessly, for her skill at lying. She remembered the games they had played as children, where pretending to be other people had formed the backbone of their play. She remembered the way he was forever trying to rescue her, and she constantly chafing to have her own adventures. A coil of rage arose in her—it was not for women to have adventures, because they were women and they were weak, passive treasures to be desired. Desired, toyed with—*hunted*. But Ned was not to blame for this.

So in the following days, they aimed themselves at Korrit, which by all accounts was even more a backwater than Dynmar.

"My guess is he is picking up supplies there before he heads into the mountains," said Ned. "Everyone believes that that is where Darien went. That's where the Path is said to be."

"Do you believe in the Path?" Rianna asked, picking desultorily at her skirts.

"I don't know . . . and I don't much care," Ned said shortly.

"You sound angry."

"Songs are nothing to me," said Ned. "Once I tried to believe they mattered, because you love them so. But now I understand I care nothing for words spun to music by a man removed from danger. A blade sings louder."

Rianna crooked a smile and said nothing. She knew she owed Ned quite a lot, and it would therefore be rude to point out that his views were more vehement than necessary. She wondered if he would ever forgive her, but it was too wearying a thought to pursue. Ned Alterra was his own man; it was not her place to dictate to him how to spend his days.

But there was an unmistakable kernel of truth in what he'd said. *A blade sings louder.* Each evening when they stopped for the day, she practiced with her dagger. Ned once offered to help her, but she pretended not to hear. And she tried not to think too much, as each motion triggered the release of a memory. *A knife is intimate in the kill*, she heard Rayen Amaristoth say, one of the echoes that rebounded in the smooth-walled cell of her mind.

Ned watched her, and she wondered if he felt what she did: that in those moments he may as well have been miles distant, a speck on an ever-receding shore.

Perhaps, around her, he had always felt that way.

One night, when the echoes became a cacophony that she could not escape, Rianna began spinning with her dagger in a series of slashes that did not even make sense, yet she could not stop; as the trees stood in vast disapproval and the frigid wind whipped at her face, she whirled faster and faster. Their tiny fire threw wavering light so she could see the ground, the stones, but nothing else beyond the black curtain of night. Ned was no more than a shadow, and then not there at all, as she spun and spun.

And then her blade clanged as it hit something hard, and she saw that Ned had entered the light and intercepted her knife with his own, stopping her dead. She glared; it had been a week that they had traveled and never had he dared interfere. "Leave me."

"You'll have to fight me first."

There arose in her an unprecedented fury. Without a word, she attacked him, and later she wondered if she might have killed him that night, if he had not fought well. She hissed as she plunged her knife toward his knees—a blow that would maim. He leaped to avoid her blade and then swiped at her knife, knocking it from her grasp. Her fingers stung as the hilt was torn away and she nearly fell, gasping for breath and clenching her hands in fruitless anger.

"There are a few things I can teach you, if you'll let me," said Ned.

"Why—because I'm a girl, I need lessons from you?"

Ned bent to the ground to retrieve her dagger and presented it to her with a slight bow. In the faint light the insignia of her father's house gleamed like a reminder, or reproach. "I am no weapons master," he said. "But I learned a few tricks abroad. We share a common purpose—shouldn't we help one another?"

"Are you saying there are things I can teach you?" she said, half mockingly.

Ned's face remained expressionless, as if considering the question. At last, without looking at her, he said, "Many things."

Rianna felt ashamed then, though still inexplicably angry. She turned away, but the next evening, she allowed him to join her within the circle of the firelight. No longer could she lose herself in the whirl of her own dance; that was lost to her. But she understood that to learn, she needed help, and Ned now seemed to have knowledge. Nothing could make him graceful, but there was a steady adeptness in his movements now, and speed.

"You know it's likely that Rayen will kill us both," Rianna said one night when they were done.

"I know," said Ned. "Can I dissuade you from accompanying me?"

"That's what I was going to ask you."

"He is one of the finest swordsmen in the kingdom," said Ned.

"Alas," said Rianna, sheathing her knife and bending smoothly at the waist to collect sticks for firewood. "What a loss that will be for the kingdom."

Most days, though, they did not speak. She was too preoccupied with her private world—and she suspected that he had his, as well. Rianna was awakened one night by Ned crying out in his sleep, a continuous wail that she knew would have shamed him to have her hear it. She could have gone to him, held him in her arms. Perhaps more— what did it matter now? Instead she turned over on her side and tried to sleep.

In the morning, Ned showed no sign that he remembered his nightmare—for so it must have been—and she wondered how much he held back from her now. He had been to the lands beyond the Blood Sea, faced the nameless perils there. In another time, she might have been jealous, demanded to hear detailed descriptions of the places so far beyond the scope of her experience. Now something held her back. Just as she would never tell him how it was to bed Rayen or to love Darien, there were myriad dark threads of thought that he might never share with her. This was something she now understood, without ever having to ask.

IT was in the second week of their journey that Ned found Rianna crying. She had gone into the woods to relieve herself and not returned, and he, becoming worried, at last followed where she had gone and called out for her.

"I'm here," she said shakily, where she stood clinging to a tree. "There is nothing wrong."

"Are you sure?"

Rianna raised her skirt to the level of her knee, exposing her bare leg to the cold. A trickle of dried blood stained her leg all the way down to her boots. "Do you see that?" she said. "Do you understand what it means?"

In that moment Ned thought he might cry, too. "All this time, this was worrying you?"

Rianna choked a laugh. "Worrying me?" she said. "I thought, if a child of his was inside me, I might need to use the knife on myself."

"I am glad that won't be necessary," said Ned.

She laughed again, more merrily this time. "Ned," she said. "Will you wet a rag for me in the stream? I would like to clean this up."

THE day they reached the village of Korrit it was raining, the skies a haze of unrelieved grey. Wrapped in their cloaks against the weather, they trudged to the village gates through mud. The road was desolate, and as they hurried through the narrow streets—if indeed the dirt paths could be called thus—they met few passersby.

"If not for the shoemaker, I'd have never heard of this place," said Ned. "And now I understand why."

They made their way toward the inn. Rianna had begun to shiver violently; when Ned noticed, he motioned that they retreat to the shelter of a large tree.

"Rianna, what's wrong?" he asked. "Are you cold?"

She shook her head so hard that droplets spat from her hood. "No. I just realized—he could be here now."

"You're right," he said. "We'll find concealment for you, and then I'll find out what I can at the inn. Rayen has never met me."

They decided she would hide in an abandoned shed that was near enough to the inn that if she called out, there was a chance he would hear. She crouched in the shadows as he left and swept the cloak across her face for concealment.

When he returned some time later, she was still there. She jumped to her feet. "Did you find out anything?" Her eyes were focused on his face so intensely that Ned could imagine them burning through him, yet he knew that this had nothing to do with him at all. She would burn through anyone, anything, on the bright lethal beam of her purpose.

"I had a drink with the barkeep."

She clenched her teeth with impatience. "And?"

Ned drew a breath and let it out again, suddenly reluctant. "Rayen passed through here yesterday."

"And?" she urged again.

"He was heading north on the road, through the woods and towards an outlying property. I got a description of the place. But there is more." Ned paused, wondering how best to continue. There were implications to what he had heard, if his guess was correct. Rianna was watching him, letting her lifted eyebrow speak volumes of her irritation. Finally, Ned went on. "Rianna, the man told me Rayen wasn't alone when he passed through," he said. "He has a prisoner."

CHAPTER
31

COLD was seeping into all their days, into his dreams at night. Darien Aldemoor would wake to find himself curled tight as a coiled spring in his blankets, his cloak providing an extra layer of tenuous protection. It wasn't enough, and he knew the true chill of winter had yet to set in.

If Lin shared his concerns, she didn't speak of them or of much else, lost as she seemed to be in her own thoughts. Ever since the night he had summoned Edrien Letrell, there had been an air of deep quiet about her, as if she were sinking away from him, like a stone down a well. She was unresponsive, almost docile, when he changed her bandages each day, her gaze fixed somewhere past his shoulder.

Yet it was due to her that they seemed to have given the Ladybirds the slip; in these woods, she was at last in her element. Once, she told him, she and Rayen had competed to find an elusive white wolf that was preying on a nearby village. It had been winter, and the wolf blended with the blanketing snow, making the hunt all the more challenging. For days, she told him, they had each subsisted alone in the woods, foraging where they could, in search of the beast.

"Who won?" Darien had asked, as Lin trailed off. It had been at night that they'd talked about this, each facing a different direction as they sat with their backs together. There was scant warmth to be had from this, but sometimes Darien imagined he could feel the small scared rhythm of her heartbeat, like that of a bird, through the drum-taut muscles of her back.

Though he could not see her face, he could hear the wry smile in her voice. "Neither of us," she said. "When I returned home, starving and near frozen after five days, Rayen was waiting, feet propped up and with a glass of wine by the fire. He laughed at me, said, 'Anyone else would have known when to stop.'"

"Rayen's a charmer," said Darien, and felt as if the blackness of the wood swallowed his small words. All she told him of her former life, he thought, was from some nightmare country beyond the use of language, even the finely wrought use of it in which Darien was skilled.

His shirt that they used to make bandages was nearly gone, but thankfully her bleeding was subsiding. Darien was no physician, but in his time with Marlen on the road, they had occasionally been forced to tend to their own wounds. Though none had been so deep as the small, expert cuts Lin had made in her own wrists.

Why did it still hurt to think of Marlen?

Darien thought perhaps the cold and solitude of the woods, and Lin's pale silence, were forcing him too much into his own head.

"I need to talk to you," he said finally one day as they were walking. It was a better day than usual for her; she seemed to be regaining the use of her hands, and once in a while she had broken from reverie to smile abstractly at him, as if he were an amusing child she did not quite have time for.

"What is it?" she said, immediately stopping in her tracks.

"Let's sit a minute," said Darien. "Please."

She dropped obligingly to a sitting position on a fallen log, stretching out her legs. He sank to the ground nearby.

"Lin," he said, and he suddenly wondered what he wanted to say. "This journey—what has it brought us? And with winter coming . . ."

"I think I know what you are going to say." She enunciated the words with an odd disconnectedness, as if each were separate from the one that came before.

"Do you?" He wondered how she could know, when he was scarcely sure himself.

"You want to be quit of all this," she said. "To stop seeking the Path. And escape to Kahishi, I suppose? There would be no life for you in Eivar, the way things stand."

Darien stared at his hands rather than look at her. He wondered when he had become someone who could be this sad, this torn within himself. "It seems like ever since we began, only terrible things have happened," he said. "And I fear I am becoming something terrible. What I did to you . . ."

"What about Rianna Gelvan?"

"What about her?" Darien said tiredly. "I'm sure I could get her out of the country somehow. If she'll still have me after the mess I've made of things."

He felt pressure on his shoulders and looked up, surprised. Lin had risen, in catlike silence, and made her way to him as he stared at his hands. She rested a hand on each of his shoulders, a phantom smile on her face. "Darien, it's not for me to tell you what you should do," she said. "If you want to stop now, that is certainly your right. Just as it is my right to keep going, if I choose."

"You can't go alone," Darien protested.

Lin shrugged, moved away from him like a boat adrift, hands loose at her sides. The bandages at her wrists were like tattered bracelets. Her face was turned up to the small bursts of light that were breaking through the trees; there was a cold yellow sun today. "That's not your concern," she said. "So tell me. Have you decided?"

"I must think on it," Darien said heavily.

Lin nodded, ran a hand through her hair. It brushed her shoulders now, but was grimy and matted from days on the road without washing. "I think I'll go stretch my legs a moment."

"I'll come," said Darien, beginning to pull himself up.

"No, thank you," said Lin. "I won't be long. I think both of us should have some time alone."

"Why?"

Lin smiled. "For one thing, you just said you wanted to think about your choice. So I suggest you do that while I'm gone. Think." Before he could say another word, she melted into the trees in that maddening way she had.

Darien wished it were safe to play his harp. It was only with his fingers to the strings that the densely tangled problems in his mind took on a pattern and shape. Perhaps that was the answer, then: Kahishi, a land of golden desert, mountains and remote gardens; a place where Darien could build his life anew, his music freely sounding amid foreign sands and stones.

LIN felt strangely light, as if her legs were not a part of her, as she flitted from one tree to the next. It was not how she usually navigated the forest terrain, but today—she did not feel entirely in possession of her body. She didn't know if it was fatigue, or the shock of Darien's words . . . though if she were honest, she had to admit that it had not really been a shock. The only surprise was that he had persisted this long, in light of all that had befallen them. What Path could be worth so much loss, so much pain?

For her it was different, of course.

She had meant to end her own life that night in the woods. She still didn't know how to feel, that she was still here, her baffling life still unfolding. She didn't know how to live her life now that she knew what it was to have a dead man fill her, down to the dregs of her soul; to feel his essence and dreadful agony like a thousand-ton rock.

In the moments that Edrien Letrell had possessed her, it was as if she had swallowed in one terrible rush every thought, every experience and loss in the course of his life. Images and sensations raced one into another: a golden court, the sharp taste of Kahishian rice dishes, the silk and scent of women in the dark, one woman's eyes large with pain—and it was as if these eyes were the center: they kept reemerging throughout the rest of the memories, cropping up amid sensations of taste, of music, of erotic conquest. If Edrien's life could be compared to a song, there had been a recurring theme.

In her waking life, that was all Lin could remember. Sometimes a cobweb of memory would drift through her consciousness, and it took a moment for her to realize that it was not one of her own memories.

Nights were another story. When she slept, the life of Edrien Letrell came calling, events haunted with familiar melody. His songs had different meanings for him than they'd had for Lin, and now she could feel that, too. She would awaken exhausted as if she had actually lived these events—a life not her own.

For that reason Lin drifted through the days, unspeaking; she was afraid of what she might say if she did speak. She was afraid of this new life devouring hers, and battled to hold fast to her own thoughts, her own memories. Her own music. Her songs were the essence of her; and never had Lin understood this more than she did now, with another man's music vibrating from the depths of her skull down to the root of her spine, memory and music together.

I need Valanir Ocune, she thought more than once during those days. Not even the Academy Masters had his knowledge of the enchantments. Perhaps he would be able to tell her if she was losing her soul.

Now in the depths of the wood, mulling her conversation with Darien—for she had given him a half-truth; she needed to think, as well—Lin wondered if she could give up the search for the Path now. Something deep and obscene had happened to her the night Darien had used her blood, and the Path might be the only place where it could be made right.

If it could be made right.

She knew that if she could consciously explore the pattern of Edrien's memories, she would find clues to the Path. But that was a part of what was so disturbing: she could not control the access she had. And she guessed that the events of the Path were buried deep, as Edrien Letrell had wished them to be.

She thought she knew what Darien's decision would be. He had done his best. But with the Tower of the Winds out of their reach and the summoning of Edrien Letrell unsuccessful, what was left for him to do? And perhaps he was right. Valanir Ocune had clearly been wrong about Lin—perhaps that meant he had been wrong about other things.

Lin turned to make her way back, a cold weight of certainty in her heart. She would give him her blessing to seek a new life. He would soon forget her, and she would get lost in the mountains and find the Path, or not. *More likely not.* The nightmare of their journey together, she and Darien Aldemoor, would trail away into oblivion, without the satisfaction of an ending.

Later, Lin would think it was the heaviness of these thoughts and the effort of keeping Edrien Letrell's memories at bay that distracted her, made her vulnerable to what came next.

SHE was flying on winds that swept through the mountains, for once in a dream that was her own. Alyn was in the air beside her, golden hair dancing in the wind, smiling into her eyes. Lin smiled back, achingly happy in that instant. *You came back for me.*

His hand was on the nape of her neck, his voice as she remembered it. *I was always coming back.*

When Lin awoke, her head pounded a dull ache in her temples. She groaned, tried to move. She felt heavy in every limb, as if flattened beneath a great weight. "Darien?" Her mouth shaped the word with an effort.

"Wake, my love." A voice she had heard only in dreams this past year.

She would have screamed, had she the voice. But she realized now that he must have used some kind of hallucinatory substance on her. Her memory stopped, she realized, by the trunk of that tree. She tried to lift her head. Now she was beginning to feel a dull pain in her wrists, and she realized that they were bound, the ropes chafing at her wounds. Her legs were bound as well, and beginning to tingle unpleasantly.

"Darien," she said again, this time with dawning horror. If Rayen had found him on his way to finding her, the poet would not have had a chance.

His face appeared above her, dark hair framing the ivory carving of his face. His smile made him even more handsome, she thought, or would have if she could see him as anything but hideous. "I believe we left your friend somewhere in the more southerly part of the forest," he said. "He is a very lucky man, my love, that I did not come across him when I stole you away, or he would not have lived to harp another day. Oh—that rhymed! Perhaps I should become a poet. Was this one after my money, too?"

Lin gritted her teeth. She felt that the effort it cost to speak might kill her. "What's wrong, Rayen?" she said, though barely above a whisper. "Did you miss me so much as that?"

Rayen only laughed. He seemed genuinely cheerful, which frightened her more than anything else.

At least Darien was unharmed, though he would wonder what had happened to her.

If I could only have said farewell, she thought. She had no doubt that for making a fool of him all this past year, Rayen would kill her, here in the forest under a hushed canopy of green. Completing, at long last, what he had started years ago.

"You know," she said, "I'm honestly touched that you've spent all this time looking for me. I thought I wasn't your type."

"What is my type?"

Her stomach was a knot. *Get it over with quickly,* she thought, lifting her chin to expose her neck. That would be a quick death, if she could goad him sufficiently. "Blond and stupid," she said. "And rich."

"Alas, you're right," he said, unperturbed. "That explains the last one, certainly. I believe you may know her."

The knot tightened. "I'm sure I don't."

"I see you've guessed already," he said with a grin. "Poor Rianna Gelvan, pining for her Darien. In truth, that's why I let him live. Because it would spoil all my work if he is never to witness it." He snapped one of his gloves, a habit that had always irritated her.

Your work. She closed her eyes. It had never occurred to Lin that she herself might represent Rayen's "work." But no. She had run. That had not been a part of his plan.

"Now," he said, "I'm going to untie your legs if you behave. Unless you want to be carried very roughly and unconscious from here to where we're going."

"Why not just kill me here and save yourself the trouble?" She put a challenging edge into her tone, the goad again.

"That would be a waste of valuable resources," said Rayen. "No, my dear . . . You don't get to die yet. Not until after you're married."

A hollow laugh rattled in Lin's throat. "Married," she said with disbelief. "You intend to keep me imprisoned until I am in someone's bed?"

"Not exactly," said Rayen. "I've done Nickon Gerrard a good turn, and in exchange he has promised to use his powers in my service. For one small task."

Lin's hands clenched. "What are you talking about, Rayen?" She tried to keep her voice calm. If he knew how much he was frightening her right now, her chances of goading him to kill her would be lost. He would enjoy this torment instead, far too much.

In his gratified smile, though, she could see that she had failed. He knelt close until she could feel the warmth of his breath on the side of her face, his sibilant whisper in her ear. "Ah, at last Lin the poet has met something she fears more than death," he said. "In return for my help amassing evidence against the detestable Galician merchant, Nickon Gerrard has promised me a docile sister—a lady who knows her duties and will be a credit to our house. He cannot make you anything resembling a beauty, alas, but he can play the strings of your heart as he does his harp. So he has promised me."

Lin breathed deep, trying to calm her heart. "Rayen, what if I promise to marry whomever you choose? And whatever else you require?"

He laughed. "Too late for that, love. It's not that I don't trust you, although of course I don't. But I also really like this idea. You must admit it's intriguing. My sister the lady, her only desire to please her man—oh, and her husband, of course." He laughed again, and Lin wondered if he was as mad as their mother. "I think I'll have a tapestry woven of this hunt," he went on. "In the last panel, instead of a unicorn surrounded by spikes, there will be the foolish figure of a female poet. For Lord Gerrard has promised that although your manner will be forever changed, deep within there will be the part of you that knows—that will *always* know—which of us has won."

CHAPTER
32

WHEN Kiara dropped a gift in your lap, you could not refuse it. To do so was not only foolish—it was a display of rank ingratitude to the goddess. Whatever else Valanir Ocune did or did not believe, in the solitude of his nights of composition he at times felt distinctly the visitation of a being outside himself. Lauded as the greatest poet of the age, Valanir knew—sometimes too well—that such music was the dark murmur of the goddess in his ear. Not him at all. He was dust, and as he aged, he could no longer deny it within himself.

Yet even so, Valanir was haunted by the image of Lin Amaristoth's eyes turned up to his, liquid with trust after she had cast off her mask, and he knew some gifts were themselves a kind of trap. He knew he wanted, *needed* to see this staggering thing as a gift of the goddess. For if not, what did that make him?

So he had left the silken and gold comforts of the sultan's court, where for decades he had been an honored guest. He would not consent to be an official poet for the Kahishian ruler, insisting on his independence, on vanishing into the desert or mountains for weeks at a time; but nonetheless his standing in that magnificent court was all that he could desire. He was given a tower for composition, its great height reminiscent of the Academy cells where his journey had begun. Such had been true for Edrien Letrell as well; for centuries, the citizens of Kahishi had seen themselves as patrons of Kiara's art, though they had another name for her.

He had departed the court and set upon the great trade route that ran between Majdara and Tamryllin, the two capital cities of his life. He wasn't sure where he was headed, but so far his dreams had provided a fragile sort of guidance. His dreams, and that one night when he had awakened in a cold sweat, ablaze with the knowledge of a terrible thing that had taken place in the depths of the Eivarian north.

The road was cold, the wind that tunneled through the borderland mountains growing chillier with each passing day. Last time Valanir Ocune had made this journey had been the height of spring, when he had traveled with caravans bound for Tamryllin and the Midsummer Fair. The days had rippled with conversations with merchants, guards, and lone fortune seekers; nights came alive with the music and dancing of performers of every stripe.

Now only Valanir's thoughts accompanied him, and only the wind would do for music. The roads were nearly deserted and therefore dangerous, but most Kahishians showed reverence for a man of the harp and ring and welcomed him in their homes.

He was certainly not without defenses. It was his skill in areas outside the realm of music that had helped spread his fame. People wanted heroes, Valanir thought; they would not revere a man in possession of only a single gift. He had complex feelings about the nature of fame; he knew a true Seer should not allow such considerations to cloud his heart.

No one could see his heart, in part because Valanir Ocune had never allowed anyone to come close. But the goddess Kiara did. Perhaps that was why her gift to him now was tainted with a bitter draught; she returned to him the mingling of dark and light that throughout his life was all he had been able to give her.

It was on a day near the end of autumn, just before the border crossing amid a landscape of skeletal trees, that he discovered just how thin, how frangible had been his plans. He was Valanir Ocune, most celebrated poet of the age, revered among the poets in Eivar and in the court of Majdara; but he was only a man, for whom events beyond his control must relentlessly unfold. On that day he awoke believing he could anticipate the next twist of the road; by the day's end, he would know that there was no road at all, only a tangled wood with no light.

It began when he was assailed by a voice that rose up from within his mind yet came from outside as well. His inner defenses bypassed, for the first time in his life. *"He has her,"* said a voice that was instantly familiar. The power of it was so great, so painful in its reverberations that he fell to his knees. The mark on his eye, the Seer's mark, was liquid fire. Breathing deep, Valanir clutched at his head, bowed as if in submission to a tide.

"Are you there, Valanir?" The voice rolled over and through him. *"He has her. Help me."*

IT had not taken long for Darien to discover what had happened. At first he became anxious simply because he wanted to hurry on to the next phase of his life. Added to his anxiety was a discomfiting guilt as he thought of Lin's wounds—acquired for his sake—and how vulnerable she would be traveling alone.

As he paced the ground with the rhythmic monotony of a pendulum, Darien decided that he would suggest—no, *insist*—that she allow him to escort her to a town where she could rest, be safe. In the back of his mind, he knew it was a foolish plan: Rayen was pursuing her, as was the Crown; there was no place in Eivar where she could be truly safe.

Darien could not have said when it was that the woods started to seem too quiet, when exactly he started to worry. He began by calling her name, softly, though it was a risk. But soon he didn't care anymore for risk, and struck out to look for her, calling her name frantically. Until he came to a clearing where Lin's cloak puddled in black folds on the ground. The cry of a lone falcon as it circled and swooped overhead was the only sound.

Surprisingly, Darien's response was to grow calm. All along, he had known that this was the risk in falling in with Kimbralin

Amaristoth—for Darien didn't think for a moment that it was any-one but her brother who had stolen her away. He knew he did not have the skill to track Rayen Amaristoth through the forest. And from what Lin had said, her brother would intend something terrible for her. There was very little time.

Idiot, he chided her within his mind. *Again and again you thwart my plans.*

He had to believe she was alive. It was that, or go on his way to the eastern passes and into Kahishi before winter set its bar of ice across the border.

That was not an option now.

Darien unwrapped the papers he had taken from the Academy. They had only brought sorrow upon him and Lin; yet with them he had awakened forces he had once imagined were Kiara's province alone.

Two portals had opened for Darien Aldemoor, or so he now thought: his vision of the *khave* house in Tamryllin, and the dream that had led him to Lin Amaristoth.

Or was it three? Death was another portal that had opened for him, this time at his command, perhaps within Lin herself. For some sins, Darien thought, he would never succeed in making recompense.

Turning to the page he needed, Darien drew a shuddering breath. The woods seemed to challenge him with their silence.

"I found you once in a dream," he said aloud, as if Lin stood there beside him. He could almost see her gentle, faraway smile as she con-sidered how rash he was. She would have told him to make for the border as quickly as he could go. But then, he thought, that was her deepest flaw: that she did not think of herself.

And what was his flaw? Why, that he was reckless, of course. He had made his choice. With Lin's blood, Darien had accessed the en-chantments once. To find her, he would do so again.

"THEY were scared of us in Korrit," Marilla was saying. She rode with the grace of a noblewoman, as she did everything. How she had come to know how to do these things remained a mystery to Marlen. Perhaps it was her mystery, he considered, that had allowed him to tolerate her this long.

That, and that somehow she held the keys to him.

"You give those peasants too much credit," said Marlen. "I doubt they were clever enough to be scared."

"I know the signs," she said. They rode single file, with her following him on the narrow paths. Once leaving Dynmar, they had been forced to take the dirt roads that diverged from the king's highway and snaked into the heart of the north. Once in a while Marlen would glance back, catch a glimpse of her smile. To have those teeth flashing at his back, he thought, was little different from having a knife there. And from that thought he moved to its inevitable sequel: she had betrayed him with another man.

"People like us, Marlen," she was saying. "We are the shadow these people fear in the deepest heart of themselves."

"Or they just got a look at my blade," he said. Her words disquieted him more than he would have wanted her to know. He tied his cloak closer around his neck against the cold.

Every night of their journey, he took her with savage coldness from behind, tearing his long harper's nails into her flesh. Even when he didn't want her he did it, even though he knew that for her it was no punishment, but the opposite. Trying to exact revenge on her was like climbing a wall of slick, dark obsidian. He saw her nurse her wounds in daylight—long purple slashes on her back and shoulders—but she seemed to wear them with ease, as if she considered them a decoration. Some would leave scars. Did they mark her as his, he wondered, or did her indifference to them mean that she was always beyond him?

According to the innkeeper of Korrit, Rayen Amaristoth had last been spotted with a prisoner slung across his horse, a boy that he claimed had impregnated one of the maids at Vassilian. "I'll see that he gives the filly her due," Rayen had reportedly said with a laugh.

Marlen wasn't sure what to do about Rayen, how deeply involved he was in Nickon Gerrard's game. But he felt a kinship with the man, from the little he knew. He had hopes that he could be reasoned with. And if not, the sword.

SHE was flat on her back on the dirt floor, her wrists and ankles bound at her sides to stakes that Rayen had driven into it. The ropes bit into her wounded wrists in a continuous shrill note of pain. Green-filtered sunlight angled through the window of what she took to be an abandoned woodcutter's cottage.

He had tied her legs. He'd had to, after she had succeeded in extracting the knife from her boot, and—painfully with her bound hands—lunged at his back. A desperate move, and with the ease of a dancer he had spun, laughing, and twisted it from her grip. Though not before she had wounded him lightly behind the knee. "Naughty," Rayen had said with amusement as he cleaned and bandaged his leg. "That's my just reward for not trussing you like a pig, my dear. It won't happen again."

Now he was humming as he prepared a fire. For once, the memories of Edrien Letrell within Lin were silenced, as if her fear had banished them.

"I'd gag you, but honestly, who would care if they *did* hear you scream?" Rayen said cheerfully as he worked. "Ah Lin, did I tell you yet how much I've missed you?"

"Rayen," Lin croaked through cracked lips. "What happened to us?"

He stood above her and looked down into her face. His eyebrows were drawn together in bemusement above a half-smile. "Happened?"

"What brother and sister are like this? Have you thought of that?" Her tongue sought moisture in her mouth, her throat contracted like crumpled parchment. "It's because of Kalinda . . . surely you know that?"

He chuckled softly, knelt beside her. "Oh, Lin," he said, with what sounded like indulgent affection. Then he smacked her across the jaw with an open palm. Blackness flickered in Lin's vision for a moment, and tears sprang to her eyes. "Do you know what she once said to me, about you?" he said, still gently. "She said if she had known what you'd grow into, when you were an infant, she'd have fed you to the dogs."

Lin didn't move. "There's nothing you can tell me about her that would shock me, Rayen." Deliberately she trained her eyes on his. The tears leaked away, clearing her vision as she looked up at him. "You hear me? Nothing."

For a moment he looked as if he might hit her again. Then he smiled. "Trying to goad me, are you," he said. "Clever." He began to unbutton her shirt.

Her entire body tightened. *"What are you doing?"*

"Do you worry I'm attracted to you? Don't flatter yourself." Cold assaulted Lin's breasts and belly. She began to shiver. She saw Rayen take a small clay pot and dab his fingers into it. "I was given instructions how to prepare you," he said. His fingers came up from the pot a shocking red.

Blood. Lin froze, trying not to flinch as, with his fingertips, he drew a complex symbol on her skin, from chest to abdomen. His neat, slender fingers reminded her of her own. She couldn't see the symbol, but it seemed like a kind of knot—similar to the mark of the Seer.

"Prepare me for what, Rayen?" she forced out, watching his finger go into the pot, onto her skin, and then back again as if hypnotized. The red design was rapidly drying to rust, like a convoluted wound.

"Nickon Gerrard is sending someone here, to perform the enchantment," said Rayen. "He should arrive soon." He drew his knife, and before she could react, he had made a small, efficient cut above the cheekbone at each side of her face. Warmth trickled down her cheeks.

Rayen smiled with all his teeth, like a white wolf of the north. "There, dear," he said. "Now you're all ready."

THE mountain lake glimmered, a mirage of dancing sunlight emerging from the trees. Beyond the crystal belt of water rose the iron heights of the mountains, uncharted by any map. Their peaks wreathed in drifting, soundless white. Beyond, Rianna knew, was an ice forest of peaks that went on so far that no one had ever found an end to it. Some called it the end of the world.

The cottage was tucked in a grove of trees beside the lake. They approached as silently as they could, breaths frozen in their throats. Rayen Amaristoth's sleek grey horse was tethered to a tree outside the door, and smoke rilled from the chimney.

In the day that had passed since their departure from Korrit, Rianna felt more than ever that she drifted like a ghost beside Ned, encased in white silence. The news that Rayen had taken Lin had nearly brought her to her knees with a sudden nausea; it was unlikely, far too unlikely, that Rayen had let Darien live. But once the moment passed, she had clambered to her feet and allowed Ned to lead her on without comment.

Their plan was to lie in wait for Rayen to come out and fall upon him before he could draw blade. It was essential, Rianna pointed out, not to kill him immediately: she wanted confirmation of Darien's fate. Ned had assented with the expressionless calm she had begun to expect.

So they concealed themselves among the trees, one on each side of the door, their weapons drawn. Their primary strength would be surprise. Their only strength, really.

When Rayen finally did open the door, Rianna thought she might faint. He looked well, she thought. Not changed at all. It seemed singularly horrible. Rianna felt her body betraying her at the sight of him, filling with a wistful, wild sadness.

I loved him, a little bit, she thought wonderingly in those light-headed moments.

Ned was first to move, as they had planned; his sword aimed to strike at the other man's head. Like wind—as if he had been expecting it—Rayen Amaristoth pivoted with his dagger drawn and parried the blow. *No sword,* Rianna thought with wild hope. The blades clashed hard enough to draw sparks. With a hiss of breath between his teeth, Ned forced his blade against Rayen's shorter one, the tension locking their weapons together. He began to drive Rayen, step by step and with a trembling sword arm, back toward the cottage wall.

Rianna jumped from her concealment. Together they could pin Rayen to the wall.

Rayen laughed, the color high in his cheeks. He had seen her. "Mistress Gelvan," he said, with an indecent emphasis on the first word. "Was it *that* good for you?" His leg shot out to strike Ned in the groin.

Ned gasped and buckled at the knees. As he fell he grabbed for Rayen's leg; the two went down together. Weapons clattered on the ground as the men grappled each other. As Rianna Gelvan ran toward them, clasping her knife, the cry tearing from her was of rage or mourning, or both.

WHEN Lin first began to hear the voices in her mind, Rayen was sitting by the hearth whittling a wood carving. Her heart hammered so hard that she thought he must notice, but he continued to hum as he worked. He had a tuneful voice, like hers. The only time she had heard him sing was once, long ago, when a beautiful noblewoman had come to stay at Vassilian for a fortnight. With apparent spontaneity, Rayen had burst into a mournful refrain at dinner one evening, eyes averted from his family and their guests as though he were too distracted by some grief to notice them. His tenor voice filled the dining hall with silvery melancholy. The woman, who had been red-haired and betrothed to a southern lord, looked stricken. Kalinda Amaristoth was still alive at that time, and Lin wondered now if the performance was at least partly for her benefit. Her sensual mouth was curled in a hungry smile as she watched her son.

The voices had risen to a buzz in Lin's mind, just on the edge of hearing. Perhaps, she thought, it was the sound of going mad.

Though in that case, what took so long?

The red-haired noblewoman had departed soon after, her face dead white, to meet her betrothed for a sun-filled southern wedding. Lin had thought of saying something to her before she left, but wasn't sure if it might be better for the girl to cherish her small heartbreak for the rest of her life than to know the truth. Better not to know that the way she had wept and bled and begged would provide amusement in the cold chambers of their home for weeks after.

Did I conspire with him? Lin had never intended to help Rayen capture these women, but she hadn't prevented it, either. She had seen herself as powerless, incapable of doing more than watching the inevitable descend. And now it had happened again to someone she knew and even loved. Somehow she had come to love Rianna in the short time she had known her. For all the good it had done.

She hoped—very much hoped—that Rianna had not begged.

Myra, she thought, and saw blue eyes opening like petals to meet hers, full of wonder and hurt. She closed her own eyes and thought, *Perhaps I am already mad.*

The hum of voices in her mind suddenly sharpened, became, *Why can't she hear us yet?*

Lin sucked in a breath. She knew that voice.

She can hear us, said another voice. *Can't you, Lin?*

It was all she could do not to cry. Their words pulsed in her temples now, clear as if they stood next to her. She thought, *Why are you here? I am as good as lost.*

I knew she would say that. Darien Aldemoor, with amused exasperation.

Lin, you have the key to escape within your grasp, said the voice of Valanir Ocune. *You must know this.*

She could see them now: as if a translucent curtain had fallen over her eyes, Darien Aldemoor and Valanir Ocune hung superimposed upon her view of the cottage ceiling, and of Rayen carving beside the fire. An ache filled her at the sight of the two of them. *I know I have Edrien within me,* she told them wearily. *But I can't approach his thoughts of the Path. When I try, the images slip away.*

You never told me about this! Darien protested.

I believe we can help you, said Valanir. *Can you feel us in your mind?*

Lin thought a minute. *Yes,* she replied, a bit wonderingly. *Darien is hungry.*

Darien rolled his eyes and sighed.

And feeling conflicted about seeing me bound and exposed in this way, she went on, with a hint of mischief.

Conflicted? Darien responded. *Please. You're skin and bones.*

All right, children, said Valanir. *I notice, Lin, that you say nothing about me.*

I don't know your thoughts, said Lin. *As usual.*

Valanir nodded. He was sitting cross-legged on what looked like a bare stretch of dirt. Beyond him, Lin could make out the shapes of sunset-colored stones and a glint of sunlight that caught in the silvering strands of his hair. *Join hands with me,* he instructed. *Both of you.*

And incredibly, Lin felt a warm hand in each of her own. She tightened her fingers and felt their flesh respond, though her physical hands held nothing and were bound with rope. *It's done.*

Now recite Edrien's verses, said Valanir Ocune. *Recite them, and, as you do, the three of us must all focus together on uncovering that final verse. The one buried in your mind.*

Lin began to nod, then remembered Rayen and stopped. He, meanwhile, rose and said, "I'll be back. May as well go kill us something." He left the cottage, shutting the door behind him.

Lin let out a long sigh. In her mind, she began reciting the verses. As she did, the sensation of Darien's and Valanir's hands in hers mingled with an assault of images. Somehow even as she took in their faces and the surrounding cottage, Lin could now also see a mountain before her, its peak bathed in mist. Daggers of smaller peaks peered through the clouds, beckoning. A white wind howled between them, buffeted her with annihilating cold.

Lin heard singing and realized it was coming from her, but it was not her voice. It was a man's voice, and ragged, not golden as it had been in the royal courts and palaces that had given him his name.

She saw black eyelashes flicker open, a world of reproach in those eyes. And then they were gone, and intermingling with the sound of Edrien Letrell's voice raised in song was a tearing, gasping sound. Lin understood, suddenly, feeling the wet sting in her own eyes: he was weeping.

You must first lose everything, Edrien Letrell had told Darien, his voice tunneling like a great knife through her body from the realm of the dead.

Lin thought then of Alyn, of Leander and Hassen and Rianna and even, inexplicably, of her family. Of the brother who could have been her staunchest friend in the world, and was instead a monster.

She could write songs forever and still not begin to cut to the heart of her losses. She had no words for the core of them, for the way they twisted in her veins and clenched her heart.

And there, suddenly, was the final verse, and she and Edrien sang it together, as she clasped hands with her last friends in the world and reached, with every scintilla of her being, for the world that lay beyond.

THEY heard voices even before they reached the clearing by the lake—a man's voice raised in anger and then splitting the air, a woman's shriek. Marlen Humbreleigh wondered if it would be unwise to proceed, but Marilla urged him on, a candle of anticipation in each eye. "This is what we've come for," she said, inexplicably. Shaking his head, Marlen drew his sword. They had followed the directions to the Amaristoth property by the lake. Marlen wondered if Lin Amaristoth had tried to escape, if her brother was killing her. That would be a fitting end to the plans of one so black-hearted as Nickon Gerrard—but would be singularly inconvenient for Marlen.

On the other hand, Marlen was becoming more aware that, all along, he'd had other purposes in entering this wood. "You know I'll kill your boy if we come across him," he told Marilla.

She smiled. "You're so kind to think of all these little ways to amuse me."

Light broke through the trees as they reached the clearing; it was late afternoon, and the sun was descending toward the water and mountains on the horizon. Rose and gold light illuminated the cottage where it stood hard by the water.

The sight that greeted them distracted Marlen from any thought of the time of day.

Three people struggled at the center of the clearing. Marlen recognized Rayen Amaristoth, his neck encircled by Ned Alterra's arm as the latter stood behind him. Ned's grip bound Rayen fast in place. Rianna Gelvan held a knife to his throat.

"Two against one," Marlen said mildly. "That's hardly fair, is it?"

Rayen smiled, shaking strands of sweaty dark hair out of his eyes. "There you are," he said. His breath was coming hard. "Took you long enough."

"I was unexpectedly delayed," said Marlen with reflexive courtesy.

"Gentlemen," Rianna said, her voice piercing the air. "Lord Amaristoth and I have not finished our conversation." Her eyes as they passed over Marlen made him shiver. The skin on the left side of her forehead and on her cheekbone was scraped purple in a giant bruise. Swathing her head was a velvet snood, which had slipped to reveal delicate skullbone above one ear, carpeted with stubble.

Marlen heard a falcon cry out into the autumn air, saw its shadow flit across the ground, circling, circling.

"I left Darien alive," said Rayen, "so he could see what was left of you. And how you betrayed him."

Rianna pressed the point of the knife into Rayen's skin; a trickle of red puckered up from the flesh. He didn't flinch. "Speaking of betrayal—you betrayed my father, didn't you?" she said. "I've had a great deal of time to think, here in this wood. I think Nickon Gerrard sent you into our home to investigate him. To find out his secrets."

"For that I had help," said Rayen. "My lord Marlen Humbreleigh, who has arrived now so fortuitously, informed Lord Gerrard of your father's heretical practices. My task was to uncover evidence. Nickon Gerrard knows full well that I am a hunter."

Ned spoke for the first time. "Lord Humbreleigh . . . is there no end to your treachery?"

"I weary of this," said Rianna Gelvan.

Ned looked at her as if in deference, though it was the strength of his grasp that held Rayen Amaristoth in place. "I believe the honor must be yours."

"This is nonsense," said Rayen. "If you kill me, do you know how hard the justice of the kingdom will pursue you? I am Lord Amaristoth." His eyes fixed on Rianna. "You may think Darien could love a whore," he said. "But a whore *and* a murderess? Do you think he'll lick the blood from your hands like a little dog?" Rianna stared at him. In his silken voice Rayen said, "Will you tell him how you cornered a man without his sword? You could never have taken me otherwise; but for that, and my wounded leg. You'll sicken one such as Darien Aldemoor; he'll seek an innocent and sweet girl with pristine hands."

"Shut up, Rayen," said Rianna. She lifted the knife from Rayen's throat. Then she plunged it into his stomach and slit him open like a fish. A cry escaped both their throats at once.

Rayen's eyes bulged; his mouth gaped in a dreadful, whistling shriek. Rianna stumbled back, so pale that the veins in her face showed like spiders. Then she danced forward again and in a single motion cut his throat.

Ned Alterra dropped the gutted body to the ground. Rayen Amaristoth's staring eyes grew dim as red fountained from his throat.

Marlen felt sick. "That was a dishonorable killing."

"For a dishonorable man," said Rianna, in a hard, clear tone like a glass bell. Then she fell to her knees and began to retch. Ned leaped to her side and rested a hand on her shoulder, his gaze warily trained on Marlen Humbreleigh and Marilla as they watched from the height of their mounts.

Marlen wondered why, through all this, he had not moved to stop them. He wondered if even with his considerable skill, he could have. Something in Rianna Gelvan's thin, hungry face crept a sliver of ice down his back.

Marlen turned his attention to Ned. The man looked a mess, his lank hair wild and his face drawn as if in pain. "Lord Alterra," Marlen addressed him formally. "We must have a reckoning."

Marilla spoke then for the first time. "I don't want you to, Marlen."

Marlen's whole body jerked in the saddle toward her, and suddenly he felt dizzy. "What do you mean?" he said. "Are you not mine?" The naked vulnerability in his own words made him feel faint, as if he had exposed his neck to a knife.

"I am," she said, and for once there was no mockery in her voice. "I am and will always be yours. But I don't want you to kill him."

"So that's why you came with me," said Marlen. His fists had clenched without his noticing. He tried to steady himself. "I don't know what I think of that."

Marlen was never to know what she would have said in response—if she had a response. For in that instant, the entire clearing was bathed in light so blinding that it was as if the sun had fallen to earth. And then the light was everywhere, everything. The woods were gone.

❖❖❖

I N a swirl of blue silk skirts and chestnut curls streaming to her waist, the woman in the garden rose to greet the young man who had just entered. Surrounded by rose hedges and with a profile of symmetrical perfection, she gave the impression of a work of art. Her blue eyes were crinkled at the corners, lines that told of laughter and gave her an expression of amusement even when she was not smiling.

The man who bowed upon entering the garden was tall, with a lean and handsome face. At his side was buckled a golden harp, and his ring glittered a rose hue in the sunlight.

"*Lord Gerrard,*" Rianna heard Ned mutter in her ear. But when she tried to turn to look at him, she could not; nor could she even see her own hands in front of her.

It was true: the man was Nickon Gerrard, but without a strand of grey in his hair and with a face smooth as a babe's. "*My father's garden,*" she murmured back. But that he must have surely noticed for himself.

The woman in the garden, meanwhile, reached out a long-fingered hand to Nickon Gerrard, allowed him to kiss it. The only adornment she wore was a gold ring on the hand she outstretched to him.

"Nick," she said. "I wasn't expecting you. Gidyon isn't at home."

Nickon Gerrard straightened, took his place on the garden bench beside her. "Where is he?"

"Taking Rianna for a walk," she said, and dimples dented her pink cheeks when she smiled. "I thank the gods I married a man who is such a devoted father."

Nickon Gerrard appeared impassive. "No doubt he is grateful for his good fortune, Daria. Whatever god or gods he may thank for it."

She inched away from him in her seat, a chill crossing her face. "What did you come for, Nick?"

"To extend you an invitation," he said, his voice smooth with the awareness that her tone had changed. "Visit me sometime. I work all day, and there are days that I have trouble believing I may be Court Poet someday."

"I had thought it decided," said Daria Gelvan. "It is known that the prince favors you."

"That is true, but then there is the king," said Nickon Gerrard. "I fear I may have failed in some way to please him. He speaks of Valanir Ocune, but I know Valanir doesn't even *want* to be Court Poet. Thinks he's too good for it, no doubt."

"I am sure you are as talented as Valanir Ocune," said Daria. The mechanical tone of her voice suggested it was something she said often. "Nick, in all the years that I've known you, your troubles have remained the same."

Nickon Gerrard bared his teeth in a grimace. "What are my troubles?"

She rested a hand on his wrist, looked up earnestly into his face. "You're afraid."

A mist engulfed the scene, and the colors of the Gelvan garden in spring—green of leaf and grass, red and pink and yellow of the roses—melted into white oblivion. Rianna still couldn't see her hand before her face, but she could feel Ned's hand in hers. "I'm afraid," she said aloud.

"Don't be," she heard him say. His voice hung strangely in the air, as if contained in a small space.

"Where are we?"

"I have no idea," said Ned. "But we don't seem to be in danger."

"That was . . . my mother."

"I know. I remember her, a little. I didn't remember how much you look like her."

"If she could see me now," she said, and choked a laugh. Perhaps it was a blessing that she could not see her own hands, caked thick with blood and worse. That wet, surprisingly tough sensation of plunging the knife through Rayen's guts was a continuous echo running from the tips of her fingers to the palms of her hands. Rianna kept seeing his face in that moment, his mouth a black moon of agony, eyes bulging like glass pebbles from his skull. She closed her eyes and saw it; she opened them and there it was, too: a skeletal mask floating between her and the world.

Rayen had been right about the intimacy of the knife. One final lesson she'd had from him.

And then Ned said, "Since it seems we're not going anywhere, I have something to tell you." For the first time since he had found her in Dynmar, he sounded apprehensive. Almost like the old Ned who had been so careful around her, as if she might break.

Rianna thought she ought to relieve him at once. "You fucked Marilla."

She heard him draw a sharp breath, then expel it with a wondering sort of laugh. "You must tell me how you did that."

"Why else would Marlen Humbreleigh demand a reckoning from you?" she said. "And there was something in the way Marilla was looking at you just now. I think she loves you."

"Marilla doesn't love me," said Ned. "But yes. You were right."

"It's no concern of mine," said Rianna. "In fact I . . . I think I'm glad."

"Glad?"

Rianna felt a sting in the bridge of her nose, as if she were about to weep. "There's so little I've given you, Ned. I'm sorry."

She felt his hand on her arm, a warmth in the empty white surrounding them. "That's not true," he said. "Can you imagine if we'd never known one another all those years? I can't. I don't want to."

Rianna was searching for a reply when the whiteness around them flashed away, was replaced with an ornate chamber furnished in crimson. Tall windows hung with drapes of red velvet were grey and splattered with rain. A lonely wind keened as torrents thudded against the glass.

The room was bathed in the glow of a giant fireplace, around which shadows encroached. It was within this pool of light that Daria Gelvan and Nickon Gerrard stood. Her back was to Rianna and Ned; they saw only the rippling fall of her hair to her waist. Against the light, the Court Poet's face was awash in shadows, but there was a frantic light in his eyes and he kept running his fingers through his hair. He looked very young.

Daria held a ring up to the light. His Academy ring.

"A tiger's eye," she said. "Tell me again what it means."

Nickon Gerrard cleared his throat, clasped his hands in front of him. "*Power and fire dance within you, that must have release in the world,*" he recited.

She extended the ring to him as if it were a gift. "I thought so," she said. "Do you know what else I think?"

"I'm sure I can guess." He slid the ring back onto his finger.

"Power, Nick," she said, her voice very soft yet carrying strongly in the silence of the room. The rain danced more gently now on the windowpanes. "All the years that I've known you, it was the only thing you wanted."

"You're wrong about that," he said. "I wanted one other thing. It was taken from me."

"Gidyon didn't take me from you," she said. "Nick, our friendship means so much. Don't spoil things."

"I won't, then," said Nickon Gerrard with what was clearly a forced smile. "Come. It's too rainy to go out. Drink with me." He motioned to the decanter that had been set out, the two glasses beside it. Daria watched as he poured, and for a moment Rianna saw a shift in her expression, though it may have been the shifting light of the flames. But nonetheless, for a moment: a flicker of what looked like trepidation. The next moment she was smiling as she accepted her glass, raised it in salute.

"To you," said Nickon Gerrard with a raised glass, and drank. When he lowered the glass, there was a flush in his cheeks, his eyes like banked coals. "Daria, surely you have always desired me—in your heart?"

Daria had sipped the wine; now she set it carefully aside. "In my heart," she said, stretching her lips across her teeth in a smile. "Of course."

He grabbed her. For a long time they kissed, a strangely silent act backed only by the sound of rain. Rianna felt as if she could not breathe.

Suddenly Daria cried out; Nickon Gerrard had thrown her across the couch with a laugh, sending her tumbling. She gathered her skirts, herself, with an effort at dignity. "Nick—"

"You think I don't know?" Nickon Gerrard said. "What you're up to?"

Daria's lips parted. "I don't—"

"You do," said Nickon Gerrard smoothly. "And you've failed him. This very moment as we sit here, drinking wine, the king is being found dead in his chambers. I thought I should tell you myself."

She suddenly jumped, delivered a blow to his throat with the side of her hand, which she had stiffened into the shape of a knife. It was stunning, the speed with which it happened. Her hand caught his throat with an audible crack. Nickon Gerrard grunted. Then he delivered a blow to her chest so powerful that she reeled back with a cry, crashed to her knees. For a moment he rubbed the place on his throat where she had struck him as if in thought, swallowed. And then smiled.

"You can't kill me," he said. He grabbed her arms. "My life is not my own. As time goes on, this will be more and more true, until no weapon at all can stand against me. I'll show you why."

She struggled, but he forced her into the shadows beyond the firelight, to a wall dominated by a massive tapestry. He flung the tapestry aside and revealed a hidden door.

"My husband knows I am here," she hissed.

"So he does," said Nickon Gerrard. "Oh, don't tempt me with words like that, Ria." His arm pinioning her arms to her sides, he forced open the door.

"*Don't look,*" Ned said urgently in Rianna's ear, in a strangled voice.

Beyond the hidden door, she saw what looked like a table constructed of bones and skulls. Cut into the center of the table was a concave hollow, splattered dark. The skulls still had their hair—some of it long. Some of them were small, as if they belonged to children.

"Blood divination," said Daria in a choked voice. "As King Aldemar thought."

"The new king," said Nickon Gerrard, "will be just as weak, but far more pliable." And suddenly he threw her again, this time halfway across the room.

"Then your plan must be to kill me here," said Daria, her hair ragged across her face.

"I've already killed you," said Nickon Gerrard.

Her face whitened even before he went on. "It's a rare poison," he said in a suave voice now, as if to seduce her again. "I am immune to it, as I have become immune to most things. In the next hour, you will begin to go mad, to find yourself not knowing your own name or the faces of those you love. That will last a day. Then a fever will take you and burn away whatever of your mind is left. I am told it's painful."

"I will know my daughter," said Daria Gelvan. Her pupils had dilated until her eyes were pools of black. Sweat beaded on her forehead.

"It's the strangest thing," Nickon Gerrard said, musingly, as if in contemplation. "There was a time when my feelings for you were—everything. You were all I thought about. The king knew that, of course, when he chose you to spy on me."

She was dragging herself across the carpet, but it was with an effort; she had to steady herself on the arm of the couch.

Nickon Gerrard was staring out into the rain. "Now I feel nothing," he said. "Like all of it—that awful weakness—happened to someone else."

At last Daria reached the door handle, pulled the door open. Her breaths were a terrible grating noise.

Nickon Gerrard suddenly laughed. "Go, then. I wonder if there's a hell for traitors."

"Same as for killers," said Daria Gelvan, barely forcing it out. "I will see you there, one day." She gathered her skirts to her chest and dashed to the door then, leaving it ajar behind her. Nickon Gerrard remained motionless. Another moment, and he picked up his glass from the end table and drank, his eyes already far away.

It was a mercy when this image drained away and left Rianna and Ned back in the white place, which now seemed at once safe and sinister. "I hope that was all," said Rianna. She was trembling uncontrollably. "I want to go home."

Ned gave a short laugh. "Where is home?"

Rianna forced a smile into the whiteness, a show of bravery even though he couldn't see it. "I thought perhaps you knew."

He didn't have a chance to reply. His hand tightened on her arm as the shroud of white around them changed to black.

A THOUSAND voices and scents and colors assailed them, a cacophony of sensation that after days in the stillness of the woods felt like an attack. They stood in a city square where domed palaces of marble blocked the sky. A bronze fountain, itself nearly the size of a palace, dominated the center of the square: it was a taloned and scaled beast with enormous wings, water shooting up onto its back and rilling swiftly down. On islands of carpets spread on the paving stones merchants displayed their wares: pots of all shapes and colors, baskets piled high with shockingly bright fruit buzzing with flies, vivid bolts of jacquard and damask. Sacks of spices breathed perfumes into the choking heat of the day: cumin and rosemary and saffron, as well as other, sweeter scents Marlen could not identify.

Amid the chaos, Marilla was struck oddly still beside him—or perhaps it was not odd; she was probably shocked to find herself here, just as he was. They were not in Eivar, that much was certain. Eivar never had sunlight so powerful that it shimmered blinding white from the cobblestones, not even in summer.

Belatedly, Marlen noticed another charming detail: their horses were gone.

"Marilla," he said, "it appears that we are having a bit of an adventure."

She raised an eyebrow. The sun seemed harsh on her pale face, but she did not so much as squint against the light. "Majdara," she said.

"What?" He thought perhaps he had not heard her, above the noise.

"Majdara," she repeated. "Capital of Kahishi. That's where we are."

"You really are educated," he said. "I should have known not to trust an educated woman."

She bared her teeth at him. "My lord," she said with exaggerated courtesy, pitching her voice above the tumult of the square. "Is this truly the time and place to discuss my dalliance with Ned Alterra?"

Marlen moved nearer to her. "Is that what it was—a dalliance?"

She inhaled sharply, her teeth still bared in what was almost a smile. "I would make love to you right here in front of all these people if it would convince you—and if that would make you focus, please, on where we are. This city is dangerous."

"The lady is right," said a new voice, and Marlen felt the bottom drop out of his heart.

Standing just behind them was a tall man, distinguished, with shaggy silver-streaked black hair that fell to his shoulders. His deep-set dark eyes were lustrous, in the fine-boned mask of his face. "Stop gaping," he said with contempt. "You have ever been a disappointment to our house. And to me."

"Father," said Marlen. "You have ever uttered the same things to me, both in life and now, apparently, in dreams."

"This is no dream, idiot," said Lord Humbreleigh with a snort. "Don't you know where you are?"

"The Path," said Marilla, expressionless. "Isn't it."

In that moment a hunched man wrapped in rags lurched into her, his hands open and outstretched. Before Marlen could react, Marilla swiped at the man's head with the heel of her hand and barked something unintelligible, her face hard with scorn. The beggar went scurrying as if terrified for his life, melted into the crowds in the square.

"The Path," Marlen's father agreed. "In this case, it has chosen to bring you here. And it has chosen me as your guide, which must be some sort of joke, considering how little interest I take in your company." He was wearing the colors of their house, black and green, as if for an official occasion. The crest of House Humbreleigh gleamed gold on his breastplate and on the pommel of his sword. Even at his age, his craggy features were handsome.

"It is another sort of joke for me," said Marlen. "I was guided by you all this past year. It brought me the fame and glory that you promised, and they taste of ash and dust."

"All of it?" Marilla asked, as if with interest.

Marlen smiled. "Yes. Even you, my treacherous darling." He then glanced up at his father, suddenly confused. "But in my research, when guides on the Path were mentioned, they were always . . ."

"Dead?" said Marlen's father. "So the news didn't reach you."

The colors of the square suddenly ran together in Marlen's eyes like wet paint, and the noises of Majdara seemed to be coming to him from miles away. His knees felt weak. "How—?"

"It was the heart," said Lord Humbreleigh. "The curse of our family."

Marlen barked a laugh, though it came out shaky. "As curses go, that one seems ironic." He shook his head, trying to steady the blurring colors into their proper shapes again. "Did you—did you even know I'd won the contest?"

"Of course," said his father. "It was the first time in your life that an act of yours had pleased me. All the more so that you apparently did it without that millstone Darien Aldemoor around your neck."

"So I pleased you," said Marlen, more to himself than to his father.

"If you knew how I achieved it, I suspect that would please you even more."

"It's not truly you, is it?" Marilla asked Lord Humbreleigh. "Can the dead walk, even here?"

Marlen's father seemed to give thought to the question, according Marilla more respect than Marlen would have expected. Lord Humbreleigh's views on women and their mental capacity were no secret, and had not even exempted his own wife. "I don't know," he said at last. "I may be no more than a projection of Marlen's mind given shape. These are matters unknown even to the dead." He drew himself up, his lip curling into the dignified sneer that Marlen realized, with a shock, he would never see again in life. "But my task is to guide you where the Path dictates. Follow me, or you will be trapped here for the rest of your life." He smiled, the familiar wolfish grin Marlen saw when he looked in the mirror. "Not really much of a choice, is it?"

"Where do we go, then?" said Marlen wearily. Beside him, he felt Marilla tense like a knife, even though they weren't touching; waves of apprehension seemed to prickle from her skin to his. It surprised him; in all the time he had known Marilla, she had been horribly unafraid of everything, even of his arm against her windpipe. Perhaps the unnatural state of things shook even her.

Lord Humbreleigh indicated a street that twisted away from the square, overhung with the shadows of a great arch. "That way," he said. "Try not to get killed."

IT was euphoria that first filled her when they met, despite all the strangeness that had befallen them: in that moment, all that seemed important was that she was free and that they were together again. On a ledge overlooking a dizzying view of roiling white mist, breaking apart to reveal a carpet of dark green that was the forest miles below, they found themselves standing with joined hands. For a moment, she registered surprise that Valanir Ocune was not there, but that was eclipsed by the simple joy in Darien's face when he saw her, when he clasped her around the waist and spun her around and around in the air as if she were a child. Lin realized that, like him, she was laughing.

When her feet touched the ground, she embraced him tightly, just for a moment. "I thought . . ." she began.

He nodded, his smile fading. "I know. What did he do to your face?"

"They're shallow cuts," she said. "They'll heal cleanly. Rayen keeps his knife very clean."

Sometime in the course of their reunion she had found an opportunity to close up her shirt. She felt relief when she saw that Darien had her cloak, which, with some ceremony, he fastened around her shoulders. "Good thing I found this, or you'd be freezing in short order," he said. "As it is—do you know where we are? I wonder why Valanir Ocune didn't come through with us."

The wind was whistling among the stones as though it were alive. Lin thought of what else could be alive out there: Chamois. Mountain cats. It had been years since she'd hunted them, in what she saw now as pitiful attempts to win her mother's love. But she remembered the dangers.

"Aside from somewhere in the mountains," she said, "I have no idea. I hope he's all right."

"I wouldn't worry about Valanir Ocune," said Darien. "The man has the lives of a cat. Likely he managed to skip off to someplace warmer." The wind ruffled his hair. Darien shivered and pulled his cloak tighter around his neck.

Lin smiled. "I hope you're right. I—I am grateful to both of you." She recalled Rayen's finger coming up red from the pot, efficient, even gentle on her bare skin, and had to suppress a shudder.

"Hush," he said. "It is no less than you deserve."

It was hard for her to meet his eyes. The obscenity of the blood symbol on her chest felt like a brand, rendering her somehow unworthy. "Darien, do you think we are really on the Path? This place—it doesn't look different from the mountains. Can it be that what we did was pass through a portal to a different part of the north?" Another thought immediately followed. "Perhaps it is Valanir Ocune who is on the Path now."

As she spoke, she realized that Darien's face had become like wax and that he was no longer looking at her. His eyes were focused over her shoulder. With what seemed like an effort, he murmured, "No, Lin. We are indeed there."

She turned, dreading what she would see. And not for nothing, for the man who leaned his great bulk against a tree was not some-one she wanted to see here. "Thalion's light."

Straightening to his full height, Hassen Styr smiled. "That is surely no way to greet a friend."

"*Guides on the Path are not of the living,*" said Darien.

"True," his friend agreed. "But that was not news to you."

Darien swallowed. "Can you ever forgive me?"

"Please, Darien," Hassen held up a hand. "You're embarrassing me. Let's just get to the business of this Path, shall we?" He smiled, but looked genuinely discomfited. "No sane man wants to be a tragedy. I would prefer that you remember me for my songs."

"Always," said Lin. "We will play them wherever we go, for how-ever much time we have. And we will attribute them to our friend Hassen Styr, who was so brave."

"Lin, the one who always knows what to say," said Hassen. "I am glad Darien has you with him." His cloak was draped around his throat, concealing it—and the wound that had killed him, Lin real-ized. "Follow me," he said. "We have very little time."

"What do you mean?" Darien asked. "Little time?"

Hassen's brow furrowed, as if he heard something they could not. "I don't know," he said. "I only know what I'm told. Hurry now."

It was then that they saw that in the distance before them the trees stopped to reveal a valley filled with sunlight, the white walls of a city arising like a jewel at its center. And in that moment the forest around them began melting away, the trees vanishing to reveal the sky and sun, the undergrowth transforming into wild grass and weeds stirred in a gentle wind. A road, wide as a king's highway, wended toward the city walls.

But for such a wide road, toward such a large city, it was strangely deserted.

"Let's go, then," said Darien Aldemoor, and together they set out, the two who lived and the one did not, on a road they didn't know.

THEY had arrived on a mountain ledge, perched above a breathtaking panorama of the woods below. In the distance, dark folds of green undulated in a rhythm that was like music, or perhaps seemed so as the wind sang around them. It was cold, but in that moment Ned was so grateful to be out of the white emptiness that he felt it as a relief. In the distance he could hear the call of a bird of prey, resounding from peak to peak in the stillness.

He was even relieved to see Rianna, though she was a horrid mess of blood. She laughed unsteadily when she caught him looking at her. "I am even worse now than when you found me," she said. "Bald *and* filthy."

"Your hair will grow," he said. "And the rest—that is the price of what we did. I hope you don't hate me for letting you kill him alone. I considered doing it for you, but I thought—I thought perhaps you needed to wash your soul clean of him by doing it yourself. Was I wrong?"

Her eyes were distant, reflective. "I don't know. I don't know if I will ever be—clean," she said. "I can now imagine the journey to becoming someone who kills without regret. It's not a road I want to take."

"Nor will you, then," said Ned forcefully. "You will go back to the life you had. And be happy."

The sound she made was not quite a laugh. "You will make a good father someday." Her face grew solemn. "Ned, Lord Gerrard killed my mother."

"And now he has your father."

"If he's not dead already." Rianna's face was carefully expression-less, but Ned knew what it cost her.

"It is so much," said Ned. "What we have learned today. What we've done." He was silent, but when she didn't speak, he went on. "When we find Darien Aldemoor, there will be much to tell him. Perhaps he will have some idea how to deal with Nickon Gerrard."

Now Rianna seemed stirred to speak, though she looked away from him, toward the expanse of mountain and wood spread at their feet. The wind pried at her snood and skirts. "We must find Darien, to make certain he's all right," she said.

"And because you love him," said Ned.

Now Rianna did look at him, and in her bruised face he saw some-thing that surprised him: naked fear. Yet as he watched, her jaw firmed, as if she were steeling herself to put her head inside a lion's mouth. It touched him to see it, though he couldn't imagine the reason. *If you knew how brave I think you are,* he thought. And per-haps she somehow read it in his face, because at once she relaxed, almost smiled into his eyes in a way that reminded him of when they were children.

"I don't love him, Ned," she said, as if drawing the words from a great distance. "I love you."

He didn't know how the distance closed between them, how she was suddenly in his arms. Ned only knew, when she drew him to her—fingers caressing his hair and her lips hungrily finding his—that the world could have ended in that instant and, to him, it would have had no more significance than a distant falling star, exploding gently in its descent to earth.

CHAPTER 34

THE music of dripping water, echoing somewhere in the tunneling street, was constant. They traipsed shallow stairs, indented at their centers with gutters that pooled with shadow. The street Lord Humbreleigh had chosen was almost entirely covered in arched stone shutting out the sun. Rainbow clotheslines hung from the windows, breaking the monotony of smooth stone. It was quiet here. Smells of cooking and bittersweet *khave* drifted from windows, and underlying these, a whiff of urine. *Drip* went the trickle, in the distance.

"I don't suppose you'll finally say where you're taking us?" Marlen said. His father seemed to be deriving a perverse pleasure in revealing nothing. Once, Lord Humbreleigh would not have hesitated to strike his son for impudence, but that had been long ago.

"In a moment," said Lord Humbreleigh. "I don't suppose you'll tell me how my son, of impeccable bloodlines, came to be with a whore?"

Marilla's face did not change; she had the blank-eyed expression Marlen knew well.

"I don't pay Marilla and never have," said Marlen. "She is not my whore."

"Would she be with you if you were not next in line for Court Poet?" said Lord Humbreleigh with a dry laugh. "If you did not provide her with her own apartments, and jewels?"

That, Marlen could not answer. It was the question he had avoided asking that still burrowed into his mind like a spinning needle. She claimed to belong to him, yet she had betrayed him with another man. And what would she be without him? Well he remembered her room in the slums of Tamryllin. If not for Marlen, she would still be there.

"I don't know," Marlen said helplessly. He looked at Marilla, but she was gliding ahead. Marlen caught her wrist, stopping her. Now she looked up at him, pale, glassy eyes meeting his. He said, "Why wouldn't you let me kill him?"

"I asked you not to," she said. "As a favor."

"When have you ever minded watching a man die?"

She shrugged. "Go on and kill him, then," she said. "Cast me out into the street. If you think it is only jewels I want—I can get them. I can get many men to give me what I desire, Marlen. I don't need you for that."

"And Ned?" Marlen said. "What did he give you?"

A sound, then, like the crackle of fire; Lord Humbreleigh was laughing, head thrown back. "You know the answer to that," he said. "Oh, my son. What a fool you were not to cut this whore's throat when you had the chance." He turned suddenly. "I think the time is now right to tell you where we are going."

"Kind of you," said Marlen. "I hope that means we are almost there, and will be rid of you faster."

"Majdara has an industry that is almost unique in the world," said Lord Humbreleigh, gesturing expansively as if he delivered a lesson. The corner of his mouth was quirked in unmistakable enjoyment. "Do you know what it is?"

"Manure?"

"Flesh," said Lord Humbreleigh. "Nowhere else in the world is there so active a trade in slaves. Nowhere else can a man—or a woman, for that matter—find a selection of temptations as diverse or as valuable." He leaned forward, savoring the words. "It is here, for example, that a girl of nine, whose parents were slain by marauders, might be put to lucrative use."

"Appalling," said Marlen. "So you intend to educate us in these atrocities?"

"To educate *you*, certainly," said Lord Humbreleigh. "There are men who only find pleasure when they inflict pain. And inflicting pain on children—so much the better." He was smiling, eyes alight with a gleam Marlen knew too well. "Marilla knows what I am talking about, don't you, dear?"

Her eyes were still unreadable. "Like father, like son, Lord Humbreleigh," she said. "But when you cause harm, I see you do it with so much more—intent."

Marlen's father's voice lowered to a murmur. "The Path is not bound by time. We are now in Majdara of more than a decade past. The same year invading brigands raided border villages of Eivar, put men and women to the sword, and brought their pick of the children to this city. The pretty ones. The ones they thought might make their fortune in the trade."

Marilla was staring at him. Marlen touched her arm. "Does he mean . . . ?"

Now she reacted, flinching away, her teeth flashing at him. "Leave me be."

"As it happens, you may recognize where we are now, if you take a moment to look around," Lord Humbreleigh said. He motioned to a stone façade graced with slender pillars and a massive wrought-iron door. "In that house is where the nine-year-old girl was held for six months. Her captors introduced her to instruments of torment most people never see in their lifetimes. They were noble, you see. Their tastes were sophisticated."

"What do you mean by this?" Marlen demanded. "This is low even for you, father."

Lord Humbreleigh spread his hands. "I did not choose this destination for you," he said. "I am merely your guide. It is the Path itself that chooses."

"Very well," said Marlen. "We are here. We've seen the house. Now we can go."

"Unfortunately not," said Lord Humbreleigh. "The journey can end only inside that house. When the door is opened and its threshold crossed. I did not make these laws, son," he added at the sight of Marlen's face. "What does it matter? I'm sure you can bear the sight of a tortured child. Especially knowing as you do how very much unharmed she will emerge." He laughed again.

"As unharmed as I was by you all those years," said Marlen. "I have destroyed the only friendship that mattered to me, gained the hatred of all poets, and was party to the death of a man—a good man. But I am alive, so I suppose it can be said—I am *unharmed*."

"Marlen," Marilla said. Her voice was as he'd never heard it, soft and faintly trembling. "Please don't go in there."

"You heard him," said Marlen. "I am sorry, love. How else can we ever get home?"

"I can't bear for you—for anyone—to see me like that," said Marilla. "Please. Let me go in alone. Perhaps that will be enough." Marlen began to speak, but she silenced him with a hand at his lips, a touch surprisingly gentle. "Marlen," she said, "if you see me like that, I will have to leave you. And I don't want to leave you. Do you understand?"

Marlen ran his hands through his hair, feeling utterly out of his depth. "Go then," he said. She turned, her face tight with dread as she gazed at the wrought-iron door. "Wait," Marlen said. Pulling her back to him, he kissed her for the first time in weeks. Her response was not the violence he was accustomed to, from her; there was a tender urgency in her kiss, a desperation.

It seemed to last an age but must have been only a moment. *The Path is not bound by time,* his father had said. She tore away again, though not without a glance behind her to where he stood.

But it was with the regal posture he knew well that she advanced, with measured tread, to the wrought-iron door.

Lord Humbreleigh stood with his hands on his hips and a curled lip. "It has been my honor to guide you," he said. "There. I am forced to say that, also by law."

"I know you were forced to say it, Father," said Marlen. He saw for the first time that his father's shoulders were stooped and that he was not quite so tall as Marlen remembered. The man who had stamped an indelible mark on Marlen's face was long gone—had been gone even before his death. Yet in Marlen's mind, he had always towered, and still did.

Marilla had arrived at the door. She grasped the handle, and the great metal weight swung wide on its hinges without a sound. With the same deliberate pace, she stepped inside until she was standing on the threshold, her elegantly clad figure blocking from view whatever was inside.

For several moments she was still, arms hanging at her sides. Then she dropped to her knees with a soft cry.

Marlen cried out then too, though later he could not recall what his words had been, tearing from him as the world around them went black. Most likely, he would later think, they were, *I'm sorry.*

DARIEN expected Hassen to guide them into the city, but instead his friend began leading them away from the main road. They ventured into hills of a green so intense it was as if they had just been refreshed with rain. Dark trees swayed with slow majesty in the breeze. "Where is this?" Darien asked. "It looks like the south."

Lin raised her gaunt and bloodied face to the wind. "The light and the air here are like nothing I know."

"It is the south," Hassen confirmed. "And here we are."

Darien caught his breath. They had arrived in a place where the green hills and trees half encircled, like the setting of a jewel, the blue of the sea. The Blood Sea was so different, he thought, from the pale grey-green northern waters he had used to watch crash, in eternal repetition, from the cliffs of Academy Isle. Looming to the east was the wall of mountains that divided Eivar from Kahishi.

So hypnotized was he by the view that for a moment he didn't realize that Lin was calling to him and pointing in the opposite direction, toward a grove of trees.

"I had a wager that you'd notice it first," Hassen said to her with a grin.

Darien stared, uncomprehending. "What are they?"

"Standing stones," Lin said with a delighted smile.

Darien blinked. Indeed, he could see now that the vast pillars of rock in the grove formed the shape of a ring. "I'd thought King Eldgest dismantled them all in his crusade," he said. "Naming them blasphemous of the Three."

"Yet these remain," said Hassen. "Perhaps Eldgest died before he could complete his work. People of the nearby city—those who still, in secret, worship the old gods—sometimes come to this place. Here by the Blood Sea, gateway to the far east, some of the most ancient beliefs live on."

"Hassen, that sounds like a song," said Lin.

"So it may be," he replied. "Now watch."

THEY did not have long to discover what he meant: in that moment a woman, slender and with long dark hair, stepped out from the trees. Her skin was an unnatural white, as if the blood had been drained from her, and her dress that trailed in the grass was white. A man followed after her, greying, weary, a harp at his side.

The woman turned toward them so they could see the glint of her blue eyes. But this was not necessary for Lin, who had known them both at once.

Just as suddenly as she had looked toward them, the woman looked away, and Lin realized: *They cannot see us.*

"Did you bring me here to inflict more pain?" the man said, breaking the stillness. "I love you, Myra. You know this."

"It is so like you," she said, "to accuse me of causing you pain. Simply by wanting what every woman wants, I tortured you. Isn't that so?"

"Tell me why you have brought me to this place," he said. "Please."

The wind caught her hair, flung it in a long black banner behind her head. Even in memory, Lin thought, Edrien Letrell's paramour was not so proudly beautiful as she was in life. And then: *My thought, or his?* Lin's memories were becoming so merged with those of Edrien

Letrell that she feared she would soon not know the difference. Soon it would be as if she herself had made love to this woman in the shadow of these standing stones.

Made love to her and then left the next day. "*I'll find someone who will love me,*" Myra had said with quiet fury just before slamming shut the door to her home, and she had sent his harp flying into a wall, denting it forever.

Edrien never fixed those dents, nor ever used a different harp.

"It is not I who has brought you here, but the Path," said Myra. "I am but your guide—secondary to you here, as I was in life."

"That's where you're wrong," said Edrien. "You are not, have never been secondary. You are everything. Since you died I've had terrible dreams."

"Perhaps your dreams were whispering what the Path has brought you here to know," said Myra. The harshness had drained from her voice; it had grown soft. Still there was a thread of steel in the set of her face. Lin found herself remembering a heady mix of joy and frustration, days of passionate battling followed by nights of equally passionate reconciliation. Life with Myra had demanded everything of Edrien—perhaps that was why he had not stayed?

The uncertainty as much as the memories, Lin felt sure, were Edrien's own. Perhaps these were even the thoughts that occurred to him as he stood here now, facing his dead love on the Path.

"What must I know?" Edrien asked.

Her eyes, fixed on him, held a kind of compassion, contrasting with the rigidity of her face. "I did not die of the plague, Edrien."

"What do you mean?" But he stumbled back as if he did not want to hear. His hand sought the support of one of the moss-covered standing stones.

"It was the child you gave me, that last night here," said Myra.

The knuckles of Edrien's hand that gripped the stone had gone white. "The . . . child?"

"It came too early, just four months after you had gone," she said. "The blood wouldn't stop." She approached Edrien where he stood, and prying his hand loose from the stone, held it against her face. "I am sorry, love," she said. "I didn't want you to ever know."

IT seemed like an age but also not nearly enough time before they at last drew apart. The wind on the cliff tore at them as if it sought to sunder them from one another or send them plunging from the great height to their deaths. Ned gripped Rianna's waist in both his hands and thought she didn't feel fragile to him now. "I don't know how you can love me," he said, "but I don't want to ever let you go."

She laughed a bit breathlessly. He thought it must be a dream.

"I feel the same," said Rianna. She held up her hands to his face. The nails of some of her fingers were cracked or broken, and all were caked with blood. All traces of a smile had left her eyes as she gazed at him. She did not need to look up—they were nearly of a height. She said, "Can you love someone with these hands?"

Ned clasped them both, raised them to his lips. "I love your hands."

She pulled him close again and buried her face in his shoulder. Ned closed his eyes and tightened his arms around her. *I'll never let you go.*

"Touching," said a voice behind them.

Ned opened his eyes but did not loosen his grip. He immediately recognized the man who stood in the shadow of the trees, green eyes like arrows trained upon them.

"Forgive me," Valanir Ocune added as he advanced toward them. "Love is not to be mocked, not in this otherwise merciless world of ours." It looked to Ned as if the Seer had recently encountered this mercilessness firsthand: his face looked haggard.

"Where are we?" Rianna asked, disengaging from Ned and turning toward the Seer. "Do you know?"

"So you are real, then," said Valanir Ocune. "I am not sure whether to be pleased or not. This is a place of danger, and from what I recall, neither of you is equipped for that. I am not sure where we are," he went on, "but it is not the world we know. The Path has brought us here."

"The Path," Ned said. "Is there no way to be rid of these damned poets?"

Rianna laughed, said teasingly, "You have nothing to fear from them."

And then Marlen Humbreleigh and Marilla were there, appearing out of the air. They stared around wildly as if fearing an attack.

Marlen was first to recover, spotting Ned. His eyes narrowed. "You."

"Yes," said Ned.

"Stay away from him," said Rianna.

"I have no wish to harm him," said Marlen. He took one of Marilla's hands in his. Ned was shocked to see tears running down her face, her eyes large and blank as a doll's.

"Is she all right?" said Ned. "What's happened?"

"This gods-cursed Path had its way with us," said Marlen. "The songs of Edrien Letrell failed to mention what a sadistic exercise it is. But I daresay we still look better than you two." His eyes fell upon Valanir Ocune. "So you're here. This is starting to become interesting."

"I'm flattered," said Valanir Ocune. Then all at once his eyes widened, he backed away a step. "Marlen," he said, and it was clear he was trying to keep his voice level. "How are you feeling?"

Marlen looked confused. "What?" The next moment his face spasmed, his mouth gaping, his eyes bulging in their sockets. Rigid, drawn up to his full height, he crashed to the ground like a felled tree.

Marilla dropped to her knees, tried to turn Marlen's face to hers. In an uncharacteristically shrill tone she cried, "*Help him.*"

But when Ned and Rianna tried to run forward, Valanir cast his arm imperiously before them, bringing them up short. Marlen was making horrible strangled sounds.

"Stay back," said Valanir Ocune. He seemed to have grown taller, towering over them, his voice tight with contained fury. "He's here."

THE scene had changed again, before Darien had a chance to think; they now stood at the foot of a bare cliff that clawed empty sky far above a cobalt sea. Until now, Darien had been able to identify where they were, but this place, he sensed, was different. The sea was a blue that seared his eyes, its music so plangent he could have wept.

It was a song of loss, he thought.

"Hang on," he said, glancing at the bare stretch of stone around and about them. "Where is Hassen?"

"I will not think of the road's end," said Lin.

Darien shook his head. "What?"

She looked sad. "It's just a song." Then she said, "Look, Darien— the tree."

A lone tree sprung crookedly from the apex of the cliff. Darien had seen it at once, but had not observed anything remarkable about it. He had failed to see, at first, that its branches and leaves sparkled silver in the sunlight.

"The Silver Branch," he said. "Is this it, then? Do we take it?"

Just then Edrien Letrell appeared before them, his face turned toward the sea. Behind him, Myra stood. The white of her dress and skin seemed to fill with the sunlight like a glass chalice, her eyes sorrowful. "What I will tell you now is not what I want to tell you," she said. "But I do because I must."

Some time later, Edrien was holding a silver branch from the tree in both his hands. Myra had gone. To the whispering air and the singing sea he murmured, "Forgive me, love. I could not do it."

The next moment, Lin and Darien found themselves on a different cliff overlooking a great wood, just in time to see Valanir fling an arm in front of Rianna and Ned, commanding, "Stay back."

They saw Marlen writhing on the ground, his face dark and contorted. "No," Darien said softly, but found that he could not move. Kneeling beside his friend, Marilla had both hands clasped to her mouth.

"Darien," they heard Rianna say, looking panicked. A dark snood covered her head. She was streaked with dried blood. She looked a horror. "Darien, do as Valanir says."

"Are you all right?" Darien said. "Gods, Rianna."

"I'm all right," she said. Her tremulous smile made her look more like the girl he remembered. "It's not my blood."

And then Marlen rose to his feet, suddenly, but it was not Marlen at all. Marlen Humbreleigh was gone, though the man who stood in his place was as tall and also carried a harp.

Valanir Ocune placed himself in the man's path, sword out. "Hello, Nick," he said.

CHAPTER
35

NICKON Gerrard's eyes were aflame, his mark of the Seer blazing—a glow mirrored in the silver light that outlined his form and gleamed from his hair. He seemed to look down on Valanir Ocune from a height. As Valanir advanced toward him, blade extended, the Court Poet suddenly laughed.

"You can't be serious," he said. "A *sword*?" Nickon Gerrard muttered something under his breath.

Valanir grunted as the blade twisted in his hands and was wrenched away. As it clattered to the ground, he said, "I, too, possess other weapons. I thought to begin honorably."

"There is no beginning," said Nickon Gerrard. "Not yet. I have no desire to waste time with you, Valanir. Later, perhaps, there will be a chance to reminisce, in the comfort of the royal dungeons."

"I know what you want," said Valanir, and in a voice sternly commanding, he called, "Lin, join yourself with me. You are in danger."

The Court Poet laughed. "Have you appointed yourself her guardian? Perhaps if you had not spent the past years lounging in the *khave* houses of Majdara, you would be equipped to save her now." In a different voice, one that seemed to contain and hold the wind, he cried, "*Let the portal be born from within.*" His fingers, slender and long-nailed, extended in Lin's direction.

Lin gasped as she was lifted off her feet into the air. "Lin!" Darien shouted and tried to grasp at her, but she rose higher, out of reach. Her face was dead white as her shirt split open, and they saw that the mark on her chest and belly, intertwining in an endless knot, glowed a dull red. As they watched, it grew brighter, like a sunset that foretold bloodshed.

Lord Gerrard cried, *"Let the portal be opened!"*

"Gods, no," said Valanir Ocune with horror.

That was when Lin began to shriek. As if it were a door, the symbol on her torso had split down the middle, and only blackness showed beyond.

Rianna was clawing to break free from Ned. "I'll kill him," she was keening as he clasped her around the waist, lifting her above the ground so that she kicked the air. "No," he said, his face strained and white. "This time you can't."

"Fuck you, Seer," Darien screamed at Valanir. "Do something."

"I can't," said Valanir. His face looked sunken and old. "Lin is the key, and he has her."

Though Lin's cries were like repeated stabs of a knife in his chest, Darien Aldemoor felt a sudden peace envelop him. It was an unmistakable sensation, such as he sometimes felt before his very best performances: an absolute sureness of what he did. "Remember this," he said to Valanir Ocune, and managed a smile. *"You carry my fame to all the world."*

Raising his own arms wide, his face turned toward the sky, Darien began to sing the words to a song no poet had sung before.

On cliffs above an impossibly blue sea where a silver tree glimmered in the sunlight, Lin and Darien had watched as Myra told Edrien Letrell one last thing.

She said, "The Path has chosen you, highest among poets, to bring back the enchantments of old. But there is a price."

Edrien was watching the waves. His face was relaxed. "Of course," he said. "There is always a price."

"Your life," said Myra.

"I expected that."

And then Myra did something neither Darien nor Lin would have expected: she began to sing. Her voice was sweet and true in that emptiness of stone and sky. The song was simple yet strange, its meaning first fluttering near, then eluding comprehension.

Edrien turned to look at her. "You never sang for me before," he said, when she was done. "I did not know what I missed."

"I knew better than to sing for an Academy-trained poet," said Myra with a smile. "You'd have mocked me endlessly."

"No," said Edrien. "No, I would not have."

"That is the song that will return the enchantments to the world," she said quietly.

"At the cost of my life."

She bowed her head. "That is not what I wish. I am merely your guide here."

"I understand," said Edrien. "And what happens if I—if I choose not to do this?"

"Then you will be expelled from the Path forevermore," said Myra. "Sent back with a branch from the silver tree as a sign that you traveled the Path and at the last failed in its purpose."

"A branch to mark my failure."

"Yes."

Darien sensed a deep quiet in Lin Amaristoth as she took in these words. He wondered if she was as dazed as he felt. For some moments Edrien Letrell did not speak, and the only sound they heard was that of the waves. No gulls in these skies, no drifting cries upon these waters.

"It would be justice for me to give my life," said Edrien, finally. "Since I killed you."

"You didn't kill me, Edrien," said Myra, sharply now. "Don't be a fool."

"Surely you blamed me."

Her lips curled in a bitter smile, and her eyes met his: a mixture of hardness and grief there. "I cursed you."

Then without warning—just as Hassen had left them without warning—Myra disappeared. Edrien was alone on the cliff.

For what seemed like a very long while, he watched the waves. Their song of loss consumed the silence, a continuous refrain. At long last, Edrien gazed up into the sky and, in a firm, clear voice said, "I have chosen." His shoulders bowed, and it seemed then as if a burden fell upon him.

Edrien Letrell began walking up the cliff and toward the silver tree, where he was to cut the branch that he would bring, still coruscating with its own light, back to the world of men.

WHEN Darien Aldemoor first began to sing, Ned wondered if it was some trick, some effort to divert Nickon Gerrard's attention to himself. But he couldn't imagine what that would accomplish, not when a chasm of black was erupting in Lin's chest. He could see in Valanir's eyes that her death was now assured.

Rianna had given up struggling. Her sobs were heartbroken as a child's. "I hate you," she murmured.

He hugged her tightly to him. "I can't let you die. Forgive me."

Darien's song had grown louder, and the young poet now seemed to stand tall as a tree; a glow similar to that of Nickon Gerrard emanated from his skin. But while Nickon shone silver like the moon, Darien's light was like him: golden as the sun. His song became harsh, drowning even Lin's screams. The Court Poet was now watching with a guarded expression. His arms were upraised toward Lin, and it was clear that he could not stop Darien's song while his energies were employed in opening the portal.

Suddenly Darien paused in his song, shouted, "*Valanir! Be ready.*" Then he saw Rianna and smiled. "You're beautiful," he said. "Ned, take care of her." Lifting his head again to the sky, Darien sang the concluding notes of the song, rounding them off with a thundering crescendo. The light of him became blinding, transforming from golden to white, and then all at once Darien's legs gave way and he fell. A flash like lightning ripped through the clearing, so for a moment no one could see.

When the light faded, Darien lay on the ground. Rianna gave a wail, then broke free of Ned. "Now is our chance," she said shakily, tears coursing down her face, her dagger in hand.

Ned was not sure what she meant, but he swiftly drew blade, just in time to see that now Valanir Ocune rose to a great height and glimmered silver. His eyes blazed with rage as he shouted a single word, and in the next moment, Lin Amaristoth crashed to the ground. The mark on her chest had faded to the dull brown of dried blood.

Another intonation from Valanir Ocune, and Nickon Gerrard's sword jumped from its scabbard and shivered into a thousand glittering pieces. Rianna and Ned immediately closed on the Court Poet, their blades to his neck. Rianna hissed, "Try singing your way out of this."

Lin sprang to her feet, her eyes wild, her face a corpselike shade of grey. She ran to Darien and knelt at his side. His eyes fluttered, but he could not speak. Clutching at Darien's head in both her hands, Lin pressed her lips to his. When she let go, Darien smiled with a hint of mischief, looked about to speak. But instead the smile faded, and his eyes grew dim.

"Now to do something about . . . this," said Valanir, indicating Lord Gerrard.

But they saw that Rianna and Ned held their blades pressed to Marlen Humbreleigh's neck as he stood dazed between them. Nickon Gerrard was gone.

CHAPTER 36

VOICES came at him from the dark. It was as if he floated bodiless, could neither see nor feel; he could only hear. At first the voices were a murmur without words. Gradually they sharpened with meaning as Marlen's awareness swam back to him.

"How will I explain this?" A familiar voice, querulous. "I can't just say you're dead!"

"I *will* be dead." Another, this one arousing such terror in Marlen that he would have screamed if he could. "You will hold a funeral in which I—that is, at which *Lord Humbreleigh*, here—will officiate, as my successor."

"This is *too* strange, Lord Gerrard." King Harald, sounding as if the wrong meal had arrived for his dinner. Marlen had always wanted to slap sense into the man.

Light pierced Marlen's eyelids now. He squeezed his eyes shut, but it did no good: this was really happening. The floor was hard against his back. His limbs seemed frozen in place; he could not even feel them. The vulnerability was as dreadful as the fear. He might as well have been naked.

"You have no choice," Nickon Gerrard said. "Where are you without me, Harald?"

"You will call me by my rightful title!" said the king, but it was without conviction.

"Ah—he's awake." Nickon Gerrard's voice, smoother now, as if in anticipation. Marlen's eyelids lifted as of their own accord; he found himself staring up at the Court Poet. Now that Marlen's faculties were returning, his brain strived to recollect how he came to be here. He remembered woods. Smell of pine, piercing chill of late autumn.

And then, absurdly, it came to him what he had eaten last: bread and cheese that now roiled in him like spoiled stew on a flame.

More: Marilla's fingers, cool and smooth, threaded through his like a pact. Men's eyes fixed on him wherever he went, watching. Silent. Willing his downfall, retribution for his crimes.

A night that seemed long ago: Nickon Gerrard's gaze suddenly turning to the place where Marlen had thought himself concealed. *I will find you.*

"No," Marlen heard himself say aloud. So he could speak now.

"I regret that you will feel this," said Nickon Gerrard, and sounded genuinely regretful. When he began to sing, his voice was laden with this unaccustomed melancholy, as if some last reserves of feeling, long dormant, awakened now. The song was wordless, pure melody, an ethereal building in the Court Poet's dusky voice like the priests' chants in the Eldest Sanctuary.

Or in the Academy, what seemed an age ago now. A different life.

Marlen began to feel a prickling on his skin, as if someone teased it with a thousand needles. He gritted his teeth. The Court Poet's song had grown more complex, and stronger, pounding in Marlen's ears.

So many crimes, people he had betrayed or harmed. Darien. Hassen Styr. Leander Keyen. Master Gelvan. And those were only the ones he knew. Who could say how far the damage rippled outward.

Another memory, recent: Piet, the little weasel, bending in conference with Lin Amaristoth beside a fire one evening. They didn't know Marlen was there. Piet said, "Marlen—he will pay?" No answer from Lin. Her eyes had caught Marlen's in that instant, where he stood in the enmeshed shadows of the trees. Dark tunnels her eyes seemed to him, as they had in his dream.

The needles became knives, driving into bone. Marlen gasped. And then they were fires, thousands of them. Tearing through bone, muscle, and the soft places between.

Marlen heard his own voice, shrieking, as if from far away. *How far.*

Knives of fire, gutting him. His screams became clogged with vomit, changed to a horrible gagging he could not control.

"Lord Gerrard!" A cry. The king.

Still the song of Nickon Gerrard went on, driving the knives into him and twisting them. Twisting *him* beyond recognition. Marlen's vision blurred, began to darken. *This must be it,* he thought. *The end.*

He'd compare notes with Darien, when he got there.

Then a shout, words he could not hear. Nickon Gerrard's song stopped. The last thing Marlen heard was, *"Hold!"* A woman's voice, before black took him.

IN the moments after Darien Aldemoor fell and Nickon Gerrard vanished, Marlen had found himself staring at Rianna's dagger and Ned's sword. The memory of her last kill fresh in his mind, he'd said, "I hope we can talk about this."

He was more dazed than he wanted to let on. Though his body had been taken over by Nickon Gerrard, a corner of his mind was present; he had witnessed everything as if through a headache-inducing mist. He had seen the only man he had ever considered a friend sing away his life, and in that moment a part of Marlen died. *Now there is just the moon.*

As he stood rigid between the two blades, Marlen's mind still dwelt on Darien's face, on his smile just before the light had gone from him. *You were always better than I,* he told Darien in his mind. *I couldn't stand it. Somehow I should have tried.*

Lin wept on Darien's chest with quiet intensity, her shoulders trembling without a sound. Valanir Ocune came to her and touched her shoulder, but Lin recoiled with unexpected violence. She stared up at him with a frozen face, said, "It should have been you."

Valanir backed away. "I don't deny it." His face was pale, his mark of the Seer still a shimmer of silver. "His name will live on long after the rest of us are gone. All our names will flicker dim before that of Darien Aldemoor."

Marlen tore his eyes away to focus on his captors. "What say you?" he asked. Behind them, he could see Marilla watching with the ice of hopelessness in her face. Much as she liked violence, he supposed she was unskilled in it. And he certainly would not have recommended confronting these two, who seemed to have a sort of unvoiced death wish between them.

"Marlen," said Rianna Gelvan, in a voice surprisingly sane considering how she looked just then. Tears were running down her face. "Nickon Gerrard killed my mother. I ask that you look upon your actions and consider what sort of man you wish to be . . . how you wish to be remembered. It is because of you that one of the brightest of our poets is gone. That my father is imprisoned . . . or worse."

It did not seem safe to deny it. Marlen realized he did not wish to anyway. "Are you asking me to help you free your father?"

"I am."

"With blades at my throat, how can I refuse?"

Rianna and Ned exchanged glances. They lowered their blades. "I cannot force you," said Rianna. "I ask you as a man of honor. The man who killed my mother should not have my father too. You set in motion this chain of events . . . you can still make amends."

Marlen wondered when the world had become so bizarre a place, with a Galician merchant's daughter, soaked head to toe in blood, enjoining him to honor. But with solemnity, he nodded. "I accept."

"But there is more." Everyone turned to see Lin, still looking white, standing above Darien's body. "The Red Death is heading towards Tamryllin. We have the enchantments now—we must use them for their true purpose."

"*An anchor against the dark,*" said Valanir Ocune, from a song of long ago. Marlen found himself shuddering, though could not have said why. And then he saw the Seer's gaze was fixed on him.

"What is it?" said Marlen. "I said I'm willing to help. For what it's worth."

"I must gather the Seers," said Valanir crisply, glancing across to Lin, who still would not meet his eyes. "At this moment, Marlen, you pose a danger to all of us. And to yourself."

LATER that night, they built a large fire as if to throw into it all their memories of the past day, a day Rianna thought would never stop replaying itself in her mind and would break her heart. Worse: her mind kept twisting to find ways she might have done something different, prevented Darien's sacrifice while still saving Lin. As Valanir Ocune spoke, words mingling with the solemn roar of the flames, Rianna pressed her head into Ned's shoulder.

"I have made the arrangements," Valanir was saying. "At this moment many Seers are joined to me, concealing Marlen Humbreleigh from Nickon Gerrard. But it will take more strength than we have to maintain this for long. We must act."

Marlen looked weary, but also strangely calm. Marilla was curled into him like a sleepless cat. "So I'm to be the bait," he said.

"Not exactly," said Valanir. "You're joined to Nickon Gerrard—he has access to you. All along, his plan was to inhabit your body. The *laylan* has just about devoured his."

"So he thought, why not become young again—and a swordsman, too?" Marlen stretched. "Understandable."

"Marlen," Lin said then, sharply. The first thing she had uttered in a long while, her voice almost a croak. "Darien is dead."

Marlen looked at her, still weary. "I know." Words that fell heavily into the quiet of the woods. "And we speak of my death now. The difference is I've earned it."

She covered her face in her hands.

Valanir said, "Based on what Marlen saw, Nickon Gerrard has kept his body alive with a potion. Something he could have acquired only from the far east, where such magic is made."

"Dane Beylint was famed for procuring rare items from perilous places," said Rianna.

"Obviously he didn't know what he was dealing with," said the Seer. His face was all shadows, save where moonlight struck gleams of light from the mark on his eye. It shimmered a slow, rhythmic pulse, as if in time with his heart. "We will need the strength of every one of our people. Everyone I can gather—the Seers at the Academy, the younger poets as well." He gazed across to Lin, who sat hunched before the fire, her face raw with grief. "Lady Amaristoth—I ask that you lead them with me."

"Lead them?" she said, her voice hollow, stripped of its accustomed melody.

"Yes," said Valanir. "I want you to be in command."

FOR days, Lin and Marlen had sat squinting over maps he had drawn of the palace passageways, the secret tunnels that he had discovered to Lord Gerrard's rooms. Lin was amazed by his memory, as well as by the cleverness that had led him to find what were certainly among the Crown's most guarded secrets.

"I was bored," he said with a shrug when she remarked upon it, but she was not sure she believed that.

Yet even Marlen had not found the room Rianna Gelvan had seen on the Path. Nickon Gerrard's hidden room, where he kept the altar of bones and performed divination and murder.

She and Rianna had exchanged few words following Darien Aldemoor's death, until the evening before their arrival in Tamryllin. They were camped in the northern forests, where their numbers would be most likely to go undetected, and the plan was to travel to the capital through a portal in the morning. Such an expenditure of power would have been too great for one poet, but for the two hundred that they had amassed, joined together, it was suddenly possible. There had been a tense moment when Marlen Humbreleigh and Piet Abarda had encountered one another in the camp, but in the end Marlen had stalked away from Piet's taunts, upright and dignified with Marilla on his arm. Lin had taken Piet aside after that, had told him in no uncertain terms how she expected him to conduct himself, "snake" or no.

The snake was, after all, going to be their vanguard. The one most likely to fall.

That was the least of Lin's worries during those days. Handling the tensions between Academy masters and hotheaded young Seekers had presented yet another headache. Lin found that between planning their strategy and preventing the poets from killing each other, she was hardly getting any sleep. Valanir Ocune would accost her at various times and convince her to eat.

So it was only the night before the battle that she came upon Rianna, sitting alone at one of the fires. The girl had taken to wearing men's clothes, though they curved alluringly on her figure as they never had on Lin, and to wrapping her head in a colorful sash Valanir Ocune had from Kahishi.

There was surprising vulnerability in her face when she saw Lin, that was apparent even in the uncertain light. "Lin—are you avoiding me?"

Lin was taken off guard, then realized that there was justice in the question. "No, of course not, love. Of course not," she said, and joined Rianna by the fire. But she hovered at the other side, not venturing too near. "I have been . . . afraid, I guess, that you might hate me. For what I let happen to you."

Rianna shook her head. "You tried to protect me," she said. "You didn't know where the danger would come from, in the end. You couldn't have."

"I am so sorry about Darien."

"He was beautiful, wasn't he?" The firelight danced in Rianna's eyes. "On the Path, I understood—I realized that I had never known Darien. He was beautiful, and he was not mine. And he did not know me—no one did, not even me. Or maybe he did, and I changed."

"But you love Ned," said Lin. Ned Alterra had been a great help to her in the past weeks, training poets in the rudiments of weaponry, in case. She hoped there would be no need for drawn blades, but she was not going to send men who had never learned to fight against the palace guards without some training.

Rianna's smile was radiant in the dark. "Yes."

Lin was not certain what impelled her, though it had something to do with the stillness of the night and the memory of Darien Aldemoor and an amazement that, after all that had happened, there could be such a thing as uncomplicated as love in the world. She bent and kissed Rianna's forehead, her eyes pricking as if with hot needles. "The Three watch over and bless you both."

It was dawn when Marlen Humbreleigh found himself within a circle of chanting Seers, their voices twining like an invisible net cast around him. Once he would have joined them, added his celebrated voice to theirs just to evoke a response. Always it had mattered so much what others thought of him, how impressed they were with his talent. Now he stood silent within the circle. Beyond, he saw Lin Amaristoth and Rianna Gelvan standing together, watching quietly. Lin had her arm around the girl, as if to shield her from the sight of him.

Standing apart was Marilla, her face like stone. She had barely spoken to him since the Path. All she did was clasp his hand when they were together—not tightly but with an inextricable weave of her fingers with his.

Valanir Ocune was part of the ring of Seers. As they continued to sing, shrouded in their grey robes so that Marlen did not know them—knowing only that some had been his own Masters—Valanir stepped forward into the circle, rested his hand on Marlen's shoulder. Tired and admittedly afraid now, Marlen allowed it.

"You have shown courage these past days," said Valanir.

Marlen shrugged. "Too late."

"Once you are released from our concealment, Nickon Gerrard will have you."

"We're counting on that, aren't we?" said Marlen.

The Seer's gaze seemed to pierce Marlen to the fear he concealed. He looked regretful. "Yes, we are."

THEY heard the screams as they pelted up the stairs of the passage that according to Marlen's maps led most directly to Nickon Gerrard's chambers. Behind them, Lin heard a clatter and anguished cries and knew the guards had encountered some of the poets who followed in the rear. Her army of Seekers, who for days had practiced the simple rite of Disarming. Not all would make it through.

Grief surged in her, but she pressed on toward the screams. In her heart she cursed Valanir Ocune, who ran now beside her, for placing her in command.

When they burst into the room, the sight that greeted them was from nightmare. Nickon Gerrard's body lay tumbled on the floor, eviscerated as if his innards had been carved out. His face was drawn back in a silent howl, the eyes bare sockets.

Beside the Court Poet's hollowed body lay Marlen Humbreleigh. But what drew Lin's eye was the figure that loomed over Marlen, black as if a void had been cut into the space, edges blurred like smoke. When the face turned to Lin it was a mask of white, blue fires where the eyes should be.

"Hold!" she said, to distract the thing while Valanir ran in beside her.

Ned and Rianna were running to the corner, where the king was cowering. They had sneaked in earlier that day, disguised as palace servants. Rianna threw her arm around Harald's neck, said, "Call off your guards, or I'll kill you."

Lin and Valanir joined hands. The thing before them swooped, and Lin raised her knife with a cry; but instead it whirled at Ned and in seconds Ned's throat was slashed red and he lay on the ground. The thing that had been Nickon Gerrard held Ned's knife aloft, began chanting words over the growing puddle of crimson that ran from the wound onto the ornate carpeting. Rianna's shriek filled the room.

Lin felt her heart contracting. "Valanir, *now*."

He looked savage, lips drawn back from his teeth. "Are you ready?"

As if in answer, the room fell away around them.

"I'm afraid," Valanir Ocune had confessed to her one night in the northern woods, in a rare moment of quiet. They sat a distance apart, her anger fluttering between them.

"Of course," she said. "We all are."

"Not of Nickon Gerrard," he said. No trace in him of the charming lawbreaker she had known in Tamryllin. Now each of his words seemed imbued with the gravity that in recent days had come upon him. "I mean if we succeed. Having access to our powers, finally . . . it is what I have worked towards for more than half my life. But now I understand . . . this magic changes you. And we won't have the guidance of the Seers before us. It will change us in ways we can't foresee."

Relinquishing her anger she said, "I know." Somewhere in the recesses of her mind, a song of Edrien drifted in faraway notes of longing. "For me, it has already begun."

They were in a place of nothing, or so it seemed to Lin: no light or dark, just the fire-eyed tower of black that was the *laylan* growing larger by the moment before them. Beside her, Valanir with his hand in hers. She glanced at him a moment and experienced a shock: his face was young, hair tumbling in locks of red-gold over his forehead. The moon opal ring and his mark of the Seer shone blindingly as one.

An awakening, she thought, even as she turned back to confront what faced them.

And then she saw something else: a ring of men in grey, their hands joined, blurred in the distance as if by mist. The Seers who now stood outside the gates of Tamryllin, their magic linked to her and Valanir Ocune, their song flooding the emptiness of this place between worlds.

Valanir Ocune raised his hand, the light around him stronger, his face strangely open, exposed. His voice joined with the melody coming from Lin, from the men who surrounded them.

A blackness had begun to slit the air. A portal. As the *laylan* drew nearer to Valanir, Lin saw that its borderless substance was being pulled, almost imperceptibly, toward the void they had opened.

A night spirit could not be killed. But without a body to inhabit, it could perhaps be transported back to the Otherworld. Or so they had gathered from the writings of Seers long ago. They had staked their lives on it.

The *laylan* reached Valanir Ocune; blackness enveloped the Seer. From within the cloud, Lin could hear him scream.

"No! I've got you!" Lin cried and felt with some amazement that she could turn the *laylan* back with the full force of what was gathering in her. It recoiled and began to be drawn ever more insistently into the portal.

Valanir collapsed against her, but his hand remained firm in hers. "Once more," he gasped, and together they both cried out as the agony overtook them. Around them they could hear similar cries from the Seers, men surprised by the dreadful intensity of what this new power demanded of them in turning back the dark.

And then the *laylan* shrieked, vanished into the portal that closed behind it. And as Lin and Valanir drew breath to recover from the annihilating pain that had rolled through them, the palace returned to what it was. The Seers melted out of sight. Rianna held a bleeding Ned in her arms, and the king wept tremblingly in the corner beside the bodies of the Court Poet and Marlen on the floor.

CHAPTER 37

SHE was alone in a hallway of many doors, strewn with a light that seemed to come from everywhere and nowhere. Treading softly on a floor that kept flickering from tile to parquet to carpet and back again, as if she were in many places at once, Lin wondered a moment if this dream was hers. She listened, but heard no woman's voice, no strains of a centuries-old song.

The long corridor was hers, as it had always been.

No way out but forward, she thought, and knew what it meant: she turned the handle of the nearest door and it opened on a stream of sunlight, golden as summertime. She stood in a green meadow where patches of lavender grew among dark green bushels of sage and rosemary. The weave of their combined scent drifted toward her on the breeze. She was surrounded by waves of green that went on forever. The hall was gone.

A child was running toward Lin: a little girl, almost a baby, her golden curls bouncing in a flurry around pink cheeks. She was giggling, and Lin could see a familiar cast to her face, to the shape of her blue eyes. Before she reached Lin, the girl halted, suddenly, and turned to look behind her. A distant figure was approaching through the grass, more slowly but with a wave. The gold glint of a harp caught the sun.

Laughing again, the little girl jumped into a patch of dandelions and vanished. There was no sign that she'd ever been, not even a puff of dandelion dust or a bent blade of grass.

Darien Aldemoor was within sight now, smiling. He was clad in blue and red, the House colors of Aldemoor. As he came within earshot, he said, "I'm glad it's you."

Lin reached out her hands to him. "I miss you."

He took her hands, a familiar gesture, then raised one of her wrists to his face. A purple-brown gash ran like half a bracelet across the tender skin on the underside of her wrist. Darien winced. "I will never forgive myself for this."

"You may as well," Lin said. "You did pay the ultimate price for my life."

"I did," said Darien, his eyes earnest as they met hers. "And now you know it's up to you, don't you?"

"What is, Darien?" There were tears streaming from her eyes, when she'd thought she had already cried all the tears that were in her.

Darien stroked her cheek under one eye, brushing away the droplets there. A mischievous smile stole over his face. "Kimbralin Amaristoth, for the first time in your life, I want you to *live,* and make your music. Will you do that for me?"

Lin squeezed her eyes shut a moment, as if that way she might empty them finally for good. "I'll try. Darien—who was that child?"

His smile faded, he let go her hands. "I've finally learned where these doors lead, Lin," he said. "There are many worlds, and some of them are the lives we didn't choose, the paths we didn't take. All of them are here." He was far away now, on the next hill, though he hadn't moved. His voice carried to her on a warm breeze that rippled the grasses. "I've seen some of yours. That's why I want you to promise me that you will choose life. And your music."

Lin thought she might have said, "I promise," but her words fell into a haze as all the colors of the meadow ran together in a whorl and drained away. She stared into the sudden greyness for several moments before she realized where she was: an inn in Tamryllin, curled in a bed alone.

ONCE, Rianna Gelvan's tower had been her sanctuary, the place where she felt at peace as she gazed upon Tamryllin's rooftops set within the encircling hills and trees. Even now the wind chimes brought a wave of memory so intense she nearly had to kneel where she stood by the window, but it was a memory of a place that seemed far distant. And now in the night, all she could see from the window was the moon riding high and nearly full.

Making it more unreal was her reflection in the bedchamber mirror: a staring skull. She hadn't seen her own reflection since she left Tamryllin all those weeks past. Her eyes were wild, and her face raw from weeping.

After the *laylan* had vanished, many things had seemed to happen at once. Covered in Ned's blood, Rianna had barely been able to form a coherent word. But it turned out that the wound, though bloody, was not fatal. Valanir Ocune had bound it expertly with his shirt.

As Valanir bent over Marlen, who was grey and still, Lin addressed the king, who had collapsed into one of Lord Gerrard's red-and-gold couches. "We know your secret—about your father's death," she said. "But that is not all. Piet—bring me the commander of the guard and his men."

Piet Abarda and his Seekers, many of whom possessed skill in swordsmanship from their upbringing as lords' sons, had captured the commander of the guard and his men after disarming them. The guards stopped dead when they saw Lin's knife to the king's throat. "We will not harm him," she told them. "I want only to show you something. Rianna?"

Rianna rose to her feet. She saw with trepidation, the memory of horror still fresh within her, that the same tapestry she had seen on the Path still hung on that wall: a saccharine depiction of a royal hunting party, where even the deer seemed to be smiling. Sliding the tapestry aside, Rianna saw that there was indeed a door there.

Rianna averted her face from the sight within. She would not look again at Nickon Gerrard's altar with its multiple grins, its weave of bones. People who would not be missed by anyone important, allowing the Court Poet to practice his murderous experiments undisturbed for years.

Rianna did not need to see the horror again, but she could see it in the faces of the men who stared slack-jawed at the open doorway. Though clad in the official red and black livery of the Ladybirds, the guards looked like lost children.

"This is why we are here," Lin Amaristoth said. "This is what Nickon Gerrard has been up to for years." They were motionless, wordless. They could not speak their minds in the presence of the king. But by morning, if events proceeded as planned, news of Lord Gerrard's chamber of death would be flaring in every tavern in the city.

Lin withdrew her knife from the king's neck; he collapsed into himself like a pathetic ball of soft fat, his bearded face scrunching into his neck as he nearly sobbed. "Now we ask that your majesty release Master Gelvan," said Lin. "And then we can discuss the relationship between the Crown and the Academy, now that circumstances have—changed. We have our power again, your majesty. And we intend to keep it this time."

"Who are you?" the king finally stammered.

"I am Kimbralin Amaristoth," she said. "I believe you know—*knew* my brother, who is lately deceased. Now, where is the merchant?"

When Master Gelvan was helped into the room, painfully thin and filthy, with a straggling beard, Rianna ran to him with a cry. His eyes were narrowed to slits, as if adjusting to light. But his hands were strong on her shoulders nonetheless. "My love, what has happened to you?" He could barely speak.

Rianna forced a laugh as she hugged him to her. "That *you* would ask me that. Oh, *Avan*." She felt a catch in her voice. "So much has happened."

* * *

THAT night as he worked, he sang. His song *was* the work. His eyes were intent on the body on the bed, so near to death. For years Valanir Ocune had studied the enchantments of healing, hoping that one day they might be put to use. They worked only with enchanted wounds, which this was.

Marlen's hair was spread on the pillow; his lips were cold. In the moonlight that streamed from the window, his skin showed a purple cast. They were in Marilla's apartments. Valanir had stripped Marlen of his shirt; now he pressed his fingertips to crucial pressure points in the course of his song. As he worked, he felt a perilous falling sensation in his chest, as if the words drained something vital from him. The most urgent of the healing enchantments were, in their own way, dark. Cheating death, Valanir thought, meant you had to play its game.

He wondered if Kiara watched over him here, as she had all his life. Guiding, whispering, and ultimately bestowing upon him the gift of deepest insight into his own soul when through Lin Amaristoth, he had reached the Path.

If it was a gift.

When he and Marilla had first mounted the stairs with Marlen's long, graceful form sprawled in their arms, she had asked, in an even tone, "Can you save him?"

"There is a chance, lady." He had come to know Marilla as a shadow figure at Marlen's side. For someone whose reputation was so savage, she seemed strangely shy. "But you know that even if I can save him, this life, this wealth"—he gestured around the apartments—"they're finished for him."

"I know, *Erisen*." Moonlight reflected from her pale eyes. She adjusted Marlen's feet at the edge of the bed; he was almost too tall for it. "I have lately been thinking of the lands near the border of Kahishi, where my family once had a home. I am thinking of farming again."

THE wedding took place after the snows melted, when the first of the spring crocuses were peering from the new grass of Master

Gelvan's garden. Still, a chill stood in the air, stirring color to the cheeks of the bride as she waited beneath the Galician wedding canopy that Lin had embroidered with her own hands. The bride's dress was green and gold brocade—her mother's wedding dress, saved by Master Gelvan for this occasion. A gold veil fell around her face and trailed in the grass.

For a wedding so vital to the social fabric of Tamryllin—one of its wealthiest daughters, wed to one of the most important families—it was shockingly small: other than Lin Amaristoth and Valanir Ocune, the only other guests were Ned's family. Such had been the request of the couple, and so relieved were their parents simply to see their children alive, they could not refuse.

Master Gelvan's hair had frosted utterly grey while he was imprisoned; he would not speak of what had befallen him there. At times Rianna regretted that the former Court Poet was beyond her revenge. She would have liked to have killed him more slowly, if possible. She knew her father had nightmares. And now she understood him in ways that she never had before.

The day before the wedding, Rianna had suddenly turned to him and said, "She was loyal to you."

Master Gelvan had been in the midst of looking over accounts in his study while she read on a bench beside the window. She was in here a great deal now, when she wasn't with Ned; she had a need to be near her father, as if to assure herself that he was indeed unharmed.

But she had not told him of the Path, fearing to hurt him more than he had already been hurt. She could still feel, jangling in her bones, the moment Nickon Gerrard's knife had punctured Ned's throat; she could only imagine how it would feel to have that moment go on and on for weeks, months, years. She wanted to protect her father now from anything else that might come after.

But a realization came to her: that a secret, held forever by death, was its own source of pain. And it could be her gift to him, perhaps, to dispel it.

So she told her father of what she had seen. And she saw that it hurt him, but she saw also a peacefulness came over him. "You are right," he said at last, when she was done. "I didn't want to think ill of her, but there was no way to know for certain. Rianna . . . thank you for this."

"Do you think you'll ever remarry, *Avan*?" she asked. "I want you to be happy."

He laughed, but turned serious after a moment. "For years, I was intent on revenge, and my grief . . . it would have been impossible," said her father. "And now . . . well, I'm old, Rianna."

"You aren't," she said stubbornly. "Besides, you know what this city is like. You'd need to fight women off. To find the one with gold in her heart, and not her eyes."

Her father had laughed at this, too. He did not say anything about metaphors or poets, and for that she was grateful.

LIN had heard countless jests growing up—mostly from servants in the kitchen—about the nervousness of grooms at weddings, but she had never seen Ned as relaxed as he looked now, standing tall between the bent figures of Master Gelvan and Lord Alterra as they escorted him to the marriage canopy.

They performed the ceremony without clergy; instead, Rianna had asked Lin to officiate. Sprinkling water from a blessed spring on the couple and reciting the Ellenican prayer—blessing their union in the light of Thalion, Kiara, and Estarre—Lin had been able to forget for a moment all the responsibilities that awaited her beyond the walls of this garden. At Master Gelvan's request, she also murmured a marriage sacrament in the forbidden tongue of the Galicians, in undertone, so that none should hear—a secret from all but Rianna and Ned. Sunset cast a copper glow over everything, itself a benediction.

Ned's father had been unnerved by the idea of a woman performing the ceremony, but Ned had convinced him that a woman of rank was different. Lin felt self-conscious as she raised her arms above the couple, as it caused her six-colored cloak to flare in the breeze. It was not the cloak that had belonged to Nickon Gerrard—to wear anything that the blood-soaked poet had touched would have been unacceptable. But Valanir Ocune had advised that, as Court Poet, it was vital that she make her authority absolutely clear. "No one else will, if you do not," he had said, and she had known it was true.

It was uncertain if Marlen Humbreleigh and Marilla would have been invited to the wedding—Lin knew Rianna was ambivalent about both of them. But they had departed the city in exile months before, heading south to the village where Marilla's family had lived.

"There is good farming in the south, and Marilla wants to see if any of her family survived," Marlen had explained with a tired smile. Since the injury, he had seemed tired a great deal of the time. Valanir had told him it would take months for the effects of Nickon Gerrard's rite to dissipate. Marilla thought the southern lands would warm his languid blood.

In the time following Nickon Gerrard's death, Lin and Valanir had met with the king, their army of poets at their backs. Most of the poets had stayed within the palace walls the first night, almost as if they truly were a conquering force. In that night, the balance could have shifted with disastrous results if the guards had decided to reassert themselves. But Lin had counted on the gruesome crimes of Nickon Gerrard to turn the guards in the poets' favor, and so they did: when she and Valanir arrived at the gates the next morning, they were escorted to the king's chambers. The king was under siege from more than just the poets, and he knew it.

"These are our conditions," said Lin that day, as they stood before Harald in a secret meeting that was no secret at all, not with hundreds of guards and poets standing outside in the corridor. Lin and Valanir had agreed that she would be the one to state them, because she did not have a history of rebellion against the Crown—and because Amaristoth blood ran in her veins. "The laws controlling the content of poets' songs will be revoked. The Crown's direct authority over Academy procedures—revoked. In exchange, all graduating Academy students will swear an oath of fealty to the Crown. And every year, the Academy will pay a tithe to the Eldest Sanctuary in recognition of its ultimate authority."

The king had leaned forward, clearly attempting to assert some dominance in the conversation. "There must be more," he said. "I must have a Court Poet at my side who will stand as assurance that these conditions will be met and that the Academy will stay loyal to the Crown."

Lin had thought of this, already knew what she would say. Yet before she could speak, Valanir did. "I recommend Lady Kimbralin Amaristoth for the position," he said, sending a cold shock to Lin's spine. "She is sole heir to the lands of Amaristoth and their wealth. It would be to your advantage to have her close."

"But a woman," the king had protested, with a furrowed brow. "There are no female poets."

"Your majesty, until this winter, there were no enchantments," said Valanir Ocune. "The game has changed forever."

LATER that evening, at the inn, she confronted him. "I thought it would be you," she said. "I don't even know if I want this. In truth . . . I do know. I don't."

"It has to be you," said Valanir. His voice was gentle, but there was steel in it, too. Laughter and song echoed through the floorboards from below, where—incredibly, to Lin—life in Tamryllin was proceeding as usual. The old enchantments had been brought back through Darien's life, the Court Poet was dead, and the new one would be a woman. And yet the same drunken songs, the same laughter, rocked the walls of the inn as on the previous night.

Such was the reality of a city that had perched like a white gem above the harbor for hundreds of years. Lin realized, suddenly, what it would mean to be Court Poet in that palace, where Eldgest had once dismembered Academy poets, cutting out their tongues. No longer was history just words on a page. It was a song ringing out on a midsummer night; it was, just now, like the planks of a ship jarring beneath her feet in a storm.

Valanir's voice called her back from her thoughts. "What happened today can all still come to nothing. It was a coup, and the success of a coup depends on what comes after, when the storms are done. There will be grave difficulties ahead, negotiating the balance between the Academy and the Crown. The Court Poet in the coming years will be pivotal to that negotiation. And only you possess both the skills and the background with which to do it."

"Only me?" Lin said. "I can't imagine that is true."

"You are a poet, and an Amaristoth," said Valanir.

Feeling as if the breath had been pummeled out of her, Lin sat on the bed. She thought of Darien and the promise she had made to him. *Does this keep it, or break it?* Aloud, she said, "So it is the palace for me, then. And you? Where will you go, Valanir Ocune?"

"Not far," he said. "I will be at the Academy. We will need to open new classes for all poets, even the graduates. Everyone must learn how to control these techniques and not abuse them."

"We've seen what can happen," Lin said softly, her eyes dropping to the backs of her wrists and the half bracelets there. She knew they would scar, unlike the marks Rayen had cut in her face, which had faded. "Will you visit me here?"

Valanir took her hand. "I will come often," he said. "I must help mediate between the Academy and the Crown. In truth, Lin, it's not what I want, either. I was born to wander, as Edrien was."

"Yet it was your song that was the beginning to . . . all of this," said Lin.

"I helped set events in motion," said Valanir. "As did you."

Lin met his eyes. It was becoming easier to do that. Her voice was pitched so low he would have had to strain to hear as she said, "So it is to be walls, then, for both of us. Walls and rooms. You know I used to dream of taking to the road with you."

She allowed her words to hang there in the silence. Below, the singing and the laughter continued. The life of Tamryllin on a winter evening, as outside it began softly to rain.

THAT winter, the Academy held a funeral for Darien Aldemoor, Hassen Styr, and the five poets who had fallen in the attack on the palace, interring them with much ceremony in a shrine on Academy Isle.

Buried, too, were the remains of Lord Gerrard's altar to blood div-ination, after Valanir Ocune and other Seers performed the rite of its destruction in the Court Plaza before all the people. A detail Lin Amaristoth had suggested: that the people would know that the threat of the Red Death would now be lifted from Eivar—and what had caused it.

In that same spot before the palace gates, for thirty nights and a day, the harp and ring of Darien Aldemoor were displayed on a plat-form watched by palace guards. Candles lined the platform, a prayer to speed Darien's soul to the gods' embrace. At all times of night, poets kept silent vigil by the flames.

As for Marlen Humbreleigh, he had vanished south with his strange lady; none had heard from him since.

IN early autumn of that year, Lin visited the Gelvan home to see the girl child Rianna Alterra had brought into the world. Lank brown hair like Ned, blue eyes like Rianna. Of course, these things changed all the time until children were of a certain age, but even so . . . Lin thought of a golden-haired little girl skimming through fields of lav-ender, rosemary, and sage and closed her eyes a moment as she pressed her lips to the infant's cheek.

This girl would learn knives and poetry from an early age. Rianna was jesting from her bed, where her father threatened that she had better stay if she knew what was good for her. "You can't punish me anymore, *Avan*," she said sweetly to Master Gelvan's departing back. "That's Ned's duty now."

The father of their newborn flushed red as a poppy and practically fled the room, mumbling something about a hot water bottle. Rianna flashed a mischievous grin at Lin, and Lin was again reminded of Darien.

Drawing herself up amid the pillows, Rianna took the baby back from Lin and held it to her breast. "We're calling her Dariana," she said. "I hope she will be strong. And that a certain Court Poet will teach her what she needs to know, when the time is right. As once she taught me."

Lin took Rianna's hand. She saw the girl was paler than the sheets she lay upon and that new lines strained around her lips. Lin said, "I swear to you that any child of yours shall have my protection and love, for as long as I live."

IT was in a somber mood that she returned to her rooms at the palace. The day had been blessedly uneventful, which was a rarity. Usually she was running from meeting to meeting—between Academy Masters with requests and court nobility with grievances—baffled as to how anything in government could ever be accomplished with so many meetings to attend.

And through it all, there was Edrien Letrell to contend with, his memories and music threading with hers. It was a burden she would have to bear all her life, Valanir had told her. There was no known enchantment that could disengage Edrien from within her, and as time went on, they would grow ever more intertwined.

That was something she preferred not to think about as she went about her numerous daily tasks.

"Who let you in without my permission?" she said when she saw the figure by the window, gazing out at the waves below. Lin's tower room boasted a view of the harbor, where she could pretend—sometimes, when she was happier—that she was a student at the Academy, with the waves crashing in a slow music to the words she composed by candlelight.

Most treasured of all to her was the golden harp on a table beside the window. Some nights, when the ghosts of memory—hers or otherwise—threatened to overwhelm her, Lin sought refuge in precise and passionate melody. Sometimes, when she thought she could bear it, she played to the dark the song that Darien Aldemoor had begun to shape in their time at the Academy. *Never shall we see such times again.*

Valanir Ocune shrugged without turning from the window. "I suppose your attendants thought you wouldn't mind. I told them it was urgent that I see you."

"You do charm your way into whatever you want—and whomever you want," said Lin acidly, throwing herself onto her couch with a sigh. It was a relief to sit here in her chambers, to not have all eyes on her, just for a moment.

"Except you," said Valanir, now turning to her. "It must be that chilly northern blood."

"What did you want to see me about?" She tipped her head back and closed her eyes, hoping she could stay awake long enough to hear him out. He'd be wanting something for the Academy, no doubt; these days, with the immense changes that were happening, they always wanted something. But in exchange, she was demanding they start accepting women as students, even if the numbers would be small at first.

This particular subject had been debated at several of the innumerable meetings. Lin was surprised sometimes by how enraged she felt when she confronted the Academy Masters on this, as if any experience in her life could have led her to hope for anything else. Any experience but one: that a woman now sat as Court Poet in the palace of the king. Yet to the Academy Masters, entrenched in centuries of immovable tradition, Lin's existence was no more than a fleeting anomaly. In such meetings, Lin sometimes felt her fingers stealing toward the hilt of her knife.

"I never told you—or anyone, for that matter—what it was that I saw on the Path," said Valanir Ocune. She heard him take a seat across from her. It was a sparsely furnished room; Lin thought that here, in her own chambers, she could adhere to her northern roots. "And in truth, I still cannot tell you."

"All right," Lin said, her eyes still shut. "So what *did* you want to tell me, then?"

She heard Valanir shift in his seat. "I can't tell you what I saw, because that would be too much, like letting you inside my gut," he said. "But it's begun a journey for me. To undo some of the harm I have done—or, make amends for that which I ought to have done, and did not."

"That sounds very high-minded," she said drowsily, almost drifting off.

"Lin. Open your eyes," said Valanir, gently.

Reluctantly, and with effort, Lin did. For a moment, her eyes needed to adjust to the light—the room was almost dark. It took another moment for her to see that this was not her chamber at all but a round bare room of stone, a single window revealing a slit of violet sky and a sprinkling of stars.

"Where have you brought me, Valanir?" said Lin. Her fatigue had fallen away. "Where is this?"

In a low voice he said, "This is the Tower of the Winds. In the chambers beneath this room, students weave songs from the night. But here, in the topmost chamber, we of the Academy perform one of the oldest of the enchantments."

"You can't mean . . ."

"It's time," he said. A breeze from the window ruffled his hair. The sea winds were chilly this far north, but imbued with millennia of music.

"Do the Masters know?"

"They will know once it is done," he said.

"I don't have the knowledge—"

"Lin, you have more than earned the right. And besides, we need you."

She shook her head, bemused. "What must I do?"

"The work is mine—as your initiator in this rite," said Valanir Ocune. "We will be linked to one another from now until death. And after all that I have done in my life that I regret, and that which I ought to have done . . . I will know that there was at least one thing I brought to the world that was good."

Her eyes met his, and Lin suddenly found her mind skipping back to a firelit night in midsummer, green eyes watching her through a mask of Thalion. *There has been no end to the road,* she thought. *Not yet.*

"Close your eyes, dear Lin," said Valanir.

She did as she was bid. With her eyes closed, Lin had the sensation that there were other people in the room who watched the proceedings. Darien. Hassen. Perhaps, in some twist, even Rayen. And the Seekers who had fallen on the day they had retaken the palace—following her command. She did not know if she felt their presence because of some magic invoked by Valanir, or if it was simply the intensity of her desire for what could not be.

Not in this of the many worlds.

There was nothing in life, she thought, that was purely light, or dark.

As in a chant, Valanir spoke. "I will begin the enchantment now, a song of seven verses. You entered this Tower a poet, but shall emerge with a power even greater."

The presence of Edrien Letrell in her mind grew quiet, seemed to have receded with Valanir's words. It would soon return, she knew. Someday she would pay a reckoning for that night of forbidden magic. But not yet . . . not tonight.

I will remember this night for always, Lin thought. *And I will always remember that it was* mine.

Valanir traced a symbol on her closed right eyelid. A warmth flooded through her from that eye, a sensation both pleasant and on the edge of pain. Much as she had come to expect of such things. "This song will be for you and will change you. Kimbralin Amaristoth," murmured Valanir Ocune, and sea winds took the words. "Court Poet. Seer."

Acknowledgments

My first readers, who offered tempered criticism and discerning praise when this book was in its rawest form, will always have my gratitude. They are: Rachel Beitsch-Feldman, Harel Feldman, Carolyn Kephart, Ville V. Kokko, Rena London, Devorah Moskowitz, Tova Moskowitz, Batya Ungar-Sargon, Jeffrey Schindler, Stephanie Whelan, Shlomo Winkler, and Aron Wolinetz. Professor Richard Van Nort provided invaluable consultation in matters of combat—any mistakes are my own.

To my agent, John Silbersack, and my editor at Tor, Marco Palmieri, I am deeply grateful.

At the center of everything is Yaakov—life partner, best friend, and hero. You light every day of my life.